ALBERT CAMUS: PHILOSOPHER AND LITTÉRATEUR

ALBERT CAMUS: PHILOSOPHER AND LITTÉRATEUR

Joseph McBride

St. Martin's Press
New York

© Joseph McBride 1992

The following have been cited with the permission of Librairie Gallimard, Paris:

Material from Albert Camus' *L'Etranger* copyright © 1962, Editions Gallimard.

Material from Albert Camus' *Caligula* copyright © 1962, Editions Gallimard.

Material from Albert Camus' *Le Malentendu* copyright © 1962, Editions Gallimard.

Material from Albert Camus' *Le Mythe de Sisyphe* copyright © 1965, Editions Gallimard and Calmann Lévy.

Material from Roger Quilliot's introduction to Albert Camus' "Métaphysique chrétienne et Néoplatonisme" copyright © 1965, Editions Gallimard and Calmann Lévy.

English Language translation of Albert Camus' "Métaphysique chrétienne et Néoplatonisme" copyright © 1965, Editions Gallimard and Calmann Lévy.

The following have been reproduced by permission of Hamish Hamilton Ltd.:

Material from Albert Camus' *The Outsider*, trans. by Stuart Gilbert, Harmondsworth: Penguin Books, 1961. Copyright © Estate of Albert Camus, 1942.

Material from Albert Camus' *Notebooks* 1935-1942, trans. with an introduction and notes by Philip Thody, London: Hamish Hamilton, 1963. Copyright © 1962 by Librairie Gallimard. Translation copyright © 1963 by Hamish Hamilton Ltd., and Alfred A. Knopf Inc.

Material from Albert Camus' *Caligula and Cross Purpose*, trans. by Stuart Gilbert, Harmondsworth: Penguin Books, 1965. Copyright © Librairie Gallimard, 1947.

Material from Albert Camus' *The Myth of Sisyphus*, trans. by Justin O'Brien, Harmondsworth: Penguin Books, 1975.

The following has been reproduced by permission of Oxford University Press:

Material from John Cruickshank's *Albert Camus and the Literature of Revolt*, London: Oxford University Press, 1959.

Grateful acknowledgement is also made to the following for permission to use material reproduced in this volume:

Catholic University of America, Washington, D.C., for material from works of Saint Augustine contained in the *Fathers of the Church*, ed. L. Schopp, D. J. Deferrari, et al. (Catholic University of America Press, 1947- .)

Alfred A. Knopf, Inc., New York, for material from Albert Camus' *The Stranger*, trans. Stuart Gilbert, copyright © 1946 by Alfred A. Knopf, Inc. Reprinted by permission of the publisher.

For material from *The Myth of Sisyphus and Other Essays*, by Albert Camus, trans. J. O'Brien, copyright © 1955 by Alfred A. Knopf, Inc. Reprinted by permission of the publisher.

For material from *Notebooks, 1935-1942* by Albert Camus, trans. P. Thody, copyright © 1963 by Hamish Hamilton Ltd. and Alfred A. Knopf, Inc. Reprinted by permission of the publisher.

Herbert R. Lottman for material from *Albert Camus: A Biography*, London: Weidenfeld and Nicolson, 1979.

Elaine Greene Ltd., London, for material from Conor Cruise O'Brien's *Camus*, Fontana Books, 1970. Copyright © 1970 by Conor Cruise O'Brien.

Harper Collins Publishers, London, for material from Conor Cruise O'Brien's *Camus*, Fontana Books, 1970.

All rights reserved. For information, write:
Scholarly & Reference Division,
St. Martin's Press, Inc., 175 Fifth Avenue,
New York, NY 10010
First published in the United States of America 1992
Printed in the United States of America
ISBN 0-312-07597-9

Library of Congress Cataloguing-in-Publication Data
McBride, Joseph.
Albert Camus : philosopher and littérateur / Joseph McBride.
    p. cm.
Includes bibliographical references and index.
ISBN 0-312-07597-9
1. Camus, Albert, 1913-1960—Criticism and interpretation.
2. Authenticity (Philosophy) in literature. 3. Absurd (Philosophy)
in literature. 4. Metaphysics in literature. I. Title.
PQ2605.A3734Z72134 1992
848'.91409—dc20   92-12753
                                                   CIP

To My Mother

CONTENTS

PREFACE

In the form which it finally assumes, a book of this kind is the end product of many years of work. While it goes without saying that the academic labours which produced it are those of its author, it is sometimes forgotten that a philosopher is, in at least one important respect, just like other men in that he needs not only money, but a great deal of advice and encouragement as well. It is only proper, therefore, that the author of *Albert Camus: Philosopher and Littérateur* should say a word of thanks both to the executors of the Maynooth Travel Fund, who afforded him an opportunity to pursue a period of research at the University of Oxford in 1989, and to the College Executive Council of Saint Patrick's College, Maynooth, whose generosity helped to defray the expenses incurred in the production of this book.

The author wishes to acknowledge, in particular, his very great debt and considerable gratitude to an old friend, Father James McEvoy, professor of ancient and medieval philosophy at the Université Catholique de Louvain, whose encouragement and advice he has found invaluable over many years. He also wishes to thank Mr. Michael McBride and Dr. Bríd O'Doherty, who read his translation of Camus' "Métaphysique chrétienne et Néoplatonisme," and Mrs. Ann Gleeson, who typed the final manuscript, and Dr. Michael O'Dwyer, who helped with the proof-reading. The author is deeply appreciative, too, of the help given him by the staff of the libraries of the Queen's University, Belfast, St. Patrick's College, Maynooth, the Bodleian Library at Oxford and the Bibliothèque Nationale at Paris.

INTRODUCTION

The serious, nonjournalistic work of Albert Camus, it is sometimes said, falls into three categories: literary, political and philosophical. This division is, however, a highly arbitrary one, for it is rarely possible to separate literature from philosophy in Camus: he himself said that anyone who wishes to philosophize should write novels and that all great novels are metaphysical ones. Many of his dramatic works also are of a basically philosophical nature. Moreover, Camus refused to separate politics from ethics, just as he refused to separate morals from metaphysics. It seems highly desirable, therefore, that the theme of this book and the works which are centrally relevant to it should be located within some more rational and adequate schema than the tripartite one just mentioned.

When Camus met his tragic death near Villeblevin, on 4 January 1960, he was carrying with him a black leather briefcase. In it was a dossier, which, Camus' biographer tells us, was later found to contain (along with Friedrich Nietzsche's *The Joyful Wisdom* and the French translation of Shakespeare's *Othello*) Camus' own journal and the manuscript of *Le Premier Homme*. A notebook entry, written between 17 and 25 June 1947, tells us that this last work was to constitute (along with *"Le Jugement,"* almost certainly the original title of *La Chute*) the third of the five cycles of which his entire work was to have been composed. What this cycle of works, together with the fourth and fifth "series," would have brought we do not, of course, know in any degree of detail. We can say with certainty, however, that the second cycle deals with the theme of revolt, and that the works that are central to it are *La Peste* (1947) and *L'Homme révolté* (1951). We know too that the first "series" is about the absurd, the subject matter of *L'Etranger* (1942), *Le Mythe de Sisyphe* (1942), *Caligula* (1944) and *Le Malentendu* (1944).

The aim of this study is to present Camus' thinking on the absurd as it is expressed in *Le Mythe de Sisyphe* and *L'Etranger*, and to trace the origins of this concept in the philosophies of Saint Augustine and Friedrich Nietzsche. It also underlines the importance of Camus' diploma dissertation of 1936, "Métaphysique chrétienne et Néoplatonisme" ("Héllenisme et Christianisme: Plotin et Saint Augustin"), for an understanding of the two works to which we have referred. In so doing, *Albert Camus: Philosopher and Littérateur* will clearly reveal that the proper understanding of Camus' early work requires that it be read not merely as literature but as philosophy as well.

Camus' early philosophy, however, is not merely about the meaningless-ness of human life; it is also about authentic human existence. Authenticity, after all, is demanded of *l'homme absurde* by the meaningless nature of his mortal condition. There is always, in Camus' mind, an intimate connection between the notion of absurdity and that of authenticity, the theme of *l'exil* and that of *le royaume*. Our study is also devoted to a critical examination of this second concept, authenticity, as it is expressed in the two works to which we have referred.

Albert Camus: Philosopher and Littérateur is made up of three parts, each of which has three chapters. Part 1 is devoted to a presentation of the absurd in *Le Mythe de Sisyphe* and *L'Etranger*. Chapter 1 uncovers the double origin of the absurd in Nietzsche's atheism and Saint Augustine's concept of natural desire for God. Chapters 2 and 3 are devoted, in turn, to Nietzsche's rejection of Christianity and to Saint Augustine's thinking on "the place of happiness."

Part 2 of our study is devoted to an exposition and critical appraisal of Camus' early thinking on authenticity. Chapter IV reveals a Promethean ethic, which is nihilistic and which has its origins in the moral philosophy of Nietzsche. The latter's existential ethic is explicated in Chapter V. Chapter VI provides an evaluation of Camus' thinking on authenticity.

The third part of this book is devoted to Camus' "Métaphysique chrétienne et Néoplatonisme," and to its intellectual setting, both of which are centrally relevant to the concerns of *Le Mythe de Sisyphe* and *L'Etranger*. Camus, as we shall see, was preoccupied, even in his student days, with what Malraux called "the human condition," and with the nature of the "kingdom" that is available to man. Chapter VII charts the historical and intellectual background to Camus' dissertation and describes its main themes. An English translation of "Métaphysique chrétienne et Néoplatonisme" is to be found in Chapter VIII. The final chapter contains the bibliography which Camus appended to his diploma thesis.

There is, of course, a great deal more to Camus' philosophy than that which is contained in *Le Mythe de Sisyphe* and *L'Etranger*. Our study is, therefore, a limited one. The former book is, however, Camus' first major philosophical product, while *L'Etranger* is his most famous philosophico-literary work. Moreover, the themes of our study have not been chosen arbitrarily: they are, in fact, crucial for an understanding of Camus' early thought, and indeed for an adequate appreciation of many of his later intellectual preoccupations as well. I believe that by elucidating Camus' thought about authenticity and the absurd in the light of its origins, and by revealing the intimate relationship between literature and philosophy in Camus, I will have contributed to the voluminous output already available on this writer a work that is original and of some value.

PART 1

THE ABSURD AND ITS ORIGINS

Chapter I

The Absurd in the Early Works

THE ABSURD IN *LE MYTHE DE SISYPHE*

Camus' first major philosophical work, *Le Mythe de Sisyphe*, was completed early in 1941[1] and published in November of the following year. It represents an attempt "to resolve the problem of suicide."[2] At a more fundamental level, however, *Le Mythe de Sisyphe* is designed to treat with philosophical rigour the theme which has so often been taken to define the early thought of Albert Camus, that of the absurd.

Camus opens this essay with the startling claim that "there is but one truly serious philosophical problem, and that is suicide. All the rest—whether or not the world has three dimensions, whether the mind has nine or twelve categories—comes afterwards." Suicide is a *philosophical* problem, because it is related to the question of life's meaning. "Suicide has never been dealt with except as a social phenomenon. On the contrary, we are concerned here, at the outset, with the relationship between individual thought and suicide."[3] It is a philosophical *problem*, because Camus has yet to decide whether suicide is the authentic response to the human condition. And suicide is the *one truly serious* philosophical problem, because human existence is meaningless. We are therefore introduced, at the very beginning of *Le Mythe de Sisyphe*, to "the absurd" and the question of authentic human existence, the major themes not only of this essay but of Camus' entire philosophy.

Human existence is meaningless. There are, however, three questions that must be asked if we are to arrive at a precise understanding of Camus' views concerning the nature of the human condition and of the philosophical presuppositions underlying those views: Why exactly does Camus regard man's existence as absurd? What are the logical implications of an acceptance of the absurdist stance? What precisely does Camus mean when he says that human existence is meaningless?

Before answering these questions, however, we must draw attention to what are almost certainly the two most fundamental distinctions made by Camus in Le Mythe de Sisyphe. The first is the distinction between the "fact" of absurdity and the awareness that some people have of this "fact." It is one which can easily be grasped and needs no explanation. Man's existence, says Camus, is meaningless, but not everyone is aware that this is so. The second distinction, that between "the feeling of the absurd" and "the notion of the absurd," is one which is not so easily understood but which is nevertheless of considerable importance to him. "The feeling of the absurd is not, for all that, the notion of the absurd."[4] The difference between the two can be understood by reference to Sartre's claim that "the absurd is not, to begin with, *the object of a mere idea; it is revealed to us in a doleful illumination.*"[5] For what Sartre is saying here, at least implicitly, is that Le Mythe de Sisyphe distinguishes the content of an intellectual grasp of the absurd from a largely affective, and relatively vague, awareness of it. The latter Camus calls "le sentiment de l'absurde"; the former, "la notion de l'absurde."

It would be a mistake, however, to assume that this "feeling" is an unimportant one, for in Le Mythe de Sisyphe Camus deals with it at some length before treating "the notion of the absurd" and lists the experiences which give rise to it. He insists, furthermore, that it is "le sentiment de l'absurde" that gives rise to the notion of life's meaninglessness.[6] Our concern, however, is with the "fact" of absurdity. It is in relation to this "fact" that our three questions must be asked.

Why does Camus say that life is without meaning? It is absurd not, as has usually been suggested,[7] precisely because of the limitations of human reason when it confronts, for example, the physical universe, but because man has a desire for understanding and the limitations of his reason do not, in this context or in any other, allow for the satisfaction of that desire. Whereas Nietzsche traces the pursuit of knowledge back to a will to power, Camus locates its origin in man's desire for happiness. "There is no happiness if I cannot know."[8] In fact, this desire for happiness is taken by Camus to be man's essential attribute:

> The mind's deepest desire, even in its most elaborate operations, parallels man's unconscious feelings in the face of his universe: it is an insistence on familiarity, an appetite for clarity . . . If thought discovered in the shimmering mirrors of phenomena eternal relations capable of summing them up and summing them-selves up in a single principle, there would be seen an intellectual joy of which the myth of the blessed would be but a ridiculous imitation. That nostalgia for unity, that appetite for the absolute illustrates the essential impulse for the human drama.[9]

For Camus, then, it is not the world but the human condition that is absurd. The world in itself is simply unintelligible.[10] And human existence is absurd, not because man by nature desires to know *or* because knowledge is not to be had, but because man has a natural desire for understanding *and* knowledge is unavailable to him. Logic, psychology and physics provide man with truths, but do not give him truth.[11]

At this point in his argument, however, Camus is on very weak ground, for "the absurd" is in his view a permanent feature of the human condition, whereas man's inability to answer the type of question to which he refers is only partial. "There are," as Sartre says, "only relative absurdities, and only in relation to 'absolute rationalities.' "[12] Camus would therefore appear to be in a better position when he traces the meaninglessness of life to the passage of time and the fact of human mortality:

> . . . if, bridging the gulf that separates desire from conquest, we assert with Parmenides the reality of the One (whatever it may be), we fall into the ridiculous contradiction of a mind that asserts total unity and proves by its very assertion its own difference and the diversity it claimed to resolve. This other vicious circle is enough to stifle our hopes. These are again truisms. I shall again repeat that they are not interesting in themselves but in the consequences that can be deduced from them. *I know another truism: it tells me that man is mortal.*[13]

Many commentators have, of course, pointed out that death is, for Camus, a source of absurdity. It is significant, however, that few philosophers seem to realize that death is, for him, not merely *a* source of absurdity but *the* source of meaninglessness in man's world and that even fewer commentators have posed our second question, let alone adverted to its significance: What are the logical consequences of Camus' assertion that death renders man's existence meaningless? This question is a crucial one, for it not only reveals the intimate connection that exists between "the absurd," on the one hand, and, on the other, the atheism and the philosophical anthropology of Camus, but it throws considerable light on what he means when he speaks of the absurdity of life.

The first consequence is that death must, in the mind of Camus, be annihilation: There must be, in his view, no God and therefore no possibility of immortality with God. The second is that death must be, as Aquinas says,[14] the annihilation of a creature that is naturally made for God. Both these points are well made by one philosopher:

> We have said above that death can be the source of the absurdity of life if it involves complete annihilation. But in fact that is not entirely accurate. Only the death of a *creature who needs or desires immortality* renders *that* creature's life absurd.

> The real source of absurdity for Camus, therefore, is his refusal to accept that immortality with God is possible, his belief that death is the annihilation of a creature who needs immortality with God. Death is the focal point of absurdity rather than the cause of it . . .[15]

But what does Camus mean when he says that man's existence is absurd? This also is a crucial question, but one that philosophers have almost invariably answered either inaccurately or with insufficient precision. Gorchov, for example, is mistaken when he claims that "absurdity" may be characterized as "the complete otherness of man and the world"[16]; so also is Cruickshank, when he asserts that it is "the conclusion arrived at by those who have assumed the possibility of a total explanation of existence by the mind but who discover instead an unbridgeable gulf between rationality and experience."[17] And Sartre is less than entirely precise, though not altogether inaccurate, when he says that the absurd is "nothing less than man's relation to the world. Primary absurdity manifests a cleavage, the cleavage between man's aspirations to unity and the insurmountable dualism of mind and nature, between man's drive toward the eternal and the *finite* character of his existence, between the 'concern' which constitutes his very essence and the vanity of his efforts."[18] To be absolutely accurate, one would have to say that when Camus speaks of the meaninglessness of man's life he intends to say not that it is altogether meaningless, but that it does not have the kind of meaning it would have if God existed and immortality were possible for man. This point too is made clearly by Mackey:

> He is quite clear on this: the fact that man must die and in dying cease altogether to exist is the fact that renders his whole life meaningless. But, let us repeat, to say that an *annihilating death takes meaning from life is an overstatement. To be more accurate, Camus would have to say that this fact deprives life of a certain kind of meaning, namely, the meaning that would derive from some destiny in an after-life, the meaning that corresponds to man's desire for the absolute. At the back of Camus' mind there is always the alternative: either annihilating death or something similar to the Christian heaven.*[19]

A relatively recent study of Camus therefore expresses a profound insight into his thought when it points out that, while the absurd represents for him "a victory over the previous state of suicidal mysticism," it remains nevertheless "a religious vision because man does not forget his need for God. . . . Camus simply could not give up the images of eternity which he had depicted in *L'envers* and in *La mort heureuse*."[20]

Human existence, then, is absurd, and it is in death that this absurdity has its "focal point," for man has a natural desire for a nonexistent God. While it is true that Camus does not provide a detailed argument for his atheism in *Le Mythe de Sisyphe*, he does clearly indicate there what his fundamental objections to religious belief are. These objections are to be found in a passage which might have been written by Nietzsche himself, for it summarizes very neatly the essence of the latter's case for the nonexistence of God. This case rests on the claim that if man is to have a destiny in *this* world and a moral code which has its origin not in the dictates of an alien God but in the will of man himself, then he must dispense with religious belief.

> ... to the extent to which I hope, to which I worry about a truth that might be individual to me, about a way of being or creating, to the extent to which I arrange my life and prove thereby that I accept its having a meaning, I create for myself barriers between which I confine my life. I do as do so many bureaucrats of the mind and heart who only fill me with disgust and whose only vice, I now see clearly, is to take man's freedom seriously.[21]

The thinking which lies behind Camus' atheism is also revealed in the enthusiasm which he displays for the "absurd reasoning" of Kirilov, the hero of Dostoevsky's *The Possessed*.[22] The major influence on this aspect of Camus' philosophy was, however, the atheism of Nietzsche, with its emphasis on the alienation of man, which it regarded as an inevitable concomitant of religious belief and acceptance of Christian morality.

While Camus insisted that God does not exist, he was equally insistent that man was made for God and that the human nostalgia for God is man's essential attribute. He refers frequently to man's desire for God, not only in *Le Mythe de Sisyphe* and other "absurd" works of this period, but in the early lyrical essays which go to make up *L'envers et l'endroit*. It is significant also that in his treatment of "philosophical suicide" in *Le Mythe de Sisyphe* he criticizes Kierkegaard and Chestov, not for insisting that man is made for God, but for making the leap from that desire to God's existence[23]; and that in the thesis on Christian Neoplatonism, which Camus submitted to the Université d'Alger, in 1936, for the *Diplôme d'études supérieures*, he quotes from Saint Augustine, in terms that might well be applied to his own philosophical anthropology:

> In all these things which I run through in seeking Thy counsel, I find no safe place for my soul, except in Thee, where my scattered parts are gathered together and no portion of me may depart from Thee. Sometimes, Thou dost introduce me to a very unusual inner experience, to an indescribable sweetness which, if it reaches perfection in me, will be beyond my present knowledge.[24]

The philosophic influence[25] on this aspect of Camus' work derived from the philosophy of Saint Augustine, which he studied, with varying degrees of enthusiasm, in preparation for the thesis *Métaphysique chrétienne et Néoplatonisme.*

Before I conclude this section, one final point should be emphasized. Camus was what Jacques Maritain calls an "absolute, positive atheist":[26] His aim was not merely to reject religious belief and the meaning that Christianity seeks to give to life, but to replace these by a philosophy which would give man's life a secular meaning, locating his destiny within this world and making him, at the moral level, master in his own house.[27] This aspect of Camus' philosophy will be considered in Part 2 of the present study, which deals with the question of authenticity. Before turning to that question, however, I propose to examine his treatment of the absurd in *L'Etranger* and to consider critically those aspects of the philosophies of Nietzsche and Saint Augustine which are so important for an understanding of the nature and origins of Camus' thinking about the absurd.

THE ABSURD IN *L'ETRANGER*

L'Etranger, which was completed in the spring of 1940 and published in June 1942 (five months before the appearance of *Le Mythe de Sisyphe*), is one of the most widely read, and arguably the most influential, philosophical novel of this century. It is, however, a work whose meaning has not always been well understood, for while it is generally agreed that its hero, Meursault, is an absurd character, it has rarely been made clear what the precise nature of the absurd in *L'Etranger* is and where its philosophic matrix lies. Insufficient attention has been paid to the fact that *L'Etranger* deals not only with the absurd but with authenticity, the second major theme of Camus' philosophy. These defects will, to some extent at any rate, be remedied in the present study; this section will deal, for the most part, with the nature of the absurd in *L'Etranger,* while Part 2 will be devoted to the theme of authenticity. The precise sense in which *Le Mythe de Sisyphe* is, to use the words of Sartre, a "parallel commentary" on *L'Etranger* will at the same time be clarified considerably.

It is, of course, widely accepted that *L'Etranger* deals with the meaninglessness of human life. While agreement on this point is general, however, it is by no means universal.[28] When the novel was first published, for example, few commentators interpreted it in this way. Even in 1946, three years after the appearance of Sartre's famous review of *L'Etranger* (in the *Cahiers du Sud* of February 1943), Cyril Connolly claimed that the novel was the story of a typical

"Mediterranean man, as once he was in Corinth or Carthage . . . as he is today in Casablanca or Southern California."[29] It might be well, therefore, before dealing with the nature of the absurd in *L'Etranger*, to establish, however briefly, that absurdity is indeed the theme of Camus' first *récit*.

The point at issue is one that can easily be substantiated, for there is more than ample evidence to support it. This evidence derives from three sources: the very detailed biographical research done on Camus by Herbert Lottman; Camus' own notebooks for the period 1937 to 1942; and the text of *L'Etranger* itself. It might be useful to say something about each in turn.

In *Albert Camus: A Biography*, Lottman recalls the details of a conversation which took place toward the end of 1938 between Camus and Christiane Galindo,[30] who had been his secretary during the period when the novel was being written and who had been responsible for typing the manuscript of *L'Etranger*. It suggests that Camus' first novel, like *Le Mythe de Sisyphe* and his play, *Caligula*, is an absurd work:

> On Christmas Day, 1938, Camus told Christiane Galindo that he had begun work on "l'absurde." He was also making notes for the third panel of his triptych on the absurd: the play *Caligula*.
>
> Now, although apparently he had not yet spelled this out to friends (or even to himself in his journal), Camus had developed the strategy which would serve him for all his future writing. On a given theme—for the moment it was the Absurd—he would write, simultaneously, three works in three different genres: a philosophical essay, a novel, a play. *Le Mythe de Sisyphe, L'Etranger*, and *Caligula* were started at approximately the same time, the writing would be carried on simultaneously, and if possible they were even to be published together. He knew that in outlining such a program he was in for years of effort, but this was the way it was going to be.[31]

A number of entries in the notebooks for the years 1937 to 1942 are equally illuminating and strongly corroborate Lottman's claim, for many of them not only refer to *L'Etranger* but also make it clear that absurdity is its central theme. We need mention only two of them. The first, which was written in December, 1937, could serve as a useful summary of the novel:

> The man who showed all kinds of promise and who is now working in an office. He does nothing apart from this, lying down and smoking until dinner time, going back to bed again and sleeping until the next morning. On Sundays, he gets up very late and stands at the window, watching the sun or the rain, the passers-by or the silent street. The whole year through. He is waiting. He is waiting for death. What good are promises anyway, since in any case. . . .

The passage ends at this point, but we might legitimately complete Camus' statement with a sentence from *Caligula*:

Men die; and they are not happy.[32]

The second entry was made in his journal in December 1938. It is no accident that it is followed immediately by one which reappears almost verbatim toward the end of *L'Etranger*.[33]

There is only one case in which despair is pure: that of the man sentenced to death (may I be allowed a short illustration?) A man driven to despair by love might be asked if he wanted to be guillotined on the next day and would refuse. Because of the horror of the punishment? Yes. But here, the horror springs from the complete certainty of what is going to happen—or rather, from the mathematical element which creates this certainty. Here, the Absurd is perfectly clear. It is the opposite of irrationality. It is the plain and simple truth. What is and would be irrational is the fleeting hope, itself already near to death, that it is all going to stop and that this death can be avoided. But this is not what is absurd. The truth of the matter is that they are going to chop his head off while he knows what is happening—at the very moment when his whole mind is concentrated on the fact that his head is going to be chopped off.

Camus insisted, moreover, that he himself was one of the people who entered into the making of *L'Etranger*[34] and it is useful to recall that, in a notebook entry that we have already quoted, he referred to *Le Mythe de Sisyphe* as one of the "three absurds."

If we turn, finally, to *L'Etranger* itself, we can see that its hero, as Sartre puts it, "belongs to a particular species for which its author reserved the word 'absurd.' "[35] This point is most vividly illustrated at the close of the novel when "Meursault talks about himself and entrusts something of his secret to the reader."[36] Since, however, we will have occasion to refer to this passage on a later occasion, we shall confine our attention to two passages which are to be found in the early part of the novel. The first of these reads:

Marie came that evening and asked me if I'd marry her.

I said I didn't mind; if she was keen on it, we'd get married.

Then she asked me again if I loved her.

I replied, much as before, that her question meant nothing or next to nothing—but I supposed I didn't.

"If that's how you feel," she said, "why marry me?"

I explained that it had no importance really but, if it would give her pleasure, we could get married right away.

I pointed out that anyhow the suggestion came from her; as for me, I'd merely said "Yes."

Then she remarked that marriage was a serious matter.

To which I answered: "No."[37]

The second says:

Just then, my employer sent for me . . . He wanted to discuss a project he had in view, though so far he'd come to no decision. It was to open a branch at Paris,. . . and he wanted to know if I'd like a post there.

. . . I told him I was quite prepared to go; but really I didn't care much one way or the other.

He then asked if a "change of life," as he called it, didn't appeal to me, and I answered that one never changed one's real life; anyhow, one life was as good as another and my present one suited me quite well.

. . . I returned to my work. I'd have preferred not to vex him, but I saw no reason for "changing my life." By and large it wasn't an unpleasant one. As a student I'd had plenty of ambition of the kind he meant. But, when I had to drop my studies, I very soon realised that all that was pretty futile.[38]

L'Etranger, then, is about the meaninglessness of human life. But what is the nature of the absurd in the novel? Does *L'Etranger*, as Sartre insists, deal only with "le sentiment de l'absurde" referred to in *Le Mythe de Sisyphe*, and not with "la notion de l'absurde"? And what, in any case, does "the absurd" mean in this context? Is the hero of the novel a man for whom life is altogether meaningless, or merely one whose existence lacks a certain kind of meaning? These are the questions which must now be considered.

The first major review of *L'Etranger* was written by Jean-Paul Sartre and published, as we have said, in 1943. It is in many respects a perceptive essay, but one which contains serious errors, some of which have continued to influence a host of commentators on this novel right up to the present time.[39] The most significant of these is the suggestion that while *L'Etranger* deals with the absurd, its concern is not with the notion of the absurd but with the feeling of absurdity:

Camus distinguishes, as we have mentioned, between the *notion* and the *feeling* of the absurd. He says, in this connection, "Deep feelings, like great works, are

always more meaningful than they are aware of being. . . . An intense feeling
carries with it its own universe, magnificent or wretched as the case may be."

And the author goes on to say that

"The feeling of the absurd is not the same as the *idea* of the absurd. The idea is
grounded in the feeling, that is all. It does not exhaust it." *The Myth of Sisyphus*
might be said to aim at giving us this *idea*, and *The Stranger* at giving us the feeling.[40]

There are, however, many passages in the novel that cannot properly be
understood in terms of truth-of-feeling alone, for they also express what,
for Meursault and Camus, is truth-of-being. They express, in other words,
the truth, namely that human existence is meaningless, and not merely the
fact that the hero of *L'Etranger feels* it to be so. The most important of these
passages, and the most obvious, is the one which describes Meursault's
encounter with the priest. Camus himself insists that this passage is crucial
for the proper understanding of the novel,[41] which centres around his hero's
belief that death, the great leveller, is, in fact, the focal point of life's
absurdity:

Nothing, nothing had the least importance, and I knew quite well why. He, too,
knew why. From the dark horizon of my future a sort of slow, persistent breeze
had been blowing towards me, all my life long, from the years that were to come.
And on its way that breeze had levelled out all the ideas that people tried to foist
on me in the equally unreal years I then was living through. . . . As a condemned
man himself, couldn't he grasp what I meant by that dark wind blowing from my
future?[42]

To suggest, therefore, that *L'Etranger* deals merely with "le sentiment de
l'absurde" is a mistake. The hero of Camus' novel is concerned not merely
with "truth-of-feeling," but also, and especially, with "truth-of-being."
Meursault's aim, in confronting the chaplain, is to tell him not merely how
he *feels* about life, but what he *thinks* about his existence. And the meeting of
the hero with the priest underlines Meursault's absurdism.

There are other occasions on which Meursault expresses his belief that
life is meaningless. He says it with equal cogency, though less obviously,
when he insists that the killing of the Arab was neither a sin nor a crime.[43]

That he refers at this point to a "criminal offence" rather than a crime is
significant. Elsewhere he makes the same point even more clearly:

. . . he gazed at me intently and rather sadly.

"Never in all my experience have I known a soul so case-hardened as yours," he said in a low tone. "All the criminals who have come before me until now wept when they saw this symbol of our Lord's sufferings."

I was on the point of replying that was precisely because they *were* criminals. But then I realised that I, too, came under that description. Somehow it was an *idea* to which I never could get reconciled.[44]

There is, of course, no question of denying that these passages describe what *Le Mythe de Sisyphe* refers to as an "absurd sensibility." What is equally obvious, however, is that they express an absurdist philosophy. Human existence, for Meursault, is in fact absurd. The claim that *L'Etranger* deals with "le sentiment de l'absurde" but not with "la notion de l'absurde," is therefore an inaccurate one.

The absurd in *L'Etranger* is an idea as well as a feeling. But what does it mean to say that life, for Meursault, is meaningless? This is the second question that must be asked, if we are to arrive at a precise understanding of the nature of the absurd in *L'Etranger*. It is one which is best answered by drawing attention to the logical implications of a second point which is made unambiguously by Meursault, in that section of the novel to which we have just referred. The point in question is that it is death which renders human existence meaningless. The implications of this assertion are, first, that death must be, in Meursault's view, annihilation: there must be no God and therefore no possibility of immortality with Him; second, that man must, in the opinion of Camus' hero, naturally be made for God.

These are two points which Meursault accepts, for he states explicitly that he, like others, has a natural desire for immortality with God:

. . . all of a sudden he swung round on me, and burst out passionately:

"No! No! I refuse to believe it. I'm sure you've often wished there was an after-life."

Of course I had, I told him. Everybody has that wish at times. But that had no more importance then wishing to be sick, or to swim very fast, or to have a better-shaped mouth. It was in the same order of things.[45]

He is, however, equally insistent that there is no God and that immortality is therefore unattainable:

"Why," he asked, "don't you let me come to see you?"

I explained that I didn't believe in God. . . .

. . . Thereat he stood up, and looked me straight in the eyes. His voice was quite steady when he said: "Have you no hope at all? Do you really think that when you die you die outright, and nothing remains?"

I said: "Yes."[46]

We can now see what is meant by the absurd in *L'Etranger*. The hero of the novel is a man for whom life is meaningless, but not absolutely so; rather, it lacks a particular kind of meaning, namely, that which "would derive from some destiny in an after-life, the meaning that corresponds to man's desire for the absolute"; for Meursault, and for Camus, "there is always the alternative: either annihilating death or something similar to the Christian heaven."[47] Once again, this point is made explicitly in *L'Etranger*, when its hero meets the examining magistrate.[48]

It should perhaps be pointed out, in conclusion, that the absurdity of life, for Meursault, is not focused on death alone. In terms that are reminiscent of the scepticism of *Le Mythe de Sisyphe*, Meursault insists that there are no grounds for any of man's certainties, other than that of his mortality.[49] And this, of course, implies that the unintelligibility of the physical universe is, for man, a source of obscurity. We are also reminded in *L'Etranger* (and this too recalls *Le Mythe de Sisyphe*) that Meursault is a stranger to other men. This is stated by Camus at least once in the novel[50] and is such an important theme of *L'Etranger* that many commentators continue to see in it the sole motif of that work. There can be no doubt, however, that while Meursault is "man confronting the world" as well as "man among men,"[51] he is also one who, as William Barrett said in a talk on Heidegger, "inhabits his own skin as a stranger."[52] Nor can there be any doubt that, as far as Camus is concerned, this "strangeness" has its focal point, if not its cause, in human mortality. This is what must be clearly understood, if we are to grasp the nature of the absurd in *L'Etranger* and to understand its philosophic matrix.

Chapter II

The Influence of Nietzsche

THE REJECTION OF GOD

Walter Kaufmann, perhaps the best-known commentator on the work of Friedrich Nietzsche in the English-speaking world, said some time ago in an article entitled "Nietzsche and Existentialism":

> Nietzsche's critique of Christianity is at least in some of its aspects part of a much larger undertaking that one might call a critique of *Weltanschauungen*, a critique of "world views." The "world view" that he writes about the most is Christianity, because it has had a particularly fateful importance for the Western world. Continuous with that we find an analysis of "nihilism." What interests Nietzsche beyond nihilism is possible attitudes that man might adopt towards an absurd world—again a theme that you find in Heidegger, Sartre and Camus.[1]

Kaufmann is saying two things, and on both scores he is correct: that it was Nietzsche's aim to provide a critique of world views and in particular to criticize the Christian view of things, but that he was equally concerned, like Camus, to consider the possible responses that a man might adopt to the absurd.

There are, however, two important points which Kaufmann does not make, or at any rate does not emphasize, in this article. First, Nietzsche's critique of world views, and of Christianity in particular, is dictated by the belief that they are a source of human alienation, and so prevent man being at one with himself and the world in which he lives. For Nietzsche, as for Camus, the question of the existence or nonexistence of God is, as Feuerbach says, the question of the existence or nonexistence of man. Second, there is a moral as well as a metaphysical aspect to Nietzsche's thinking on the question of human existence. It is, in his view, the acceptance of conventional morality, as well as of religious belief, that results in man's alienation. This section of the present chapter will be devoted to an exposition of the metaphysical aspect of Nietzsche's thinking on alienation. It will be followed immediately by a consideration of his views on the relationship between Christian morality and human estrangement.

Nietzsche's first major work, *The Birth of Tragedy*, is concerned, ostensibly at any rate, with the origins of Greek tragedy, which was born, he insists, of the union of Dionysus and Apollo. The two Greek deities, Apollo and Dionysus, are gods of art. Apollo represents the world of beauty. If we look down into man's lowest depths, however, below the sphere of thought and imagination, we come upon a world of terror and rapture: This is the realm of Dionysus and of the art which derives its name from him. It is man's desire for measure and proportion which gives rise to Apollonian art; the art of Dionysus represents that which is in flux and in chaos.

> The word "Apollonian" stands for the state of rapt repose in the presence of a visionary world, in the presence of the world of beautiful appearance designed as a deliverance from becoming: this word "Dionysus," on the other hand, stands for strenuous becoming. The first-named would have the vision it conjures up eternal.[2]

Now Nietzsche is more concerned with life than with art, for the views expressed in *The Birth of Tragedy* are metaphysical or, more accurately, metaphysico-artistic. They promote an ideal of life that Nietzsche takes to be original and truly human. And it is, he insists, the acceptance of this ideal that leads man to resist the claims made upon him by Apollo, on the one hand, and Dionysus, on the other. The former tempts him with his other-worldliness; the latter with an excessive realism that would have man accept what is, at the price of what ought to be. And just as true culture was born of the union of Dionysus and Apollo, so authentic living demands that man identify himself with the culture of the tragic artist.

Nietzsche insists, however, that when the culture of pre-Socratic Greece[3] had reached its zenith, the philosophers upset the delicate balance of intellect and life by insisting upon "reason at any price."[4] Historically, this decline is said to have begun with the advent of Socratic philosophy and to have culminated in Christianity. Nietzsche's hostility to "the fall" that began with the triumph of reason is undeniable. "With Socrates Greek taste veers round, in favour of dialectics. What actually occurs? In the first place, a noble taste is vanquished."[5] Nietzsche would not deny reason a place in life, but he thinks that the philosophers have carried things too far. Reason is, in their view, synonymous with life, and everything other than reason is banished to the realm of unreality. The "preponderance of the logical faculties is indicative of decadence,"[6] for when philosophy triumphs, "man finds it necessary, as Socrates did, to create a tyrant out of reason."[7] The philosophers followed the cue of Socrates in equating reason, virtue and happiness, "the weirdest equation ever seen, and one which was essentially opposed to all the instincts of the older Hellenes."[8]

Nietzsche opposes philosophy, reason and Socratism, because philosophy is, in his view, the tool of Apollo, and because it is, in some respects at least, escapist. It belongs to the realm of form and must come under the sway of Dionysus if it is to contribute to human living. This task, however, is not one the philosophers will perform, for it is essential to their calling that they remain the disciples of Apollo and betray the earth. Indeed, Nietzsche speaks of the "constraint of concepts, species, forms, purposes and laws,"[9] and defines the philosophers as "idolaters of concepts,"[10] who give a "false realism to a piece of fiction."[11]

Socratic philosophy upset the balance of the tragic culture and alienated man by denying to this world the reality it accorded to concepts. "In all ages the wisest have always agreed in their judgement of life: *it is no good* . . . Even Socrates' dying words were: 'To live means to be ill a long while: I owe a cock to the god Aesculapius.' "[12]

Plato carried this rationalism a step further. For him, the objects of the senses were not really real but *eidola;* the senses give man opinion but do not provide him with knowledge. Only the forms are truly knowable, because only they are really real, and it is not by the senses but by reason that man knows the forms. "In reality, my distrust of Plato is fundamental. I find him so very much astray from all the deepest instincts of the Hellenes, so steeped in moral prejudices, so pre-existently Christian—the concept 'good' is already the highest value with him." The whole of Platonism Nietzsche calls " 'superior bunkum,' or, if you would like it better, 'idealism.' " Plato is "that double-faced fascination called the 'ideal,' which made it possible for the more noble natures of antiquity to misunderstand themselves and to tread the bridge which led to the 'cross.' "[13] He blames Plato for creating "ideal happiness"[14] and the "ideal man"; he is the philosopher king, the prince of devils who "are prejudiced *against* appearance,"[15] who lack "a sense of history, a knowledge of physiology,"[16] who "have always trusted concepts as unconditionally as they have mistrusted the senses."[17] Plato marks the point of transition from philosophy to Christianity, from the Apollinism of reason to that of dogma.

Nietzsche, then, blames the philosophers for destroying the balance achieved by the tragic culture. They took the side of Apollo, he insists, and so betrayed the earth. The criticisms which he makes of the philosophers are applied in even greater measure to Christianity, for two reasons: first, because in Nietzsche's view Christianity is merely a popular form of Platonism which has brought to the level of the general public the philosophic speculations of Socrates and Plato; second, because it has not only perpetuated but brought to completion the hatred of life begun in Socratism and carried on in Platonism.

Nietzsche clearly regards Christianity as Apollonian. In one place, for example, he contrasts the God of "the last two thousand years" with the Greek gods, to the detriment of the former.[18] The Greek gods were superior men but not the enemies of the earth; the Christian God is infinitely greater than man and reduces him to nothingness. When Greek culture declined, there came the philosophers "with their negation of the world, their enmity to life, their disbelief in the senses."[19] And they were followed by the Christians, typified by the "ascetic priest" who is "the incarnate wish for an existence of another kind, an existence on another plane—he is, in fact, the highest point of this wish, its official ecstacy and passion."[20]

Nietzsche writes:

> To shatter the strong, to spoil great hopes, to cast suspicion on the delight in beauty, to break down everything autonomous—all instincts which are natural to the highest and most successful type of "man" . . . to invert all love of the earthly and of supremacy over the earth into hatred of the earth and of earthly things—*that* is the task which the Church imposed on itself, and was obliged to impose, until according to its standard of value "unworldliness," "unsensuousness," and "higher man" fused into one sentiment.[21]

The view of Christianity which Nietzsche expresses here is that of Feuerbach, but while the latter thought that the "truth" of Christianity should be restored in the name of authenticity, Nietzsche was of the opinion that religion should be totally rejected. "To be sure, except you become as little children you shall not enter into *that* kingdom of heaven. And Zarathustra pointed aloft with his hands. But we do not at all want to enter into the kingdom of heaven: we have become men—*so we want the kingdom of earth.*"[22]

This aspect of Nietzsche's philosophy is a significant one. Its influence is to be seen not only in the works of Christian writers such as Bonhoeffer,[23] Robinson,[24] and Ricoeur,[25] who argue that an acceptance of the death of the god of metaphysics is an absolute precondition for Christianity, but especially in the thought of philosophers such as Camus, in whose eyes the acceptance even of the god of faith must inevitably result in man's alienation.

This brings us to Nietzsche's ethical reflections and to a consideration of the role which morality plays in his concept of alienation.

THE REJECTION OF MORALITY

Nietzsche's critique of what might be called Christian metaphysics is a forceful one. It is, however, considerably less virulent than his assault upon conventional morality. The latter critique, in fact, is what defined his life's work: "Have you understood me? That which defines me, that which makes me stand apart from the whole of the rest of humanity, is the fact that I *unmasked* Christian morality."[26]

And it must be "unmasked," because it is an even greater threat to authentic human existence than is the acceptance of the Christian God:

> Oh my brethren! With whom lieth the greatest danger to the whole human future? Is it not with the good and the just?—and whatever harm the wicked may do, the harm of the good is the harmfullest harm.
>
> And whatever harm the "world-maligners" may do, the harm of the good is the harmfullest harm.[27]

Morality is the primary source of man's alienation from his true character. But what is it that leads Nietzsche to this conclusion? We have already noted that he takes Christianity in general to be Apollonian; now, most commentators suggest that his opposition to conventional morality derives from an assumption that ethical values likewise are other-worldly. This point is not an inaccurate one, but it needs to be qualified, for morality is, in Nietzsche's view, Apollonian only in the sense that it is linked to belief in God and the acceptance of an afterlife. Immortality, God and ethical values stand, or fall, together. In this respect they are other-worldly, and it is for this reason that the destruction of morality follows upon the death of God. The virulence of Nietzsche's opposition to moral values, however, does not derive (not primarily at any rate) from the belief that they are Apollonian in origin, but from the conviction that they are alienating in effect. Nietzsche is convinced, in other words, that the acceptance of ethical values inevitably entails the living of an unauthentic existence. For it is, as we shall see, the exercise of will to power beyond good and evil that leads to the cultivation of the finer nature. Nietzsche defines life as "nothing more nor less than the instinct of growth [and] . . . of power,"[28] and insists that morality is directed "precisely against the life instincts."[29]

For Nietzsche, then, morality is inimical to life. This, however, is his conclusion; we must examine the arguments that he adduces for it.

Nietzsche opposes the Christian ethic not primarily because he regards it as untrue but because of the psychology which he takes to be inseparable from Christian belief. Conventional morality, in his view, is accepted for the wrong reasons and has a detrimental effect on the lives of those who accept it. "The question concerning the mere truth of Christianity is quite beside the point so long as no inquiry is made into the value of Christian morality."[30] And although it is not until *Human, All-Too-Human* that he begins to treat morality in some detail, *The Birth of Tragedy* already indicates the direction of his subsequent thought. At one point, for example, it describes Christianity as "the most extravagant burlesque of a moral theme to which mankind has hitherto been obliged to listen."[31]

How, then, does Nietzsche view the psychology of the believer? His reply is unambiguous. Religion is nothing but an opiate. Men accept it through fear, hope, laziness, because they cannot bear existence without it or, most important of all, through "resentment."

One of the main considerations that Nietzsche advances to argue for the particular virulence of Christianity is that the morality it promotes is one that it is easy to live by. The desire for comfort is what lies at the back of much that passes for virtue. It is, he says, "the faint-hearted devil in thee, which would fain hold its arms, and place its hands on its bosom, and take it easier: the faint-hearted devil persuadeth thee 'there *is* a God!' "[32] Indeed, this view of Christianity as the work of the "faint-hearted devil" seems to have played an important part in Nietzsche's outlook from a very early period in his life. As early as 1865 he wrote:

> Is it then a matter of arriving at a concept of God, world, and atonement which will give us a feeling of the greatest smugness? When exploring, are we looking for rest, peace, happiness? No, only truth, even if it were most repelling and ugly. It is here that the paths of men part.
>
> Should you long for peace of the soul and happiness, then by all means believe. Should you want to become a disciple of truth, then search.[33]

The religious man, of course, contends that his values are not easily realized but are in truth the highest to which man can aspire. This, however, is simply because "our vanity would like what we do best to pass precisely for what is most difficult to us"; it is, moreover, "the origin of many systems of morals."[34] The Christian would have us adopt an "ideal which . . . appeals to all the cowardices and vanities of wearied souls":[35] We must recognize that conventional morality appeals to what is lowest in us and that it marks the parting of the ways for the weak and the strong.

There are some who adopt the Christian ethic because it provides them with something secure on which they can stand amid the insecurities of life. In this respect they are like Socrates, whose object in moral philosophy was to provide a bulwark against the moral relativism of the sophists. Such people need only keep to the rules; they need not ask whether these precepts do justice to man. In this respect Christian morality can be accommodated easily within the general spirit of Christianity, which is nothing more than "a great treasure-chamber of ingenious consolations"[36] and the expression of man's "metaphysical need."[37]

There are also those who accept morality through fear or hope. In *The Will to Power*,[38] Nietzsche tells us that the "holy lie" invented

1. a God who *punishes* and *rewards*;
2. an *After-Life*, in which, alone, the great penal machine is supposed to be active—to this end the *immortality of the soul* was invented;
3. a *conscience in man*;
4. morality . . . as the interpretation of all phenomena as the effects of a moral order of things (that is to say, the concept of punishment and reward).

Nietzsche's thinking on this point is clear. He is underlining his view of the relationship between religious faith and morality, and is saying that moral values are accepted out of fear of eternal damnation or hope of eternal reward. And this amounts, in his view, to accepting a pseudomorality out of hope for, or fear of, what is illusory. The only reality to which man ought to aspire, and the only thing of which he need fear the loss, is that of his "finer nature," which only a life beyond good and evil can realize.

There is another reason for the widespread acceptance of morality, and this Nietzsche calls "resentment." This concept is of the utmost importance in his account of the genesis of morals and consequently in his thinking on alienation. It is in *Beyond Good and Evil* and *A Genealogy of Morals* that "resentment" is treated in greatest detail.

Beyond Good and Evil has a great deal to say about the development of moral attitudes. It claims that in the ancient world there was no "morality of love of one's neighbour."[39] The Romans, for example, were often sympathetic toward one another and acted in a virtuous manner; but acts of this kind "do not as yet belong to the domain of moral valuation [sic]—they are still *ultra-moral*." Moral actions contribute "to the welfare of the whole, to the *res publica.*"[40] This was because the situation demanded that the state protect itself against threats from external forces.

When the fabric of society "is secured against external danger, it is fear of our neighbour which again creates new perspectives of moral valuation [*sic*]." The danger is not now from other states but from other individuals, with the result that "the lofty, independent spirituality, the will to stand alone, and even the cogent reason, are felt to be dangers; everything that elevates the individual above the herd and is a source of fear to the neighbour is henceforth called evil."[41]

That is called "evil," then, which is to be feared, whether it be another state or another person within the state. "If one could at all do away with danger, the cause of fear, one would have done away with this morality at the same time."[42] And this leads him to say that "*morality* in Europe today is herding-animal morality,"[43] of a kind which is designed to make all men equally strong so that no one will have anything to fear from any other.

It is a short step from the claim that those who term "evil" what is a threat to them will call "good" any type of action which need be no danger to them. It is a one which Nietzsche is not slow to take.[44] He insists, as does Plato's Callicles, that men are not in fact equal, for there are the strong and the weak, and consequently there is a morality of the strong and a morality of the weak. The strong oppose "good" and "bad"; the weak think in terms of "good" and "evil." The difference is more than a linguistic one. In the case of the powerful man, "good" means that which is noble, or which proceeds from the powerful man, while that conduct is "bad," which is performed by the despicable (that is, the weak) man. The impotent look on things rather differently. For them, that is "good" which does not pose a threat to their impotence; they favour a morality which terms "good" virtues such as sympathy and charity. At the same time, the powerless call "evil" the instincts of the powerful, whose conduct is detrimental to them. "The slave has an unfavourable eye for the virtues of the powerful."[45]

This point of view is expounded in greater detail in *A Genealogy of Morals*, where much is made of "resentment." Nietzsche opposes the view of certain "English psychologists" that the word "good" was originally applied to altruistic acts by those who benefitted from them and that gradually the origin of the word has been forgotten.[46] His view of the genesis of moral notions is that, originally, those actions were called good which were performed by the good man, where by the good man he means the powerful one; while those were called "bad" which were opposed to these: "The chronic and despotic *esprit de corps* and fundamental instinct of the higher dominant race coming into association with the meaner race, the 'under race,' this is the origin of the antithesis of good and bad."[47] Egotism and altruism have no relevance to moral epithets, for they enter only with "the *decay* of aristocratic values,"[48] and have to do with the pseudomorality of the herd. As Nietzsche continues, he develops these themes: "Everywhere 'aristocratic' 'noble' . . . is the root idea out of which has necessarily developed 'good,' in the sense of 'with aristocratic soul'. . . . a development which invariably runs parallel with that other evolution by which 'vulgar,' 'plebeian,' 'low' are made to change finally into 'bad.' "[49]

Nietzsche also claims that the etymology of the word "bonus" favours his thesis: it is derived from "duonus," meaning a warrior.[50] This Nietzsche considered an important point, for he wrote to his friend Peter Gast:

> I am glad to hear that the Danish philologists approve of my derivation of *bonus* and accept it. Considered in itself it is quite a feat to derive the concept "good" from the concept "warrior." No philologist would ever have been able to hit upon such an idea without the presuppositions I furnished.[51]

The obvious question to be raised at this point is the following: If the account of the genesis of morals is as Nietzsche claims it to be, how does it happen that most people regard altruistic actions as virtuous and are of the opinion that there need not be anything particularly virtuous about the "warrior?" It is precisely at this point that Nietzsche makes use of "resentment." The weak, he says, found it necessary to take revenge upon the strong, because they could not endure their subservience. To avenge themselves against their masters they brought about a transvaluation of values, out of "resentment." Thus "the revolt of the slaves in morals begins in the very principle of *resentment* becoming creative and giving birth to values."[52] Historically, Nietzsche traces this act of "cleverest revenge" to the Jews, whom he calls "that priestly nation of resentment *par excellence*."[53] It was they who, in opposition to the aristocratic equation of good, aristocratic, beautiful, happy . . . said that "the wretched are above the good; the poor, the weak, the lowly are alone the good. The men of power are evil, accursed."[54] This is truly a transvaluation of existing values, for in answer to the question "Who is really evil according to the meaning of the morality of resentment?" he replies: "just the good man of the other morality, just the aristocratic, the powerful one."[55] The slaves are forced in the name of their own safety to impose upon the strong an ethic that is to their own advantage. The result is that

> the impotence which requites not is turned to "goodness," craven baseness to meekness, submission . . . to obedience. The inoffensive character of the weak, the very cowardice in which he is rich . . . gain here fine names such as "patience,"

which is also called "virtue," not being able to avenge one's self is called not wishing to avenge oneself, perhaps even forgiveness.[56]

Morality then is an instrument by which the slaves, who are the majority, control the strong, who are the few. "Good" is what is useful to the slaves, "evil" is what is a threat to them. The "higher men" and the slaves have a will to power, and while that of the masters is expressed in a morality *beyond* good and evil, that of the slaves is expressed in a morality *of* good and evil. And while the master morality represents an exercise of the will to power over oneself, that of the slaves involves the exercise of this will to power over others.[57] The supermen, moreover, have been overthrown by the will to power of the slaves; the outcome of this power struggle finds its expression in the Christian ethic.

In Nietzsche's conception of the fall, then, it is Christianity that plays the main role, for it was this religion that effected a transvaluation of values and put the slaves above the masters. It is the work of those with a herd mentality; it extols values which express what is worst in man. Conventional morality reduces man to the level of mediocrity, where he is alienated from his true self. Christianity is "the reverse of the principle of selection"; its virtues put men "in the fetters of false values," and the inevitable consequence of its acceptance is that "the maximum potentiality of the power and splendour of the human species [is] never to be attained."[58]

Nietzsche's whole attitude to established values may be summed up as follows: "My view: all the forces and instincts which are at the source of life are lying beneath *the ban* of morality; morality is the life-denying instinct. Morality must be annihilated if life is to be emancipated."[59]

The acceptance of conventional ethical norms results in man's alienation; authenticity demands that morality be rejected.

The ethical aspect of Nietzsche's thinking on the question of human alienation has been particularly influential. Its impact is readily discernible, not only on the works of Sartre, but on those of all contemporary atheistic humanists who accept as a fundamental tenet of their thought that conventional morality is a source of human alienation. It is to be seen most clearly in the uncritical endorsement by Camus of Nietzsche's claim that traditional moral values have their origin in the dictates of God, are intimately related to other-worldly sanctions and reduce all who accept them to a level that is less than truly human. For Camus as for Nietzsche, the acceptance of Christian ethics results at best in the vilification of man, at worst in nihilism.

Chapter III

Saint Augustine: The Place of Happiness

PLOTINUS AND ST. AUGUSTINE

Whoever possesses God is happy.

—*The Happy Life*, 5,34

Saint Augustine's name appears only infrequently in Camus' writings. He is mentioned explicitly in *La Peste* (1937)[1] and implicitly in *L'Homme révolté* (1951)[2]; and his name appears, for example, in a notebook entry dated October 1946[3] as well as in an interview published in the *Revue du Caire* (1948).[4] If Augustine's name appears only rarely in Camus' writings, however, Augustinian themes abound in those same writings. *Le Mythe de Sisyphe* and *L'Etranger* have, as one of their major concerns, the theme of human autonomy. *La Peste* is about the problem of evil, and contains an explicit rejection of Augustine's free will defence.[5] *L'Homme révolté* has as one of its main themes that of a substitute universe and is concerned, to a large extent, with the Augustinian notion of moderation. *La Chute* is about Original Sin. And in a talk which was delivered in 1948 and published as *L'Incroyant et les Chrétiens*,[6] Camus mentioned, as Archambault says,[7] two themes which were of great concern to him: that of man's desperate need of grace and that of the damnation of unbaptized children. He insisted, moreover, that he himself was not the author of those themes.

> It is not I who invented the wretchedness of creatures, nor the terrifying formulas of divine malediction. It is not I who cried this *Nemo bonus*, or who proclaimed the damnation of unbaptised children. It is not I who said that man was incapable of saving himself by his own efforts alone, and that, from the depths of his misery, his sole hope lay in the grace of God.[8]

What is particularly significant, however, is the centrality and ubiquity of the Augustinian concept, natural desire for God, in the thought of Camus. As we have pointed out, it is not possible properly to understand Camus' thinking on the absurd, as it is expressed in *Le Mythe de Sisyphe* and *L'Etranger*, without realizing that, in his opinion, man is made for "something similar to the Christian heaven." This point is at least implicit in his assertion that existentialism has its origins in Saint Augustine.[9] In *La Peste*, moreover, Camus claims that man is made for totality; and in *L'Homme révolté* he insists that it is man's desire for God that drives him to create a substitute universe.

The purpose of this chapter is twofold: to say something of Camus' *Métaphysique chrétienne et Néoplatonisme*, insofar as it relates specifically to Augustine's thought[10]; and to elucidate the meaning of the concept of the natural desire for God in Camus' philosophy, by examining the part it played in Saint Augustine's philosophical anthropology.

The final chapter of Camus' thesis is devoted entirely to the thought of Saint Augustine. It has three sections, which deal in turn with "Saint Augustine's psychological experience and Neoplatonism," "Hellenism and Christianity in Saint Augustine," and the latter's thoughts on "faith and reason." The second of these sections is divided into two parts which deal respectively with Augustine's reflections on the closely related notions of evil, grace and freedom, and with his thoughts on the Trinity.

The first section of Camus' final chapter is concerned, essentially, with the extent of Saint Augustine's Platonism, or, more precisely, with the role of Plotinus in Augustine's conversion. Camus argues that the Plotinian influence on Augustine was considerable and, in particular, that it was Augustine's encounter with the *Enneads* of Plotinus that provided him with the conceptual framework he needed in order to understand and formulate the Christian doctrine of the Logos, as that is expressed in the prologue of Saint John's Gospel. The second hypostasis of Plotinus, he says, became one with the *verbum caro factum* of Saint John.[11]

If, according to Camus, Augustine was indebted to Plotinus for his doctrine of the Word as mediator between God and man, he was no less indebted to him for his teaching on the nature of physical evil. The problem of evil had, of course, been a particularly difficult one for Augustine; to such a degree, indeed, that it explained his lengthy adherence to Manichaean philosophy. It was Plotinus who enabled Augustine to find an answer to this problem, for the former taught that evil was "linked to matter" and that its reality was "entirely negative."[12]

Camus' reflections on his chosen theme do not end, however, with the influence of Plotinus on Augustine's conversion, but with the psychological makeup of Augustine himself. In what is an extraordinarily illuminating remark, Camus points out that the curious feature of the author of the *Confessions* is that his personal experience remains "the constant point of reference for all his intellectual inquiries."[13] Augustine's conversion came, as a result, not with the reading of the *Enneads* alone, but with the acknowledgement of his own moral inadequacy and with an experience of grace so profound that it brought abut a conversion which Camus describes as an "almost physical" one.

The second part of Camus' final chapter is intended "to elucidate, in Saint Augustine's thought, the basic themes of Christianity."[14] More precisely, however, it is an attempt to elucidate some fundamental Christian themes, as treated by Augustine, and to determine the extent to which they concur with Hellenic thinking on those same themes. Camus' initial reflections are devoted to the topics of evil, grace and freedom; he then turns to Augustine's teaching on the Logos and the Trinity.

Camus' exposition of the problem of evil in Augustine draws attention to the latter's principle of plenitude and his free will defence, though Camus does not name these as such. Physical evil is regarded, in Plotinian terms, as a privation, and is said to contribute to the harmony of the universe in a way that is similar to the contribution which the dark areas of a painting make to the beauty of that same painting taken as a whole.[15] Moral evil is, for Augustine, a greater problem than natural evil, but for all that it is one which he does not shirk. Sin, he insists, is imputable to all men and is the result of a primeval fall.[16] Original Sin, moreover, has destroyed man's freedom to do good and left him only the power to do evil and to trust in the grace of God, which, though gratuitous, is always necessary for salvation.[17]

After treating of the problems of sin, grace and freedom, Camus turns to Augustine's teaching on the Trinity. His aim, in so doing, is to determine the extent to which this fundamental Christian doctrine, as understood and expounded by Saint Augustine, is influenced by "Platonic authors."

This aspect of Augustine's thought owes much, Camus insists, to Plotinus, who, as we have seen, provided him with "a conception of the Word" that was "purely philosophical," and thereby gave him the apparatus he needed in order to come to terms, intellectually, with a doctrine otherwise incomprehensible to him. "The ideas," for Plotinus, "participate in all that is divine. They are in him [the One], and yet he is superior to them."[18] It is, says Camus, the principle of participation that is crucial here, and this just as much for Augustine as for Plotinus. He feels justified therefore in quoting a "robust text" of *The Trinity* which shows clearly the extent of Plotinus' influence on this aspect of Augustine's thought:

> Hence, because there is the one Word of God, through which all things were made, which is the unchangeable truth, all things in it are originally and unchangeably simultaneous, not only the things which are now in this whole creation, but also those which have been and are to be. In it, however, these things have not been, nor are they to be, they only are; and all things are life, and all things are one, or rather it is one thing alone which is, and one single life.[19]

Augustine's thinking on the Trinity, then, owes much to Plotinus. While his debt to the latter is great in this regard, it is nonetheless far from being total, for there are, says Camus, fundamental differences between the positions of the two authors on the subject of the Trinity. The first of these differences is, of course, that the Plotinian system does not allow for the Incarnation.[20] The second is that Augustine regards God the Father not, in Plotinian terms, as "the origin of the two other essences, but as the source of the unique nature of the Trinity."[21] Camus quotes Augustine's *Against the Discourses of the Arians*: "The one God is the Trinity itself, and so the one God is somehow or other the sole creator."

What Camus says of Augustine's position on the Trinity is not, of course, profound, but it is at least accurate. He goes on, however, to write an extraordinary passage, one which, as Paul Archambault says, reveals his inability to distinguish "theological fact . . . from misinterpretation and sheer fantasy."[22] This passage tells us that Augustine's trinitarian teaching can be adequately summarized as follows:

> The three persons are therefore identical. Three basic conclusions follow from this: the three persons have merely one single will and one single operation. "Where there is no nature, there is no diversity of wills." "It is not, then, the Word alone who appeared on the earth, but the whole Trinity." "In the Son's Incarnation it is the Trinity in its entirety which is united to the human body."[23]

The closing part of Camus' final chapter deals with the relationship between faith and reason in Augustine. Camus in fact summarizes, very briefly, Augustine's solution to what he describes as the conflict between reason and revelation, and underlines its historical importance.

Augustine's contribution to this problem was, according to Camus, to enlarge the scope of human reason or, as he puts it, to make reason more "flexible," by submitting it to the light of revealed truth.[24] Augustine's philosophy, he insists, is the combination of a progressive "compromise" between Hellenic philosophy and Christian faith. In Augustinian thought, which constitutes a "second revelation," metaphysics and religion, the Word and the Flesh, are reconciled without the original physiognomy of Christianity being lost in the process.[25] The historical importance of Augustine's approach to the problem of the relation of reason to revelation was that it transformed Christianity into a philosophy and, in so doing, guaranteed its widespread acceptance.[26]

Camus' reflections on Augustine's thought are, as we have hinted, sometimes wide of the mark. However, they are rarely unimportant for the understanding of Camus' own philosophy. Of particular importance is Camus' understanding of the nature of Augustine's conversion, in the year 386, for this understanding, or more precisely the implications of it, throw considerable light upon the meaning which Camus attached to the concept of natural desire for God in the thought of Augustine and, as we shall see, upon how this concept is to be understood in Camus' own philosophy. It would therefore be useful to ask how Camus viewed Augustine's conversion and to look at the implications for Camus' own thought of his understanding of that conversion.

The fourth chapter of Camus' thesis opens with a comparison of a number of Augustinian texts with similar ones from the *Enneads* of Plotinus.[27] This comparison leads Camus to the conclusion that the influence of Platonism on Augustine's thought is very great indeed.[28] It is extremely significant, however, that after making this point, Camus immediately goes on to say that while the influence of Plotinian philosophy on Augustine's conversion was immense, this influence was by no means inestimable, and to refer to Alfaric's conclusions on this question as "unwarranted."[29] In Camus' opinion, then, Augustine was converted in 386 not to Christianity nor, as Alfaric claims, to Platonism but to Christianity *and* Platonism.[30]

The importance of this point for the proper understanding of Augustine's reflections on man's natural desire for God, or at any rate on Camus' understanding of Augustine's thinking on this question, could scarcely be exaggerated, for it has two crucial implications. The first is that Augustine accepted, in Camus' opinion, the essence of Plotinus' thinking on the Platonic theme of "conversion," and this as early as A.D. 386. Man carries with him, for Augustine as for Plotinus, the memory of a lost homeland.[31] The second implication is that, in Camus' opinion, the God whom man naturally desires is not in Augustine's eyes the One of Plotinus, but the Christian God.

What Augustine demanded, along with Faith, was truth; along with dogmas, a metaphysic. So too did the whole of Christianity. But if he embraced Neoplatonism for a short time, he was soon to transform it. And with it the whole of Christianity.

That place which Christianity uniquely accords to Christ and the Incarnation should therefore be retained in Augustine's thought. The figure of Jesus and the problem of the Redemption are going to change everything.[32]

Camus' understanding of Augustine's thinking on the concept *desiderium naturale* is scarcely in doubt: Man is naturally made for God. This understanding is, I would suggest, extremely important, not only for a grasp of Camus' reflections on Augustine but for a proper appreciation of the early thought of Camus himself. In the opinion of the latter, human life is absurd; it lacks the kind of meaning it would have if God existed and immortality were available to man. Human existence can only be absurd, however, if, as we have suggested, man is made for something similar to the Christian heaven, and if such does not exist.[33] Camus' philosophy of man is therefore precisely that of Augustine, at any rate as the former understood that anthropology. There can be no doubt, moreover, that it has its origins in the study of Augustine's thought which Camus pursued for his *Diplôme d'études supérieures*.[34] It only remains now for us to consider Augustine's philosophical anthropology, with a view to elucidating more fully the absurdist philosophy of *Le Mythe de Sisyphe* and *L'Etranger*.[35]

DESIRE FOR GOD

It has been said by some scholars that the central theme of Augustine's thought at Cassiciacum was "interiority."[36] This is not entirely accurate, however, for "interiority" was for Augustine not so much a theme as a method. "Interiority" means "a search of one's heart, of one's own interior, of the life of one's own consciousness."[37] It was, in short, a means which Augustine employed in order to arrive at an understanding of himself and, by implication, of man. And the insight which is perhaps most important in Augustine's early thought is precisely what the use of this method revealed to him: that man is a being who naturally desires happiness. The central theme of the early Augustine, therefore, is not interiority but happiness.[38] It is one that is of crucial importance in all the Cassiciacum dialogues; and it was to the question of happiness that Augustine devoted his first major philosophical work, *The Happy Life*. It is to that theme and to the analysis of it there that we first turn.

The Happy Life is notable, among other things, for Augustine's insistence that while no man can be happy who does not have what he desires, a man may well have what he desires and yet not be happy. The problem of happiness in *The Happy Life* therefore centres, as it does also in the *Soliloquies,* on two questions: What should a man desire in order to be happy? How is he to attain the object or goal that would bring him happiness?[39] It is to be noted, however, that Augustine does not ask, in this work or in any other, whether happiness is indeed what man desires: that man does wish to be happy is, in Augustine's view, simply a truth[40]; it is with this truth that Augustine's anthropological reflections begin. We therefore find him stating quite explicitly in *The Free Choice of the Will* (which was written about the same time as the Cassiciacum dialogues) that while all men do not attain to happiness, all truly desire it:

> *Aug.*   But do you not think that every man wills and desires the happy
>   life in every way possible?
>
> *Evod.* Undoubtedly.
>
> *Aug.*   Hence when we say that men are unhappy by their own choice,
>   we are not saying that they want to be unhappy but that their
>   will is such that unhappiness results of necessity and even
>   against their will. Hence this does not go counter to our earlier
>   conclusion that all men want to be happy, though not all
>   succeed because they do not all have the will to lead an upright
>   life, and it is this will which alone can merit the happy life.[41]

Augustine might therefore appear to be at odds with the proposition expressed by Aristotle at the beginning of the *Metaphysics,* and endorsed by many of the greatest thinkers in the history of philosophy, that "all men by nature desire to know." Augustine's early thought, however, reveals that while the difference between himself and, for example, Aristotle on this particular point is considerable, it is not as great as might be expected; for there is in Augustine's thought, as Gilson says, "a close relationship between the idea of happiness and that of truth."[42]

The precise nature of this relationship, and indeed of the truth in question, will, of course, have to be determined in this chapter, but it is important, before doing so, to point out that the Cassiciacum dialogues are unambiguous on two fundamental points: that happiness is related *in some way* to truth; and that the question of how these are related to one another is, for Augustine, an extremely important one. Both these points are borne out clearly in *Answer to Sceptics,* for one of the interlocutors, Trygetius, claims that man cannot be happy without the knowledge of truth,[43] while another, Licentius, says that happiness is to be found in the mere search for truth.[44] Augustine himself insists that "the question in debate is a matter of the utmost importance" and that it is therefore "worthy of diligent discussion."[45]

What is the relationship between happiness and truth? Is happiness to be found in the search for knowledge, or in the attainment of it? What kind of knowledge is it that gives man happiness? Is it, for example, mathematical knowledge, the reliability of which Augustine never doubted, even in his most sceptical moments? These are the questions that must now be considered. The first is answered unequivocally in *Answer to Sceptics*,[46] the second in the *Soliloquies;* much of what is said in *The Happy Life* is centrally relevant to both questions.

The view that happiness comes with the quest for knowledge is put very succinctly by Licentius in *Answer to Sceptics*. "Our ancestors," he says, "whom we credit with having been wise and happy, lived upright and happy lives by the mere fact that they were searching for truth."[47] It is, however, the position adopted by Trygetius that is endorsed by Augustine[48]: A man cannot be happy if he does not have wisdom, and one who is searching for truth cannot be wise: " . . . we require that a happy man be perfect, a sage in all respects. But, whoever is still searching is not perfect. Therefore I utterly fail to see how you can call him happy."[49]

The argument which Augustine employs against the sceptics in *The Happy Life* is a similar one: No man is happy who is not in possession of that which he desires to have; one who is searching for truth but has not yet found it cannot therefore be happy:

" . . . these [the Academics] strive for the truth, and so must wish to find it . . . But they do not find it; consequently, they do not possess what they wish, and therefore cannot be happy. No-one, however, is wise if he is not happy. Therefore, the Academic is not wise."[50]

For Augustine, happiness comes with the acquisition of knowledge. But what is the nature of the knowledge to which he refers at this point? This is a question to which, as we have said, the *Soliloquies* and *The Happy Life* address themselves. In the first of these works Augustine insists that happiness does not come with sense knowledge, which in his view does not constitute real or true knowledge at all. There can, he says, be no knowledge without truth, and the senses do not give man truth.[51] He goes on to argue, moreover, that the truths of mathematics, which are grasped by the intellect and which do constitute genuine objects of knowledge, are not the source of happiness; the latter, he insists, comes only with the knowledge of God.[52] In fact, the unique feature of this knowledge is that it alone confers happiness upon the one who attains to it.

> . . . no matter how forcibly you press and prove, I still dare not say that I want to know God as I know these things [the objects of mathematics] . . . if the knowledge of God and of these things were the same, I would rejoice over knowing them as much as I anticipate my joy in the knowledge of God. But, on the contrary, in comparison with Him I have such a low opinion of them that it sometimes seems to me that if I ever know Him and, if I ever see Him in the way in which He can be seen, all these things will vanish from my consideration. Even right now, by reason of the love I have for Him, they scarcely come into my mind.[53]

This is also the conclusion at which Augustine arrives in *The Happy Life*: All men, he says, naturally desire happiness. One of the major tasks of this work is (as we have said) to determine *what* a man should desire in order to be happy. At one point in the dialogue this question appears to be answered unambiguously, for Augustine insists that he who wishes to be happy should desire to possess God, who alone exists eternally and cannot be taken from man by any misfortune.[54] At this point, however, the question arises: What does it mean to possess God? Augustine's reply to this question *is* unambiguous: It means to grasp the Truth intellectually and so attain to wisdom:

> This, then, is the full satisfaction of souls, this the happy life: to recognize piously and completely the One through whom you are led into the truth, the nature of this truth you enjoy, and the bond that connects you with the supreme measure.[55]

In Augustine's view, then, happiness is attained not in the pursuit of truth nor even in the acquisition of it, but in the possession of wisdom, the knowledge of things divine.[56] *The Happy Life* tells us, moreover, that the awareness of this fact constitutes "the very kernel of philosophy."[57] Augustine makes this point very forcibly in *The Free Choice of the Will*, when he delivers his panegyric on truth and insists that happiness comes only with the knowledge of God:

> I had promised to show you, if you recall, that there is something higher than our mind and reason. There you have it—truth itself! Embrace it, if you can, and enjoy it; "find delight in the Lord and He will grant you the petitions of your heart." For what more do you desire than to be happy? And who is happier than the man who finds joy in the firm, changeless, and most excellent truth?[58]

Augustine's position is clear: Man can be happy only in the knowledge of Truth. But can such knowledge be had? Can in fact any knowledge at all be had? And why is this happiness to be attained only in the knowledge of Truth? These questions will bring us to the heart of Augustine's anthropology and clearly reveal the affinity that exists between this aspect of his philosophy and that of Camus.[59]

The problem of certitude, at any rate as that has been defined since the time of Kant, does not occupy the central place in Augustine's epistemology.[60] However, to assume that he was not in any way concerned with this problem would be to make a mistake of alarming proportions, for the Confessions tell us that Augustine himself was for a time attracted, if not seduced, by the scepticism of the New Academy and that he was brought to a state of despair by the thought that truth might not be attainable.[61] It is significant too that his first concern, after his conversion to Christianity in A.D. 386, was to refute that scepticism which he looked upon as an insuperable obstacle to the attainment of truth, and therefore of happiness.[62] This refutation is to be found in Answer to Sceptics[63] and in the second book of The Free Choice of the Will.

In the former work Augustine argues that even the sceptics, who think it probable that truth is not to be found, are certain of some truths. They do not doubt, for example, that there is either one world or more than one, and that if there is more than one world, then the number of worlds must be either finite or infinite. They hold, then, that of two disjunctive propositions one must be true and the other false. The truth of the principle of contradiction is therefore not placed in question.[64]

Again, Augustine argues that the sceptic must admit the truth of his subjective impressions. He may well be deceived if he judges to be objectively the case that which his senses tell him. But sense knowledge, considered as simple appearance, is infallible. When the sceptic's eyes tell him, for example, that towers are in movement, they do not deceive him, for towers do sometimes appear to move.[65]

We can also be certain, says Augustine in The Free Choice of the Will, of mathematical truths. When a person says that seven and three make ten, he does not say that they may make ten or that they ought to do so, but that they do make ten. And what he has in this case is knowledge:

> ... whenever anyone affirms that the eternal ought to be valued above the things of time, or that seven and three are ten, no one judges that it ought to be so, but merely recognises that it is so. He is not an examiner making corrections, but merely a discoverer, rejoicing over his discovery.[66]

Augustine says, moreover, that certain knowledge is not confined to the area of mathematical truths and abstract principles, for a man can be certain of his own existence. Even if he were to doubt the existence of other material things and of God, he would nevertheless be doubting; but the very fact that he doubts proves that he exists, for he could not doubt, if he did not exist.[67] Nor is there anything to be gained by suggesting that one might be deceived into thinking that one existed for, Augustine argues (in terms that anticipate those subsequently employed by Descartes[68]): If one did not exist, one could not be deceived.

> . . . to begin with what is most evident, I will ask you whether you yourself exist. Possibly, you are afraid of being mistaken by this kind of question when, actually, you could not be mistaken at all if you did not exist?[69]

What Augustine is saying in *Answer to Sceptics* and *The Free Choice of the Will*[70] is unambiguous: The sceptics may be right when they question the reliability of sense knowledge, but they cannot invalidate the certain knowledge that comes not through the senses but by way of the intellect. Now, it is the intellect that tells a man that he exists, lives and understands. The essence of Augustine's position is put very succinctly in *The City of God:*

> . . . we are, and we know that we are, and we love to be and to know that we are. And in this trinity of being, knowledge, and love there is not a shadow of illusion to disturb us. For, we do not reach these inner realities with our bodily senses as we do external objects.[71]

For Augustine, then, truth can be reached: man can obtain certain knowledge of the fact that he exists, lives and understands. But can he know Truth? This is the question which must now be considered. It is answered in the second book of *The Free Choice of the Will,* for example, where Augustine expounds his most famous argument for the existence of God, that taken from the eternity of truth, and insists that it is possible for man to obtain a natural knowledge of God's existence.[72]

The crux of this argument is expressed in similar terms by Eugène Portalié and Charles Boyer. The former writes:

> La raison de l'homme occupant le plus haut degré de la hiérarchie des êtres de ce monde, si elle découvre un être plus parfait, cet être sera Dieu. Or, ma raison constate qu'au-dessus d'elle, il y a la vérité éternelle et immuable, qu'elle ne crée pas, mais qu'elle contemple, qui n'est ni mienne, ni en moi, puisque les autres la contemplent aussi bien que moi et hors de moi. Cette vérité est donc Dieu lui-même ou, si l'on suppose un être, source de toute vérité.[73]

And Boyer says:

> Le raisonnement fondamental de saint Augustin revient à ce syllogisme: s'il est
> quelque chose au-dessus de notre raison, Dieu existe. Or, il est quelque chose
> au-dessus de notre raison. Donc, Dieu existe.[74]

It seems to me, however, that while, for example, Portalié's presentation of Augustine's proof is remarkably clear and unusually precise, it does not do justice to the latter's argument, the complexity of which cannot be expressed adequately in syllogistic form.[75] Augustine's demonstration of God's existence begins precisely where his refutation of the sceptics ended, that is, from the certainty that he exists, lives and understands, and proceeds by a very detailed line of reasoning to the conclusion that God exists. A careful analysis of this process of argumentation shows that it contains five steps.

Augustine argues, first, that existence, life and knowledge form an ascending scale of being and that knowledge is to be placed at the top of this scale, because it alone implies life and being:

> Ev.   . . . while these are three in numbers, existence, life and under-
> standing, and though the stone exists and the animal lives, yet
> I do not think that the stone lives or that the animal understands,
> whereas it is absolutely certain that whoever understands also
> exists and is living. That is why I have no hesitation in conclud-
> ing that the one which contains all three is more excellent than
> that which is lacking in one or both of these . . .[76]

He suggests, second, that man has senses and intellect or, more precisely, external senses, internal sense and reason. The greatest of these is reason, for "it knows itself and, unlike the senses, has knowledge in the strict sense." Moreover, it can judge not only the external senses but the internal sense, which is superior to those:

> Aug.   See now whether reason also judges the inner sense. I am not
> asking whether you have any doubt that reason is better than
> the inner sense because I am sure that this is your judgement.
> Yet I feel that now we should not ever have to ask whether
> reason passes judgement on the inner sense. For in the case of
> things inferior to it, namely, bodies, the bodily senses, and the
> inner sense, is it not, after all, reason itself that tells us how one
> is better than the other and how far superior reason itself is to
> all of them? This would not be possible at all unless reason were
> to judge them.
> Ev.   Obviously.[77]

Augustine argues, third, that if there is anything superior not only to reason and the data of reason, but to all else as well, this would be God:

> *Aug.* But suppose we could find something which you are certain not only exists but is also superior to our reason, would you hesitate to call this reality, whatever it is, God?
>
> *Ev.* If I were able to find something which is better than what is best in my nature, I would not immediately call it God. I do not like to call something God because my reason is inferior to it, but rather to call that reality God which has nothing superior to it.
>
> *Aug.* That is perfectly true.[78]

He insists, fourth, that there is something, namely, Truth, which is superior not only to reason but to the data of reason, because it is the Ground of their being.[79] These data are, of course, the necessary, immutable and eternal truths of, for example, mathematics and morals, which are common to all the minds that grasp them and superior to reason, which discovers them to be true and is therefore subject to them:

> *Aug.* You would in no way deny, then, that there exists unchangeable truth that embraces all things that are immutably true. You cannot call this truth mine or yours, or anyone else's. Rather, it is there to manifest itself as something common to all who behold immutable truths, as a light that in wondrous ways is both hidden and public.[80]

Augustine argues, finally, that God, who is Truth itself, therefore exists:

> *Aug.* You granted that if I could prove that there was something above our minds, you would admit that it was God, provided that there was still nothing higher. I argued and stated that it would be enough for me to prove this point. For if there is anything more excellent, then this is God; if not, then truth itself is God. In either case, you cannot deny that God exists, which was the question we proposed to examine in our discussion.
>
> *Ev.* I accept all this, overwhelmed as I am with an incredible joy which I am unable to express to you in words.[81]

Knowledge of Truth, in Augustine's view, *is* available to man. But why does happiness come only with the attainment of such knowledge? This is the question that must now be examined, and it is, as we have said, a crucial one. In his early thought, Augustine answers it at two levels. The relevant texts are *The Happy Life* and *Divine Providence and the Problem of Evil.*[82]

The first of these works is designed to show that happiness is to be found only in the knowledge of God, and the argument which Augustine employs in an attempt to establish this would appear to be a relatively simple one. For he insists first that man is composed of soul and body,[83] and that the food of the soul is knowledge.[84] He then argues that the only kind of knowledge that will satisfy the soul and make man happy is the knowledge of something that is permanent and that cannot be taken away from him. This, of course, can only be the knowledge of God.[85] This argument is, however, a deceptively simple one, for there underlie it certain metaphysical and ethical presuppositions which are not explicit in *The Happy Life*. These can best be brought to light if we turn our attention to the third and arguably the most important of the Cassiciacum dialogues.

Divine Providence is fundamentally a work of theodicy. More precisely, it is an attempt to reconcile belief in God with the existence of physical evil.[86] What concerns us, however, is not Augustine's address to the problem of evil but the emergence in the course of this work of a general view of things which, transcending as it does anthropological issues, helps us better to understand the conclusions at which he arrives in *The Happy Life*.

What, then, is the *Weltanschauung* of *Divine Providence* and what picture does it paint of man's nature and his place in the scheme of things? Augustine's answer to this question is unambiguous. Man has a rational soul and is therefore superior to physical creation and to the brute beasts.[87] He is, however, inferior to God, who is the originator of the order which, Augustine insists,[88] is all-embracing:

> "Would that you were not far astray," Trygetius said, "from that order which you defend, and that you were not so heedlessly (to put it mildly) borne against God. Indeed, what more hideous statement could be made than that evil things themselves are comprised in order, for surely God loves order?"
>
> "Of course, he loves it," Licentius replied. "From Him it comes, and with Him it is. And if anything can be more fittingly said of a thing so exalted, think it over by yourself, I say, for I am not competent to teach you such things now."[89]

The notion of order is, of course, a crucial one in the early writings of Augustine, such as *The Happy Life* and *Divine Providence*, as well as in the later ones, for example, *The Literal Meaning of Genesis* and the *City of God*. Augustine constantly insists (as he does in *Divine Providence* 2, 2, for instance) that while all created things are subject to the divine order, God "governs himself by means of order." Now this carries with it the implication that it is God, "the measureless measure of all measures," not man himself, who is the measure of man. This is stated as early as *The Happy Life* (4, 35), where Augustine says, as we have seen, that happiness is to be found in the knowledge of God, who is Himself nothing less than "the supreme measure."

For Augustine, then, the soul has its own place in the scheme of things: It is superior to the body and the material world but inferior to God. There is, however, another point to be made; it is the crucial one which underlies what Cayré describes as the "latent theocentrism" of Augustine's thought and it is therefore centrally relevant to our third question.[90] This point is that the Augustine not merely defines order as "that by which are governed all things that God has constituted,"[91] but describes it as a necessary precondition of the attainment of human perfection: "Order is that which will lead us to God, if we hold to it during life; and unless we hold to it during life we shall not come to God."[92]

Order, therefore, is not simply a *datum;* it is, for the soul, a challenge as well.[93] This challenge is met, to an ever-increasing extent, as man grows in the knowledge of God.[94] This is the point which Augustine makes very forcibly in *Divine Providence,* when he says, for example, that to be wise is to be with God and that "to be with God" is to grasp Him intellectually;[95] it is the very same point which he makes toward the end of this work, when he insists that the soul is perfected in the knowledge of Truth, in which its love of beauty attains to satiety in the vision of God himself: " . . . when the soul has properly adjusted and disposed itself, and has rendered itself harmonious and beautiful, then will it venture to see God, the very source of all truth and the very Father of Truth."[96]

Our reflections on Augustine's philosophy of man have, of course, been confined for the most part to the thought expressed in his philosophical dialogues, written at Cassiciacum in the course of the year 386-387. It is therefore important to draw attention, at the conclusion of this chapter, to the suggestion that Augustine was converted, in 386, not to Christianity but to Neoplatonism and that the happiness of which he speaks in, for example, *The Happy Life* is, as it were, the natural happiness that comes from a purely philosophical knowledge of God.

There are, it seems to me, two points which should be made in relation to this claim. The first is that it is simply an inaccurate one: Gilson is undoubtedly correct when he says that it is arrived at as a result of a mistaken interpretation of "certain equivocal expressions" employed by Augustine in *The Happy Life.*[97] For while Augustine does say in the *Soliloquies,* for example, that the knowledge of God is a unique form of knowledge and that it alone brings complete happiness,[98] he clearly identifies the happy life, in this dialogue as elsewhere, with the unending possession of that knowledge.[99]

The second book of the *Soliloquies* is, in fact, largely devoted to the discussion of immortality, and it is impossible to make sense of that discussion outside of that context. Moreover, Augustine says unequivocally in the first of the Cassiciacum dialogues that the happy life is the perfect one and that it is given only to those who do not solely love (and therefore know) God, but who hope for Him as well.[100] This teaching is substantially repeated in *The Retractions*[101] where Augustine refers to a comment made in *Soliloquies* (1, 7, 14) and writes: "I am not pleased with the remark that, in this life, the soul is already happy in the knowledge of God, unless, perhaps, through hope."

The second point that should be made is that Augustine's thought *in toto* makes it clear that while the philosophical knowledge of God does, in his view, bring man happiness, it is a kind of happiness which is perfected only in the direct Vision of God; and beatitude is, of course, attained only in the afterlife. This is the point which Augustine emphasizes not only in his *Commentaries on the Psalms*[102] and his *Sermons*[103] but in the *Confessions* as well.[104] It is, however, most obviously expressed in the *City of God*:

> Meanwhile, and always, the supreme good of the City of God is everlasting and perfect peace and not merely a continuing peace which individually mortal men enter upon and leave by birth and death, but one in which individuals immortally abide, no longer subject to any species of adversity. Nor will anyone deny that such a life must be most happy, or that this life, however blessed spiritually, physically, or economically, is, by comparison, most miserable.[105]

Augustine's anthropology is constructed on lines of admirable clarity. Man, in his view, is made for the Vision of God; nothing that is of this world can make him entirely happy. It is my contention that the Augustinian philosophy of man was adopted by Camus and enlisted to serve, alongside the atheism of Nietzsche, as the basis of his argument for the absurd.[106] In the case of Camus, however, man's desire for totality is, of course, firmly located outside of the religious context.

PART 2

AUTHENTICITY

Chapter IV

Authenticity in the Early Works

AUTHENTICITY IN *LE MYTHE DE SISYPHE*

Le Mythe de Sisyphe, as we have seen, opens with the claim that "there is but one truly serious philosophical problem and that is suicide." Camus' "problem" is to determine what the appropriate human response to the absurd is. *L'homme absurde* has, we are told, three options open to him: "philosophical suicide," "physical annihilation" and "revolt."[1] Most of Camus' essay is devoted to a consideration of the relevant merits of these three possibilities and to an explication of the moral code entailed by "revolt." This section of the present study will examine each of these options in turn.

The first of them, "philosophical suicide," is considered by Camus in some detail. It is in the context of his treatment of this notion that he deals, albeit very briefly, with the absurdist philosophies of, for example, Heidegger and Jaspers, or at any rate with the "absurd" aspects of their philosophies.[2] The work of Kierkegaard, Husserl and Chestov is treated in greater detail, however, with a view to illustrating what Camus means by "philosophical suicide" and why he regards it as an unauthentic human response to the absurd. For our purposes, it will be sufficient to consider his reflections on Husserl and Kierkegaard.

Both of those philosophers recognized clearly, says Camus, the absurdity of the human condition.[3] While they recognized the absurd, however, Husserl and Kierkegaard, like the other existentialists, refused to preserve it, and resorted to "philosophical suicide." They performed "the movement by which a thought negates itself and tends to transcend itself in its very negation."[4] The movement to which Camus refers at this point is identified, in the case of Kierkegaard, with the leap of faith, and in that of Husserl, with the elaboration of an "intentional" philosophy. The former, says Camus, "makes of the absurd the criterion of the other world"[5]; the latter elaborates a theory of "extra-temporal essences" in which "all things are not explained by one thing but by all things."[6]

The first "solution" considered by Camus, then, is "philosophical suicide." It is, however, an unauthentic one. Now, there would appear, at a casual reading of *Le Mythe de Sisyphe*,[7] to be only one reason why he rejects it: Camus considers it illogical to leap, as Kierkegaard did, immediately from man's desire for God to His existence, or to embrace, as Husserl did, an "abstract polytheism" which immediately satisfies that longing. To commit "philosophical suicide" is not to resolve the problem posed by the absurd but to dissolve it, by destroying the human mind and thereby negating one of the terms of the absurd equation:

> My reasoning wants to be faithful to the evidence that aroused it; that evidence is the absurd. It is that divorce between the mind that desires and the world that disappoints, my nostalgia for unity, this fragmented universe and the contradiction that binds them together. Kierkegaard suppresses my nostalgia and Husserl gathers together that universe. It was a matter of living and thinking with those dislocations, of knowing whether one had to accept or refuse. There can be no question of masking the evidence, of suppressing the absurd by denying one of the terms of its equation.[8]

The second "solution" examined by Camus is suicide. Unlike "philosophical suicide" and "revolt," however, this term is not used in any technical or esoteric sense; it simply refers to voluntary self-annihilation. Camus' concern at this point is to ask whether the absurd man can live only with what he "knows," namely, that life is meaningless, or whether suicide is the only appropriate response to the absurdity of his condition:

> It is essential to know whether one can live with it [the absurd] or whether, on the other hand, logic commands one to die of it. I am not interested in philosophical suicide but rather in plain suicide. I merely wish to purge it of its emotional content and know its logic and its integrity.[9]

Camus, however, is as unhappy about suicide as he is about faith.[10] The reasons for this dissatisfaction would once again appear, on a relatively superficial reading of *Le Mythe de Sisyphe*, to be entirely related to what he regards as the logical demands which the human condition makes upon the absurd man. For while logic demands a solution to the problem posed by the absurd, suicide involves the physical annihilation of the questioning subject. And "to negate one of the terms of the opposition in which he lives, amounts to escaping it."[11] Furthermore, the absurd demands "revolt," and suicide entails the acceptance of life's meaninglessness:

> This is where it is seen to what a degree absurd experience is remote from suicide. It may be thought that suicide follows revolt—but wrongly. For it does not represent the logical outcome of revolt. It is just the contrary by the consent it presupposes. Suicide, like the leap, is acceptance at its extreme.[12]

The third option open to *l'homme absurde* is "revolt." This is a relatively difficult concept and one whose meaning has not always been properly understood.[13] It is defined, negatively, by the rejection of suicide as well as of faith and, positively, by the absurd man's decision to live his life in conscious awareness of its meaninglessness. Camus therefore describes it as "a constant confrontation between man and his own obscurity"[14] and as "the certainty of a crushing fate without the resignation that ought to accompany it."[15] And while suicide and faith are firmly rejected in *Le Mythe de Sisyphe*, "revolt" is unambiguously declared to be the only acceptable response to the meaninglessness of the human condition. Camus describes it as "one of the only coherent philosophical positions"[16] and insists, as we have seen,[17] that it is revolt which gives to life its value and its majesty.

Why, then, does Camus conclude that authenticity is to be realized in "revolt"? There are, in fact, two lines of argument which lead him to this conclusion. Since the second of these will be dealt with in some detail later in this chapter, it will be sufficient at this point to concentrate on the first line of argument. It amounts essentially to the claim that "revolt" is the only response that is logically coherent in an absurd world:

> If I hold to be true that absurdity that determines my relationship with life, if I become thoroughly imbued with that sentiment that seizes me in face of the world's scenes, with that lucidity imposed on me by the pursuit of a science, I must sacrifice everything to these certainties and I must see them squarely to be able to maintain them. Above all, I must adapt my behaviour to them and pursue them in all their consequences.[18]

More precisely, however, Camus' argument contains four steps and is highly reminiscent of that used by Descartes to establish his own existence as a thinking thing. Camus argues, first, that he can be certain of one thing only, namely, that human existence is absurd.[19]

He contends, secondly, that he can derive from this basic certainty a rule of method, to the effect that whatever is known to be true ought to be "preserved." To retain oneself the truth that one has would appear, therefore, in Camus' mind, to be *"la règle de méthode."*[20]

Camus goes on to say, thirdly, that the absurd ought therefore to be "preserved."[21] He argues, finally, that if the absurd is to be "preserved," then what is required is not suicide or its philosophical equivalent, but "revolt":

> There can be no absurd outside the human mind. Thus, like everything else, the absurd ends with death. But there can be no absurd outside this world either. And it is by this elementary criterion that I judge the notion of the absurd to be essential and consider that it can stand as the first of my truths. For me the sole datum is the absurd. The first and, after all, the only condition of my inquiry is to preserve the very thing that crushes me, consequently to respect what I consider essential in it. I have just defined it as a confrontation and an unceasing struggle.[22]

Authenticity then is to be realized neither in "philosophical suicide" nor in physical annihilation, but in "revolt." But what form is this "revolt" to take? Camus insists that the authentic life works itself out in "freedom" and "passion."[23] It remains, therefore, to explain what he means by these terms and to show how they are related to that "revolt" which he sees as the first consequence of his "sceptical metaphysics."[24]

"Revolt," as we have seen, is defined, negatively, by the absurd man's rejection of suicide as well as of faith and, positively, by his decision to live his life in conscious awareness of its absurdity. This means that life does not have for *l'homme absurde* any religious meaning; there is, in his view, no God and no possibility of an afterlife with God. Belief in the possibility of a total freedom which, as Camus puts it, "draws a cheque on eternity" is, therefore, in the eyes of the absurd man, a mere illusion. There comes with this "awareness," however, and with the "revolt" of which it is, of course, an integral part, the only freedom that is available to man. It is, Camus admits, a freedom that is severely limited, analogous to that of the condemned man on the day of his execution. But it is a very real freedom,[25] and it is in the exercise of this liberty that man finds his strength and his only consolation.[26]

The "revolt" of which Camus speaks is then a source of liberation. It frees the absurd man from "the false hopes of an afterlife, the requirements of which would somehow restrain the present life."[27] But it also allows him the freedom to live his life as befits the man who is aware of the absurdity of his mortal condition and is therefore conscious of the absence of moral values. This means that the absurd man is free to live each passing moment to the full.[28] "Passion" or "intensity" is what follows upon the exercise of freedom.

It should, of course, be noticed that in Camus' judgment the absurd man who lives out his life in "revolt," "freedom" and "intensity" is invariably innocent. This is a simple point, and it is not difficult to see how he arrives at it. "Revolt" brings with it the awareness of a world from which God is absent and in which no absolute ethical norms are to be discovered. There are, therefore, no absolute moral standards in the light of which the absurd man's action can be appraised. *L'homme absurde*, Camus insists, may well be a responsible man, but he can never be a guilty one.[29]

Camus goes on, however, with a singular lack of logic, to insist that the moral stand demanded by revolt is not a nihilistic one and that ethical limits can, therefore, be set to the life of the absurd man:

> The absurd does not liberate; it binds. It does not authorize all actions. Everything is permitted does not mean that nothing is forbidden. The absurd merely confers an equivalence on the consequences of those actions. It does not recommend crime, for this would be childish, but it restores to remove its futility. Likewise, if all experiences are indifferent, that a duty is as legitimate as any other. One can be virtuous through a whim.[30]

There is one final point to be made, and this too is of some importance. At the end of his treatment of authenticity in *Le Mythe de Sisyphe*, Camus acknowledges, at least implicitly, the debt which his reflections on "revolt" and the absurdist ethic owe to Nietzsche:

> Thus I draw from the absurd three consequences which are my revolt, my freedom and my passion. By the mere activity of consciousness I transform into a rule of life what was an invitation to death—and I refuse suicide. I know, to be sure, the dull resonance that vibrates throughout these days. Yet I have but a word to say: that it is necessary. When Nietzsche writes: "It clearly seems that the chief thing in heaven and on earth is to *obey* at length and in a single direction: in the long run there results something for which it is worth the trouble of living on this earth as, for example, virtue, art, music, the dance, reason, the mind—something that transfigures, something delicate, mad, or divine," he elucidates the rule of a really distinguished code of ethics. But he also points the way of the absurd man.[31]

There can be no doubt, therefore, that Camus' thinking concerning authenticity was, like his philosophy of the absurd, greatly influenced by the existentialism of Nietzsche.[32] A later section of this chapter is devoted to a consideration of the origin and nature of that "distinguished code of ethics," which left such a deep impression on the young Camus and which resulted from Nietzsche's decision "to obey at length and in a single direction." Before turning to Nietzsche, however, it would be useful to give some space to Camus' treatment of authenticity in *L'Etranger*, his most famous philosophico-literary product.

AUTHENTICITY IN *L'ETRANGER*

L'Etranger is about the meaninglessness of human life. Its hero, Meursault, is an absurd character. But *l'homme absurde* is not simply a man whose existence is meaningless; he is also one who "does not hesitate to draw the inevitable conclusions from a fundamental absurdity"[33] and to live his life in accordance with those conclusions. To understand the concept of authenticity in *L'Etranger* is to understand the nature of the absurd man's conclusions and the extent of Meursault's adherence to what he regards as their truth.

The first conclusion arrived at by Meursault is that the absurd demands of him the kind of response which Camus describes in *Le Mythe de Sisyphe* as "revolt." For while the hero of *L'Etranger* admits to only one certainty, that of death, he refuses to become resigned to it.[34] Life, he insists, is to be lived and its absurdity is to be acknowledged:

> . . . Actually, I was sure of myself, sure about everything, far surer than he; sure of my present life and of the death that was coming. That, no doubt, was all I had; but at least that certainty was something I could get my teeth into—just as it had got its teeth into me. I'd been right, I was still right, I was always right.[35]

To suggest that authenticity demands revolt is, of course, to make two negative suggestions, for if life is to be lived, suicide cannot be the authentic response to the absurdity of man's condition; and if authenticity demands not only that life be lived, but that a conscious awareness of its meaninglessness be maintained, then there can be no place in Meursault's scheme of things for the philosophical suicide of *Le Mythe de Sisyphe*. The first of these points is made, indirectly but forcefully, by Meursault in *L'Etranger*, for the hero of the novel dies only because death is forced upon him, and this of course implies that he would continue to live if he could. The suicide, Camus insists, is the opposite of the man condemned to death:

> I was going on in the same vein, when he cut in with a question. How did I picture my life after the grave?
>
> I fairly bawled out at him: "A life in which I can remember this life on earth. That's all I want of it." And in the same breath I told him I'd had enough of his company.[36]

The second negative implication is drawn, explicitly and with equal force, in *L'Etranger*:

"Why," he asked, "don't you let me come to see you?"

I explained that I didn't believe in God.

"Are you really so sure of that?"

I said I saw no point in troubling my head about the matter; whether I believed or didn't was, to my mind, a question of so little importance.[37]

What is demanded by the absurd is neither faith nor suicide, but revolt. The posture in which authenticity consists can be negatively as well as positively defined, for it refers, on the one hand, to the rejection of suicide as well as of faith, and, on the other, to the retention of an absurdist awareness. For *l'homme absurde*, therefore, life does not have a religious meaning. There is, in his view, no God and therefore no possibility of an afterlife with Him. It is precisely this "awareness," however, which confers freedom upon him. This is the second conclusion which Meursault draws from the absurd: "I'd passed my life in a certain way, and I might have passed it in a different way, if I'd felt like it. I'd acted thus, and I hadn't acted otherwise; I hadn't done x, whereas I had done y or z."[38]

The absurd man is free. The revolt of which Camus speaks is, for him, a source of liberation: it frees Meursault from "the false hopes of an after-life, the requirements of which would somehow restrain the present life," but it also allows him the freedom to live his life as befits a man who is aware of the absurdity of his mortal condition and of the absence of moral values. He is therefore free to substitute a quantitative ethic for a qualitative one, and to live each passing moment to the full. This, in Meursault's view, is the third consequence of the absurd[39]: "He seemed so cocksure, you see. And yet none of his certainties was worth one strand of woman's hair. Living as he did, like a corpse, he couldn't even be sure of being alive."[40]

The absurd man who revolts in freedom and passion is, moreover, invariably innocent. This is the fourth of Meursault's conclusions. It only remains to explain the nature of this innocence and to show how it is related to that revolt which Meursault sees as the first consequence of life's meaninglessness.

What, then, does it mean to say that the hero of *L'Etranger* is innocent? It means that he is, like Nietzsche's *Übermensch*, a being whose actions are not to be judged by conventional moral standards. In this sense too Meursault is an outsider, and while, as Camus says in *Le Mythe de Sisyphe*, he may be responsible, he can never be guilty. His innocence is therefore of a moral kind. It is for this reason that he regards all actions as morally equivalent and is prepared to describe the murder of the Arab as a criminal offence but not as a sin.[41]

The relationship between Meursault's innocence and his "revolt" is an obvious one. The posture in which authenticity consists brings with it, as we have seen, the awareness of a world from which God is absent and in which no ethical standards are to be discovered. There are in this universe of thought no moral criteria, in the light of which man's conduct can be appraised. "God," as Dostoevsky says, "is dead and all is permitted." Man's moral state is one of total innocence. It is this that Meursault affirms when he denies his fallen state and endorses the sentiment expressed by Camus in *Le Mythe de Sisyphe* and in his early essay, *L'Eté à Alger*: "There are words whose meaning I have never really understood, like that of sin."

For Meursault, then, life is meaningless, but its absurdity is to be lived out in freedom, passion and innocence. The demands which Camus makes upon *l'homme absurde*, however, are extensive, for he is required not merely to draw the appropriate conclusions from the absurd but to maintain a rigorous adherence to the "truth" of those conclusions. We have now to consider the extent to which Meursault measures up to the second of the demands posited by Camus.

This would appear to be a matter which has already been more than adequately investigated. In a lengthy preface to an English-language edition of *L'Etranger*, in which he explains the meaning of the novel, Camus himself tells us that Meursault is condemned because of his total commitment to "the truth" of the absurd and to what is intellectually and emotionally demanded by that truth. The extent of this commitment has, however, been questioned by a number of commentators.[42] Conor Cruise O'Brien, for example, claims that "there is just one category of phenomena about which Meursault will not lie and that is his own feelings,"[43] and that therefore "Camus is rigorous in his treatment of the psychology of Meursault—in the novel, not in his retrospective commentaries on it."[44] A critical examination of O'Brien's arguments will lead us to the heart of the matter in question and to the essence of Camus' thinking on authenticity, as artistically expressed in *L'Etranger*.

After giving a brief account of this work, O'Brien quotes Camus on the meaning of the novel:

> Years later, in a preface to an English language edition of *L'Etranger*, Camus wrote: " . . . the hero of the book is condemned because he doesn't play the game. In this sense he is a stranger to the society in which he lives; he drifts in the margin, in the suburb of private, solitary, sensual life. This is why some readers are

tempted to consider him as a waif. You will have a more precise idea of this character, or one at all events in closer conformity with the intentions of the author, if you ask yourself in what way Meursault doesn't play the game. The answer is simple: He refuses to lie. Lying is not only saying what is not true. It is also and especially saying more than is true and, as far as the human heart is concerned, saying more than one feels. This is what we all do every day to simplify life. Meursault, despite appearances, does not wish to simplify life. He says what is true. He refuses to disguise his feelings and immediately society feels threatened. He is asked, for example, to say that he regrets his crime according to the ritual formula. He replies that he feels about it more annoyance than real regret and this shade of meaning condemns him.

Meursault for me is then not a waif, but a man who is poor and naked, in love with the sun which leaves no shadows. Far from it being true that he lacks all sensibility, a deep tenacious passion animates him, a passion for the absolute and for truth. It is a still negative truth, the truth of being and of feeling, but one without which no victory over oneself and over the world will ever be possible.

You would not be far wrong then in reading *The Stranger* as the story of a man who, without any heroics, accepts death for the sake of truth. I have sometimes said, and always paradoxically, that I have tried to portray in this character the only Christ we deserved. You will understand after these explanations that I said this without any intention of blasphemy and only with the slightly ironic affection which an artist has the right to feel towards the characters whom he has created."[45]

O'Brien quotes Rachel Bespaloff:

Though he [Meursault] does not condemn social oppression nor try to fight it, he denounces it through his quiet refusal to conform to the defiant attitudes one expects of him. One realises that this indifferent man is intractable in his respect for truth. On this point he exhibits a surprising and even heroic firmness, since in the end it will cost him his life.[46]

O'Brien's first point is clear, namely, that many commentators on *L'Etranger*, including Camus himself, portray Meursault as an honest man who died because he would not lie, and that some even suggest that he was also the enemy of social oppression. He then argues that "the Meursault of the actual novel is not quite the same person as the Meursault of the commentaries . . . it is simply not true that Meursault is intractable in his absolute respect for truth"; and this becomes clear when we remember that "Meursault in the actual novel lies. He concocts for Raymond the letter which is designed to deceive the Arab girl and expose her to humiliation, and later he lies to the police to get Raymond discharged after beating the girl up"; that "there is just one category of phenomena about which Meursault will not lie, and that is his own feelings"; that

> logically there is no reason why this should be so. There is no reason why he should not use lies to get himself out of the trouble which he got himself into by lies. Indeed, in the second case the motivation is (one could imagine) infinitely stronger than in the first. Yet it is in the second that he resists. The reason can only be that his own feelings, and his feelings about his feelings, are sacrosanct. They, are the God whom he will not betray and for whom he is martyred. His integrity is that of the artist, a Nietzschean integrity.[47]

O'Brien is correct when he claims that Meursault contributes to social oppression. The examples which he gives bear this out clearly. But there is no mention in Camus' commentary of social oppression; he claims only that his hero died for truth. The question, therefore, is this: Does O'Brien show that the hero of Camus' novel is "as indifferent to truth as he is to cruelty" and that therefore "Camus is rigorous in his treatment of the psychology of Meursault—in the novel, not in his retrospective commentaries on it"?

This, I would suggest, is something which O'Brien does not succeed in showing, for the arguments which he adduces to establish the unreliability of Camus' own commentary are based on a misunderstanding of its meaning. To say that Meursault is honest only about his feelings is, as we shall see, inaccurate. It is, therefore, incorrect to suggest that the hero of the novel is in this respect inconsistent. And to fail to understand Meursault's honesty is to fail to appreciate the extent of his commitment to the absurd.

Meursault, says Camus, "refuses to lie." O'Brien claims that in concocting the letter and giving false evidence to the police Meursault does in fact lie, and he therefore concludes that the hero of the novel is not the Meursault of Camus' commentary. Is he right? O'Brien certainly is correct when he says that Meursault is not concerned in these instances to say what is objectively true. He is likewise right when he claims that an honest man does not lie, especially when to do so is harmful to others. He is wrong, however, to conclude that Camus in his own commentary paints a false picture of Meursault, for O'Brien does not realize that the novel operates at two levels of truth, with the result that when Camus describes his hero as an honest man he is speaking at one level, O'Brien at the other.

What are these two levels of truth? There is, first, the commonsense level at which Meursault might refuse to lie. He might, for example, refuse to lie to the police on Raymond's behalf. At this level, Meursault is dishonest, as

O'Brien has shown, for he agrees to tell the police what he knows to be objectively untrue. There is also, however, the level at which the absurd man. might refuse to lie: he might refuse, for example, to say what for him is untrue, namely, that life has meaning and that there is a scale of moral values. It is at this level that Camus is speaking when he describes Meursault as an honest man. In Camus' opinion this is not the only level of truth; it is, however, the decisive one. He knows that Meursault lies in the commonly accepted sense, but his point is that the hero of *L'Etranger* at no stage says other than what he thinks to be true or more than he thinks to be true; at no stage does he say other than what he feels or more than he feels, namely, that life is absurd and all actions morally equivalent.[48] It is the honesty of Caligula when he says that "this world of ours, this scheme of things, as they call it, is quite intolerable," and that "all [actions] are on an equal footing." To say otherwise is to fail to realize that Meursault represents for Camus the modern Sisyphus, the authentic man in a world without meaning, the one who lives out the absurd in revolt. And this demands that he live for the moment and regard all actions as morally acceptable.

It is in the context of moral indifferentism that one should read the instances which O'Brien cites in order to establish the dishonesty of the hero and to criticize the commentary of the author himself. If one looks not only at the fact that Meursault concocted the letter and lied to the police on behalf of Raymond, but also at the reason why he did so, one can see that Meursault, though dishonest at the first level, was absolutely honest at the second and that O'Brien's criticisms of Camus are in consequence wide of the mark. "I wrote the letter. I didn't take much trouble over it, but I wanted to satisfy Raymond, *as I'd no reason not to satisfy him*."[49]

Meursault makes it clear at this point why he wrote the letter, or rather why he did not refuse to write it; and what can be said of this incident can also be said of his decision to lie to the police. He did so because he had "no reason not to satisfy" Raymond. This is not merely an assertion of friendship. It is a clear acknowledgement on the part of Meursault that he could provide no reason, moral or otherwise, for refusing his friend's request. He could not refuse the request on moral grounds, because he believed that in an absurd world the authentic man is not bound by any moral code. Meursault decided to help Raymond, because his own "revolt" would permit no reason, moral or otherwise, why he should refuse to do so.

Meursault's decision was, within the terms of his own philosophy and that of the early Camus, a moral one. The hero of *L'Etranger* was absolutely honest when he took the side of Raymond. Had he refused to help his friend on moral grounds, because he had, ethically speaking, a reason not to satisfy him, he would have been acknowledging implicitly that he was bound by a scale of moral values. In other words, he would have been lying. That he was not prepared to do.

It might be said by way of rejoinder that in this case Camus contradicts himself, or rather that he commits his hero to a contradictory position, for he is saying on the one hand that for Meursault all actions are morally equivalent and, on the other, that his decision to help Raymond was dictated by a desire to be authentic, that is, by a need not to say what for him "is not true" or "more than is true." This, however, is not O'Brien's point. In fact, it is a criticism which can legitimately be made only if Meursault *is* honest; O'Brien, however, maintains that he is not.

The real weakness in Camus' position is therefore very different from that suggested by O'Brien. It is that Meursault *is* honest, even though at one level only, when he believes that all actions are equally without moral significance. It is a weakness in Camus, only because his description of his hero as an honest man *is* an accurate one.

What then of O'Brien's second claim, to the effect that "there is only one category of phenomena about which Meursault will not lie, and that is his feelings"? This also can be seen to be inaccurate. There are many passages in the novel which cannot be understood in terms of truth-of-feeling alone. The most important of these is, as we have seen, the one in which Camus' hero describes death as a leveller, and goes on to add:

> What difference could they make to me, the death of others, or a mother's love, or his God; or the way one decides to live, the fate one thinks one chooses, since one and the same fate was bound to "choose" not only me but thousands of millions of privileged people who, like him, called themselves my brothers? Surely, surely he must see that? Every man alive was privileged; there was only one class of men, the privileged class. All alike would be condemned to die one day; his turn, too, would come like the others. And what difference could it make if, after being charged with murder, he were executed because he didn't weep at his mother's funeral, since it all came to the same thing in the end? The same thing for Salamano's wife and for Salamano's dog. That little robot woman was as "guilty" as the girl from Paris who had married Masson, or as Marie, who wanted me to marry her. What did it matter if Raymond was as much my pal as Céleste, who was a far worthier man? What did it matter if at this very moment Marie was kissing a new boy friend?[50]

Meursault is not concerned, at this point, with truth-of-feeling alone. He is also concerned, and especially so, with "truth-of-being." O'Brien refers to "the strained rhetoric of the scene with the chaplain and the conclusion."[51]

But Meursault's meeting with the priest in fact provides the key to the proper understanding of the novel. It explains Meursault's otherness. He is "an outsider," because he sees annihilating death as something which renders human life meaningless. His attitude to human life is very much that of Sartre toward physical reality: it has no meaning. Since it has no meaning for him, he shows no great sorrow at his mother's death; he regards it as "coming to the same thing" whether he shoots the Arab or not; and he, with perfect consistency, puts no great significance even on his own life.[52] Had O'Brien realized this, he would not have restricted Meursault's honesty to the truth-of-feeling, nor would he have insisted that Camus' hero shot the Arab because he regarded *him* as less than a man[53]: he did so because he regarded everyone, himself included, as, in one sense, less than a man:

> ... my grip closed on the revolver. The trigger gave, and the smooth underbelly of the butt jogged my palm. And so, with that crisp, whip-crack sound, it all began. I shook off my sweat and the clinging veil of light. I knew I'd shattered the balance of the day, the spacious calm of this beach on which I had been happy. *But I fired four shots more into the inert body, on which they left no visible trace.* And each successive shot was another loud, fateful rap on the door of my undoing.[54]

There are, of course, in these passages and in others, obvious references to Meursault's feelings; that they contain besides an honest expression of the hero's view of things is, however, scarcely in doubt. The claim that Meursault is honest only about his feelings is, therefore, an inaccurate one. There are no grounds for the charge of inconsistency, nor is there any need for an appeal to "artistic truth" or "Nietzschean integrity" to explain it. We have no need, as Laplace once said in a different context, of this hypothesis.

Meursault, moreover, is consistent, not only in his truth of feeling, but in his feelings and in his behaviour. In every case, the feelings which he does express are such as we would expect from the absurd man: feelings of indifference. He invariably acts in a way that is consistent with, and even reveals, what he believes and what he feels, for he behaves as if nothing mattered and all actions were morally equivalent. This is what he does when he smokes in the presence of his mother's dead body. "But I wasn't sure if I should smoke, under the circumstances—in Mother's presence. I thought it over; really it didn't seem to matter, so I offered the porter a cigarette and we both smoked."[55] This is likewise what he does when he lies on behalf of Raymond.

O'Brien is wrong, then, when he says that the Meursault of Camus' commentary is not the hero of the novel. Meursault is, in Camus' sense, absolutely honest. He is honest about his view of life and about his own feelings. His feelings and his actions are, furthermore, perfectly in line with his view of life. It is, as Camus says, his stubborn honesty, his refusal to say either explicitly or implicitly what, as far as he is concerned, is "not true" or is "more than is true," what he does not feel or "more than he feels," that leads to his death. It is a form of honesty which would not be ours, and which indeed was not for very long that of Camus himself; but a form of honesty it was. To fail to understand this is to fail to grasp the extent of Meursault's commitment to "the truth" of the absurd and to what he sees as the inevitable consequences of that truth.

Chapter V

Authenticity in the Philosophy of Nietzsche

There is, as we have seen, a negative side to the philosophy of Nietzsche. It consists, for the most part, in a critique of *Weltanschauungen* and, in particular, of the Christian world view. Nietzsche's thought also has a positive aspect, however, for his primary philosophic concern is not merely to proclaim his atheism but to erect an existential ethic on the basis of a death of God position.[1] This section will be devoted to a consideration of the nature and origin of that ethic which left such a deep impression on the young Camus. While it is the product of Nietzsche's mature philosophy, it has its roots in *The Birth of Tragedy*.

Nietzsche's thought is set within the framework of a rejection of God and Christian morality, on the one hand, and an attempt to provide an alternative to them, on the other. His sister, Frau Förster-Nietzsche, tells us that in the notes for the year 1878, in which he recalls his state of mind at the time of writing *The Birth of Tragedy*, Nietzsche comments:

> The Gods are evil and wise, they deserve to go under. Man is good and stupid—he has a more beautiful future and can attain to it only when the Gods have at last entered the twilight of their days.—Thus would I have formulated my *credo* in those days.[2]

And of *The Birth of Tragedy* he himself writes:

> It was against morality therefore that my intercessory instinct for life turned in this questionable book, inventing for itself a counter-dogma and counter-valuation [sic] of life, purely artistic, purely *anti-Christian* . . . I called it Dionysian.[3]

It was with considerable justification, therefore, that Nietzsche wrote to his mother in a letter of 1887: "If people had understood one word of the first thing I wrote, they would have been afraid and crossed themselves forthwith." While Nietzsche opposed the views of those who held that Christian morality did most justice to man, he was not prepared to accept what many regarded as the only reasonable alternative to it, namely, the complacent attitude of the "culture-philistine," for he regarded that as being, like Christianity, the expression of a refusal to be "engaged" in the world. It is neither the Christian nor the "culture-philistine" who is the embodiment of authentic human values, but the tragic artist.

> He who has glanced with piercing eye into the very heart of the terrible destructive process of so-called universal history, as also into the cruelty of nature, and is in danger of longing for a Buddhistic negation of the will—Art saves him, and through art life saves him for itself.[4]
>
> Here in the extremest danger of the will, *art* approaches as a saving and healing enchantress.[5]

Nietzsche's first attempt to provide an alternative to Christian values produced the "metaphysico-artistic" attitude of *The Birth of Tragedy*. The philosophy which he expounds in this work is termed "artistic," because it finds its expression in Greek art; it is metaphysical, because it is not confined to art but, as Henri de Lubac points out, "embraces a whole conception of the world and of man and a whole ideal of life."[6] Nietzsche sees in what he takes to be the culture of ancient Greece the only one that is worth restoring, because it alone "aims at the production of the great man"[7] who can turn his back upon Christian morality and refuse to adopt a "nay-saying" attitude to life.

As a means, in part, of promoting an alternative culture, then, Nietzsche published *The Birth of Tragedy*, in which he not only rejected Christian values and Christian optimism but repudiated any form of optimism dictated by an attitude of noncommitment. Both Christian and optimistic outlooks, he claimed, are inferior to the tragic culture of the Greeks, whose pessimism, based as it was upon strength, was one not of renunciation but of health. To give an idea of what he meant, Nietzsche employed the new terms "Dionysan" and "Apollonian."

Each of these types of art represents at the same time a way of life. The Apollonian artist contends that authentic human values are expressed in the culture of which Apollo, with his associations of form, ideal beauty and dream, is the deity; the Dionysian artist maintains that all one can do is to preserve a passive identification with the flux and pain of unformed life. Though Nietzsche says that Christianity is "neither Apollonian nor Dionysan" but "nihilistic,"[8] the general weight of evidence in his writing points to his inner conviction that

Christianity is Apollonian, for it teaches that there are fixed moral values and an afterlife, thus disparaging this world. As far as he is concerned, it is no more than a popular form of Platonism.

Tragic art, Nietzsche insists, is the alternative to both Christian Apollinism and passive renunciation. Greek tragedy, he says, was born of the union of Dionysus and Apollo; it can be identified neither with the one nor with the other, but contains an element of each. "An idea—the antagonism of the two concepts Dionysian and Apollonian—is translated into metaphysics . . . In tragedy this antithesis has become unity."[9] The man who looks to tragic art as an aesthetic expression of the values which are really authentic will refuse to give allegiance to either Apollo or Dionysus; he will succumb to neither temptation: escapism or renunciation. He will be like those men of old who created the Greek tragedies, the very type of all art which represents a triumphant response to the suffering of life. This response is the cry of one who says "yes" to life, by creating a meaning for human existence out of his great need. This is the task of the tragic artist for whom "it is only as an aesthetic phenomenon that existence and the world appear justified."[10]

The notes which were written late in Nietzsche's life and were compiled to form much of what was published posthumously as *The Will to Power* express a position which appears at first sight to be simply a reiteration of his earlier views on the nature and function of tragic art. We are once again told that it is art which provides the clue to the living of the authentic life:

> Our religion, morality and philosophy are decadent human institutions. The counter-agent: art.[11]

> Art is the metaphysical activity of life, the only task of life.[12]

On closer examination, however, *The Will to Power* can be seen to contain more than a restatement of those earlier views. In his former reflections on Greek culture, Nietzsche had been content to insist that it is in tragic art that we find the expression of authentic human living. In *The Birth of Tragedy* Nietzsche had distinguished between "nature" and "finer nature"; he had insisted that the acceptance of Christian ethics prevented man from cultivating this finer nature and that human existence demanded that art be taken as the criterion of authenticity. However, that was essentially all he had to say on the question of authentic human living, at that point.

There were, moreover, three crucial questions which Nietzsche had left unanswered in his early attempt to solve his value problem.

1. Why does the acceptance of traditional morality result in human alienation?
2. Why must tragic philosophy be regarded as the truly human philosophy?
3. What is the basis of the distinction between "nature" and "finer nature"?

An attempt to answer these questions is to be found in Nietzsche's later thought. In *The Will to Power*, we are again told that art is the "counter-agent to religion, morality and philosophy," but it is of significance that, at this stage in Nietzsche's philosophic development, art has been shown to have its basis in man's will to power. The position adopted in *The Birth of Tragedy* is altered in accordance with this conviction. The philosophy of the tragic artist is opposed to Christianity, because it is not religion but tragic art which symbolizes man's exercise of will to power.[13]

It is to the concept of will to power, then, that Nietzsche must appeal to answer the three questions which arose out of his early attempt to solve his value problem. Will to power is therefore a notion of the utmost importance in Nietzsche's moral philosophy. Before taking up the analysis of this concept, however, we must turn to Nietzsche's reflections on philosophy and the philosophers, for these reflections, as Cunningham argues,[14] are of crucial importance for the understanding of his thinking on the question of authenticity.

In the second book of *The Will to Power*, Nietzsche surveys the views of traditional thinkers and asks, "What prospect has he of finding what he seeks, who goes in search of philosophers today?" He does not hesitate to say, in reply, that there have as yet been no genuine philosophers. "Is it not probable that he will wander about by day and night in vain?"[15] If we ask why Nietzsche is of this opinion, we find an answer which is, in the present context, of crucial significance: they have all been "contemptible libertines hiding behind the petticoats of the female 'Truth.' "[16] Nietzsche traces the failure of philosophers back to the delusion, common to them all, that it is the business of the philosopher to know. They think, with Aristotle, that it is the impulse to knowledge which lies at the basis of philosophy. However, Nietzsche claims that there is no truth and that there are no "moral facts": there is only a moral interpretation of facts. The true philosopher will recognize that truth is not relevant to his task and that the impulse to knowledge must be repudiated. 'The falseness of an opinion is for us not any objection to it.... the question is, how far an opinion is life-furthering."[17] *"The real philosophers,"* he insists, *"are commanders and lawgivers;* they say 'thus shall it be' . . . Their 'knowing' is *creating* . . . their will to truth is—Will to Power."[18]

In man, then, there is both a creature and a creator. Authenticity is to be realized not in the discovery of one's ethical code but in the creation of one's own moral values, "beyond good and evil." The passages to this effect are numerous throughout the works of Nietzsche, from *Thus Spake Zarathustra* to *The Antichrist.*

> This somnolence did I disturb when I taught that *no-one yet knoweth* what is good and bad—unless it be the creating one.
>
> It is he who createth man's goal.[19]

> The noble type of man regards *himself* as the determiner of values; he does not require to be approved of. . . . He knows that it is he himself alone who confers honour on things, he is the *creator of values.*[20]

Nietzsche's ethic is an existential one, born of will to power. But what is this will to power? This is the question which must be asked, if we are properly to understand Nietzsche's moral philosophy. It is one which Walter Kaufmann's *Nietzsche* answers to some extent, for Kaufmann's examination of the genesis of this notion in the philosopher's writings shows that the will to power is a psychological concept which, in Nietzsche's view, explains much of man's behaviour.[21] To say that Nietzsche bases his ethic on a psychological principle is, however, to tell only part of the story, for the will to power is not merely a psychological notion but a psychobiological function. This will be clearly demonstrated by an examination of the role which Nietzsche assigns to this concept in those spheres of life which lie outside the realm of philosophical anthropology.

Any analysis of Nietzsche's discussion of will to power in nature must draw attention to his claim that the basic drive behind philosophy[22] and contemporary science, with its insistence on the concept of energy,[23] is not an impulse to knowledge but a will to power. This analysis might also underline his convictions that freedom of the will has its basis in the desire for power[24] and that monarchy, aristocracy and democracy can all of them be explained in the same terms.[25] For our purposes, however, it will be sufficient to point out that "all organic functions [and] the solution of the problem of generation and nutrition" are explained by Nietzsche in terms of "the development and ramification of one fundamental form of will, namely 'will to power.' "[26] It is this will that distinguishes "nature" from "finer nature"; we shall now show that Nietzsche "finds 'will to power' the most suggestive name for the primeval life force out of which all organic and psychological functions have evolved and whose generic traits they retain."[27] That link between biology and the psychological principle which is central to Nietzsche's anthropology will, at the same time, be clearly established.

That such a link does indeed exist can best be illustrated by Nietzsche's criticisms of Darwin. Nietzsche is at pains to emphasize that life is dynamic and that Darwin's insistence on adaptability and the influence of environment does little justice to the aggressiveness which is such an obvious feature of living things. To give adaptability the importance which Darwin does is "to throw doubt and suspicion upon life and the value of life."[28] In Darwinian theory, he insists, "the influence of environment is nonsensically *overrated*: the essential factor in the process of life is precisely the tremendous inner power to shape and to create forms, which merely *uses, exploits*, environment."

> Greater complexity, sharp differentiation, the contiguity of the developed organs and functions, with the disappearance of intermediate members—if that is perfection then there is a Will to Power apparent in the organic process by means of whose *dominating, shaping* and *commanding* forces it is continually increasing the sphere: it *grows* imperatively.[29]

Each organism, Nietzsche argues, has its own will to power, and their unending conflict contributes most to the process of natural development. Creation and destruction go hand in hand. "The bond between the inorganic and the organic world must lie in the repelling power exercised by every atom of energy. 'Life' might be defined as a lasting form of *force-establishing processes*, in which the various contending forces, on their part, grow unequally."[30]

> Physiologists should bethink themselves before putting down the instinct of self-preservation as the cardinal instinct of an organic being. A living thing seeks above all to *discharge* its strength: "self-preservation" is only one of the results thereof.[31]

In this context, Nietzsche criticizes Darwin's view that evolution favours the survival of the fittest. It is not the fittest forms which survive in the struggle for life but those which reach a higher level of existence, through the exercise of will to power. "Biologists reckon upon the struggle for existence, the death of the weaker creature and the survival of the most robust, most gifted combatant," but in the process of evolution, "the richest and most complex forms perish more easily."[32] It is in will to power that we find "the ultimate reason and character of all change," and it is this will which "explains why selection is never in favour of the exceptions and the lucky cases." The principle of adaptation "explains nothing." It serves "not as an explanation but only as a designation for the identification of a problem."[33] "I see all philosophers and the whole of science on their knees before a reality which is the reverse of the 'struggle for life,' as Darwin and his school understand it."[34]

Nietzsche insists, moreover, that the will to power is selective and purposive,[35] and that it demands on the part of life, at the subhuman and at the human level, what he calls "self-surpassing." Two passages in *Zarathustra* show clearly that there is in Nietzsche's view a "self-surpassing" in the process by which all living things rise to a higher level of existence.

> Good and evil, and rich and poor, and high and low, and all names of values: weapons shall they be, and sounding signs, that life must again and again surpass itself.
>
> Aloft will it build itself with columns and stairs—life itself: into remote distances would it gaze and out towards blissful beauties—*therefore* doth it require elevation. And because it requireth elevation, therefore doth it require steps, and variety of steps and climbers. To rise striveth life and in rising to surpass itself.[36]

> That is your entire will, ye wisest ones, as a Will to Power. Hearken now unto my word, ye wisest ones. Test it seriously, whether I have crept into the heart of life itself, and into the roots of its heart. Wherever I found living things, there found I Will to Power. . . . And this secret spake Life herself unto me. "Behold," she said, "I am that *which must ever surpass itself.*"[37]

What Nietzsche says of the will to power in nature is, I would suggest, of the utmost importance. It shows clearly that the principle that he claimed to be psychological, which he used as a basis for distinguishing between "nature" and "finer nature," and which he called "once more the key to the fundamental problems," was a principle that he understood not only to apply at the human level but also to hold good of plant life and the animal world.[38] One philosopher claims that while "much of Nietzsche's later writing employs biological language and abounds in acute comment on the scientists he read, it would be a serious error to suppose that the will to power theory grew out of such studies, or to file it away in some allegedly separate 'positivistic' compartment of his thought."[39] But this same thinker admits that the will to power is a biological function found in the nonmoral spheres of life, when he says that "if we look for his [Nietzsche's] evidence that life is will to power, we encounter first the spectacle of life amid nature . . . Nietzsche remarks that a generalisation intended to cover all life must apply to plants and animals."[40] He quotes Nietzsche as follows:

> . . . in order to understand what life is, and what kind of tension life contains, the formula should hold good not only of trees and plants, but of animals also. What does the plant strive after?—to what end do trees of a virgin forest contend with each other? "For happiness"—for power.[41]

The principle that Nietzsche substitutes for Darwin's hypothesis of Natural Selection, in order to explain the upward movement of life in nature, is the same principle which he applies to man and enlists to serve as the criterion of moral living. That Morgan should fail to detect the significance of this identification seems particularly remarkable, when we recall what he says of Nietzsche's aesthetics, the importance of which could scarcely be overrated in any worthwhile study of Nietzschean ethics: "Nietzsche bases his theory of beauty and ugliness upon biological values";[42] his is a "biocentric aesthetics";[43] "aesthetics is a natural science"; and "Apollonian and Dionysian are natural forces."[44]

Nietzsche, then, for all that he criticizes Darwin, attempts to base an "ethics of evolution" on what he takes to be the "evolution of ethics."[45] While Darwin is prepared to admit that there are moral qualities which cannot be accounted for in terms of the hypothesis of Natural Selection, and Huxley says that "the ape and tiger methods of the struggle for existence are not reconcilable with sound ethical principles,"[46] Nietzsche tries to construct an existential ethic on the basis of the principle which he takes to lie behind the evolutionary process, and so attempts to make the will to power "the kernel of the transvaluation of values."[47] He agrees with Huxley that traditional morality does not fit the demands of the cosmic process; he concludes from this, however, not that we should distinguish morality from the force which lies behind evolution, but that human existence demands that man create his own ethical code out of a will to power, to which the evolutionary process owes its very existence. In other words, the will to power, which is in itself no more than a psychobiological function, provides Nietzsche both with an account of organic development and with a criterion of moral worth.[48] It is the basis also of that existential ethic of which Nietzsche made so much.

This, then, is the moral position at which Nietzsche arrived as a result of his decision "to obey at length and in a single direction." It was, moreover, his persistent and unwavering pursuit of the Promethean "flame" that produced *that* moral code to which the young Camus[49] referred as a "really distinguished code of ethics."

Chapter VI

Authenticity: An Evaluation

The last few decades have seen the publication of a great deal of literature on Camus' writings, the greater part of which has little philosophic content. This judgment however, could not reasonably be extended to John Cruickshank's monumental work, *Albert Camus and the Literature of Revolt*, which addresses, with a considerable degree of penetration, some of the central problems of Camus' philosophy.

Two chapters of this highly influential book provide an exposition and critical analysis of *Le Mythe of Sisyphe*. Here we will evaluate Camus' treatment of authenticity in the first of his philosophical works by examining, for the most part, the more important criticisms which Cruickshank makes of Camus in those chapters.

Cruickshank's first objection is a logical one. He argues that the question with which Camus opens *Le Mythe de Sisyphe* is tautologous and therefore "philosophically unsound":

> . . .does intellectual recognition of the absurd *logically* entail suicide? Schopenhauer did not do away with himself, but was he required by logic to do so? Camus puts this question in a compressed form by saying: " . . . *y a-t-il une logique jusqu'à la mort?*" Behind this terse question, at least as put by Camus, there lurks, I suspect, some kind of tautology or circular argument. In the immediately preceding sentences he speaks, not of thinking logically, but of being logical. In particular he raises the problem of being logical to the utmost limit. Indeed, in the whole of the argument up to this point, it is clear that he means by logic a rigorous measure of consistency between thought and action. This being so, Camus' question, at least as he put it, ceases to be a meaningful one. His use of the term "logical" prior to this point means that when he asks whether the absurd logically entails suicide he is in effect asking whether consistency of thought and action is entailed by consistency of thought and action.[1]

And he continues:

> Therefore, if one is to treat the essay seriously, some way must be found of getting round the tautology. The most obvious way seems to be to accept, at least provisionally, the fact of a certain discrepancy between Camus' feeling and his thought. It may still be that his feeling that a problem exists is correct even though he has not expressed the problem in a way that would satisfy the requirements of formal logic.

Cruickshank is correct when he argues that "the question which Camus has asked, *at least in the way he puts it,*" is philosophically unsound. Unfortunately, he makes no contribution to the proper understanding of Camus' aims in *Le Mythe de Sisyphe* (or at any rate of one of his aims), when he asserts that if this tautology is to be circumvented and the essay treated seriously, we must accept, at least provisionally, "the fact of a certain discrepancy between Camus' feeling and his thought," and when he adds: "It may still be that his feeling that a problem exists is correct even though he has not expressed this problem in a way that would satisfy the requirements of formal logic."[2]

Now, Camus does not pose the problem of suicide solely out of a feeling that there is such a problem, or in an attempt to arrive at a purely logical solution to it, but because of his conviction that the absurd demands of the authentic man a response that is truly human. His concern at that stage in the development of his thought is not merely with logic, but with what the fourth of his *Lettres à un ami allemand* called the "truth of man." That is why "revolt," the solution which *Le Mythe de Sisyphe* offers to the problem of suicide, is said by Camus to be not merely the logical response to the absurd but the source of life's meaning.[3] And it is for this same reason that he quotes, at the very beginning of *Le Mythe de Sisyphe*, Pindar's third *Pythian Ode*:

> O my soul, do not aspire to immortal life, but exhaust the limits of the possible.

This point will be considered in greater detail when we have examined Cruickshank's second objection.

The second criticism, or set of criticisms, is directed not against the question with which Camus opens *Le Mythe de Sisyphe* but against his solution to the problem of suicide. Cruickshank insists that the sole aim of this essay is to provide a logical answer to the problem posed by the absurd, and that Camus' attempt to deal with the question of suicide in this way is conspicuously unsuccessful.

In the first place, the whole enterprise of making the absurd intelligible, of using it as a source of values, seems to involve a *petitio principii* . . . Secondly, Camus gives the notion of the absurd three different meanings during the demonstration of his *cogito;* (i) it is the whole tragic paradox of the human condition and a subject of scandal and complaint; (ii) it is a situation that we are called upon to maintain as fully as we can; (iii) it is an attitude of revolt (the wager of the absurd) which somehow requires us to use the absurd in sense (ii) above against the absurd in sense (i) above. These different meanings of the term "absurd" involve three different kinds of relationship and are both confused and confusing. . . . Throughout the whole argument there is a disturbing lack of clarification or definition of terms. Lastly, it is difficult not to feel that Camus' enthusiasm for the absurd, on the basis that it testifies to the truth of its own existence and that this truth must be preserved, is rather too formal an argument.[4]

Cruickshank is again correct when he claims that the argument that Camus employs in order to derive "revolt" from the absurd is both sophistical and excessively formal. He is therefore on firm ground when he criticizes Camus for insisting that "revolt" is the only response that is open to the absurd man, because it is the only one that is logically consistent with the facts of the absurd. Cruickshank also is correct when he goes on to claim that "revolt" could more reasonably be regarded as the product of "reasoned choice" than as the fruit of logical deduction. At this stage of his argument, however, Cruickshank makes two crucial points which are inaccurate, and which are, moreover, closely interrelated. He suggests, first, that "revolt" is not for Camus the product of "reasoned choice," and, secondly, that the "truth of man" is no part of Camus' concern in *Le Mythe de Sisyphe*.[5] On both these scores, however, he is profoundly mistaken, for while admittedly Camus says on many occasions that the absurd demands a logical response and that "revolt" is therefore the only solution that is acceptable to him, it is clear that he does not always say this. At one point, for example, he describes "revolt" as *"le pari déchirant et merveilleux,"*[6] and a little later, after appealing for "revolt" on grounds that appear to be entirely logical, he makes obvious references to the "truth of man."[7] At another point he describes Kierkegaard's leap of faith and Husserl's elaboration of an "abstract polytheism" not only as intellectually indefensible but as a "sin," indeed, the only sin that is open to man in an absurd world.[8]

In his thesis on Christian Neoplatonism, moreover, Camus insists that "the world is not oriented towards the 'all things are always the same' of Lucretius, but that it serves as the setting for the tragedy of man without God."[9] He clearly endorses too "the Greek view," that in an absurd world man should resort not to faith and the meaning that religion gives to life, but to the creation of a secular meaning in a universe from which God is absent. For the Christian he says:

> History has the meaning which God has chosen to give it; the philosophy of history, a notion that is alien to a Greek mind, is a Jewish invention. Metaphysical problems are embodied in time, and the world is merely the physical symbol of this human striving towards God. Whence the crucial importance of faith. It is enough for a paralytic or a blind man to believe—and behold he is cured. Faith is essentially consent and Renunciation. And faith is always more important than works.[10]

This is not the dispassionate language of the logician but the word of a philosopher whose thought is, in one respect at least, no different from that of certain other existentialists, whose main concern is not for logical consistency but for the need to meet the demands that the human condition makes on those who would live an authentic existence. The last word on this crucial question should therefore be left not to Cruickshank but to Roger Quilliot, whose comments on Camus' *Métaphysique chrétienne et Néoplatonisme* go to the very heart of the latter's early thought.

> . . . il projette sur l'hellénisme comme sur le christianisme ses propres difficultés et ses propres aspirations: l'un et l'autre lui composent des paysages conceptuels, et catalysent ses réactions spontanées. Camus a peut-être plus appris sur lui-même en écrivant ce diplôme que sur les pensées grecque et chrétienne: elles l'ont simplement aidé à nommer ses problèmes.[11]

The existential aspect of Camus' early philosophy brings us immediately to another of Cruickshank's criticisms, for after pointing out that the absurd man is, in Camus' view, responsible but never guilty, he writes:

> If *l'homme absurde* is asked to make the leap of faith he can find no evidence that would justify his doing so. If he is then told that he is guilty of the sin of intellectual pride this notion of sin is without meaning for him. He remains similarly unmoved and uncomprehending when told that hell and eternal damnation await him. Such ideas remain utterly alien to one who is aware of the absurd; they cannot survive the test of lucidity. At this point Camus continues, speaking of *l'homme absurde*: "He is asked to admit his guilt. He feels himself to be innocent. Indeed his complete and utter innocence is all that he feels."
>
> Camus does suggest, however, that the notion of sin can have meaning for *l'homme absurde* in one single situation. It is sin to reject lucidity and turn one's back on the evidence it provides.[12]

And he continues:

> Camus can still only claim that evasion of lucidity is a sin by using some moral standard lying entirely outside the world of the absurd. It is impossible for him to produce from a world without transcendence, such as lucidity reveals, any standards by which he can assert that either acceptance or rejection of lucidity is sin. In fact, all these objections indicate again that an emotional determination to retain the absurd at all costs lies behind much of Camus' apparent logical detachment. It is worth mentioning here, incidentally, that even the pressure on *l'homme absurde* to choose lucidity and, later, to exercise freedom, makes of freedom and lucidity moral absolutes of the very kind that his fundamental innocence is held to deny. Camus claims to derive from the absurd values which the absurd, by definition, cannot recognize.[13]

This criticism is a correct one, for in an absurd world nothing can be morally unacceptable. It is significant, however, that Cruickshank's inability to see in *Le Mythe de Sisyphe* anything other than Camus' concern with logic leads him seriously to distort Camus' thinking yet again. For the latter's reflections upon "lucidity" are not based upon "logical detachment"; nor do they spring from "an emotional determination to retain the absurd at all costs." These reflections are, on the contrary, intimately related to what Camus sees as *"la vérité de l'homme."* The "truth of man" and of the world is, according to Camus, revealed by "lucidity." And when he insists that there is only one sin that the absurd man can commit in a meaningless world, he is saying that there is no evidence to suggest that the world is intelligible and human existence meaningful, and that to advocate, as Kierkegaard does in these circumstances, the leap of faith, is to do what in the eyes of the absurd man is intellectually indefensible as well as morally unacceptable. Now that, though inaccurate, is a point which can be properly evaluated only in its true context, that of "la vérité de l'homme."

Cruickshank turns, fourthly, to Camus' reflections on freedom and argues that there is something unsatisfactory, not only about the liberty which is recommended in *Le Mythe de Sisyphe* but also about the way in which Camus argues on its behalf.

> This freedom is also severely limited. It is freedom to complain about the absence of absolutes but not freedom to fill this metaphysical void. It is freedom to act capriciously here and now (without fear of the consequences in an after-life, for instance), but not freedom that can outlast death. Camus describes it as a freedom that cannot draw cheques on eternity. He then goes on, in a sombre image, to compare it to the freedom experienced by the condemned man on the day of his

execution. This really gives the case away. The condemned man's freedom of which Camus speaks is, I imagine, something like the freedom defined by Spinoza as consciousness of necessity—what we may call freedom in sense A. Such freedom is clearly not lack of restraint—the meaning normally given to the term and what we may call freedom in sense B. Camus is unconvincing when he claims, in his enthusiasm for the absurd, that freedom in sense A is superior to freedom in sense B. Indeed, the reverse would seem to be true, since freedom in sense B is always free to become freedom in sense A, whereas freedom in sense A can never choose to become freedom in sense B. The whole treatment of freedom in *Le Mythe de Sisyphe* is unsatisfactory and fails to justify Camus' eventual assertion

. . . death and the absurd are thus the principles underlying the only reasonable kind of freedom: that which a human heart can experience and put into practice.[14]

What Cruickshank is saying at this point is quite accurate, for the kind of freedom that Camus recommends is "quite unsatisfactory": it is not real freedom but "consciousness of necessity." He is also correct when claiming that *"la liberté"* of which Camus speaks is akin to that experienced by the condemned man on the day of his execution, and that it is therefore "severely limited." His contention that there is "something very unsatisfactory . . . about the way in which Camus argues on its behalf" is also an accurate one. Cruickshank, however, does not reflect accurately what Camus is actually saying when he endorses this limited freedom at the expense of the "metaphysical freedom" he rejects; nor is he sufficiently precise about the shortcomings of Camus' argument on its behalf. For Camus is not saying, or at any rate he does not intend to say, that the freedom that accompanies religious belief is "inferior" to that which goes with "revolt," but that the latter, though severely limited, is the only real freedom that is available to man, whereas "metaphysical freedom" is an illusion.[15] The argument which he advances on behalf of this limited freedom is not "unsatisfactory" precisely because of his belief (mistaken though it is) that the *liberté* which he endorses is superior to that which he rejects, but because the argument itself rests on the assumption that the "metaphysical freedom" to which he refers is simply illusory. For *Le Mythe de Sisyphe* does not show that there is no God, and Camus is mistaken when he claims that the acceptance of conventional morality is necessarily destructive of human freedom.

The absurd man, then, lives out his life in "revolt," "freedom" and "intensity." He is fully aware of the moral equivalence of all actions, of his own innocence, and of the fact that "all is permitted." But Camus claims that the belief that 'all is permitted' does not carry with it the conviction that nothing is forbidden. Cruickshank's remaining objections are logical and moral ones, and are directed for the most part against Camus' attempt to show that his absurdist ethic is not a nihilistic one.

Cruickshank begins by reminding us that, in Camus' opinion, the moral attitude required by the absurd is not the monopoly of Don Juan, the actor and "the conqueror," and that "a model of chastity, a civil servant or a prime minister can equally well live lives consistent with the awareness of the absurd"; all that consistency demands is "lucidity and honesty about the human condition." He then argues that Camus is in this respect inconsistent and that he "is taking back with one hand what he had given with the other."[16]

What Cruickshank says at this point is essentially correct, for Camus' attempt to defend the absurdist ethic does indeed force him into ethical formalism. Moreover, Camus is conspicuously unsuccessful in his attempt to show "that what normally pass for the opposite types of ethical behaviour could equally well be derived from the same absurdist position, if this position were soundly held." It is surprising, however, that Cruickshank does not push this second point a step further and pose an objection even more fundamental than either of those that have just been mentioned: even if Camus could justify the claim that "what normally pass for the opposite types of ethical behaviour could equally well be derived from the same absurdist position," he would still be faced with an inevitable nihilism. For if the absurd man is free and "all is permitted," then what Cruickshank calls the "opposite types of moral behaviour" might "*equally well* be derived" from the absurdist position, but they could never be reasonably demanded by it. The absurd man, as Camus says in *L'Homme révolté*, may give his life to the cure of lepers; but he is also free "to flame the crematory fires." While Camus may therefore be right when he says that "the absurd does not recommend crime," he is surely mistaken in his claim that "all is permitted does not mean that nothing is forbidden." This has rightly been described as "the language of a man who realizes that some law or limit must be set but has not in the conceptual framework he has so far built up, the means to set such a limit." In the last analysis "the 'all is permitted' must be taken literally, provided only that man realizes consciously the condition of his existence and action, and freedom is then equivalent to licence. Duty is as legitimate 'as any other,' that is to say, as crime. But no more."[17]

No evaluation of Camus' early thought would be complete without at least a mention of a further point, and indeed a crucial one, which Cruickshank makes in the third chapter of his much-acclaimed study. It amounts to the rather surprising claim that the ideas outlined in *Le Mythe de Sisyphe* were not in fact those of Camus, and that this essay "is more concerned with public stocktaking than with public advocacy."[18] The radical nature of this claim could scarcely be exaggerated, for it implies that the weaknesses of this work (and of course its strengths) are not those of its author but belong to ideas which Camus indeed expressed, but did not himself endorse.

> In a brief preliminary note to *Le Mythe de Sisyphe,* he [Camus] states clearly that he is not elaborating a *"philosophie absurde"* but describing the *"sensibilité absurde."* He adds that his attitude towards the absurd is a provisional one. Nevertheless, the majority of readers have taken no notice of these remarks. They have continued to equate the various—and sometimes conflicting—ideas of *L'Etranger, Caligula* or *Le Malentendu* with Camus' own private beliefs. The result is that he is still most widely known as the author of *L'Etranger* and *Le Mythe de Sisyphe.* He continues to be described as a writer or philosopher of the absurd.
>
> Camus was sufficiently incensed by this situation to write an essay about it in 1950. . . . While admitting that a part of him was tempted by the absurd, and still responds to it, he claims that what he primarily did in *Le Mythe de Sisyphe* was to examine the logical basis and intellectual justification of that "sensibilité absurde" which he found expressed in various forms by so many of his contemporaries.[19]

The view that Cruickshank expresses at this point is, of course, an eccentric one.[20] There are good reasons for suggesting, moreover, that it is a profoundly mistaken view and that *Le Mythe de Sisyphe* truly is concerned as much with "public advocacy" as with "public stocktaking." We shall confine our attention to three of these reasons.

The first and most obvious is that Camus himself states, in the preface to the English edition of *Le Mythe de Sisyphe* (1955), that the aim of the essay is not merely to describe a Godless world but to construct an absurdist ethic which would not founder on the reef of nihilism. He also goes on to insist that this was the purpose not only of his essay on Sisyphus, but of all his subsequent works.[21]

Secondly, while Camus does say in his brief preliminary note to *Le Mythe de Sisyphe* that this work is primarily concerned not with an "absurd philosophy" but with an "absurd sensibility," and that "no metaphysic, no belief is involved in it," the essay itself makes it clear not only that man is made for an absent God and that his existence is therefore absurd, but that man can give his fundamentally meaningless existence the sole kind of meaning it can have only by following the example of Sisyphus and adopting the posture of "revolt."[22] It elaborates, in other words, an absurdist philosophy which has its metaphysic of unbelief and its atheistic ethic. It must be remembered too

that this metaphysic was dictated in no small measure by a sceptical epistemology which was clearly his own,[23] and that Camus went to great lengths
to defend the moral position into which he was forced by the logic of "revolt."

Thirdly, there is an intimate connection between the ideas expressed in
Le Mythe de Sisyphe and the events of Camus' own life. This, as Lottman points
out, was clearly recognised by Pascal Pia, to whom the essay was dedicated,
as well as by André Malraux, who was closely associated with Camus at the
time *Le Mythe de Sisyphe* was published.

> At times it seems veritable autobiography, a portrait of the artist as a young man.
> When the book opens with the now familiar proposition that "There is only one
> philosophical problem which is really serious: suicide. To decide whether life is
> or is not worth living," one can imagine that one is reading Camus' journal.
> Remarkably, the section of the book which describes models of behaviour limits
> these to three: Don Juanism, the actor, the conqueror. Each description contains
> concepts which will make most sense to the reader who has gone this far in
> Camus' biography . . .
>
> One man who knew as much of Camus' biography as anyone was instrumen-
> tal in seeing these books through to publication: Pascal Pia. Another man was
> capable of understanding this product of lived experience if only because he had
> travelled the same path through intuition and invention: André Malraux.[24]

To suggest, therefore, as Cruickshank does, that Camus' first philosophical work was more concerned with "public stocktaking" than with "public
advocacy" is to adopt a position that is not merely eccentric but utterly
untenable. The thought of *Le Mythe de Sisyphe* is indeed that of its author.

PART 3

CHRISTIAN METAPHYSICS
AND NEOPLATONISM

Chapter VII

Background and Themes

Albert Camus' academic training began, not in his native village, Mondovi, but in Belcourt, the working-class area of Algiers, to which he had moved in 1918, after his father's death. Camus attended, first, Belcourt's kindergarten, and then its primary school, the Ecole Communale.

At about the age of ten Camus entered the second year of the école's *cours moyen* and, in so doing, became a pupil of Louis Germain, a specialist in French and an outstanding teacher, to whom he was to acknowledge, all his life, a debt of profound gratitude.[1] Germain quickly recognized his pupil's exceptional intellectual ability,[2] and persuaded Camus' family to allow him to prepare for the examination that was to provide him with a scholarship to the Lycée Bugeaud.[3] Camus took this examination in June of 1924 and four months later became a pupil of the Bab-el-Oued grammar school. He was to remain there until 1933[4] when, after successfully completing his baccalauréat and hypokhâgne year,[5] he became a full-time student of philosophy at the University of Algiers.[6]

Camus' acquaintanceship with philosophy began, however, not at university but at the lycée,[7] and can be traced, essentially, to two closely related factors: the nature of the educational system of the lycée itself,[8] and the influence of Jean Grenier, the teacher whom Camus was subsequently to describe as his *maître à penser* and to whom he was to dedicate no less than three of his works.[9] It might therefore be useful to say something, however briefly, of these two influences.

Camus entered the lycée in 1924 with the intention of becoming a teacher. He took, as a result, the academic course which, while it included subjects such as English and mathematics, was heavily biased in favour of French and Latin literature. He therefore became acquainted, and this at an early age, not only with Cicero and Vergil, and with the French classical authors, but also with contemporary French writers such as Gide and Malraux whose interests were both literary and philosophical.[10] Camus' interest in that philosophico-literary genre of which Malraux was such an able exponent was later to be encouraged by his most famous teacher. It was, moreover, to be a matter of lasting concern to him.

Jean Grenier was born in Brittany in 1898. After a brilliant student career, dedicated in large measure to philosophy, he took his *agrégation* in 1922 and went to work for the publishing house of Gallimard. Grenier's interest in teaching, however, took him first to Albi in southwest France and then, in 1930, to North Africa, where he became professor of philosophy at the Lycée Bugeaud and at the University of Algiers.[11] He first met Camus in October of that year when the latter entered the final year of his studies for the *baccalauréat*.

The influence which Grenier exerted, even on his lycée pupils, was immense, for he was a brilliant and unorthodox teacher who encouraged his students to read extensively and to publish their most promising essays.[12] It was he who introduced Camus to his own favourite thinkers, Bergson and Nietzsche, and to his chosen literary figures, among whom were Gide and Dostoevsky. Even more importantly, however, Grenier familiarized Camus with the main themes of his own philosophy, so beautifully expressed in his *Les Îles*, and, in so doing, exposed him to the possibility that man, whose existence was truncated by death, might be open to "the sacred" and "the mysterious."[13]

Camus was to reflect a great deal on these themes during his undergraduate years.[14] He was also to interest himself at that time, and profoundly so, in those authors to whom Grenier had introduced him. These reflections, and these same authors, were to produce, with the help of René Poirier[15] and of Jean Grenier himself,[16] in 1936, Camus' *Métaphysique chrétienne et Néoplatonisme*, the diploma dissertation which is, at the same time, an historical thesis on the relationship of reason to revelation and a comparative study of Greek and Christian views on the nature and destiny of man.[17] It is to this thesis that we shall now turn our attention.

Camus began his studies for the *Diplôme d'études supérieures* in 1935, immediately after the completion of his *licence en philosophie*. The theme he chose to investigate for his diploma was that of the relationship between Hellenism and Christianity.[18] His approach to this question was to be an historical one. "How had Hellenism and Christianity, with their supposedly opposite visions of the universe, ever managed to fuse into one another?"[19] Such was the problem that Camus attempted to resolve.

There were, according to Camus, four stages in the process which led to the progressive Hellenization of Christian thought. There was, to begin with, the Christianity of the Gospels, which was entirely "religious" and totally uninfluenced by philosophical notions. Thereafter the meeting of Greek rationalism and Christian revelation produced Gnosticism. The third stage was that of Neoplatonism. The philosophy of Plotinus, in particular, provided Augustine with the "ready-made formulas" he needed in order to convert the message of the gospels into a philosophy. The fourth and final stage was that of the Augustinian *second revelation,* which transformed Christianity into a metaphysic and represented the culmination of the process of Hellenization. Each of these stages corresponds to one of the four chapters of Camus' thesis, which are entitled, in turn, "Evangelical Christianity," "Gnosis," "Mystical Reason," and "The Second Revelation." The last of these chapters has, of course, been dealt with in that part of our study which relates specifically to the thought of Saint Augustine. We shall now consider the first three chapters of Camus' dissertation.

The opening chapter of "Christian Metaphysics" is devoted to evangelical Christianity. It has three sections, which deal in turn with the themes of early Christianity, its literature and personalities, and the causes of its historical evolution. Each of these sections, brief though it is, deserves some consideration.

Evangelical Christianity has as its "privileged theme" the Incarnation, which Camus describes as "the point where the divine and the flesh meet in the person of Jesus Christ."[20] There went with this fundamental religious belief, moreover, a number of specifically religious concerns. The early Christians were plagued, for example, by the thought of death and had a passionate belief in the Second Coming of Jesus. "This idea of an imminent death, linked closely to the parousia of Christ, obsessed the first generation of Christians in its entirety."[21] They believed too in the universality of sin and in the worthlessness of man. Saint Paul's "nemo bonus, omnes peccaverunt" is reechoed in Augustine's "non posse non peccare," and their moral life expressed a commitment not to man but to God alone. "What belongs to Caesar is the penny on which his image is imprinted. What belongs to God is the heart of man alone, when it has broken every attachment to the world."[22]

If the early Christians were pessimistic about man and the world, they were not, for all that, without hope. The logic of the Incarnation, Camus insists, demanded of evangelical Christians not only a tragic vision of life but a profoundly optimistic one as well, for it brought with it the hope that accompanied Redemption, a new understanding of the Kingdom of God and a philosophy of history. Camus dwells to some degree on the Redemption and emphasizes Saint Paul's insistence that this latter and the Incarnation are, as it were, two sides of the same coin.

> The will of God has in his [Saint Paul's] view one sole end: to save mankind . . .
> The only way to save us was to come to us, to take our sins from us by a miracle
> of grace, namely Jesus, of our race, of our blood, who acts on our behalf and has
> taken our place. Dying with him, and in him, man has paid for his sin, and the
> Incarnation is at the same time the Redemption.[23]

Nothing, then, is more Christian than the doctrine of the Incarnation. The belief that God became man is not, however, a philosophical notion but a specifically religious one. It is not surprising therefore that the early Christians should have been so contemptuous of human reason and so insistent upon the importance of revelation.[24] This point, which Camus makes frequently in his thesis, serves as a useful transition to the second part of his opening chapter, which is concerned, to a large degree, with evangelical faith.

In the next section of his first chapter, entitled "The Men of Evangelical Christianity," Camus turns to the literature of the second and third centuries and to the Christian communities of this same period. His aim in so doing is to show that the themes that we have just described reappear in the writings of this period and that they reflect the concerns of the Christian milieu in which they were nurtured. The works to which he refers are those which compose the "apostolic literature" developed by, for example, Saint Clement and Saint Polycarp.

Camus has no difficulty in establishing that the literature to which he addresses himself is "exclusively practical and populist" and that its spirit and characteristics faithfully reflect the teachings of the apostles. He points out, for example, that while the first epistle of Saint Clement has "one sole aim, to restore peace to the Church of Corinth," his second letter, like the *Shepherd* of Hermas, has to do with penance. He insists, too, that the epistle of Polycarp and the *Fragments* of Papias have a purely practical purpose, and that they share "an anti-Docetic Christology, a classical theory of sin and the exaltation of faith."[25] This leads him to conclude that these writings faithfully reproduce the familiar themes of evangelical Christianity and that they show, in particular, a profound dislike of all speculation.

Camus' greatest concern at this point, however, is not with the works of Clement or Polycarp but with those of Ignatius, who "combats fiercely the Docetic tendency at the heart of Christianity" and "has the most lively feeling for Christ made flesh."[26] Ignatius is not content to emphasize the Christian preoccupation with faith and love. Rather, he pushes one of the themes of early Christianity, that of the primacy of faith, as far as it will go, and insists that no one can be, at the same time, both a believer and a sinner. His *Epistle to the Ephesians* is therefore illustrative of that fanaticism which, according to Camus, is such an obvious feature of Christian faith.

> The carnal person cannot live a spiritual life, nor can the spiritual person live a carnal life, any more than faith can act the part of infidelity, or infidelity the part of faith. But even the things you do in the flesh are spiritual, for you do all things in union with Jesus Christ.[27]

If the writings of the Apostolic Fathers reflect the teaching of the Gospels, they also manifest, and no less obviously, the concerns of the religious milieu in which they were developed. For the Alexandrian Christians were disdainful of all speculation and insisted, as did Tertullian, that "faith is sufficient for man" and that "all else is literature." It is not surprising therefore that Clement of Alexandria, an ardent supporter of Greek culture, should have described the Christian thinkers of his time as "simpliciores" who, as he put it, "are fearful of Greek philosophy, as children are of a scarecrow."

In the final section of his opening chapter, Camus deals, for the most part, with the causes of the evolution of evangelical Christianity and with the difficulties faced by the Christian apologists in their attempt to reconcile Greek philosophy with Christian revelation. After providing a brief historical introduction in which he informs his readers of the obligations imposed upon Christian thought by its rupture with Judaism and its entry into the Greco-Roman world, Camus approaches his task in three stages. The first of these is devoted to the Greek "conversions" to Christianity; the second and third stages are concerned, respectively, with the opponents of philosophico-religious syncretism and with the problems involved in the very construction of a Christian philosophy.

There were, according to Camus, two reasons for the historical evolution of Christianity. The latter needed, in the first place, "to satisfy the Greeks who had already been won over to the new religion." The early centuries of the Christian period saw the conversion to Christianity of a number of highly cultivated Greek writers such as Aristides, Miltiades, and Athenagoras. These thinkers, while firmly committed to their new faith, were, at the same time, too firmly rooted in Greek culture to abandon entirely the intellectual climate in which their thoughts had been nurtured. They therefore became the first apologists whose main concern was "to present Christianity as conforming to reason." Faith, in their view, "perfects what Reason provides, and it is not unworthy of a Greek mind to accept it."[28]

Camus dwells, in particular, on the influence of Justin Martyr who "goes very far in this direction," and whose *Dialogue with Trypho* was designed to establish the accord of "Christian truth" with the New Testament and the Prophets. Saint Justin, says Camus, underscores the similarities between Christian thought and Greek philosophy and accepts wholeheartedly the view, widespread in his time, that Greek philosophers were inspired by the Old Testament. Justin insists too that the Logos was manifested to man in the person of Jesus, but that the Word existed before its incarnation and inspired the philosophy of the Greeks.

If Christian thinkers of the second and third centuries found it necessary to come to terms with the apologists, they were also faced with the task of evangelization. It was necessary for them, as Camus puts it, "to attract the others." In order to do so, however, they were forced to speak in terms comprehensible to the pagan world, or, more precisely, to express the Kerygma "in formulas that could be understood, and thus to pour into the suitable moulds of Greek thought the unco-ordinated aspirations of a very profound faith."[29] This, in Camus' view, was the second reason for the evolution of Christian thought. Before outlining the problems which inevitably accompanied such a pursuit, however, he points out that the challenges to the work of the apologists came not only from Christian writers such as Tatian, Hermas, and Tertullian, but also from those pagan thinkers who sought to divert the religious enthusiasm of their time from Jesus to figures such as Aesculapius, Hercules or Bacchus.[30]

Camus deals finally, in this first chapter, with the problems faced by the apologists in their attempt to rationalize the deposit of faith. Christian dogmas, he says, emerged from the union of Greek metaphysics with evangelical faith. The courtship of reason and revelation was a long one, however, and the obstacles to their eventual marriage were very great. The Christian notion of creation "ex nihilo," for example, had to be reconciled, as Saint Augustine knew only too well, with the Greek belief in the eternity of matter. "It is difficult to understand the substance of God, which makes changeable things without any change in itself, and creates temporal things without any temporal movement of its own."[31]

The task begun by Clement of Alexandria and Origen, difficult though it was, culminated nonetheless in the Christian Platonism of Saint Augustine. It did so, however, only with the help of Plotinian thought and with the lessons learned from the "false conciliations" of Gnosticism. These philosophic movements form, each in its turn, the subject matter of the second and third chapters of "Christian Metaphysics." It is to these chapters that we shall now turn our attention.

The second chapter of Camus' dissertation, which is entitled "Gnosis," is designed, according to its author, to describe the defining themes of Gnosticism and to reveal the origins of these themes. These tasks, however, are performed, successively, in the second and third parts of this chapter, which opens with an introduction and ends with a short section on the role of Gnosticism in the evolution of Christian thought. We shall treat, in turn, of all four sections.

Camus' initial reflections on Gnosticism define this latter movement as "one of the first attempts at Greco-Christian collaboration,"[32] as "a Greek reflection on Christian themes," and as a movement which "poses problems in a Christian manner" and "resolves them in Greek formulas."[33] Before going on to provide a detailed account of Gnostic themes, however, Camus outlines these themes with a view to justifying, in particular, his claim that Gnosticism is both a Christian phenomenon and a Greek one. The Gnostics, he says, were Christian in their belief in the Incarnation and in their acceptance of the Redemption. They were convinced too of the importance of evil. The Gnostics, however, were Greek in their belief that salvation comes with knowledge and in their conviction that such knowledge can be gained from men. Salvation, on the Christian and Gnostic view of things, is humanly attainable. For the Christian, however, such is in the hands not of man but of God, and is gratuitous; for the Gnostic, on the other hand, salvation is contemporaneous with the very knowledge of God, which is available, for example, to "the spirituals" of Valentinus: " . . . they built on the few simple and impassioned aspirations of Christianity, as on so many solid pillars, a complete setting for a metaphysical kermesse."[34]

Gnosticism, then, is an attempt to combine knowledge and salvation. Our author proceeds immediately to provide a detailed account of this attempt.

Camus opens the second section of this chapter, entitled "The Themes of the Gnostic Solution," with the claim that four fundamental themes appear, with varying degrees of emphasis, in every Gnostic system: the problem of evil, the Redemption, the theory of intermediaries, and the ineffability of a God with whom man cannot communicate. This part of his study is designed to elucidate Gnostic thought by providing an exposition of the systems of Basilides, Marcion and Valentinus, and by offering some comments on the minor Gnostic sects such as the Naassenes, Perates, and Sethians.

Basilides typifies the Gnostic concern with evil. (Camus, in fact, dismisses the claim made by Hippolytus in the *Refutations* that Basilides elaborated a metaphysical cosmology.) "If it is true that the problem of evil is at the centre of all Christian thought, no one was as profoundly Christian as Basilides."[35] The latter, says Camus, was incapable of thinking in abstract terms; his sole concern was with the human side of problems and with man's relationship to God.

Camus, relying for the most part on Clement's *Miscellanies* and on *Against Heresies* of Epiphanius, says that Basilides proposed a theory of Original Sin, or at any rate, of a "natural predisposition" to evil on the part of man. Basilides went on to say, moreover, that suffering, which has a redemptive value, is the inevitable consequence of sin. He had no alternative therefore but to claim not only that the martyrs, whose fate was of great concern to him, had sinned, but that Jesus too had done so. "No one," he insisted, "is without sin." While Christ himself did not escape "the universal law of sin," he showed man nonetheless that redemption could be found in suffering.

Having dealt with the problem of evil in Basilides, Camus turns to Marcion whom he describes as a "religious genius" rather than a "speculative thinker," and whose work he refers to as "exegetical" rather than "original." His aim, in so doing, is to illustrate, in particular, Marcion's concern with Redemption, the second of the Gnostic themes. Camus, however, does not treat this matter in isolation from Marcion's thought as a whole, but rather locates it within the context of the Gnostic's three pivotal concerns: God, Redemption through the person of Jesus, and morality.

There are, for Marcion, two divinities: a superior God who rules the invisible world and an inferior God or demiurge who is the author and master of the material world. The former, the God of the New Testament, was revealed to man not by creation, which Marcion regards as evil, but by Jesus Christ; the latter is the God of the Old Testament "who persecuted Job in order to prove his power to Satan, who made use of blood and battles and who oppressed the Jewish people with his law."[36] The unending struggle of good and evil, to which Saint Luke so clearly alludes, is waged, Marcion insists, between these two divinities.

The role played by Jesus in Marcion's drama is a very radical one. Christ is the envoy of the superior God who wages war against the evil divinity, thereby freeing man from his domination. Jesus redeems mankind by combating the work of the wicked God. In Marcion's system, therefore, Christ is the emancipator and redeemer who effects "a sort of metaphysical coup d'état."

Marcion's thoughts on God and redemption culminate in his moral teaching which, according to Camus, embodies "asceticism of the most extreme kind." This world and its goods should be despised out of hatred of the "cruel and warlike judge" who is their author. And sexual abstinence should be practised in defiance of the latter's "increase and multiply." Marcion's theory foreshadows that metaphysical rebellion which is such an obvious feature of modern thought.

The first generation of Gnostics, to which Basilides and Marcion belonged, was content, according to Camus, to locate God in the invisible world and to regard Him as ineffable. The tendency toward negative theology in the thought of some Gnostics did not appeal to Valentinus, however, whose most original contribution to Gnostic thought was his theory of intermediaries. It is to this theory that Camus now turns. He begins his reflections on Valentinus, however, by pointing out that his attempt to bridge the gap between God and the world should properly be understood in the context of a system of thought which is not merely theological but moral and cosmological as well.

The God of Valentinus lies beyond time, is uncreated, and, by virtue of his very perfection, diffuses Himself. The immediate product of his superabundance is the Dyad of Spirit and Truth. These latter, in their turn, produce the Word and Life, which give birth to man and the Church. From these six principles come the entire pleroma which Valentinus places between God and the world. This pleroma is composed of two groups of angels or aeons, one of which has ten members, while the other has twelve members. These groups are called, in Gnostic language, the Decade and Duodecade.

The cosmology of Valentinus is also an elaborate one. The world, in his view, emerges from the creative action of the demiurge who imposes form upon the matter of which the universe is composed. If the demiurge is the author of the world, he is also responsible for the creation of man whom he fashions out of grief, ignorance, fear and despair, the passions born of Sophia's rebellion against God. And men are divided, according to the extent of their awareness of their origins, into three categories: the spirituals, hylics and psychics.

The groups of people to whom we have referred can, according to Valentinus, be distinguished from one another easily. The "spirituals" have no interest in the material world and aspire only to God. The "hylics," on the other hand, have no knowledge of their origins and are drawn only to the things of sense. The "psychics," whom Camus places between these two latter groups, are torn between, on the one hand, their longing for a life of sensuality and, on the other, a disquiet of a profoundly spiritual kind. All three groups, however, bear the marks of their birth (fear, ignorance and grief) and are therefore in need of redemption. This latter is effected, moreover, not by Jesus but by the Spirit who reveals, to the "spirituals" at any rate, the knowledge of themselves and of their origins in which salvation consists.

The moral teaching of Valentinus is directly related to his cosmology, for the conclusion which he draws from this latter is an utterly simple one: "There is no freedom in the human soul by virtue of the sin of Sophia." Man, like the highly imperfect world in which he lives, is, in large measure, the product of a primeval fall, and sin is imputable not to God but to man himself. "I came to accept the truth of what the tragedies told us, I am convinced that they give us merely the truth. I believe in the longing of Oenomaüs while he was in a frenzy, I do not think it incredible that two brothers could have fought with each other. And I could not find within me the strength to say that God was the author and creator of all these evils."[37] The gnostics or "spirituals" alone will be saved, and this through knowledge of their origins, though the "psychics" too may attain salvation by submitting themselves to the will of God.

The remainder of this section is devoted to a brief consideration of the more obscure Gnostic sects such as the Naassenes, Perates and Sethians whom Camus classifies with some degree of precision. He points to the richness and variety of Gnostic thought and to the multitude of later Gnostic schools. At the same time Camus insists, however, that their teachings on the origin of the physical world, the nature of man, the Incarnation and the Redemption owe a great deal to the reflections of Basilides and Marcion, and even more to the cosmology and aeonology of Valentinus.

Camus opens the next section of this chapter entitled "The Elements of the Gnostic Solution" with the rather blunt assertion that Gnosticism is the product of the juxtaposition of very disparate themes, drawn from different sources, and that it can therefore make no legitimate claim to originality. His aim, at this point, is to summarize these themes and to throw some light on their origins.

A great number of Gnostic themes can be traced to Plato, or at any rate to the tradition that he represents. The emanation of intelligences from the bosom of the Divinity, the suffering of souls estranged from God, and regeneration through a return to original sources are all Platonic notions. The Greeks moreover applied to their moral philosophy, as much as to their aesthetics, the notion of moderation, and this, too, profoundly influenced the Gnostics. Sophia, like Prometheus, is the victim of excess.

If the Gnostics drew heavily upon Platonic sources, they borrowed a great deal from Christianity as well. Basilides, Marcion and Valentinus, like other Greek thinkers, were obsessed with evil and with the Incarnation and the Redemption. They were also indebted to Christianity for their philosophy of history and for the view that truth, which was salvific, should not be, as many Greek philosophers had held, merely an object of contemplation. "Truths are not to be contemplated. Rather we wager on them, and with them on our salvation." This latter point leads Camus to conclude that, in some respects at any rate, the Christian influence on Gnosticism is more of an emotional than of a doctrinal kind. "The Christian influence at this point consists not so much in a group of dogmas as in a state of soul and an orientation."[38]

Gnosticism, then, is the product of Greek and Christian influences. There were, however, other factors at work as well. In the notion, for example, of a higher knowledge that constitutes wisdom, Camus sees the influence of the mystery religions. The Gnostics owe to Philo, moreover, the notion that the universe was created by intermediary beings and the suggestion that the visible world is a reflection of the invisible world. These suggestions lead Camus immediately to the conclusion of his second chapter, which deals with the place of Gnosticism in the historical evolution of Christianity.

Camus begins his final reflections on Gnosticism by summarizing its general characteristics. The Gnostics, he says, were obsessed with the problem of evil and pessimistic about the world. They worshipped an inaccessible God and identified salvation with knowledge. Over a period of more than two hundred years, in fact, they gathered together "all the ideas which were abroad at that time and used them to construct a hideous Christianity, made up of oriental religions and Greek mythology."[39] Gnosticism is very much a Christian heresy.

The fact that Gnosticism is a Christian movement as well as a heretical one leads Camus to draw two conclusions, which, while very different from one another, are historically of some importance. He concludes, in the first place, that Gnosticism was "one of the ways in which the Greek and the Christian could be combined," and so "marks an important stage [in the evolution of Christianity], an experiment which could not have been passed over in silence."[40] If Gnosticism was one possible form of Greco-Christian synthesis, it was nevertheless an undesirable one, which added a rational explanation to the Gospels and showed Christianity "the road not to follow." It was for this reason that Tertullian tried to stem the Christian advance toward the Mediterranean. The excesses of Gnosticism, moreover, led later Christian thinkers to borrow from the Greeks "their formulas and modes of thought" rather than their "emotional postulates" which could neither be reduced to evangelical thought nor set alongside of it.[41]

Camus leaves Christian thought at this point and turns immediately to Neoplatonism, which was to play such an important role in the philosophy of Saint Augustine.

The third chapter of Camus' dissertation, which is entitled "Mystical Reason," is devoted to the thought of Plotinus. It has three sections which bear, respectively, the titles "Plotinus' Solution," "The Opposition" and "Meaning and

Influence of Neoplatonism." The first of these sections, which contains an outline of Plotinus' thoughts on emanation and conversion, opens with a short but crucial introduction which sets the scene for Camus' treatment of Neoplatonism. It is with this introduction that we shall now begin.

Camus opens this chapter by stating that Plotinus is interesting on two scores. He is, in the first place, the very embodiment of the drama of Christian metaphysics in its attempt to marry the religious and mystical aspirations of Christianity with its need for a rational explanation of things. It is, says Camus, "the longing for God" that animates him. "But Plotinus is also a Greek . . . he has the taste for a rational explanation of things. And in this respect his own tragedy reflects the drama of Christian metaphysics as well."[42] According to some commentators, the Plotinian synthesis furnished Christian thought if not with a doctrine, at least with "a method and a way of looking at things."

Plotinus' concern for the destiny of the soul and his taste for rationality were harmonized in "mystical reason," a crucial concept on which Camus lays some emphasis. Knowledge, for Plotinus, consists not in construction but in contemplation and inner recollection. "To know is to worship with Reason's accord."[43] And if Plotinus' reason is based on his belief that the world is intelligible, the principles or hypostases that underlie this intelligibility are to be understood, nonetheless, in mystical as well as in cosmological terms. In this respect Plotinian thought is like psychoanalysis: diagnosis coincides with treatment. To reveal is to heal, and to know the first hypostasis is to return to one's homeland. "The demonstrations of the Good," says Plotinus, "are also means of rising to him." This leads Camus to the themes of emanation and conversion, but only after he has provided some reflections on Plotinian aesthetics.

For Plotinus the world, which is intelligible, is grasped not by reason but by contemplation. If Plotinus' thought is religious, however, it is also aesthetic. The things of this world, in his view, are intelligible, but only because they are beautiful. And the beauty of the visible world merely reflects that of the higher world, the object of Plotinian striving. "All that comes here below from up there, is more beautiful in the higher world."[44] What Plotinus seeks then is not appearance but, rather, that "reverse side" of things that is his lost paradise. In this respect, Plotinian philosophy differs profoundly from Christian thought, which substitutes history for harmony and separates truth from beauty, thereby conferring on reason not a mystical role but a purely "legislative" one.

Plotinus, then, is not merely a mystic and an aesthete, but a rationalist as well. The world, in his view, can be understood. What underlies this intelligibility, moreover, is the fact that there are two principles in the Plotinian system, namely Intellect and World-Soul, which link sensible things to the One, the first of Plotinus' hypostases. In the third chapter of his dissertation Camus outlines Plotinus' demonstration of the One and explains how Intellect and World-Soul proceed from the first Plotinian hypostasis.

Camus' exposition of Plotinus' "demonstration" is a succinct and accurate one, which immediately evidences the latter's concern with the beauty of the visible world and his insistence that such can be adequately explained only by reference to an ultimate being who is simple, intelligent, ineffable and the very source of order and beauty.

> If the world is beautiful, it is because something lives in the world. But it is also because there is something that gives order to it. This spirit which animates the world is the World-Soul. The higher principle which keeps this logos within determinate boundaries is Intellect. But the unifying principle of order is always superior to that order. There is therefore a third principle superior to Intellect, which is the One.[45]

The visible world owes its existence proximately to the World-Soul and ultimately to the One. But how is the creativity of the first hypostasis to be understood? Does the One, like the Christian God, produce things out of nothing, or is his creative action akin, for example, to that of Plato's demiurge? Plotinus' answer is unambiguous. Visible things proceed from the One, neither by a process of creation, which separates "the heaven and the creator,"[46] nor in the manner of Plato's *Timaeus*, but by virtue of a "procession" or "emanation" which unites the One with the visible world "in the same sweet movement of superabundance."[47] The One, which is the Good and the Beautiful as well, and which is perfect and is beyond being, superabounds and produces Intellect "in the way that a fire gives off its heat or a flower its fragrance."[48] And Intellect, the second Plotinian hypostasis, which, according to Camus, is identical with the world of Platonic ideas, produces the World-Soul intermediate between the sensible world and the intelligible realm, as the One engendered Intellect itself. "All things which exist, as long as they remain in being, necessarily produce, from their own substances," says Plotinus, "a reality which is directed to what is outside of itself and is dependent upon their present power . . . as fire produces heat and snow does not retain all its cold."[49]

Intellect and World-Soul, then, both are and, at the same time, are not identical with the One. They are, indeed, to be identified with Him as their common origin; they are, however, distinct from the first hypostasis as they become fragmented, Intellect in duality, World-Soul in multiplicity.[50] The Plotinian system preserves unity as well as diversity, identity as well as difference. And what is crucial to this system is not the principle of contradiction but that of participation. This brings us immediately to Camus' account of "conversion" and "ecstacy" in Plotinus.

All things, according to Plotinus, proceed from the One by a process of emanation. But does the first Plotinian hypostasis transcend the things He has created, or is He immanent in them? Plotinus' answer to this question, says Camus, is vital for an understanding of "conversion." The God of Plotinus is at once a transcendent being and an immanent one, for while He "produces without exhausting Himself," the One is also "present in all his works," though not spatially so. And this means, of course, that the whole of creation, except matter, has a natural knowledge of the One and a natural desire to be united with Him. This union is achieved by turning back to the First Principle and contemplating it. Camus makes this point by referring specifically to the human soul and to Intellect, the second hypostasis.

The soul, like Intellect, desires "to be and to be one." It therefore carries within itself a desire for God and the memory of its homeland. Life without God is a mere shadow of life. In terms that anticipate Saint Augustine's ascent of the soul to God and of his distinction between "cognitio" and "notitia," Plotinus insists that the soul, in its knowledge of the One and its desire to know the first hypostasis better, strives to ascend from the world of sense, first to the realm of ideas and then to the First Principle itself. Beauty and virtue are not sufficient for the soul, nor is it satisfied even with Intellect. "If it halts at Intellect, the soul undoubtedly sees things that are beautiful and noble. It does not, however, for all that, altogether possess what it is looking for. Like a face which, in spite of its beauty, cannot attract glances, for it does not reflect the grace which is the flower of beauty."[51] The Plotinian hypostases are therefore to be viewed not merely in metaphysical or in cosmological terms, but in spiritual or religious ones as well, for they form the stages in "the soul's journey to its metaphysical homeland" where it is at last happy in the attainment of the One.[52]

Camus concludes this section of his third chapter with a brief account of how, according to Plotinus, this "union with the One" or "ecstacy" is to be achieved: it requires interiority and personal ascesis. The human soul bears within itself the three hypostases and the memory of its origins. Its ascent to God must therefore begin with a withdrawal into itself and a flight from that body, one which paves the way for its union first with Intellect and then with the One itself. "We must not batten on what is not the soul, though it is in the soul; rather we must return to that homeland the remembrance of which tinges our souls' disquiet."[53] This union "so complete and so unusual" is ecstacy, which Camus describes as the very heart of Plotinus' thought, and the point at which the latter's reflections end in the silence that is so appropriate to the mystic.

It only remains for Camus to consider, as he puts it, the attitude of Neoplatonism to Christianity, and to extrapolate the basic themes of Plotinus' philosophy, with a view to determining the role of these themes in the evolution of Christian metaphysics. These tasks are performed, respectively, in the second and third parts of this chapter.

The nature and extent of the Neoplatonic opposition to Christianity, says Camus, can be gauged usefully from Plotinus' assault upon the Christian Gnostics and from the views expressed by Porphyry, his most famous disciple, on what he took to be Christian eschatology and obscurantism.

In *Ennead* II, 9, which is written against those who claim that "the demiurge of the world is evil and the world bad," Plotinus opposes his own coherent and harmonious cosmos to the romantic universe of the Gnostics who scorn "the world, the gods and all the beauties of the cosmos." More precisely, however, Plotinus criticizes the Gnostics, with varying degrees of emphasis, on four points. They despise, in the first place, the created universe and insist that a new world is waiting for them.[54] The Gnostics believe, moreover, that they are the children of God, and substitute for the harmony of the universe a product that will satisfy their egotism. What most annoys Plotinus, however, is the "humanitarianism" and "anarchy" of the Gnostics. The former, he says, gives the name of brother to "the most worthless of men" while denying this same privilege "to the sun, the stars in the sky or even the World-Soul."[55] Their "anarchy" substitutes for the virtue of the sage the idea that salvation is arbitrary, an opinion that, according to Camus, "cannot be reconciled with a doctrine in which beings act according to the needs of their nature, and not, as Plotinus protests, at one moment rather than another."[56]

These criticisms, it might be said, were directed not against Christian thought but against the Gnostic heresy, which was, after all, a mere caricature of Christianity. This, however, is a point which Camus is not prepared to concede. Plotinus' concern in this instance, he insists, was not so much with doctrinal details as with "an attitude to the world," which he took to be Christian rather than Platonic. And the Neoplatonic opposition to this same "attitude" is to be found not merely in Plotinus but also in Porphyry, who chided the Christians on their "irrational faith," and whose aesthetic sense was outraged by Christian eschatology.[57]

If the Plotinian reaction to Christianity was a negative one, Neoplatonism was to play, nonetheless, an important role in the subsequent development of Christian thought. Camus' immediate task is now to define that role by looking at the meaning of Neoplatonism and at its influence on the evolution of Christian metaphysics.

Plotinus, says Camus, was a highly original thinker, for while his *Enneads* are Hellenic works, the influence of the Greek philosophers on these writings was far from overriding. In the thought of Plato, for example, the myths on the destiny of the soul are set alongside of a purely rational explanation of things; for Plotinus, on the other hand, philosophy and mythology are inseparably interconnected and bear upon the same reality. (The Plotinian hypostases, Camus repeats, have a religious significance as well as an explicative value.) Plotinus, moreover, reconciled, with the help of the principle of participation and of a logic divorced from space and time, the "contradictory" notions of divine transcendence and the immanence of God.

Neoplatonism was not merely an original mode of reflection, but also an influential one that profoundly affected the future development of Christian thought by providing it with a "method" and a direction for its subsequent evolution. The orientation to which Camus refers is, of course, a philosophic one; the "method" that made it possible for an essentially religious world view to be reconciled with Greek metaphysics was, according to Camus, the principle of participation.

> . . . what Neoplatonism contributed to Christianity so as to allow it subsequently to evolve was, in fact, a method and a direction for its thought.
>
> A direction for its thought, because by providing Christianity with frames of reference already fashioned to religious ways of thinking, Neoplatonism strongly inclined it toward the perspectives within which these frames of reference had been created. Alexandrian thought encourages Christianity to progress toward the conciliation of a metaphysic and a primitive faith. But in this regard, there was little to be done, as the movement was under way. The method, however, arrived at the right time. Christianity is going to resolve its great problems, Incarnation and Trinity, by employing the principle of participation.[58]

The influence of Neoplatonism on Christian thought, Camus concludes, is that of "a metaphysical doctrine on a religious way of thinking: a model to follow, once ambitions are aroused."[59] And Plotinus is, in this context, the key figure who "prepared and moulded formulas which were found ready-made at the very time they were needed."[60] He therefore played a vital role in the development of that Christian philosophy which was fully articulated in the thought of Saint Augustine.

Chapter VIII

Métaphysique chrétienne et Néoplatonisme
by Albert Camus

In the paintings of the Catacombs the Good Shepherd willingly assumes the face of Hermes. But if their smile is the same, its import is quite different. Christian thought, which had to be expressed in a coherent system, thus tried to mould itself into the contours of Greek ideas and to express itself in the metaphysical formulas that it found fully constructed. But at least it transformed them. This is why, in order to understand what is original in Christianity, we must reveal the source of its profound meaning, and why, for historical purposes, we must return to its sources. That is the aim of this present work. But if research of any kind is to be coherent, it must follow one or two basic lines of thought. This introduction will help us to define these thought patterns, in so far as it will highlight certain constants which emerge, despite its complexity, in the historic material with which we are concerned.

What, it has often been asked, constituted the originality of Christianity with regard to Hellenism? As well as having obvious differences, they still have a good many common themes. The fact of the matter is, however, that in every case where a civilization is brought into being (and to give birth to a civilization is man's greatest task), there is a movement from one plane to another, rather than a substitution of one system for another. It is not by comparing the dogmas of Christianity with Greek philosophy that we begin to see how they differ, but rather by noticing that the emotional plane on which the evangelical communities found themselves is alien to the classical aspect of Greek sensibility. That which is original in Christianity is to be found on the emotional level, where the problems are posed, and not in the system which is devised in order to meet these problems. Christianity, in its initial stages, is not a philosophy in opposition to a philosophy, but a whole gamut of aspirations, a faith, which moves on a certain plane and looks for its solutions within this plane.

It is appropriate at this point, however, before speaking of what is irreducible in the two civilizations, to introduce some distinctions and to take account of the complexity of the problem. It is always arbitrary to speak of a "Greek mind" as opposed to a "Christian mind." Aeschylus and Sophocles, the primitive masks and the Panathenaic games, the oil flasks of the fifth century and the metopes of the Parthenon, and finally the mysteries and Socrates, all serve to emphasize, alongside of the Greece of light, a Greece of darkness, less classical but equally real. On the other hand, there can be no doubt that a certain number of chosen themes are discernible in any civilization, and that it is possible, with the help of Socratic thought, to trace within Greek philosophy a certain number of privileged patterns whose composition implies precisely what is called Hellenism. Something in Greek thought prefigures Christianity, while at the same time something else rejects it in advance.

A. *THE DIFFERENCES*

The Greeks and Christians can thus be shown to have had utterly divergent attitudes to the world. As it is formulated toward the first centuries of our time, Hellenism implies that man is self-sufficient and that he himself has the ability to explain the universe and his destiny. His temples are built to his stature. In a certain sense the Greeks believed that existence could be justified by reference to sport and to beauty. The shape of their hills, or a young man running on a beach, revealed to them the whole secret of the universe. Their gospel said: our kingdom is of this world. It is the "Everything is fitting for me, my Universe, which fits your purpose" of Marcus Aurelius.[1] This purely rational conception of life, that the entire world can be understood, leads to moral intellectualism: virtue is something that is learned.

Without always admitting it, the whole of Greek philosophy makes the sage equal to God. And God being no more than a superior form of knowledge, the supernatural does not exist: the whole universe is centered around man and his endeavour. If, therefore, moral evil is a lack of knowledge[2] or an error, how can a place be found in this view of things for the notions of Redemption and Sin?

In the realm of nature, moreover, the Greeks also believed in a cyclical world, eternal and necessary, which could not be reconciled with creation *ex nibilo* and therefore with an end of the world.[3]

Convinced in a general way that only the idea is really real, the Greeks could not comprehend the dogma of bodily resurrection. Celsus, Porphyry and Julian, for example, cannot be scornful enough of this idea. Whether in physics, morals or metaphysics, the whole difference lay in the way the problems were posed.

At the same time, however, they continued to have some points in common. Neoplatonism, the final thrust of Greek philosophy, cannot be understood, nor can Christianity, without considering the source of their common aspirations, to which the entire thought of this period tries to be equal.

B. *THE COMMON ASPIRATIONS*

Few periods were as troubled. In an unusual mixture of races and peoples the old Greco-Roman themes intermingled with that new wisdom which was coming from the East. Asia Minor, Syria, Egypt and Persia were sending ideas and intellectuals to the Western world.[4] The jurists of the time are Ulpian of Tyre and Papias of Herese. Ptolemy and Plotinus are Egyptians, Porphyry and Iamblichus are from Syria, Dioscorides and Galen are Asians. Even Lucian, that renowned "Attic" mind, is from Commagene, on the frontier of the Euphrates. And this was what made it possible for the sky to be filled at the same time with Gnostic aeons, the Jewish Jahveh, the Christian Father, the One of Plotinus and even the old Roman gods, still worshipped in the rural areas of Italy.

It is certainly true that political and social causes can be found for that: cosmopolitanism[5] or the very real economic crisis of the period. But there is also the fact that a certain number of passionate demands begin to burgeon and that these will try to be satisfied by any means. And the East alone is not responsible for this awakening. If it is true that Greece had by that time euhemerized[6] the gods, if it is true that the problem of the destiny of the soul had given way to the ideas of the Epicureans and Stoics, it remains true nonetheless that the tradition to which the Greco-Roman world was returning was a real one. But something new is making itself felt all the same.

In this world where the desire for God becomes stronger, the problem of the Good loses ground. The humility of souls in search of inspiration replaces the pride in life that animated the ancient world. The aesthetic plane of contemplation is hidden yet again by the tragic one, where hopes are confined to the imitation[7] of a God. The mournful drama of Isis in search of Osiris is enacted.[8] One dies with Dionysus[9] and is reborn with him. The priest follows Attis in his worst mutilations.[10] Zeus is united with Demeter, at Eleusis,[11] in the person of the high priest and a hierophant.

At the same time, moreover, there is the idea that the world is not oriented toward the "all things are always the same" of Lucretius, but that it serves as the setting for the tragedy of man without God. The problems themselves begin and the philosophy of history takes shape. There is less reluctance to accept, from this time on, that change which the Redemption brings to the world. It is not a matter of knowing and of understanding, but of loving. And Christianity will only serve to give rise to the idea, though there is little Greek about it, that the problem for man is not to perfect his nature but to escape from it. Desire for God, humility, imitation, aspirations toward a rebirth—all these themes cross and countercross in the mysteries and in the Oriental religions of Mediterranean paganism. Since the second century in particular (the worship of Sybil was introduced into Rome in 205) the leading religions continued, by their influence and growth, to prepare the way for Christianity. In the period which concerns us, the new problems are posed in all their acuity.

C. STATE OF THE PROBLEM AND PLAN OF THIS WORK

To regard Christianity, therefore, as a new form of thought which follows rapidly upon the heels of Greek civilization would be to evade the difficulties. Greece is continued in Christianity, which is itself preformed in Hellenic thought. It is too easy to see in Christian dogmatics a Greek infiltration that was in no way legitimized in the evangelical doctrines. One cannot deny the contribution which Christianity makes to the thought of the time, and it seems difficult to exclude entirely the idea of a Christian philosophy.[12] They have one thing in common, namely, a disquiet which gives birth to problems: the same process of evolution leads from the practical concerns of Epictetus to the speculations of Plotinus, and from the inner Christianity of Paul to the teaching of the Greek Fathers. Is it possible, however, in spite of all this, to glean from such confusion that which constitutes the originality of Christianity? That is where the whole problem lies.

Christian teaching is, from the historical point of view, a religious movement, born in Palestine, inscribed in Jewish thought. At a time that is difficult to determine precisely, but which is certainly contemporaneous with the point at which Paul authorizes in principle the admission of Gentiles and exempts them from circumcision,[13] Christianity breaks away from Judaism. At the end of the first century, John proclaims that the Lord and the Spirit are one. Between 117 and 130 the Epistle of Barnabas is already decidedly anti-Jewish. This is the crucial point. Christian thought is divorced from its origins at this point and pours in its fullness into the Greco-Roman world. The latter, prepared by its anxieties and the mystery religions, ends by accepting it.

It is no longer of interest, from that time onward, to make a rigid distinction between the two doctrines, but rather to look into the way in which they combined their efforts and to see what each managed to retain, in spite of their collaboration. But what an Ariadne's thread has to be followed in order to make one's way through this morass of ideas and systems! The theme which constitutes the irreducible originality of Christianity is that of the Incarnation. Problems take flesh and immediately assume the character of the tragic and of necessity, which is so often absent from certain games of the Greek mind. Even when the Jews had rejected Christianity and the Mediterranean had accepted it, the profoundly original character of Christianity survived. And Christian thought, which had to borrow from the already existing philosophy some fully articulated formulas, nevertheless transfigured them. The role of Greece was to make Christian thought universal by orienting it toward metaphysics. The mysteries had prepared her for this role, as had a whole tradition which has its origin in Aeschylus and the Doric Apollos. This is the explanation of a movement in which the Christian miracle managed to assimilate the Greek miracle, and to lay the foundations of a civilization so lasting that we are still thoroughly impregnated by it.

Our enterprise and the approach we shall take to it have now been outlined: to follow in Neoplatonism the attempt of Greek philosophy to provide a specifically Greek solution to the problem of the era; to outline the Christian effort to adapt its dogmatics to its own original religious life, until the time when, encountering in Neoplatonism metaphysical formulas already moulded upon a religious thought, Christianity blossomed into that second revelation which was Augustinian thought. But there are three moments in the evolution of Christianity: the Christianity of the Gospels from which it originates; the teaching of Augustine where it culminates in the union of the word and the flesh; and the deviations into which it let itself be drawn in its attempt to identify knowledge with salvation, namely, the heresies of which Gnosticism provides a perfect example—the Gospel, Gnosis, Neoplatonism, Augustinian thought. We shall study these four stages of an evolution that is common to Greece and Rome, in their historical order and in the relationship that they maintain with the movement of thought in which they are inscribed. Evangelical Christianity scorns all speculation and instead starts with the Incarnation theme. Gnosticism pursues a solution of its own in which knowledge and redemption are identical. Neoplatonism strives to achieve its objectives by attempting to reconcile rationalism with mysticism, and, with the help of its formulas, allows Christian teaching to become, in Saint Augustine, a metaphysic of the Incarnation. At the same time, Neoplatonism functions at this point as a reference-doctrine. The movement which animates it is the very one which enlivens Christian thought, but the notion of the Incarnation remains alien to it.

As early as the sixth century, this movement is completed: "Neoplatonism died with the death of Greek philosophy and of culture in general, and the sixth and seventh centuries were marked by a profound silence."[14]

CHAPTER ONE
EVANGELICAL CHRISTIANITY

It is difficult to speak en bloc of "evangelical Christianity." But it is at least possible to reveal a certain state of mind from which its subsequent evolution derives. The privileged theme, that very one which is at the centre of Christian thought and toward which everything converges, the natural solution to the aspirations of that period, is the Incarnation, that is, the point where the divine and the flesh meet in the person of Jesus Christ: the extraordinary adventure of a God taking upon himself man's sin and misery, humility and humiliations being presented as so many symbols of Redemption. This notion is, however, the crowning point of a group of aspirations that we have to define.

The Christian, as depicted in the Gospels, has two states of mind: pessimism and hope. Humanity, evolving on a certain tragic plane, finds no rest at that time but in God, and placing all hope of a better destiny in His hands, aspires only to Him, sees only Him in the universe, loses interest in everything but faith and makes God the very symbol of that aching, longing for transports. One must choose between the world and God. These are the two aspects of Christianity that we will have to examine, one after the other, in the first part of our dissertation. The study of the milieu and literature of the period will then reveal these different themes in the Gospel Christians.

The most reliable approach is to return to the texts of the New Testament itself. But a second method can be employed in support of this one, namely to appeal, whenever possible, to a pagan polemicist.[15] Their reproaches give us a very precise idea of those Christian teachings which would have shocked a Greek, and therefore tell us what was new in the contribution made by Christianity.

I. The Themes of Evangelical Christianity

A. *The Tragic Plane*

Lack of knowledge and contempt for all speculation characterize the mentality of the first Christians. Facts blind them and weigh them down. So too does death.

a) At the end of the fourth century, moreover, Julius Quintus Hilarianus, proconsular bishop of Africa, reckons in *The Length of the World* that there are 101 years of life left on earth.[16]

This idea of an imminent death, linked closely to the parousia of Christ, obsessed the first generation of Christians in its entirety.[17] What we have here is the sole example of a collective experience of death.[18] In the world of our experience, to realize this idea of death amounts to bestowing a new meaning upon our lives. It implies, in fact, the triumph of the flesh, the terror that the body feels at this revolting conclusion. Is it surprising then that Christians should have felt such a poignant sense of humiliation and of bodily affliction, and that these notions could have played a crucial role in the elaboration of Christian metaphysics? "My flesh is clothed with worms and dirt; my skin hardens, then breaks out afresh. My days are swifter than a weaver's shuttle, and come to their end without hope."[19] It is clear that the Old Testament was already setting the tone with Job[20] and Ecclesiastes.[21]

But the Gospels placed this sense of death at the centre of their devotion.

It is not sufficiently recognized, in fact, that Christianity is built around the person of Christ and his death. Jesus has become an abstraction or a symbol. The true Christians, however, are those who have realized this triumph of martyred flesh. Since Jesus was a man, the whole emphasis was placed upon his death. Scarcely anything more physically terrible can be imagined. We must turn to certain Catalan sculptures, with their torn hands and shattered limbs, in order to imagine the terrible picture of suffering that Christianity erected into a symbol. But then again, it is enough to consult the celebrated pages of the Gospel.[22]

A further proof, if such be needed, of the importance of this theme in evangelical Christianity, is the indignation of the pagans: "Leave her, then, confirmed in her groundless errors, to celebrate, with discordant lamentations, the obsequies of this dead God, condemned by just judges and handed over in public to the most ignominious of punishments."[23]

And again: " . . . He let himself be struck, spat upon, crowned with thorns . . . if he had to suffer, as God ordained, he should have accepted his punishment, but should not have endured his passion without directing some bold statement, some strong words of wisdom towards Pilate his judge. He allowed himself, instead, to be insulted like any one of the mob at the street corner!"[24] But this is enough to show the importance of death and its bodily content in the thought which concerns us.

b) "We like," says Pascal, "to relax in the company of those who are like us: wretched like us, powerless like us, they will not help us: we will die alone." A certain attitude, very difficult to define, accompanies the experience of death. There are indeed numerous texts of the Gospels where Jesus recommends indifference toward his relatives or even hatred of them as a means of arriving at the kingdom of God.[25] Is this the basis of an immoralism? No, but of a higher kind of morality: "If any one comes to me and does not hate his own father and mother and wife and children and brothers and sisters, yes, and even his own life, he cannot be my disciple."[26] These texts teach us, nevertheless, the extent to which the "render unto Caesar" is indicative of a scornful concession rather than of conformism. What belongs to Caesar is the penny on which his image is imprinted. What belongs to God is the heart of man alone, when it has broken every attachment to the world. This is the mark of pessimism, not of acceptance. These rather vague themes and mental attitudes, however, are realized and summed up, as one might expect, in the idea of sin, which is a specifically religious notion.

c) In sin man becomes conscious of his wretchedness and pride. "No one is good,[27] all have sinned."[28] Sin is universal. But few of the important[29] texts of the New Testament are as rich in meaning and as revealing as this passage of the Epistle to the Romans:[30]

> I do not understand my own actions: For I do not the good I want, but the evil I do not want is what I do. Now if I do what I do not want, it is no longer I who do it, but sin which dwells within me. So I find it to be a law that when I want to do right, evil lies close at hand. I delight in the law of God in my inmost self, but I see in my members another law at war with the law of my mind and making me captive to the law of sin which dwells in my members.

This is where the "to be unable not to sin" of Saint Augustine is developed. At the same time the pessimistic view which Christians have of the world becomes evident. It is to this way of looking at things, and to these aspirations that the constructive part of evangelical Christianity responds. But it was good to note this state of mind in advance. "Imagine a number of men in chains, all under sentence of death, some of whom are each day butchered in the sight of the others; those remaining see their own condition in that of their fellows, and, looking at each other with grief and despair, await their turn. This is an image of the human condition."[31] But just as this thought of Pascal, at the beginning of the *Apology*, serves to underline his final commitment to God, so the hope that should have sustained them emerges from those who have been condemned to death.

B. *Hope in God*

a) "I desire to know God and the soul," says Saint Augustine, "nothing more—nothing whatever."[32] This is true also, and in large measure, of the Gospels where all that matters is the Kingdom of God, which can be attained only by renouncing so much that belongs to this world. The idea of the Kingdom of God does not first appear in the New Testament. The Jews were already familiar with the word and what it represented.[33] In the Gospels, however, this kingdom has nothing terrestrial about it.[34] It is spiritual. It is the contemplation of God himself. Outside of the context of this search, no speculation is desirable. "I say this, so that no one may lead you astray with seductive speeches . . . See to it that no one makes a prey of you by philosophy and deceitful orations that rest upon human tradition, upon the elemental spirits of the universe, and not upon Christ."[35] The humility and simplicity of little children should be man's goal.[36] It is therefore to children that the kingdom of God is promised, but also to the educated who have succeeded in renouncing their learning so as to grasp the truth of the heart, and have thereby added to the virtue of simplicity the precious reward of self-effort. In *Octavius* Minucius Felix has Caecilius, the defender of paganism, speak as follows: "Should we not be annoyed that people who have not devoted themselves to study, who are strangers to literature and ill-equipped even for menial tasks, utter categorical statements about everything that is most exalted and majestic in nature, while philosophy has disputed them for centuries now."[37] This disdain for all pure speculation is expressed in the writings of those who regarded being poured into God as the end of all human endeavour. A certain number of conclusions follow from this.

b) If pride of place is to be given to man's striving for God, everything must be subordinated to this movement. And the world itself is oriented in this direction. History has the meaning that God has chosen to give it. The philosophy of history, a notion that is alien to a Greek mind, is a Jewish invention. Metaphysical problems are embodied in time and the world is merely the physical symbol of this human striving toward God. This is why faith is crucial.[38] It is enough for a paralytic or a blind man to believe—and behold he is cured. This faith is essentially consent and renunciation. And faith is always more important than works.[39]

Reward in the other world continues to be of a gratuitous kind. It is so valuable that it surpasses what merit demands. And it is a question of justifying humility in this case as well. Preference must be given to the sinner who repents, rather than to the virtuous man filled with pride in himself and his good works. The labourer of the eleventh hour will be paid a penny, as will those of the first hour. And the prodigal will be welcomed with open arms in his father's house. For sinners who repent, eternal life. This very important phrase, eternal life, is understood in its wide sense, to mean immortality, every time it is used.[40]

c) This is where we find the notion that interests us. If it is true that man is nothing and that his entire destiny is in the hands of God, that works are not enough to guarantee man his reward, if the "no one is good" is justified, who then will attain to this kingdom of God? The distance between man and God is so great that no one can hope to bridge it. Man cannot reach God, and only despair is open to him. But the Incarnation provides the answer. Man being unable to rejoin God, God comes down to man. Universal hope in Christ is born at this point. Man was right to depend upon God, for God has given him the greatest possible grace.

This doctrine is first expressed in a coherent manner in Paul.[41] The will of God, in his view, has one sole end: to save mankind. Creation and redemption are merely two manifestations of His will, His first and second revelations.[42] The sin of Adam has corrupted man and brought death upon him.[43] He no longer has the ability to do anything of himself. The moral law of the Old Testament merely provides man with an ethical guideline. It does not, however, give him the strength to live as he should. The law then makes him culpable on two scores.[44] The only way to save us was to come to us, to take our sins from us by a miracle of grace, namely Jesus, of our race, of our blood,[45] who acts on our behalf and has taken our place. Dying with Him and in Him, man has paid for his sin, and the Incarnation is at the same time the Redemption.[46] But for all that the omnipotence of God is not diminished, for the death and Incarnation of His son are graces, not payments that are owed to man's efforts.

This factual solution resolved all the difficulties of a doctrine and established a uniquely distant gap between God and man. Plato, who wanted to unite the Good and man, was forced to build a whole scale of ideas between these two terms: he therefore created a science. But here no reasoning at all, merely a fact. Jesus has come. To Greek wisdom, which is merely a science, Christianity stands opposed as a concrete fact.

In order to understand, finally, the complete originality of an idea which has become too familiar to our minds, let us ask the pagans of that time for their opinions. A mind as cultivated as Celsus is uncomprehending. His indignation is real. Something eludes Celsus because it is too original for him:

What does it matter, he says, that some Christians and Jews claim that a God, or a son of God, has yet to come down, while others insist that he has come down. This is the most outrageous of claims. . . . What meaning could a journey of that kind have for a God? Would it be to discover what men are doing? But is he not omniscient? Is he then incapable, in spite of his divine power, of bettering them without dispatching someone in bodily form for this purpose. . . . And if, as Christians say, he has come to help men to return to the right path, why has he adverted to these obligations of his only after leaving them in a state of uncertainty for so many centuries?[47]

The Incarnation seemed unacceptable to Porphyry as well:

Even if we were to suppose that the Greeks, for example, were so stupid as to believe that the gods inhabited statues, this would still be a less adulterated notion than the one which says that God came down into the womb of the Virgin Mary, that he became an embryo, that after his birth he was wrapped in swaddling-clothes, all soaked in blood, bile and even worse.[48]

And Porphyry is amazed that Christ could have suffered on his cross, since he had to be naturally incapable of suffering.[49]

Nothing then is as specifically Christian as the idea of the Incarnation. The obscure themes we have tried to delimit are, in fact, summed up in this notion. It is on this argument, factual and immediately comprehensible, that the thought processes whose development we must now scrutinize in those they animated, come to an end.

II. The Men of Evangelical Christianity

A. *The Writings*

Dislike of speculation, concern for the practical and the religious, primacy of faith, pessimism about man and immense hope born of the Incarnation, these are the themes which come to life again in the men and works of the first centuries of our era.

One must, in fact, be Greek to believe that wisdom is learned. Christian literature has no moralist from its beginnings to the time of Clement and Tertullian.[50] Saint Clement, Saint Ignatius, Saint Polycarp, who elaborated the doctrine of the twelve apostles and that of the apocryphal epistle, attributed to Barnabas, are interested only in the religious aspect of problems. The literature which is called "apostolic"[51] is exclusively practical and populist. We shall have to examine it in detail in order to determine, with any degree of precision, its nature and characteristics. This literature was developed between the years 50 and 90, and can therefore claim to reflect the teaching of the Apostles. It is made up, in any case, of a number of things: of the first epistle of Saint Clement (93-97) written undoubtedly in Rome; of the seven letters of Saint Ignatius (107-117), at Antioch and along the coasts of Asia Minor; of the Apocryphal epistle[52] of Barnabas, in Egypt between 130 and 131; of the teaching of the twelve apostles, probably in Palestine (131-160); of the *Shepherd* of Hermas, in Rome (140-155); of the second epistle of Saint Clement, in Rome or in Corinth (150); of the fragments of Papias, in Hierapolis in Phrygia (150); of the epistle of Saint Polycarp and of his *Testimony*, in Smyrna (155-156). But let us look at each of them instead, so as to rediscover there, in their pure state, the impassioned postulates to which we have already drawn attention.

a) The first epistle of Saint Clement has one sole aim, to restore peace to the Church of Corinth. It is of a purely practical nature. Clement insists upon the filiation that exists between the head of the Church and the Apostles, then between the Apostles and Jesus Christ whose Incarnation has saved us.[53] In his desire to have the Corinthians submit to their spiritual masters, he tells them that the source of their divisions lies in envy, and he uses this as a pretext to speak of humility and of the virtue of obedience. He delivers there a eulogy on charity.[54] Humility brings forgiveness for our sins. A second specifically evangelical attitude can be located at this point: the elect are not chosen because of what they have done, but because of their faith in God.[55] A little later, however, Clement speaks of the need of works and of the fact that faith, without deeds, is not enough.[56]

b) The letters of Saint Ignatius[57] are merely circumstantial writings, foreign to all methodic speculation. Saint Ignatius is, however, the Apostolic Father who had the most lively feeling for Christ made flesh. He combats fiercely the Docetic tendency at the heart of Christianity. Jesus is "Son of God by the will and power of God, really born of a Virgin."[58] "Of the line of David according to the flesh he is son of man and son of God."[59] "He affirms the real motherhood of Mary . . ."[60] "Really born of a virgin." . . . "Under Pontius Pilate and Herod the Tetrarch He was really nailed to the cross in the flesh for our sake."[61] "He suffered in reality, as he also really raised himself from the dead. It is not the case, moreover, as some unbelievers say, that his suffering was merely apparent."[62] Ignatius stresses even more, if such be possible, the humanity which Christ took upon himself. Christ, he says, came to life again in the flesh. "I know that He was in the flesh, even after the Resurrection, and I believe that he is in the flesh even now. And when he came to those who were with Peter, he said to them: 'Take, feel me and see that I am not a bodiless ghost.' They touched him and, through this contact with His Flesh and Spirit, immediately believed . . . And, after the Resurrection, He ate and drank with them like a being with a body, though spiritually one with the Father."[63]

Ignatius establishes the unity of the Church and the rules of the religious life on this communion of Christ with us. Faith and love, in his view, are what count: "Faith and Love are paramount—the greatest blessings in the world."[64] He even pushes one of the themes of early Christianity, to which we have already alluded, as far as it will go and says that faith makes sin impossible: "The carnal person cannot live a spiritual life, nor can the spiritual person live a carnal life, any more than faith can act the part of infidelity, or infidelity the part of faith. But even the things you do in the flesh are spiritual, for you do all things in union with Jesus Christ."[65] This is typical of that fanatical Christianity which we have already described, extreme in its faith and in the conclusions which it presupposes: moreover, it will not be surprising to find echoes of the most impassioned mysticism in the writings of Saint Ignatius: "My Love has been crucified, and I am not at all inflamed with love of earthly things. But there is a living and eloquent water which says within me: 'Come to the Father.' "[66]

c) The epistle attributed to Saint Barnabas[67] is above all a polemical work directed against Judaism. It has virtually no doctrinal elements and is of little interest. Its author is content to stress the Redemption with great realism; and this is what we have to note. We are redeemed because Jesus has given up His body to be destroyed and has sprinkled us with His blood.[68] And baptism allows us to partake of this Redemption: "We go down into the water, laden with sins and filth, and we emerge from it, bearing fruit, possessing the hope of Jesus in our hearts and in souls."[69]

d) "There are two ways, one of life, the other of death, but there is a great difference between the two ways."[70] The teaching of the twelve Apostles relates only to the way of life and to the means necessary for the avoidance of the road which leads to death. It is a catechism, a liturgical formulary which does not contradict our suggestion that all this literature is of a purely practical kind.

e) The *Shepherd* of Hermas and the second epistle of Clement are above all works of penance.[71] Their common theme is that of penance which Hermas grants only to sins committed up to the time he is writing. And from then on the teaching on penance becomes imbued with a rigour that is peculiar to pessimistic teachings. Hermas assigns this penance only once to the Christians of his time.[72] He establishes a tariff, according to which one hour of unholy pleasure has to be atoned for by thirty days of penance, and one day of such pleasure by a year of penance. Evildoers, he says, are doomed to the flames and anyone who does evil, in spite of his knowledge of God, will atone for it eternally.[73]

The second epistle of Clement is a homily similar, in many ways, to the *Shepherd* of Hermas. It too has a purely practical purpose: to exhort the faithful to Charity and Penance. Chapter 9 establishes that the Incarnation of Jesus was a real and tangible event. What follows describes the punishments which will be inflicted or the rewards which will be granted after the resurrection.

f) The epistle of Polycarp, the account we have been left of his martyrdom, and finally the fragments of Papias teach us nothing that is obviously new.[74] These works, devoted to practical ends, are grouped around an anti-Docetic Christology, a classical theory of sin and the exaltation of faith. They sum up, in fact, what we already know about the apostolic literature and its disdain for all speculation. We shall simply ask ourselves in what milieu this preaching was developed.

B. *The Personalities*

The thought of the Apostolic Fathers, it can be said, reflects the true face of the period in which they lived. The first evangelical communities shared these concerns and entertained no intellectual ambition. Nothing illustrates this state of mind more clearly than the efforts of Clement of Alexandria to dispel these prejudices. If we remember that Clement lived at the end of the second century,[75] we can see with what tenacity Christianity clung to its origins, especially as the fantasies of Gnosticism should not lure minds back toward philosophy.

Clement of Alexandria,[76] who was Greek in his intellectual makeup and cultural formation, met the strongest opposition in his milieu, and his whole aim was to reestablish pagan philosophy which was in disrepute and to habituate Christian minds to it. But this is of a different order. And the interest which the *Miscellanies* often arouse lies in the fact that they show us, through their author's spleen, how acute the hostility of his society was toward all speculation. Those whom Clement calls the "simpliciores" are undoubtedly the first Christians, and we find again in them the postulates of apostolic preaching: "The common people are fearful of Greek philosophy, as children are of a scarecrow."[77] But rancour makes itself felt: "Some people who believe themselves to be cultured, think that we should have nothing to do with philosophy or logic, and that we should not give our attention even to the study of the universe."[78] Or again: "Some people object: What good does it do to know the causes that explain the movement of the sun or of other stars, or to have studied geometry, logic or the other sciences. These things serve no purpose when it comes to determining what our duties are. Greek philosophy is merely a product of human intelligence: it does not teach the truth."[79]

The opinions of the Christian community of Alexandria were therefore very clear. Faith is sufficient for man and all else is literature. Let us compare especially an assertion of Tertullian, a contemporary of Clement, and one of the latter's texts. They reinforce each other exactly. "What is common," says Tertullian, "to Athens and Jerusalem, the Academy and the Church. . . . So much the worse for those who have developed a Stoic, Platonic, dialectical Christianity. We, for our part, have no curiosity after Jesus Christ, no research after the Gospel."[80] And Clement writes: "I am not unaware of what is constantly said by some uninformed people, who are frightened at the least noise, namely that we should confine ourselves to the things that are essential, to those which have to do with faith, and that we should ignore those things which come from outside and are redundant."[81] But these purists adhered rigidly to the holy Books. Saint Paul had warned them against "deceptive words."[82] No one wanted to be lacking in charity, sounding bronze or clashing cymbal. That is why in the fourth century Rutilius Namatianus defined Christianity as the "sect which reduces souls to the level of beasts."[83] Clement of Alexandria is merely annoyed at this; Celsus is indignant.[84] Certain proof of the liveliness of a tradition that he seems thus to have now established.

III. The Difficulties Faced by Evangelical Christianity and the Reasons for Its Development

It must be said, then, in retrospect, that early Christianity is summed up in some basic but persistent themes around which communities gathered. The Christian communities, moreover, were imbued with these aspirations and tried to give them substance by their example or their preaching. Robust and harsh are the values implemented by this new civilization. This accounts for the excitement that accompanies its birth and the richness which it arouses in the heart of man.

But an evolution is prepared on these foundations. Already, from Matthew to John, its design is apparent. The kingdom of God gives way to eternal life.[85] God is spirit and it is as spirit that He must be worshipped. Christianity has already become universal. The Trinity, still incomplete, is nevertheless half-expressed.[86] The fact is that Christianity has already encountered the Greek world, and, before passing to other aspects of its evolution, we must dwell upon the causes which forced it constantly to grow in depth and to propagate its teachings under the Greek mantle. New obligations were imposed on Christian thought when it broke with Judaism and embraced the Mediterranean spirit: to satisfy the Greeks who had already been won over to the new religion, to attract the others by showing them a less Jewish Christianity and, in a general way, to speak their language, to express itself in formulas that could be understood and thus to pour into the suitable moulds of Greek thought the uncoordinated aspirations of a very profound faith. Our task is now to say what these needs are.

A. *The Conversions*

Christianity included among its members, from this period and throughout the whole of the second century, the most cultivated Greeks.[87] Aristides, whose *Apology to Antoninus* is dated between 136 and 161, Miltiades (around 150), Justin, whose first *Apology* is dated between 150 and 155, his second between 150 and 160, and whose famous *Dialogue with Trypho* was published about 161, lastly Athenagoras (*Prayer for Christians* 176-178), are all minds converted to the new religion who concretize the union of a speculative tradition with a sensibility that is still new in the Mediterranean basin.

Their concern, from that time on, is to reconcile their minds, which education has Hellenized, with their hearts, which Christian love has penetrated. Historically speaking, these Fathers are apologists, for their whole endeavour is effectively to show that Christianity is consonant with Reason. Faith, according to them, perfects what Reason provides and it is not unworthy of a Greek mind to accept it. The two civilizations meet, therefore, on the plane of philosophy.

Justin, in particular, goes very far in this direction. He dwells upon the similarities between Christian teaching and Greek philosophies: the Gospel is a continuation of Plato and the Stoics.[88] And Justin sees two reasons for this agreement. In the first place, the idea, widespread at that time,[89] that the Greek philosophers had gained their knowledge from the books of the Old Testament and that they were inspired by these books (an unwarranted assumption, but one that won extraordinary favour). Secondly, Justin believes that the Logos was revealed to us in the person of Jesus Christ, but that He existed before this incarnation and inspired the philosophy of the Greeks.[90] This does not prevent our author concluding that there is a need for Revelation at the moral level, because of the incomplete nature of pagan speculation. At the time when the Apologists were drawing near to the Greeks, they were distancing themselves more and more from Judaism. The hostility of the Jews toward the new religion was reason enough. But there was another reason of a political nature: the role that the accusations of the Jews had played in the persecutions.[91] The whole argument of the *Dialogue with Trypho* is to establish the accord between the Prophets and the New Testament, from which Justin derived his prescription of the Old Testament and the triumph of Christian truth.[92]

B. *The Adverse Reactions*

At the same time, however, the adverse reactions were growing. We know, moreover, of Tertullian's scorn for all pagan thought. Tatian[93] and Hermas[94] also became apostles of this particularist movement. But the most natural drive is expansion, and the reactions to which we refer are those of the pagans. It can be said without contradiction that these reactions contributed greatly to the victory of Christianity. P. de Labriolle[95] strongly insists that the pagans, at the end of the second century and the beginning of the third century, made it their business to direct the religious enthusiasm of the period toward figures and personalities modelled on Christ.[96] This idea had already occurred to Celsus when he set Aesculapius, Hercules, or Bacchus in opposition to Jesus. Within a short time, however, this system became a polemical one. At the beginning of the third century Philostratus wrote the remarkable history of Apollonius of Tyana which seems on many points to copy the Scriptures.[97] Then Socrates, Pythagoras, Hercules, Mithra, the sun, the Emperors will misappropriate the favour of the Greco-Roman world and depict one by one a pagan Christ. The approach had its dangers and its advantages, but nothing illustrates more clearly the extent to which the Greeks had understood the power and seductiveness of the new religion. This Christianization of decadent Hellenism, however, also shows that the reactions were beginning to take on an ingenious form. Christianity, there-fore, had once more to adapt, to expound its great dogmas on eternal life, the nature of God, and thus to introduce metaphysics into them. This role fell yet again to the Apologists. And let no one be mistaken. This work of assimilation was coming from an earlier source. It goes back to Paul, born at Tarsus, a Greek university town. It is particularly clear, though from a Jewish point of view, in Philo. We have confined our attention to the Apologists merely because it is the first time in history that this movement assumes a coherent and collective form. We shall merely look at the problems that resulted from it.

C. *The Problems*

The Christian dogmas emerged from this union of evangelical faith and Greek metaphysics. Bathed in this atmosphere of religious tension, moreover, Greek philosophy gave birth to Neoplatonism.

But this did not happen in one day. If it is true that the antagonisms between Christian and Greek ideas had been lessened by the cosmopolitanism to which we have drawn attention, it is the case, nonetheless, that many of these tensions remained. Creation "ex nihilo," which ruled out the hypothesis of matter, had to be reconciled with the perfection of the Greek God, which implied the existence of this matter. The Greek mind saw the difficulty of a perfect and immutable God creating things which are temporal and imperfect. As Saint Augustine wrote much later: "It is difficult to understand the substance of God, which makes changeable things without any change in itself, and creates temporal things without any temporal movement of its own."[98] In other words, history made it necessary for Christianity to become more profound if it wanted to become universal. This was to create a metaphysic. Now, there can be no metaphysic without a minimum of rationalism. The mind does not have the ability to regenerate its themes when emotion undergoes an endless number of changes. The attempt at conciliation inherent in Christianity will be to humanize, to intellectualize, its emotional themes and to lead thought back from those boundaries in which it was struggling. For to explain is, up to a point, to control. Christianity had therefore been founded in order to reduce, to some degree, this lack of proportion between God and man. It certainly seems, on the contrary, that in its initial stages Christian thought, under the influence of these values of death and suffering, in the fear of sin and punishment, had arrived at the point where, as Hamlet says, time is out of joint. It behooves understanding now to provide Christianity with its visa.

This was the task, to a fairly limited degree, of the first theological systems, those of Clement of Alexandria and Origen, of the councils which were reacting against the heresies, and above all of Saint Augustine. But at this very point thought deviated. Christianity was entering into a new phase, and the question was whether it would whittle down its profound originality for the sake of popular appeal or, on the other hand, sacrifice its power of expansion in order to safeguard its purity or whether, finally, it would succeed in reconciling these equally understandable preoccupations. But its evolution was not a harmonious one. It followed dangerous paths which taught it prudence. There was Gnosticism. It availed of Neoplatonism and its comfortable frames of reference in order to accommodate a religious way of thinking. Definitively separated from Judaism, Christianity found its way into Hellenism by the door that the Eastern religions were holding open. And on this altar to the unknown God,[99] which Paul had met in Athens, several centuries of Christian thought were to erect the image of the Saviour on the Cross.

CHAPTER TWO
GNOSIS

If this Christianization of the Greek Mediterranean is accepted as an established fact, then the Gnostic heresy must be regarded as one of the first attempts at Greco-Roman collaboration. Gnosticism is in fact a Greek reflection on Christian themes. This is why it has been disowned by both sides. Plotinus writes "against those who say that the universe is evil."[100] And Tertullian reproaches the Gnostics, in *Against Marcion* (as Augustine does later in the case of the Manichees), for the belief that a rational explanation can be appended to the Gospel. It is true, nonetheless, that the Gnostics were Christians. The theme of the Incarnation is found once more in their writings. They are obsessed with the problem of evil. They understood the complete originality of the New Testament and therefore of the Redemption. But instead of having regard to a Christ made flesh, symbolizing suffering humanity, they give body to a whole mythology. Though their postulates were authentic, they gave themselves over to all the subtle games of the Greek mind. And they built on the few simple impassioned aspirations of Christianity, as on so many solid pillars, a complete setting for a metaphysical kermesse. But a difficulty arises on the historical plane. Gnostic schools succeeded each other for more than two centuries.[101] The speculations of Gnostics over several generations had followed diverse paths. Valentinus and Basilides are minds as different, when all allowances are made, as Plato and Aristotle. How then is a Gnosticism to be defined? This is a difficulty which we have already met. If it is true that only gnosticisms can be defined, it is possible nonetheless to characterize a gnostic. The first generation of Gnostics,[102] that of Basilides, Marcion, and Valentinus, provided a weft that the disciples wove. The small number of themes they held in common will enable us to provide an insight into the meaning of this heretical solution. Gnosticism is, in fact, from an historical point of view, a philosophical and religious teaching, dispensed to initiates, based upon Christian dogmas, mixed with pagan philosophy and taking into itself all that was glorious and striking in the most diverse religions.

Before outlining the themes of the Gnostic solution, however, and revealing the origins of these themes, we must determine how this solution finds its way into the movement of thought with which this work is concerned. This is, moreover, to define gnosis once more, but this time on the metaphysical plane. Gnosticism poses problems in a Christian manner; it resolves them in Greek formulas. Basilides and Marcion are convinced of the ugliness of this world. But to exaggerate the carnal side of things, to load the picture with sins and blemishes, is to dig an ever-deepening trench between man and God. There will come a time when no penance of any kind, and no sacrifice, will be capable of bridging such a gap. In order to be saved, it is enough to know God.[103] If not, what works or other resources could draw man from his nothingness. There is, as we have seen, the Christian solution: salvation through the Incarnation. This is also, in a sense, the Gnostic solution. But Christian grace bears the stamp of divine capriciousness. The Gnostics, misunderstanding the profound meaning of the Incarnation, limited its importance and transformed the notion of salvation into that of initiation. Valentinus, in fact, divides mankind into three groups:[104] the hylics, attached to the goods of this world; the psychics, suspended between God and matter; and the spirituals who, alone, live in God and know him. These spirituals are saved, as later the Chosen ones of Manes shall be saved. At this point the Greek notion makes its appearance. The spirituals are saved only by gnosis or knowledge of God. But they obtain this wisdom from Valentinus and from men. Salvation is learned. It is therefore an initiation. But if, at first sight, these two notions appear to be similar, analysis can reveal differences that, while undoubtedly subtle, are nonetheless fundamental. Initiation gives man a right to the kingdom of God. Salvation admits him to this kingdom, without his playing any part in attaining it. One can believe in God without being saved for doing so. For the mysteries of Eleusis contemplation[105] was enough. Baptism, on the contrary, does not entail salvation. Hellenism cannot abandon the hope, tenaciously guarded, that man has his destiny in his own hands. And, in the very heart of Christianity, the initiation theory tended little by little to take on the notion of salvation. Just as the Egyptian fellah slowly wrested from the Pharaoh the right to immortality, so the Christian, through the mediation of the Church, had finally between his hands the keys of the Kingdom of Heaven.

We have good reason, then, to consider Gnosticism as one of the solutions, one of the Christian stages of the problem we were elucidating: gnosis is an attempt to reconcile knowledge with salvation. But let us now examine this attempt in detail.

The Themes Of The Gnostic Solution

Four fundamental themes, variously emphasized by different authors, recur in every Gnostic system and are basic to each of them: the problem of evil, the redemption, the theory of intermediaries and a notion of God as an ineffable being with whom we cannot communicate.

a) If it is true that the problem of evil is at the centre of all Christian thought, no one was as profoundly Christian as Basilides.

This original figure is a relatively unfamiliar one. He is known to have lived under the reigns of Hadrian and Antoninus Pius (that is, toward 140) and to have begun to write, probably, about the year 80. The sole bibliography of his work that is at all complete is now thought to be ill-founded. It is that of the *Refutations* which probably treats of a pseudo-Basilides. Our most important source remains Clement of Alexandria's *Miscellanies*. Irenaeus speaks of Basilides in his catalogue, Epiphanius in his *Against Heresies* (ch. xxiv). And Origen alludes to him.[106]

"The source of this bad teaching, and its cause," says Epiphanius, "is the investigation of the problem of evil and the debate about the same problem."[107] This is evident from the little we know of Basilides' thought. Estranged from all speculation, he concerns himself solely with moral problems or, more precisely, with that which arises from the ways in which man stands in relation to God. What interests him is sin and the human side of problems. He makes, even of faith, something that belongs to nature and is concrete. "Basilides appears to be incapable of thinking in abstractions. He has to clothe them in something concrete."[108]

Basilides develops his thought from this perspective and takes it upon himself to construct a theory of original sin. This idea, of course, is not to be found in his writings, but at least we do find there the idea of a natural predisposition to sin. He goes on to make two complementary statements: sin always entails a punishment; amendment and redemption can be obtained through suffering. These three themes are attributed indiscriminately to Basilides and to his son, Isidore.

Be that as it may, Basilides is forcibly struck by the fate of the martyrs. Suffering, he says, cannot be futile. And all suffering demands a sin which precedes it and legitimizes it. The inevitable conclusion is that the martyrs have sinned. Moreover, this state is perfectly consistent with their sanctity. It is precisely their privilege to be able to atone so completely for their past. But who is the greatest of the martyrs but Jesus himself? "If I am forced to do so, I will say that a man *by whatever name*, is still man, while God is just. For no one, as they say, is without sin."[109] The reference is absolutely clear, and we can understand why, in the eyes of Epiphanius, this is bad teaching. Christ does not escape the universal law of sin. But at least he shows us that the Cross delivers us from it. Basilides and his son Isidore were, for this very reason, the first to favour a certain asceticism.[110] Isidore indeed had to do so, since he is the author of the theory of related emotions. The passions do not proceed from ourselves, but cling to the soul and take advantage of us.

Isidore saw very clearly that a theory of this kind could lead evil-doers to pose as victims rather than as sinners. This is why his rule of life was an ascetical one.

This is what remains of Basilides' philosophy. One can scarcely see how these various teachings could have been reconciled with the list provided by Hippolytus in the *Refutations*.[111] Basilides, he tells us, would have believed in an abstract God, residing in the ogdoade separated from our world by the universe in between or the hebdomade. He would have identified the God of the intermediary world, the great Archon, with the God of the Old Testament. "The ogdoade is ineffable but the name of the hebdomade can be spoken. This Archon of the hebdomade spoke to Moses as follows: 'I am the God of Abraham, Isaac and Jacob and I have not revealed the name of God to them, that is of the ogdoade who is ineffable.' "[112]

This metaphysical cosmology seems scarcely compatible with the profound inclinations of our author, especially when one attributes to him (a) the idea that Christ did not die on the Cross, but took the place of Simon of Cyrene; (b) the grandiose eschatology which the following passage predicts: "When all that is definitively completed, when all the forms that have been intermingled have been separated and restored to their original place, God will extend an absolute ignorance over the whole world so that all the beings which make it up may remain within the limits of their nature and wish for nothing beyond it."[113] The problem of evil and, to speak anachronistically, of predestination is at the centre of Basilides' meditations. The earlier doctrines are too developed, too decadent, as it were. One single statement of Hippolytus would be enough to make us suspect this: when he attributes to his author the idea that the soul has no more freedom of action than freedom of thought. It is naturally given over to sin and will inevitably fall.

The importance of the problem of evil can be gleaned from the writings of even the least known Gnostic. The same is true of all Gnostic sects.[114] It will not be surprising, therefore, to find the closely related problem of the Redemption given the same prominence.

b) Marcion[115] is the gnostic who was most conscious of the originality of Christianity. Indeed, he was so conscious of it that he constructed a moral system for himself in defiance of the Jewish law. Marcion is not a speculative thinker but a religious genius. He is not known to have had a system like that of Valentinus. He founded neither church nor school, his books are not original but exegetical.[116] In general his thought revolves around three points: first, God; second, the Redemption and the person of Christ; third, Morality.

There are, in Marcion's view, two divinities: one, the superior divinity, is lord of the invisible world. The other, his subaltern, is the God of this world. "Our God was not revealed from the beginning: he was not revealed by Creation; he has revealed himself in Jesus Christ."[117] This is because the second God, a cruel and warlike judge, is the God of the Old Testament who persecuted Job in order to prove his power to Satan, who made use of blood and battles, and who oppressed the Jewish people with his law. No Avestic influence is to be found there. It is not a question of two opposed principles of equal strength whose struggle sustains the world, but of a God and a demiurge between whom the struggle is unequal. In this way, Marcion strove for orthodoxy and relied upon the Gospels (or rather on the only Gospel he admitted, that of Luke): "No one tears a piece from a new garment and puts it upon an old garment."[118] And again " . . . a good tree does not bear bad fruit, nor again does a bad tree bear good fruit."[119] He mentioned, in particular, the "Epistle to the Galatians." Marcion believed, moreover, that the unending opposition that Paul draws between the Law and the Gospel, Judaism and Christianity, would show that the two books were inspired by different authors. In Valentinus, too, we shall again find this idea of a creator who is different from the one God. This solution is, however, a logical one, demanded by the problem of evil. In Marcion, on the other hand, the vital sense of the newness of Christianity gives rise to this radical opposition. In this sense, it was right to speak of a political thought[120] in Marcion rather than of a metaphysical one.

It is already clear how important Christ is to become. He is nothing less than the envoy sent by the Supreme God to do battle with the wicked God, the creator of the world, and to free man from his domination. Jesus accomplishes a revolutionary mission here below. If he redeems our sins it is because he combats, in them, the work of the cruel God. Emancipator and Redeemer, he is the author of a sort of metaphysical *coup d'état.* "Marcion claims that there are two Christs; one was revealed by an unknown God in the time of Tiberius, and was sent to save all peoples; the other was destined by the Creator God to restore Israel, and was to appear one day. He contrasts these two Christs as strongly as he does the Law and the Gospel, Judaism and Christianity."[121] Marcion cites a large number of texts in support of this extraordinary theory. He takes these texts, for the most part, from Saint Luke's Gospel and interprets them in his own way. "What father among you, if his son asks for a fish, will instead give him a serpent; or if he asks for an egg, will give him a scorpion? If you then who are evil, know how to give good gifts to your children, how much more will your heavenly Father give the Holy Spirit to those who ask him."[122] This strange interpretation finds its culmination in morality. The rule of life which Marcion proposes is an ascetic one. But its asceticism is based upon pride. The goods of this world should be scorned out of hatred of the Creator: Marcion's ideal is to allow him least scope for his power. From this comes the most extreme asceticism. And if Marcion preaches sexual abstinence it is because the God of the Old Testament has said: "Increase and multiply." In this pessimistic view of the world and this arrogant refusal to accept it we find the resonance of a sensibility that is altogether modern. This too arises from the problem of evil. Marcion regards the world as bad, but refuses to believe that God could be its author. If his solution centres around the Redemption, it is because he envisions the role of Jesus in a more ambitious manner than do Christians themselves. The issue, as far as he is concerned, is nothing less than the complete destruction of a creation.

c) The last two Gnostic themes cannot be dissociated from one another. For if we make of God a being whom we cannot contact, one who is outside of time, we do not, for all that, abandon the belief that He is interested in the world. It is therefore necessary to explain these relations between God and man, and, being unable to establish contact between this nothingness and this infinite, to admit at least one or several intermediaries who share at the same time in the infinity of God and in our finitude. To find these middle terms is virtually *the* great problem of the first centuries of our era. The Gnostics certainly did not fail to give their attention to it. They even did so with inordinate splendour and ostentation.

The first generation of Gnostics was happy to think of God as ineffable and indescribable. But at least they believed firmly in Him. Their successors went even further and some of their expressions often call to mind the Brahman of the "Upanishads" who can be defined only by: no, no. "This God," says the pseudo-Basilides, "was when nothing was, but this nothing was not one of the things that now exist, and, to speak openly, in simple terms and without subtlety, nothing was all that existed. Now when I say that it existed, I do not mean that it really existed, I merely want to clarify what I am thinking."[123] And again, "He who was speaking did not exist, and, what is more, that which had then been created did not exist; therefore the seed of the world was made from that which was nonexistent; I mean, that word which was spoken by the nonexistent God: let there be light; and this is what is written in the Gospel. He is the light which enlightens every man who comes into this world."[124] Hippolytus sums this up as follows: "So God, who did not exist, created a nonexistent world out of nonexistent elements by issuing a single seed which had all the seeds of the world within itself."[125] We must make allowances for the views of Hippolytus, however, and this extraordinary subtlety is not the rule among the Gnostics. It seems, on the contrary, that Valentinus had a very vivid sense of the divine nature. It is only in the doctrine of intermediaries that he gives free rein to his imagination.

d) Valentinus is the Gnostic we know best.[126] But, on the other hand, we know nothing about his life. In fact, our ignorance, in this regard, is so great that it is possible to have doubts about his existence. His system, which is a very coherent one, can be divided into a theology, a cosmology, and an ethic. It is the strangest example of that incarnation of mythology of which we have spoken. The pleroma which Valentinus places between God and the world is in fact a Christian Olympus. At least Christian in intent, but Greek in shape and imagery. Valentinus' philosophy is a metaphysic in act, an immense tragedy which is played out between heaven and earth and, in the infinity of Time, a conflict of problems and symbols, something like the "Roman de la Rose" of Gnostic thought.

In the first place, Valentinus' God[127] is uncreated and is outside of time. But, alone and perfect, He superabounds by virtue of His perfection. In so doing He creates A Dyad, that of the Spirit and Truth. These two in turn engender the Word and Life, which produce Man and the Church. From these six principles the pleroma will emerge in its absolute entirety, and it will be composed of two groups of angels or aeons, the one of twelve, the other of ten, in other words, in the language of the Gnostics, the decade and duodecade.[128] The Spirit and Truth, in their desire to glorify the divinity, create a choir of ten aeons whose mission is to give homage to God. These are in turn: the Abyss, the Mixture, He who is ageless, the Union, He who is of His own nature, Pleasure, He who is immobile, the Mixture, the only Son, Happiness. The Word and Life in their turn create the twelve, but this time in order to glorify the acting Spirit. This is made up of twelve aeons arranged in syzygies, or couples: male and female. They are: the Paraclete and Faith, the Paternal and Hope, the Maternal and Love, Prudence and Intelligence, the Ecclesiastical and the Very Happy, the Voluntary and Wisdom. The totality of these aeons compose the pleroma, halfway between God and the world. Valentinus, however, will tell us about the nature of this world and about how it relates to this theology and aeonology.

Secondly, it is remarkable that up to this point God has produced by himself, without the aid of a female principle. He alone is perfect. He alone superabounds. It is by virtue of their union that Spirit and Truth or the Word and Life succeeded in engendering respectively the decade and the duodecade. Now, the lastborn of the aeons, Sophia or Wisdom, turned from the bottom of the ladder of principles and chose to look upon God.[129] And this is how she discovered that He had created by Himself. She tried, out of pride and envy, to do likewise. But she merely succeeded in bringing a formless being into the world, that very one of whom Genesis says: "The earth was without form and void."[130] Sophia, then, became unhappy when she realized her ignorance and, overwhelmed by fear, lost all hope. These four passions made up the four elements of the world. And Sophia lived her life forever united to this formless fetus to which she had given birth. But God had pity upon her and again created a special principle, Horos[131] or limit. The latter, came to the help of Sophia, restored her original nature and rejected the world outside of the pleroma, thereby reestablishing the initial equilibrium. At this moment a demiurge intervenes, arranges matter, and creates the cosmos out of it. He utilizes the passions of Sophia and he makes men out of them. These men are divided into three groups according to their awareness of their origin[132]: the spirituals who aspire to God, the hylics who have no memory of their origins and therefore no concern about these origins, and between these two groups, the psychics, who are undecided and oscillate between the coarse life of the senses and the most exalted concerns, without knowing where to anchor themselves. But they all carry the mark of their birth: they have come into being out of fear, ignorance, and grief. It is for this reason that a redemption is needed. But this time the Spirit has come in order to deliver man from his woeful origins, after transforming Himself into Christ. Things become more complicated when it is learned that the redeemer was not Jesus. He is born of the gratitude that the aeons have for God who had reestablished order. They therefore regrouped their forces and offered in thanksgiving to God the being who had been made in this way. The redemption on the other hand is a work of the holy spirit who has revealed to men that part of them is divine, and who has brought about in them the death of their sinful part. This is undoubtedly the meaning of that puzzling text of the *Miscellanies*: "You are immortal since the beginning; you are children of eternal life, and you would have your share of death so that you may consume and exhaust it, and so that death may die in you and by you. For when you dissolve the world and are not yourselves dissolved, you are masters of creation and of all decay."[133]

Thirdly, the moral teaching of Valentinus is directly linked to his cosmology. And the latter is merely a solution to a problem which obsesses Valentinus: the problem of evil. "I came to accept the truth of what the tragedies told us, I am convinced that they give us merely the truth. I believe in the longing of Oenomaüs while he was in a frenzy, I do not think it incredible that two brothers could have fought with each other. And I could not find within me the strength to say that God was the author and creator of all these evils."[134] It is therefore the problem of evil which inclined

Valentinus toward these speculations. And the conclusion which he draws from his cosmology is an utterly simple one: there is no freedom in the human soul, by virtue of the sin of Sophia. The Gnostics or spirituals, who regain an awareness of their origins, will alone be saved. Salvation is contemporaneous with knowledge. The psychics too, for their part, can also be saved, but they must become reconciled to the will of God.

In this way Valentinus' thought rejoins the source that is common to all the Gnostics. But his aeonology and cosmology had, in turn, to achieve a very high degree of success in the mass of small schools in which Gnosticism culminated. We have yet to characterize these schools, if we are to complete our study of Gnosticism.

If we adopt what appears to be the best informed classification, that of M. de Faye, the themes which we have just outlined reappear in three groups of schools: a group which is studied by those who concern themselves with heresies, and which can be called the Disciples of the Mother. These themes were then transmitted, through the mediation of the latter, to the Gnostics, most of whom are mentioned in the *Refutations*, and to a group of Coptic Gnostics of whom the *"Scroll"* of Bruce and the *"Pistis Sophia"* give us a reliable picture. This filiation is entirely theoretical, however, for if it is true that in large measure the Disciples of the Mother precede chronologically the last two groups, then each of the three schools is composed of such a large number of sects that they probably overlapped and had interwoven themes. But the intellectual link is a real one, and the requirements of our exposé make this classification absolutely necessary. In order to complete our picture of Gnostic thought, we will, moreover confine our attention to some pointers and texts.

The Disciples of the Mother derive their name from the fact that they claim, almost without exception, that there is a female principle at the origin of the world. But the Barbelognostics (Barbelo is the name of the female principle), the Orphites of whom Hippolytus speaks and the "Gnostics" of Irenaeus can be included even under this heading. They stress, for the most part, the rivalry between the first principle, the Mother, and a male principle, or Iadalboath. The latter created man and the mother corrected what was calamitous in this creation by putting a divine principle into man. This is the origin of the classical story of the Redemption according to Valentinian themes.

The *Refutations* quotes and comments upon a large number of Gnostics whom it would be useless to mention again individually, only to rediscover ideas we have already met. It will be simpler to refer to some texts whose strangeness or unusual aims will explain, to some degree, the teachings of

Valentinus, Basilides or Marcion, as a pastiche often conveys the spirit of a work. They give us, at the same time, a very precise idea of a way of thinking that was quite widespread at that period, strange, often censured, but sometimes suggestive.

The Naassenes[135] complain of pessimism about the world and modify the theology: "This is the God of whom a Psalm speaks, the God who inhabits the flood and who, from the depths of the many waters, raises his voice and cries. The waters are where many varied generations of mortal men dwell. There he cries out to the man whom no form defines. He says: 'Deliver your only son from the lions.' It is to him that this word is spoken: 'You are my son Israel, do not be afraid when you pass through rivers, they will not drown you; if you cross fire, it will not destroy you.' "[136]

The Perates stress the Redemption and have it consist of an attraction that the Son exercises on everything which resembles the Father. It is the theory of Prints: " . . . as he brought from on high the Father's marks, so he brings these marks of the Father up from here when they have been restored."[137]

For the Sethians the higher world is that of light and our world is that of darkness. And they explain our search for the divinity as follows: "These things are like the pupil of the eye. On the one hand it is dark; the fluids which lie beneath it make it so; on the other hand, a breath lights it up. As the darkness of the pupil clings to this brightness and wants to keep it and to use it in order to see, so the light and the mind fervently seek once more their strength, which has been lost in the darkness."[138] Justin, the Gnostic of whom Hippolytus speaks, is rather a head of a religious brotherhood. Sexual symbolism plays an important role in his speculations. Consequently, there are three parties in the world: the good God, Elhoim, the creator father, and his wife Eden, who shapes the world. Tragedy results from the fact that Elhoim, attracted by the good God, abandons Eden. The latter creates man evil, so as to avenge herself. That is why the Redemption is needed. "Elhoim cries: Open the doors for me, so that I may enter and see the Lord. For I believed till now that I was Lord. From the depths of the light a voice was heard saying: 'Here is the Lord's gate, the Just shall leap over it.' The door is opened immediately and the Father, without the angels, goes through it and makes his way toward the Good. And he sees things that eye has not seen and ear has not heard, and that have not been revealed to the heart of man. Then the Good says to him: 'Sit down on my right.'"[139]

We remember, finally, a Gnostic well versed in equally obscure ideas who describes the Resurrection in the following terms: "This is how the only-begotten Son, seeing from on high the ideas transmuted into evil bodies, chose to save them. Knowing that even the aeons would be unable to bear the sight of the pleroma in all its fullness, that they would be utterly dumbfounded and would, as a result, become mortal and perish, he became small like the light beneath the eyelids: then he made his way toward the visible sky: he touched the stars there and then once more withdrew beneath the eyelids . . . This is how the Only-Begotten came into the world, without pomp, unknown, without renown. People did not even believe in Him."[140]

If we add to this list a certain Monoïmus Arabus, neo-pythagorean and juggler of figures, we will have a fairly precise notion of the diversity of sects and views.

At this point we shall draw attention solely to the teachings of the *"Scroll"* of Bruce and of the *"Pistis Sophia,"* both of which reproduce conversations of Jesus in which classical themes are extensively developed, and in which it is made clear that to possess gnosis is to know "the why of light and darkness, chaos, repository of lights, sin, baptism, anger, blasphemy, wrongdoing, adulteries, purity, pride, life, slander, obedience, humility, richness, and slavery."[141]

By limiting ourselves in this way, we have failed to include the direct disciples of Valentinus, namely Heracleon and Ptolemy, Apelles the disciple of Marcion, Marcos and his adepts, and the dissolute Gnostics. We see, then, the richness of a movement that is too often scorned. It remains for us now to distinguish, in this host of affirmations, whether moving, or unusual in their simplicity, the contributions that came from outside.

The Elements of the Gnostic Solution

This metaphysic, prevalent since the beginning of time, is still eloquent. But it can make no claim to originality.

It seems that in Gnosticism Christianity and Hellenism met without being able to come together and that they juxtaposed the most unusual themes.

Our task here will be to determine as schematically as possible the extraneous contributions.

a) A great number of themes appear to come from Plato, or at least from the tradition that he represents. Emanation of intelligences from the womb of the Divinity, the wandering and sufferings of spirits estranged from God and immersed in matter, the distress of the uncontaminated soul joined to the irrational soul in the psychics, regeneration through return to original sources, all of this is purely Greek. Horos, whose name is important, is typical in this respect, for it was he who caused Sophia to return within the limits of her nature.

Greece introduced the notion of order and harmony into morals, as she did into aesthetics. If Prometheus suffered, it is because he overstepped his nature as a man. Sophia acted in the same way and regains her peace by returning to the place she had been given.

b) Gnosticism, moreover, took its most crucial dogma from Christianity. It was happy to use this dogma for its own purposes. Every Gnostic system, however, has within it some ideas whose resonance is unmistakable. What preoccupies all our authors, as it did Basilides, Marcion and Valentinus, is the problem of evil. This is why they attempt to explain the Redemption as well. Another influence, less obvious but equally real, is the historic sense, that is to say, this notion that the world is moving toward an end, just as it is the conclusion of a tragedy. The world is a starting point. There was a beginning. Truths are not to be contemplated. Rather we wager on them, and with them on our salvation. The Christian influence at this point consists not so much in a group of dogmas as in a state of soul and an orientation. No doctrine has ever accorded to the irreducible element in man such a weight of explanation.

c) Other elements, however, very diverse and so even less discernible, were added to those influences that I have clearly illustrated in my exposition of the teachings. I propose to dwell upon these elements a little further.

1. The influence of the mysteries can be seen in this notion of a higher knowledge which constitutes gnosis. We have already defined initiation as the union of knowledge and salvation. We meet the same problem again at this point. A "spiritual" would make his own these orphic lines which were discovered on some gold tablets at Croton: "I have fled from this circle of sufferings and woes, and I am now making my way toward the queen of the sovereign places, the saintly Persephone and the other gods of Hades. I am proud to belong to their blessed family. I ask them to send me to the home of the innocent where I may hear the saving word: you shall be a goddess and you shall no longer be mortal."[142]

2. A more likely connection is that which links the Gnostics to Philo. The latter sometimes prophesies like an initiate: "Let the dullwitted in their deafness withdraw. We hand on divine mysteries to those who have undergone sacred initiation, to those who practise true holiness and are not held captive by the empty show of words or the spell of pagans."[143]

And this, even more significant still: "O you initiates, you whose ears are purified, receive that into your souls as mysteries that should never leave it. Never reveal it to anyone who is unholy; hide it and keep it within yourselves like a treasure that is totally incorruptible, like gold or silver, but which is more precious than anything else, since it is the knowledge of the ultimate cause of virtue and of that which is born of the one and the other."[144]

It is not surprising henceforth to meet in the Gnostics a fairly large number of themes that are dear to Philo: the supreme Being, source of light which radiates through the universe,[145] the struggle of light and darkness for the domination of the world, the creation of the world by intermediaries, the visible world as image of the invisible world, the theme (crucial in Philo) of the image of God, pure essence of the human soul, and the deliverance finally assigned to human existence as its end.[146]

3. Finally, it is possible to see in the midst of the Gnostic teachings the influence of a certain number of Eastern speculations and, most especially, of Zend-Avesta. Zoroastrianism, moreover, by virtue of the exile of the Jews, the protection afforded to them by Cyrus and the favour which Zoroaster showed to Zend-Avesta, played an important role in the evolution of ideas in the first centuries of our era.

The Ameshas Spentas and the Yazatas, who lead the struggle against the evil demons, themselves go to make up a pleroma, halfway between God and Earth. And Ahura Mazdah has all the characteristics of the infinite Gnostic God.

These pointers serve to reveal the complexity of Gnosticism. The conspicuous nature of this Christian heresy was obvious from the forms it took. We have still to try to summarize our inquiries by mentioning a few of its general characteristics.

CONCLUSION

Gnosticism in the Evolution of Christianity

" . . . instead of eternal acts of the divine will, sudden transformations or impassioned initiatives; faults take the place of causes; instead of the union of two natures in the person of Christ incarnate, the dispersion of divine particles in matter; instead of history, a series of unrelated happenings; the intermingling of the corporeal and the spiritual; and, to sum everything up, instead of the separation of eternity and time, a time saturated with powers that belong to eternity and an eternity traversed, scanned by tragedies."[147]

The spirit of Gnosticism could not be summed up more satisfactorily: it gathered together, over more than two centuries, all the ideas that were abroad at that time and used them to construct a hideous Christianity, made up of oriental religions and Greek mythology. But this heresy was undoubtedly a Christian one, for a definite resonance of a more raucous kind runs between the lines. Evil obsesses the Gnostics. They are without exception pessimistic about the world. They look to God with very great zeal, while nonetheless making Him inaccessible. But Christianity draws from this incalculable feeling for the divinity the idea of his omnipotence and of the nothingness of man. Gnosticism sees in knowledge a means of salvation. In this respect it is Greek, for it wants that which enlightens to regenerate at the same time. What it elaborates is a Greek theory of grace.

Historically Gnosticism shows Christianity the road not to follow. Its excesses lead Tertullian and Tatian to check Christianity as it makes its way toward the Mediterranean. It is because of Gnosticism, to some degree, that Christian thought will take from the Greeks merely their formulas and frames of reference, not their emotional postulates; for the latter are either irreducible to evangelical thought or, while similar to it in some respects, lack all coherence. One perhaps understands already why Christianity, which was implanted in the Greco-Roman world of the end of the first century, made no definitive advance until the middle of the third century. The importance we have attributed to Gnostic teachings for the evolution we want to retrace is also understandable. Gnosticism shows us one of the ways in which the Greek and the Christian could be combined. It marks an important stage, an experiment, that could not have been passed over in silence.

The excesses themselves help us to understand more clearly what was in danger of being lost in detail and subtleties. This tenacious chaff, however, Christianity mercilessly winnowed. It is, however, more difficult to dispose of one's wayward children than of one's enemies. And it is also a fact that, through a unique sense of History, the Fathers appear to have known what was going to be compromised by such excesses, however impressive they often were: the advance of Christianity toward the role for which it was destined. But let us leave Christian thought at this turning point in its history. Alexandrian metaphysics was similarly crystallizing in Neoplatonism at this time, and the material that Christian teaching will take on board is in the process of being constructed. In this way the path is prepared, in different directions, for that second revelation, which was the teaching of Augustine.

CHAPTER THREE
MYSTICAL REASON

I. Plotinus' Solution

A study of Plotinus is of interest, as far as our subject matter is concerned, on two counts. The problem on which the fate of Christianity depends is clearly posed for the first time. The Plotinian synthesis, moreover, furnished Christian thought not with a doctrine, as some authors would have it, but with a method and a way of looking at things. Plotinus' system, in fact, has its roots in the religious and mystical aspirations that are common to the whole period. It even borrows, and this frequently, the language of the mysteries.[148] It is, moreover, the love of God that animates him.[149] But Plotinus is also a Greek. And certainly by choice, for his sole wish is to be a commentator on Plato.[150] In vain, however. His World-Soul is Stoic. His intelligible world comes from Aristotle. And his synthesis retains an entirely personal tone. But the fact remains that he has the taste for a rational explanation of things. And in this respect his own tragedy reflects the drama of Christian metaphysics as well. He is concerned about the fate of the soul,[151] but he also wants, like his master, to give intellectual forms to becoming.[152] The conceptual material has not changed in Plotinus. There is one sole difference: feeling is on the alert for new discoveries. All the fragrance of the Plotinian landscape is there: a certain tragedy in that effort to pour emotion into the logical forms of Greek idealism. This again, from the point of view of style, is the source of that sluggishness, that gradual advance, that apparent mastery, which has its origin in an impasse fully accepted. And then also the profound originality of this solution and the greatness of the undertaking. For Plotinus clearly intends to do, with the help of Greek philosophy alone and without the help of Faith, what ten centuries of Christianity have accomplished with great difficulty.

This explains a sort of shimmering reflection in our author's philosophy. The fact is that each of Plotinus' doctrines reveals a double aspect whose concurrence accurately provides a solution to the problem which we highlighted above. This solution lies in confounding the fate of the soul with the rational knowledge of things. What we have here is similar to what we find in psychoanalysis: diagnosis coincides with treatment. To bring to light is to heal, and to know the One is to return to one's homeland. "The demonstrations of the Good are also means of rising to him."[153]

It is from this angle that we shall approach the study of Plotinus. We shall try to rediscover that double aspect in each moment of his teaching. But we should first note the extent to which his solution depends upon his conception of Reason. To know is to worship with Reason's accord. Knowledge is a contemplation and an inner recollection, not a construction. Plotinus' Rationalism is undoubtedly based upon the intelligibility of the world. But with what infinite suppleness. The principles or hypostases that underlie this intelligibility are important only as a balancing movement that leads them increasingly from an explanation of the cosmos to the private state of grace that each of them represents. In one sense they mark the steps of a procession, and in the other they reveal the path of a conversion. Plotinus' Reason is already, to a certain extent, the "heart" of Pascal. But this does not mean that it can be likened to a Christian philosophy, for this conception of Reason, though based upon contemplation, is inscribed in an aesthetic: Plotinus' philosophy is not merely a religious mode of thinking but an artist's way of looking at things as well. If things are intelligible, it is because things are beautiful. But Plotinus carries this extreme emotion, which seizes the artist when faced with the beauty of the world, into the intelligible realm. He admires the universe at the expense of nature. "All that comes here below from up there, is more beautiful in the higher world."[154] It is not appearance that Plotinus seeks, but that reverse-side of things that is his lost paradise. And everything here below serves as a forceful reminder of the solitary homeland of the philosopher. That is why Plotinus describes the intellect sensually.[155] His Reason is living, full-bodied, stirring, like a mixture of water and light: " . . . like a single characteristic, which encompasses and conserves all others; a sweetness which is at once a perfume; a flavour of wine which absorbs as it were all other flavours and all other colours; it has all the characteristics that can be grasped by touch or by the ear, because it is total harmony, total rhythm."[156] It is therefore the sensibility of Plotinus which lays hold of the intelligible.

But what could be regarded as a point of contact between Christianity and Neoplatonism seems to be, on the contrary, one of the points on which the two are irreconcilably opposed. For to make everything hinge upon contemplation holds good only for a world that is eternal and harmonious once for all. And for Plotinus there is, in fact, no History. But for a Christian, art is not enough. The world develops according to a divine plan; and to be renewed is to be incorporated into the movement of this tragedy. The sudden change which the incarnation effects has absolutely no meaning for Plotinus. And the difference goes even further. For a Christian who separates Reason from Beauty, the True from the Beautiful, Reason becomes merely the arbiter in questions of logic. And there can be conflicts between Faith and Reason. A Greek finds these encounters less acute, for Beauty, which is, at the same time, order and sensibility, harmonious arrangement and object of desire, remains an intelligible landscape: "Some, seeing beauty's image on a face, are transported into the realm of the intelligible; there are others whose thoughts are too sluggish. Nothing can move them. They look in vain at all the beauties of the sensible world, its proportions, its order and the spectacle offered by the stars, however distant; these people never dream of exclaiming, out of religious awe: How beautiful! From what beauty must all this beauty come!"[157] We are already familiar with this passage. It was directed against the Christian Gnostics.

A. *The Rational Explanation According to Procession*

a) If the world is beautiful, it is because something lives in the world. But it is also because there is something that gives order to it. This spirit which animates the world is the World-Soul. The higher principle which keeps this logos within determinate boundaries is Intellect. But the unifying principle of order is always superior to that order. There is therefore a third principle superior to Intellect, which is the One. Let us approach this from the opposite direction. There is no being which is not one.[158] Now there is no unity without form and logos, which is precisely the principle of unity. This is to say, once more, that there is no being without soul since the logos is necessary if the soul is to act. In the first sense we have discovered three steps in the explanation of the world; in the second, three stages of investigation of the self. These two steps coincide.[159] The metaphysical reality is the spiritual life considered in itself. One is the object of knowledge, the other of interior ascesis. When the objects coincide, however, the systems meet. To know is, to some extent, to return to the "intimior intimo meo." Knowledge is not something that one acquires; it is a striving and a desire, in a word, a creative development. From this also comes the godlike nature of the metaphysical principles. The One, Intellect, and World-Soul, the first in his plenitude, the two others as secondary manifestations, express the same divinity. The way in which this unity and multiplicity are reconciled can be seen in the procession of the three hypostases. That which underlies the rational explanation of the world naturally finds its counterpart in conversion, which is the very movement of the soul in search of its origins.[160]

We shall trace only the movement of this procession and leave aside a detailed examination of each of its moments. "All things which exist, as long as they remain in being, necessarily produce, from their own substances, a reality which is directed to what is outside of itself and is dependent upon their present power . . . as fire produces heat and snow does not retain all its cold."[161]

God Himself, in so far as He is a perfect being, beyond time, superabounds. He creates Intellect from which the World-Soul will come.

Intellect and the Soul, thus, are and at the same time are not the One. They are such in their origin and not in their final stage when they become fragmented, one in duality, the other in multiplicity. "The One is all things and yet he is not any single one of them: the One is the source of all things, for all things return to him in one way or another; or, rather they have not yet attained to his level, but they will do so."[162]

The difference between the notion of procession and that of creation can be seen at this point: the latter separates sky and creator, the former unites them in the same gentle movement of superabundance. But this divine emanation takes shape only when Intellect, which comes from God, turns again toward Him and receives its likeness from Him, and when the soul in turn contemplates the intelligible sun and is illumined by it. Each principle attains to its total fulfillment by contemplating the hypostasis above it.[163] At this juncture God merely manages to arouse His admirers. But this has been mentioned only briefly, and needs to be taken up again in detail.

b) *The First Hypostasis.* Let us confront immediately the ambiguity that we have already mentioned in the notion of the One. He is, at the same time, the rational source of explanation and that for which the soul longs. Plato says that the Good is the greatest of "sciences": he means by "science," not the vision of the Good, but the reasoned knowledge we have of him before this vision.

The analogies, the negations, the knowledge of beings that originate from the One, and their ascending gradation help us to know Him. Our purifications, our virtues, our inner harmony lead us to Him.

One comes to contemplate oneself and other things, and at the same time one becomes the object of one's own contemplations; and, having become what one is, intellect, and complete animal, one no longer sees the good from outside.[164]

These two aspects, we should note, do not coexist, they are identical. The first hypostasis is the principle of unity because it is the object of contemplation.[165] At the very moment when we look at a star it defines us and limits us to a certain extent. And to say that the One is the source of everything is to say that contemplation is the only thing that is real.

If we now attempt to define this One, we meet a great many difficulties.

1. In the first place, He is nothing, for He is pure unity, and is not a distinct being. But He is everything, as source of everything. Assuredly, He is the Beautiful and the Good all in one.[166] But these are not definitions. They are ways of speaking that have no hold on Him. For clearly He is merely a void, or rather, a meeting point.[167] But that is not where the basic difficulty lies. Why did this One who contains the whole of reality, give birth to things, and in particular, how did this unity become multiplicity?

2. "The One, being perfect, overflows, and this superabundance produces something other than itself; the thing which is engendered turns back towards the One; it is fecundated; and turning to look upon itself, it becomes Intellect; when it halts to rest in the One, it takes on being; when it returns its gaze to self, it acts as Intellect. And when it halts to gaze upon itself, it

becomes at once Intellect and being."[168] The One therefore produces in the way that fire gives off its heat or a flower its fragrance. And, object of contemplation, He gives Intellect the forms it wears.[169] But how can the One be said to be dispersed in the multiplicity of intelligibles? This is the real difficulty, and the heart of the Plotinian system. For this problem is bound up with the equally important problem of the Transcendence or Immanence of God, and with problems posed by the relationships between Intellect and intelligibles, or the World-Soul and individual souls. And at this very point a certain optic, peculiar to Plotinus, makes its appearance. We shall have to define this optic at the end of our study.

Plotinus is sometimes satisfied to describe how the operation works: "The Good is principle. By virtue of the Good, Intellect controls the beings it produces. When Intellect surveys its products, it is no longer allowed to think anything other than what the Good is. Otherwise it will produce nothing. Intellect derives from the One the strength to produce and to be satiated by the beings it produces; the One gives to intellect what it does not itself possess. *From the One a multiplicity comes into existence for Intellect: unable to contain the power that it gets from the One, Intellect divides it into fragments and multiplies it, so as to be able to sustain it in this way, part by part.*"[170] But if Plotinus moves from description to explanation, he has recourse to images. How can the One be, at the same time, dispersed in, and not dispersed in, the many? As the tree is dispersed in its branches without being found there in its utter completeness,[171] as light is divided among the rays it emits without, for all that, being concentrated in them,[172] as fire discharges heat and communicates it by means of sympathy,[173] as, finally, rivers can rise from one spring and pour into the sea waters that are at once like and unlike themselves.[174] If, in other words, creation were the issue, then the principle of contradiction could be employed, but with regard to something like procession, we must appeal to a different principle, akin indeed to that of participation, which M. Levy Bruhl attributes solely to primitive states of mind. It is within the intelligible world, however, that we must now attempt to understand this unique solution.

c) *The Second Hypostasis.* On the rational plane, to which we are now trying to confine ourselves almost entirely, Intellect is endowed with the greatest explicative power. The theory about this has not indeed been very well established. Two points of view already classical for us can be detected at the outset. While Intellect is a metaphysical principle, it remains nonetheless a stage in the repatriation of the soul. From the first point of view, it is the same as the world of Platonic Ideas. But three interpretations of the second hypostasis can be detected, alongside of one another, at the very heart of the latter notion. Intellect is, in the first place, a sort of intuitive art which is reflected on the world's crystal, as the art of the sculptor is divined even on roughly hewn clay. It is, in the second place, the perfect model on which the Forms are moulded. And it is, in the last analysis, a God, or rather a demiurge, who has informed matter. We should be careful, however, not to exaggerate the extent to which these opinions differ. And let us now take the notion of Intellect in its widest sense, as the world of ideas. At this point a problem arises that is closely related to that which we met in the theory of the One. How does Intellect overflow into the intelligibles? Are the latter different from Intellect, or are they within the form that is common to them?

Plotinus' solution is transparency. The intelligibles are in Intellect, but their relationships are not of the kind that a contemporary logic would accept. As those diamonds with identical water filling them, whose every sparkle feeds on the fires that play on other facets, so that some light repeated *ad infinitum* is definable by these fires only but is not totally contained in them, so Intellect spreads its light on the intelligibles that are in it, as Intellect is in them and it is impossible to say what belongs to them and what to Intellect. "All is transparent, nothing is dark or obscure; there every being is, to an infinite degree, visible to every being; there is light for light. Every being has all things in itself and sees all things in the other. All is everywhere. All is all. Each being is all. There below, the sun is all the stars and each of them is the sun . . . A different character is evident in each being, but all the characters are manifest in each being . . . here below one part comes from another part, and everything is fragmentary: there each thing comes at each moment from the whole and is part and whole at the same time."[175] Intellect, as a result, carries within itself all the richness of the intelligible world. Its knowledge consists entirely in knowing itself—and consequently in knowing the One. It is in this idea that the Unity of the second hypostasis, however such is envisaged, is to be found. But even here reflection is transformed, as it becomes conversion and interior ascesis, of which we shall say nothing for the moment. Let us merely note that ideally Intellect marks a state in which object and subject are one, where pure thought is merely self-reflected thought of itself. It is by a progressive concentration, by delving into itself that Intellect lays hold of its inner richness. Shall we go further? Plotinus again invokes an image. "In the single form of Intellect, which is like an enclosure, inner enclosures are to be found which limit other forms; powers are to be found in it, as are ideas and a further division which does not move in a straight line but divides it inwardly, like an all-embracing animal which encompasses other animals, then others still till it reaches the animals and powers which occupy the least space, that is, as far as the kind that is indivisible, where it comes to a halt."[176]

Intellect lays hold of its most profound truth by retreating into this enclosure. This Being which lies at the root of all things, which is responsible for the world's existence and for its true meaning, derives its unity entirely from its origin. And spread throughout the intelligibles, while knowing itself as Intellect, it is the ideal intermediary between the indefinable Good, for which we hope, and the Soul which breathes behind sensible things.

d) *The Third Hypostasis.*[177] "It occupies a middle place among beings; part of it is divided: but, located at the edge of intelligible realities and at the boundaries of perceptible nature, the third hypostasis gives the latter something of what it has in itself. The third hypostasis receives, in return, part of this nature, if it does not use only its safe part in governing perceptible nature, and if, through excessive zeal, it plunges into it, without remaining totally within itself."[178] To explain a notion amounts to determining its precise location in the stream of hypostases. This text explains clearly this first way of looking at the soul, which inherits the intelligible world in its higher part, and dips its lowest extremity into the sensible world. But the religious content of this conception is obvious at the same time, and we can see how the soul, the metaphysical principle, could serve equally as a base on which to build a theory of the Fall or of Original Sin.

This World-Soul, like the Animal of the Stoic world, defines everything that lives. But it is also, at the same time, the intelligible world, more and more divided and fragmented (as the latter pointed already to the dispersion of the One). The soul is therefore the intermediary between the world of sense and the intelligible world. There are few difficulties in its relationships with the intelligible. Intellect produces the Soul as the One engendered Intellect itself.[179] But if it is true that the World-Soul is scattered in the sensible world, if it is true that individual souls are parts of the World-Soul and that they have to play, in their respective spheres, the role which World-Soul plays on the world stage,[180] how are these parts and this totality to be united? And will this continuity of principles and Beings, which gives all its meaning to Plotinus' teaching, be preserved? A new problem arises with regard to the soul, as it did in the case of the first two hypostases.

1. Plotinus devotes three books of the fourth *Ennead* entirely to this problem, which he regards as a particularly important one.[181] Our best approach is to refer to these books. They consider two problems: the relationships between the World-Soul and individual souls, and the relationships between the human soul and the body. The latter question, which relates more particularly to psychology, will be studied in its own place,

however, and will serve as an entirely natural transition to our study on conversion.

In the ninth book of the fourth *Ennead*, Plotinus establishes the basic unity of souls and the fact that they are linked to the force that animates the world. In fact, he provides an image for this. He describes this unity as similar to that of a seminal reason containing all the organs of the body or defines it as a science containing potentially all its theorems.[182] But when this is established, there is the question of how individual souls are produced. Plotinus' solution, which he tries to explain in an image (as he already had done in the case of the One and of Intellect), has, as always, less to do with reason than with emotion. And it can be summed up essentially, according to M. Bréhier, in "the claim that souls are united to each other without losing their individuality, and that they come together without being divided."[183] The image of light appears yet again at this point.[184]

The soul is in the whole body that it penetrates, for example, in each distinct part of a plant, even in a slip which has been separated from the plant. It is, at the same time, in the original plant and in the slip, for the body of the whole is a single body, and is in it everywhere as a single body.[185] How then are we to explain the differences between individual souls? "It is because they relate in different ways to the intelligible world. They are more or less opaque. And this least transparency, which differentiates individual souls from one another as they make their way [from the One], subordinates them to one another as they return [to the One]. Contemplation is introduced, in this context, to provide once more a cogent explanation."[186]

"One soul is really united to the intelligibles, another is united to them merely by knowledge, yet another by desire; each one, contemplating different things, is what it contemplates and becomes what it contemplates."[187]

2. In short, the unity of souls is a unity of convergence which allows them all to participate in the same living reality. Their multiplicity is that of a spiritual life which gradually loses its brightness as it proceeds, till its parts are dispersed. The idiosyncrasies of individual souls are underlined by the fact that they have fallen away. Souls become gradually enveloped in darkness and sink into matter. At this final point Plotinus' thought is not definitive. Impudence[188] and blindness,[189] in his view, explain the fall of the soul. The latter interpretation seems to be the more orthodox one. The soul is reflected in matter and, taking this reflection for itself, makes its way down to be united with matter, while it should instead have risen to rejoin its origins.

3. Finally the Plotinian conception of the human soul is closely linked to all that has gone before. The principle which governs it is the following one: only in its lower part does the human soul participate in the body. But the intellect that is in it is always directed toward the intelligible world.[190] Since the soul has to direct the feeble body in the midst of the snares of sensitive nature, however, it falls from grace and gradually forgets its princely origin. The whole of Plotinus' psychology unfolds from this principle. If, in the first place, the diversity of souls is like that of the intelligible world,[191] their function is a purely cosmic one. And psychology is still physics. It also follows immediately that all knowledge which is not intuitive and contemplative shares in the conditions of bodily life: reasoned thought is nothing more than an enfeebled form of intuitive thought. Consciousness is an accident and a shadow. No part of it can belong to the higher part of the soul. Memory itself manifests an attachment to sensible forms. And when the soul arrives at the point where it contemplates intelligible things, it will have no memory of its past lives.[192] We have then, a notion of the self which, while paradoxical at first sight, is nevertheless very rich in meaning: "There is no point at which one may determine one's own limits, so as to say, 'so far it is I.' "[193] This is where we find the doctrine of conversion. In silent reflection the soul forgets its practical needs. By closing its eyes it will begin to see as Intellect does. Desire for God will animate it. The soul will climb once more the ladder of things and beings. A whole stirring of love will commune in it—and this is conversion.

We have described, then, as briefly as we could, the different moments of procession. But not everything is equally satisfactory at this point. We have not provided an exact description of Plotinus' thought. There is no movement in it. To restore that steady onward advance which leads the soul to the One, we need conversion.

B. *Conversion, or the Way of Ecstasy*

a) It is in the Soul that the source of conversion is found. The soul is desire for God and the longing for a lost homeland. Life without God is merely a shadow of life. All beings strive toward God in the scale of Ideas and try once more to return to the source from which they came. Only matter, that great emptiness, that positive nothingness, does not aspire to God, and evil originates there: "Matter is a weak and dim phantasm that cannot receive a shape. If it exists in act, matter is a phantasm in act, a lie in act, in other words a real lie, the real nonbeing."[194] It creates delusions, however, and exists basically in the blindness of souls alone. The source of conversion lies in the soul, not in matter. But what is this principle? It is the desire for God. And the religious aspect of the Hypostases, considered as so many stages on the Soul's journey to its metaphysical homeland, can be seen in every aspect of this desire. "Desire makes us discover universal being; this desire is the Love which keeps watch at the door of its beloved; always outside and always impassioned, it makes do with participating in universal being, as far as possible."[195]

Desire is also thwarted by the world. "And that is why we must fly from here and separate ourselves from what has been added to us."[196] To desire is to love what we do not have. It is to wish to be and to wish to be one. For to look for oneself is, in a sense, to recollect oneself. Even Beauty is not enough.[197] Virtue, too, is no more than a stage we must pass through in order to arrive at God.[198] And nothing is to be desired except by virtue of the One that colours it.[199] The Soul in its wild longing is not happy even with Intellect. "But as soon as the pleasant warmth descends upon the Soul from above, it regains its strength, is truly woken, spreads its wings; and in so far as there is anything beyond what is present to itself, the Soul naturally rises higher, attracted by the one who gives love; it goes beyond Intellect but cannot go beyond the Good, for there is nothing beyond the Good. If the Soul halts at Intellect, it undoubtedly sees things that are beautiful and noble, but does not, for all that, altogether possess what it is looking for. Like a face which, in spite of its beauty, cannot attract glances, for it does not reflect the grace that is the flower of beauty."[200]

b) The Soul's longing contaminates Intellect. To know, moreover, is to desire. To say that Intellect needs nothing is merely to say that it is independent of the sensible world. But Intellect leans toward the Beyond. It needs the One. "Its life is directed toward the One; it is suspended from the One; it is turned toward the One."[201] Intellect lacks something, namely its unity. It is not self-sufficient, and this lack of self-sufficiency is the cause of its suffering and of its movement. Plotinian intellect is not mathematical Reason.

Moreover, it is by virtue of the return, as we have seen, and by contemplation of the One that the soul receives its form. This advance toward God is, then, fundamental to it. And the whole of the intelligible world vibrates toward the One.

c) The crucial problem that conversion raises, however, is similar to that which we met three times when dealing with Procession. It is posed in all its starkness in one text of the *Enneads:* "That which is altogether without a share in the Good would never seek the Good."[202] That is to say: you would not be looking for me, if you had not already found me. Or, in Plotinian terms: desire requires that the thing that is desired be, up to a point, immanent in that which desires it. Will the One then be transcendent or immanent? This is a disputed question, for some (Zeller) favour pantheism in Plotinus' thought, while others discern there a doctrine of transcendence (Caird).[203] Without intending to solve this question, we can try to pose the problem in another way.

God is immanent in us. Desire demands it. Moreover, we carry the three hypostases within us, for interior recollection leads to ecstasy and Union with the One. Plotinus' God, on the other hand, transcends other beings. When He produces, He does not expend Himself utterly, but superabounds without exhausting Himself. In order to understand this contradiction, we must reverse the terms of the problem. If it is true that he who learns to know himself knows at the same time the source from which he comes,[204] if it is true that to ascend to one's origin is to contemplate oneself, then it must be said that God is not immanent in any thing, but that all things are immanent in God. "The soul is not in the universe, but the universe is in the soul . . . the Soul is in Intellect, and body is in Soul, and Intellect is in another principle; but this other principle is in no way different, wherever it is: therefore this other principle is not in anything; in this sense, therefore, it is nowhere. Where then are the other things? In it."[205] Let us, on the other hand, assume that every being has two acts: the act of being what it is, and an act which derives from this essence; the first makes it cling to itself, the second forces it to be productive and to go out of its own bosom. So it is with God. He rises out of Himself, but without ceasing to be what He is. The whole mistake of excessively rigorous interpretations is to locate the One in space. Plotinus' teaching is an attempt to express a philosophy that is not spatialised. And it is on this plane, qualitative and inexpressible, that one must try to understand it. Or else, to return in the last analysis to a psychological problem: is there an abstract philosophy of space; one that belongs to a different plane? When one tries to assimilate the Plotinian experiment, it is clear that the first principle is itself seen to be present in all its works,[206] that it is not spatially located in these works and that, in a certain sense, it transcends all things and is immanent in them[207] at the same time. Moreover, it is everywhere on condition of being nowhere, for there is no place where that which is not tied to anything, is not to be found.

d) *Ecstasy or Union with the One.* When we examine this problem we can see that, in order to rise to God, one must return within oneself. The soul must plunge into its own origins, the remembrance of which it bears within itself. From God to God, such is its journey.[208] But the soul must be purified, that is, cleansed of what has clung to it when it was coming to be. We must not batten on what is not the soul, though it is in the soul; rather we must return to that[209] homeland,[210] the remembrance of which tinges our souls' disquiet. This is why the soul is obliterated and allowed to be absorbed into Intellect which rules it, and Intellect is forced in turn to disappear, so as to leave only the One which enlightens it. This union, so complete and so unusual,[211] is ecstasy.[212] At this juncture, however, interior meditation takes place, and Plotinus stops at this point in his journey. Analyses can go no further, nor can they be more profound. This feeling, so variegated and so "full" of the divinity, this refined melancholy of certain Plotinian texts, brings us to the heart of their author's thought. "I often wake up to myself in escaping from my body."[213] Meditation of a hermit, loving the world as a mere crystal on which divinity works, thinking thoughts imbued through and through with the silent rhythms of the stars, but restless for the God who directs them, Plotinus reasons as an artist and feels as a philosopher, according to a reason utterly penetrated with light and in the face of a world in which intelligence breathes.

Before isolating the basic themes of Plotinus' philosophy, however, and above all, investigating the manner in which they helped and hindered the evolution of Christian metaphysics, let us determine, according to the texts, the attitude of Neoplatonism toward Christianity. We will then be in a position to judge the extent to which Christian thought has its origins in Neoplatonism.

II. The Opposition

The enthusiasm with which Plotinus rises toward God could mislead us. It could, moreover, have us look upon him as more Christian than he ever could be. The more categorical position of his disciple Porphyry will, on the other hand, enable us to assess carefully Plotinus' attitude toward the Gnostics, that is, toward a certain form of Christian thought.

a) In the ninth book of the "Second Ennead" Plotinus writes against a Gnostic sect which cannot be precisely identified.[214] In this book he eloquently opposes his own coherent and harmonious universe to the romantic universe of the Gnostics. We can therefore discern immediately a number of irreducible differences. Plotinus' criticisms relate for the most part to four points, not all of which are equally important. He criticizes the Gnostics for scorning the created world and for teaching that a new land is waiting for them,[215] for regarding themselves as the children of God and substituting for the harmony of the universe a providence which will satisfy their egotism,[216] for calling the most worthless of men their brothers, while refusing this name to the gods,[217] and for substituting for the virtue of the sage the idea of an arbitrary salvation, where man counts for nothing.[218]

This book in fact carries the title: "Against those who say that the demiurge of the world is evil and that the world is bad." The basic issue here is the aesthetic way of looking at the world: "However, the sky is made of things much more beautiful and much purer than our bodies: they see its order and the beauty of its harmony, and yet they complain, more than others, about the disorder of earthly things."[219] And later: "No, once more, to despise the universe, to despise the gods and all the beauties of the world is not to become a good man."[220]

b) What is offended then is Plotinus' view that the world is ordered and well managed: "If God in His providence cares for you, why would He neglect the whole universe in which you yourselves live. . . . men, you say, do not need Him to look at the world. But the universe needs Him. Therefore the universe knows its proper place."[221] Sudden changes, creation, this god who is human and attainable, are all repugnant to Plotinus. But Christian humanitarianism is perhaps even more repugnant to the aristocratic in Plotinus. "There are people who do not think it wrong to give the name 'brother' to the most worthless of men; yet they do not consider it right to give this name to the sun, to the stars in the sky or even to the World-Soul, so false is their language."[222] What lies behind Plotinus' objections, then, is the ancient Greek love of nature as well.

All these objections are undoubtedly summed up, however, in the loathing that the Greek philosopher has for Christian "anarchy." The theory that Salvation is gratuitous and irrational is at the basis of this book's every attack. This doctrine of salvation, as we have seen, implies a certain lack of interest in virtue as the Greeks understood that word. To concern oneself with God, to believe in Him and to love Him, therefore, makes up, to a great extent, for mistakes. Plotinus knew this very well, for he criticizes this precise point with extraordinary force: "What proves that they make this mistake [of misunderstanding the nature of God] is that they have no teaching about virtue. There is no point whatever in saying: look towards God, if one does not teach people how to look towards Him. It is progress in virtue within the soul, accompanied by prudence, which reveals God to us. Without real virtue God is no more than a word."[223] The arbitrary factor inherent in every doctrine of salvation cannot be reconciled with a doctrine in which beings act according to the needs of their nature, and not, as Plotinus protests, at one moment rather than another.[224]

The issue here is that Gnosticism, and these reproaches, we should note carefully, are directed against certain caricatures of Christianity. In the last analysis, however, Plotinus is combating an attitude toward the world rather than doctrinal details. The contrast is therefore between two ways of looking at the human condition. We already know enough about both of them to be able to predict the extent to which, on certain points, they remain irreconcilable.

Plotinus' disciple has, however, gone further, and has not hesitated to write an entire treatise against the Christians. He wrote this work when he was between thirty-five and forty years of age (after 208). It comprises no less than fifteen books, and we derive our knowledge of it from fragments[225] assembled by Harnack. We shall set aside detailed criticisms (improbability, contradiction) that Porphyry does not fail to mention. These criticisms are the basis of all the works of pagan polemicism. We shall merely quote some of the texts which oppose Christianity and Neoplatonism, on doctrinal points.

Porphyry complains that the Apostles were unintelligent rustics.[226] His point is a classical one, but he later reproaches the faithful for embracing an "irrational faith"[227] and expressed himself in the following terms: "It was a boon for Christ on this earth to have hidden the light of knowledge from the wise so as to reveal it to the uneducated and to nurslings."[228]

He relies upon this text of Paul for his understanding of the world. "The form of this world is passing away."[229] How will this be possible, asks Porphyry, and who will bring it about: "If it was the demiurge, he would be exposed to the charge of disturbing, of altering a harmony that had been peacefully established. . . . If the state of the world is indeed lamentable, a chorus of protests should be raised against the demiurge, for having arranged the elements of the Universe in such a troublesome way, in defiance of the rational character of nature."[230]

Christian eschatology offends not only his idea of order but his aesthetic sense as well. "And He, the Creator, would see the sky (can one imagine anything more remarkable or more beautiful than the sky?) melting . . . while the rotten, decomposing bodies of men would come to life again, among them those who before death had presented a distressing and loathsome appearance."[231]

If Porphyry is sometimes annoyed, he is also, from time to time, abusive.[232] A cultivated Greek could not embrace this way of looking at things without compelling reasons.

III. Meaning And Influence of Neoplatonism

It is time, however, to determine the meaning of the Neoplatonic solution and the role which it played in the evolution of Christian metaphysics. Our task here will be to underline the newness of Neoplatonism and to point out the ways in which it exercised its influence. Our study of Christianity will give us the opportunity to analyse this influence in detail. But let us begin by summarizing the general features of Neoplatonism in a few words.

a) It is a constant effort to reconcile contradictory ideas with the help of a principle of participation, a principle which has a place solely in a logic divorced from space and time. Mystical Reason, sensible Intelligence, God who is immanent and transcendent, the oppositions abound. However, these oppositions underline a constant movement that balances the sensible and the intellectual, the religious aspect of the principles and their explicative power. In this dialogue between heart and reason, truth can be expressed only in images. This is why comparisons abound in Plotinus. This superabundance is undoubtedly meant to meet the very same need as the parables in the Gospels: to mould the intelligibles into a shape that can be grasped by the senses, to restore to intuition what belonged to Reason. Such apparent contradictions are clarified, nonetheless, if thought is assumed to be beyond Space and Time. This is why Plotinus' originality lies above all in the method which makes these conciliations possible. But a method is valuable only in so far as it expresses a need of an author's nature. We have also shown this to be the case with Plotinus.

Where, then, is Neoplatonism to be located with regard to Hellenism and Christianity? We have satisfactorily shown, as far as the former is concerned, what was purely Hellenic in the *Enneads*. Something makes Plotinus an entirely original figure nonetheless. In Plato the myths on the destiny of the soul seem to be superadded to and set alongside of strictly rational explanations. In Plotinus, the two procedures are one, and are inextricably interwoven, since they encompass basically the same reality. A difference that must be clearly understood, for it makes Plotinus unique in his time. A difference equally applicable to Christianity since it is, on this occasion, the rational aspect that will be missing from Christian thought. Plotinus, midway between the two doctrines,[233] is to serve as a mediator.

b) What Neoplatonism contributed to Christianity so as to allow it subsequently to evolve was, in fact, a method and a direction for its thought.

A direction for its thought, because by providing Christianity with frames of reference already fashioned to religious ways of thinking, Neoplatonism strongly inclined it toward the perspectives within which these frames of reference had been created. Alexandrian thought encourages Christianity to progress toward the conciliation of a metaphysic and a primitive faith. But in this regard, there was little to be done, as the movement was underway. The method, however, arrived at the right time. Christianity is going to resolve its great problems, Incarnation and Trinity, by employing the principle of participation. But let us try to sum this up in a particular example.

Arius[234] drew upon certain scriptural texts when he affirmed the creation of the Son by the Father and the subordination of the latter to the former. "The Lord created me at the beginning of his works."[235]

For neither the angels on high nor the Son have been told the day or the hour. The Father alone knows these things. Then Arius quoted texts from John: "The Father who has sent me is greater than I."[236] "And this is eternal life, that they know you, the only true God and Jesus Christ whom you have sent."[237] "The Son can do nothing of his own accord."[238]

In order to counter this assertion, Athanasius, the defender of orthodoxy, quoted three explicit texts of John: "I and the Father are one."[239] "The Father is in me and I am in the Father."[240] "He who has seen me, has seen the Father."[241] According to these texts the son was and, at the same time, was not God. Who cannot see that the problem thus posed is the classic question of Neoplatonism? And is it surprising that Christian thought resolved the controversy in a similar manner? The Nicene Creed (325) states the principle of consubstantiality and opposes the begotten Christ to the created Jesus of Arius: "We believe in one God, the Father almighty, creator of all things visible and invisible, and in one Lord Jesus Christ, the son of God, only begotten of the Father, that is, of the same substance as the Father, God of God, light of light, true God of true God, begotten not made, of the same substance as the Father, by whom all things were made, in heaven and on earth, who came down from heaven for us men and for our salvation, was incarnate, was made man, suffered, rose again on the third day, ascended into the heavens, and will come to judge the living and the dead. And in the Holy Ghost."[242] And if this text does not seem sufficiently explicit, let us include that which Athanasius, in his "letter on the decrees of the Council of Nicea,"[243] quotes from Theognostus, head of the School of Catechetics at Alexandria, between 270 and 280[244]: "The substance of the Son has not come from outside, it has not been drawn out of nothing, it comes from the substance of the Father as brightness comes from light, steam from water, for the light is not the sun itself, the steam is not the water itself. It is not, however, an alien body, but something that emanates from the substance of the Father, without the Father being divided in any way. As the sun, remaining itself, is not diminished by the rays it emits, so the substance of the Father is not changed by the fact that His son is made in His image."

These important texts illustrate the importance of the Neoplatonic influence for the resolution of problems. A number of texts would be even more instructive in this regard.[245] But however eloquent these likenesses may be, we should not draw from them precipitate conclusions that are too generous toward Neoplatonism. Christianity is different from Neoplatonism, and has its own basic originality.

c) The sense in which we can speak of a Neoplatonic influence on Christianity is therefore clear. It is, in fact, the influence of a metaphysical doctrine on a religious way of thinking: a model to follow, once ambitions are aroused. It is with good reason, then, that we have taken Plotinus' thought as the symbol of this influence. Platonic thought prepared and moulded formulas which were found ready-made at the very time they were needed. The role of Plotinus' philosophy ended, however, with what was moving and original in it. Too many things separate Saint Augustine from Plotinus.

CHAPTER FOUR

I. The Second Revelation

A. *Saint Augustine's Psychological Experience and Neoplatonism*

a) Before showing how the evolution that we have tried to retrace finds in Augustinism one of its most telling expressions, we must address ourselves to Saint Augustine's Neoplatonism. Let us state the problem at the very beginning: the new philosophy of Plato had an influence upon the great doctor. He quotes several texts of the *Enneads*.[246] A certain number of Augustine's texts can be compared with ideas that are to be found in Plato. The most suggestive ones, in this respect, are those which deal with the nature of God.

On his ineffability: *Sermon,* 117, 5; the *City of God,* IX, 16 with *Enn.,* VI, 9,5; *On the Trinity,* VIII, 2 and XV, 5 with *Enn.,* V, 3,13; on his eternity: *Conf.* XI, 13 and *Enn.,* III, 6,7; on his ubiquity: *Sermon* 277, 13 and 18 with *E* VI, 4, 2; on his spirituality: the *City of God,* XIII, 5 and *E* VI, 8, 11. This influence has made it possible to draw unwarranted conclusions.[247] Saint Augustine's testimony is, however, sufficiently explicit. And the famous passage of the *Confessions* on "the books of the Platonists" provides a very clear statement on this matter. We will be pardoned for quoting this passage, in spite of its length. It will, as far as we are concerned, be instructive for all that is to follow: "I read that: in the beginning was the Word and the Word was with God and the Word was God. He was in the beginning with God: that the Word, God himself, is the 'true light that enlightens every man who comes into this world.'"

"But I did not read there that the Word 'was made man and came to dwell among us' . . . I did not read there that He 'emptied himself, taking on the form of a slave'; that He 'became like man by making man's sufferings His own'; that He 'humbled Himself and became obedient unto death . . .'"[248] In setting the Incarnation over against Contemplation, as he did, Saint Augustine established, for the very first time, the differences between the two philosophies and the ways in which they resembled each other.

b) But let us at least determine the extent of this influence. The remarkable feature of Augustine's philosophy is that it gathers together, in the space of a few years,[249] all the uncertainties and vicissitudes of Christian thought. As he was a very passionate man, and a sensual one, the fear of being unable to remain continent delayed his conversion[250] for a considerable period. At the same time he has the taste for rational truths. This desire for understanding is responsible for his adherence to Manicheism at Carthage in the very midst of a life of excess and pleasure. In many respects Manicheism was nothing more than a continuation of Gnosticism, but it promised proofs. This is what attracts[251] Saint Augustine.[252] But at the same time the problem of evil obsesses him: "I continued to seek the source of evil, but there was no way out."[253] And he was plagued by the thought of death: "Such thoughts I turned over within my wretched breast, which was overburdened with the most biting concern about the fear of death and [my] failure to discover truth."[254] Greek in his need for coherence, Christian in the anxieties to which his sensibility gave rise, he remained outside of Christianity for a long time. The combination of the allegorical method of Saint Ambrose and Neoplatonic philosophy won over Saint Augustine. But at the same time they did not convince him. His conversion was deferred. Consequently, it seemed to him above all that the solution was not to be found in knowledge, that the resolution of his doubts and of his distaste for the flesh did not lie in intellectual escape but in the total acknowledgment of his depravity and wretchedness. Grace would again raise him above the love of those possessions which were responsible for the extent of his corruption.

Saint Augustine is therefore to be found at the meeting place of the influences which we are trying, at this point, to ascertain. But to what precise degree? This is what we must determine.

c) What Augustine demanded, along with Faith, was truth; along with dogmas, a metaphysic. So too did the whole of Christianity. But if Augustine embraced Neoplatonism for a short time, he was soon to transform it. And with Neoplatonism the whole of Christianity.[255] The meaning of this trans-formation is what has to be determined. Plotinus, as we have seen, provides Saint Augustine with the doctrine of the Word as mediator and with a solution to the problem of evil.

Hypostasized intellect, in fact, reveals the destiny of Christ as the Word of God: "We have also heard through divine authority that the Son of God is nothing but the wisdom of God, and the Son of God is truly God . . . But, do you believe that wisdom is different from truth? For it has also been said: 'I am the Truth' " (*The Happy Life*, ch. IV, no. 34) (P.L.I 32 col. 975). As for evil, Plotinus' thought teaches Saint Augustine that it is linked to matter and that its being is entirely negative (*Conf.* VII, 12 and VIII, 13). And so all his doubts seemed to be dispelled. But for all that, conversion did not come. There is something peculiar to the author of the *Confessions*, namely, that his own experience continues to be the constant point of reference for all his intellectual inquiries. Satisfied, but not convinced, as he himself admits: what Neoplatonism could not restore to him was the Incarnation and his humility. It is only when he has understood this that an explosion of tears and joy comes to free him in the garden of his house. An almost physical conversion, so complete that Saint Augustine is going progressively to renounce the whole of his past life and to devote himself to God.

That place that Christianity uniquely accords to Christ and the Incarna-tion should therefore be retained in Augustine's philosophy. These are the formulas and themes which he sought from Neoplatonism. The figure of Jesus and the problem of the Redemption are going to change everything. We must now try to examine, in some points of his doctrine, this intermingling of Greek themes and Christian dogmas.

B. *Hellenism and Christianity in Saint Augustine*

1. Evil, Grace and Freedom. In discussing such specifically Christian problems, we shall try continually to elucidate, in Saint Augustine's thought, the basic themes of Christianity. And since we have already alluded to these themes, we need only provide a simple summary of them.

a) We shall not return to the importance of the problem of evil in Saint Augustine's philosophy. But we must remember, nonetheless, the extreme fruitfulness of this obsession. Our author was able to develop his most original doctrines by taking the problem of evil as his starting point. This very richness will force us to divide our material. Saint Augustine's philosophy is defined, on the one hand, by his teaching, and, on the other, by his reaction against Pelagius. We shall first examine his general teaching. The controversy with Pelagius will then reveal the profound leanings of Augustinism in the harshest glare of polemics. Neoplatonism says that evil is a privation, not a reality in itself. Saint Augustine agrees.[256] But we must again distinguish two kinds of evil: natural evil (wretchedness of our condition, tragedy of man's destiny), and moral evil, that is, Sin. The first is explained in the way in which dark patches are justified on a painting.[257] It contributes to the harmony of the universe. The second presents a more difficult problem. How could God have given us free will, that is, a will that is capable of choosing evil: "Because he exists as he does, man is not good now and does not have it in his power to become good, either because he does not see what kind of man he ought to be, or, though seeing this, is unable to become what he sees he ought to be."[258] Sin, which results from original sin, can be blamed on us. God has permitted us the free will of Adam, but our will has acquired the desire to make bad use of it. And we have fallen so far that the proper exercise of free will is invariably to be traced to God alone. Left to himself man would, properly speaking, be merely wicked, deceitful and sinful: "Man's sole possession is deceit and sin."[259] It is God who raises him up, when He so wishes. This is why the virtues which are kept alive in us have meaning and value only as a result of a support which we receive from God, specific and adapted to our weakness: grace. Saint Augustine puts a great deal of emphasis upon the uselessness of unaided virtue. Grace to begin with, then virtue. We recognize in this a theme of the Gospels.

The virtues of the pagans, then, are inoperative. God has bestowed these virtues upon the pagans in order to arouse within us the desire to have them when they are not ours and to lower our pride if we do have them. Never in Christianity was virtue, in the Hellenic sense, exposed to so demanding a test, and on so many occasions.[260] Moreover, these natural virtues become so many faults when man boasts of them.[261] Pride is the sin of Satan. Our sole proper duty is, on the contrary, God. And the gift which God makes of His grace is invariably a product of His generosity. This grace is gratuitous. And those who believe they can acquire it by good works have things the wrong way around. Grace would not be gratuitous if it could be earned. We must go even further. To believe in God is already to submit to His grace. Faith is the beginning of Grace.[262]

We can see to what extremes the thought of Augustine goes. It does not eschew any difficulty the problem presents. But again there is, in his view, no problem where there is submission. As is usual with regard to evil, however, this absolute dependence gives rise to serious difficulties. The grace of God is, in this context, totally arbitrary: man should simply put his trust in God. How then can one speak of man's freedom? Precisely because our sole freedom is the freedom to do wrong.[263] Saint Augustine's final avowal on this question, vital for the Christian, is one of ignorance. God's will remains intact.[264]

Saint Augustine was led to develop this theory in all its details when faced with the Pelagian heresy. In this case he was able to transcend his philosophy in order to meet the requirements of his cause. But there was also the fact that his pessimism and renunciation retained all their harshness. This is, then, in a nutshell, the meaning of his teaching on freedom.

b) A summary of Pelagius' thought will enable us to understand the ferocity which Saint Augustine brings to his struggle with Pelagianism.[265] He was affected in the depth of his experience, in his keen sense of what is bad in man.

Pelagius, a Breton monk, was basically afraid of a kind of complacency with regard to sin which can be derived from doctrines of predestination. His disciples, Celestius and Julian, were mainly responsible for the propagation of his teachings, for he himself was a man of conscience rather than of ideas.

Man, according to Pelagius, was created free. He is able to do Good or Evil as he wishes. This freedom is an emancipation from God. "Freedom of the will, by which man is freed from God, lies in the possibility of committing sin or refraining from it."[266]

The loss of this freedom was, according to Saint Augustine, a result of original sin. Some Pelagians thought, on the other hand, that Freedom was entirely under the control of the will and that man could avoid sin if he so wished: "I say that a man can be without sin."[267]

But then original sin loses all its meaning. And the Pelagians reject it totally as entailing Manichean conclusions. If Adam has destroyed us, he has done so by his bad example alone. Even the secondary effects of the Fall, such as the loss of the soul's immortality, should not be admitted. Adam was born mortal. His mistake has not been ours at all. "For newborn infants are in that state in which Adam was before he sinned."[268]

It is easy for us to sin because sin has become second nature in us.[269] Grace, clearly and properly speaking, is useless. But Pelagius always holds that creation is already a grace. The latter continues to be useful, moreover, not "ad operandum," but "ad facilius operandum."[270] It is a support, a testimonial, which God gives us. This teaching is summarized in the nine points of indictment delivered at the Council of Carthage (29 April 418).[271] In general, this teaching puts its trust in man and scorns explanations which refer to the will of God. It is also an act of faith in the nature and independence of man. All this would have annoyed a person imbued with the cry of Saint Paul: "Wretched man that I am, who will deliver me from this body of death?"[272]

But more serious consequences followed. The Fall denied, Redemption lost its meaning. Grace was a pardon, not a support. This thesis, then, was above all a declaration of man's independence of God and a denial of that persistent need of the creator that is at the basis of the Christian religion.

Saint Augustine opposes this way of looking at things and completes his speculations with a number of assertions. Adam was immortal.[273] In so far as he had the "ability not to sin,"[274] and was already the recipient of a sort of divine grace, he was free. When original sin occurred it destroyed this happy state. Scripture is explicit on this point and Augustine relies upon it.[275] Our nature is corrupted, and without baptism, man is destined for damnation (according to John II,54). Augustine finds this borne out in the desolation of the whole world and the wretchedness of our condition, which he portrays in graphic pictures.[276]

These are, however, secondary effects of original sin. Others, more closely related to it and less corrigible, will reveal the extent of our wretchedness. We have lost, to begin with, the freedom "to be able not to sin."

We depend on the grace of God. On the other hand damnation is, in principle, universal. The whole human race is doomed to the flames. Its sole hope is in the mercy of God.[277] One more point follows: the damnation of children who die before baptism.[278]

Grace, then, becomes more necessary. And we depend on it in three respects: to protect us from our fallen nature, to believe in the truths of the supernatural order,[279] and to enable us to act in accordance with these truths.[280] But our works do not merit this first grace, which is faith. Nevertheless we can earn, to a certain extent, the grace of doing good.[281] Predestination determines our whole destiny in every case. And Saint Augustine returns constantly to its gratuitous nature.[282] The number of those who are predestined, as well as of those who are damned, is determined once and for all, and is unalterable. Only then does God consider virtues and failings so as to determine how far they should be punished. What we cannot know is the reason for this. Our freedom is the freedom to reject the primary graces on the one hand and, on the other, to earn the secondary ones. Our freedom is exercised only in the context of divine omnipotence.[283]

2. The Word and the Flesh: the Trinity. We have come to the heart of the specifically Christian in Saint Augustine. If we remember Plotinus' metaphysics we shall see the infinite distance that separates the two attitudes. In so doing we shall at least avoid being misled by the many things they have in common and shall be in a position to determine the part played by Saint Augustine's Christianity in his Neoplatonism. What he got from the Platonic writers is, as we have seen, a certain conception of the Word. But his task

was to find in this conception a point of entry for Christ, and so to give pride of place to the Word made flesh of the fourth Gospel. Let us try then to determine what Saint Augustine sought from Neoplatonism. We shall then show how the doctrine of the Incarnation transformed what he had borrowed.

a) *The Word*—"In God," says Plotinus, "the pure soul dwells with the intelligibles."[284] But Saint Augustine: "The ideas are like the first forms or reasons of things, stable and immutable, not having received their eternal form, as a result, and similarly things that are always contained in the divine intellect."[285] He grasps God with his heart but also with his intellect. Clearly, then, his conception is an entirely philosophical one. For the intelligible world, at which we marvel, reveals its mystery to us. Confronted with this world, our mind performs a double movement; faced with the diversity of ideas produced by the intelligible world, it separates out the ideas which it contains. Its second endeavour, however, synthesizes these ideas in one reality that expresses them: "Not only are they ideas, but they are themselves true because they are eternal and remain ever the same and unchangeable."[286]

"This reality is God Whom Augustine grasped in this way as pure Intellect and first truth."[287] It is a Plotinian conception. The principle of participation is at work here. The ideas participate in all that is divine. They are in Him and yet He is superior to them. This kinship will be seen even more clearly in a robust text of *The Trinity*[288]: "Hence, because there is the one Word of God, through which all things were made, which is the unchangeable truth, all things in it are originally and unchangeably simultaneous, not only the things that are now in this whole creation, but also those which have been and are to be. In it, however, these things have not been, nor are they to be, they only are; and all things are life, and all things are one, or rather it is one thing alone which is, and one single life."[289] The Plotinian method is apparent at this point. As soon as Saint Augustine incorporates this doctrine of the Word intellect into his theory of the Trinity, however, things have a different meaning. Plotinus in fact makes a hierarchy of his hypostases and stresses the distance that separates the One from Intellect. Saint Augustine's exposition starts from God, not as the origin of the two other essences, but as the source of the unique nature of the Trinity: "The one God is the Trinity itself and so the one God is somehow or other the sole creator."[290]

The three persons are therefore identical. Three basic conclusions follow from this: the three persons have merely one single will and one single operation: "Where there is no nature, there is no diversity of wills."[291] "Therefore the Word alone did not appear on earth, but the whole Trinity."

"In the Son's Incarnation the Trinity in its entirety is united to the human body."[292]

Each of the three persons is equal to the Trinity as a whole and to God himself, who contains the other two persons: "The Father alone, or the Son alone, or the Holy Spirit alone is just as great as the Father, the Son and the Holy Spirit together."[293] This Trinitarian theory is therefore an attempt to reconcile equality of Persons with the view that these Persons differ from one another. A problem that already lies outside of Plotinus' thought but that launches his method. Moreover, Augustine's Christology is linked to this doctrine of the Trinity, with the result that the Word is not the Intellect of Neoplatonism.

b) *The Flesh.*—The Word has in fact been made flesh, His body is real, terrestrial and born of a woman.[294] This union of one body and one word is indestructible. Man and Christ make up one thing only. This is the whole mystery of Christianity: "The fact that the Word became flesh does not imply that the Word departed and was destroyed on being clothed with flesh, but rather that flesh, in order to avoid destruction, drew near to the Word. . . . the same one who is man is God, and the same one who is God is man, not by a commingling of natures but by a unity that comes with being a person."[295] The more Plotinian the notion of the Word is in Saint Augustine, the more it differs from Neoplatonism in so far as, with him, the union of this Word with this flesh becomes more miraculous. This is what should now be noted.

But everything is justified by a fact. If the matter is contradictory, at least the fact is obvious. Moreover, the miracle seems all the greater because the task is so great.

C. *Faith and Reason in Saint Augustine*

We did not intend, of course, to provide an exposition of Augustine's thought, and, what is more, our task does not demand that we do so. The important thing, with regard to our theme, was to consider a certain interaction of two philosophies in the writings of our author, to determine what part of them belonged to him and what part came from outside, and to draw from these philosophies some conclusions about the relationships between Neoplatonism and Christianity. That is why our study of Augustine centres around two themes that are particularly suggestive for this topic. It only remains for us to draw the conclusions from this particular study. This will enable us to retain in broad outline what we have so far looked at in detail. And, by placing ourselves at the very heart of Christian metaphysics, at this stage of its evolution, we will be able to look this evolution straight in the face and to see how all its endeavours ended, with the help of Saint Augustine, in the union of a metaphysic and a religion, of the Word and the Flesh, without, if the truth be told, the basic physiognomy of Christianity being lost in the process.

We shall merely sum up, at this point, the significance of Augustinism for the evolution of Christian metaphysics: "In all these things which I run through in seeking Thy counsel, I find no safe place for my soul, except in Thee, where my scattered parts are gathered together and no portion of me may depart from Thee. Sometimes, Thou dost introduce me to a very unusual inner experience, to an indescribable sweetness that, if it reaches perfection in me, will be beyond my present knowledge."[296] Saint Augustine ends where Plotinus' conversion culminates. They both pursue the same conclusion, but while their paths sometimes overlap, they are different nonetheless. Augustinism asserts at every step that philosophy is not enough. The sole intelligent reason is that which is enlightened by faith: "True philosophy implies an act of adherence to the supernatural order which frees the will from the flesh through grace and the mind from scepticism through revelation."[297] We could not exaggerate this point.

The dialogue of Faith and Reason was brought out into the open by Saint Augustine: it constituted the whole history of the evolution of Christianity. Some hold that Hellenic doctrine was superadded to Christian thought. This is true. Faith accepted, in the end, Reason of which it knew nothing; but, if Saint Augustine is to be believed, this was to give a very unique place to Reason.

"If you cannot understand, believe so that you may understand. Faith comes first, understanding follows. Therefore do not seek to understand so that you may believe, but believe so that you may understand."[298] This reason becomes more pliant. It is enlightened by the lights of Faith. There are, in fact, two things in Augustinian faith: the mind's adherence to supernatural truths and man's humble abandonment to the grace of Christ. It is not a question of believing in God's existence, but of total submission of the whole person to Him.

"Learning, you should realise, does not first begin with reason, and only then with faith." Reason should be humbled: "Blessedness starts with humility: Blessed are the poor in spirit, that is, those who lack arrogance and whose soul is submissive to divine authority."[299]

It is clear, then, that the Alexandrian word served the Christian faith without doing any disservice to this faith. We can see, in Saint Augustine, the whole evolution of Christianity: to make Greek reason more supple and to fuse it with the Christian edifice, but in a sphere in which it does no harm. Outside of this sphere, it is obliged to yield. In this respect Neoplatonism, Saint Augustine tells us, is at the service of a doctrine of humility and faith. Its role in the evolution of Christianity was, in fact, to support this softening of Reason, to lure Socratic logic to religious speculations and so to transmit this tool, already fashioned, to the Fathers of the Christian Church.

Augustinism can be regarded as a second revelation in this sense as well; that of a Christian metaphysic in the wake of evangelical faith. The miracle is that the two do not contradict each other.

II. Christian Thought at the Dawn of the Middle Ages

This is where the evolution of primitive Christianity ends and the history of Christian teaching begins.

Augustinism marks a conclusion and a starting point. We have sketched the paths by which evangelical Christianity arrived at this point. The crucial event in this evolution is its break with Judaism and its entry into the Greco-Roman world. From this moment they fuse with each other. Mediterranean thought, prepared by the Eastern religions, is about to be fertilized by the new civilization. If Neoplatonism can be regarded as the artisan of this fertilization, it is also true that Christianity was born of this Greco-Roman syncretism. The dogmatic formulas of Christianity grew out of a fusion of the latter with the fundamental ideas of evangelical faith. These formulas, announced by Paul and John, and developed by the Greek converts to Christianity, are fully expressed in Augustine's thought, but only after some Christians wandered into false conciliations.

The basic mystery is that this union took place, for while the sensibility of the Greco-Roman world was open to the Gospel, Reason was not prepared to admit a certain number of postulates. Belief in providence, creation, philosophy of history, taste for humility, all the themes which we highlighted were in conflict with the Greek way of looking at things. That Greek naïveté of which Schiller speaks was too thoroughly imbued with innocence and light to give way without a struggle. The task of those who tried to reconcile them was to transform the very agent of this attitude, Reason governed by the principle of contradiction, into a notion shaped by the idea of participation. Neoplatonism was the unwitting artisan of this *rapprochement*. But there is a limit to the mind's elasticity. And Greek civilization in the person of Plotinus stopped halfway. The originality of Christianity can be precisely detected in this separation. Christian thought certainly brought the Alexandrian Word into its dogmas. But this Word is not distinguished from God. It is begotten; it is not an effusion.

God is, however, in direct touch with his creatures for whom He has come to die. And what could have seemed contradictory to a Greek mind is legitimized in the eyes of Christians by a fact: the appearance of Jesus on earth and His incarnation. This word is found at the beginning and again at the end of the evolution of Christian metaphysics. It shows too that while Christianity had clothed itself in Greek ideas, it had lost none of its original flavour.

Man's ancient story of a God's journey on earth is applied for the first time, at the dawn of the Middle Ages, to the metaphysical notion of the divinity. And the more the metaphysic is developed, the greater the originality of Christianity will be, according as the distance between the Son of Man and the ideas which he transforms became more marked.

Conclusion

We undertook to solve two problems, one, very extensive, bearing on the relationship between Christianity and Hellenism, the other inscribed at the heart of the first. The latter problem had to do with the role of Neoplatonism in the evolution of Christian thought. The subject matter was too wide to allow us to hope for definitive answers. However, we have considered, on the one hand, three stages in the evolution of Christian thought and, on the other, the culmination of the work of Greek philosophy in Neoplatonism. A simple comparison furnished some conclusions.

Christianity borrowed its material from Greek thought and its method from Neoplatonism. It kept its profound truth intact by treating every problem on the level of the Incarnation. And if indeed, Christianity had not utilized this baffling method of dealing with its problems, Greece would undoubtedly have absorbed it. And not for the first time. This, at least, is true, but how many other difficulties remain: the role played by Philo in the constitution of Alexandrian metaphysics, the contribution of Origen and Clement of Alexandria to Christian teaching, the many influences which we have passed over: Kabbala, Zend-Avesta, Indian philosophies or Egyptian Theurgy. But it is enough to mention them. Let us stick to some facts. Many people speak of the Hellenization of primitive Christianity. And as far as morality is concerned, the issue is not in doubt.[300] However, Christian morality cannot be taught; it is an interior ascesis which serves to ratify a faith. We should speak, on the contrary, as our work shows, of the

Christianization of decadent Hellenism. In this context, moreover, the words have an historical and even a geographical meaning.

Is it possible, however, in the last analysis, at the end of this study, to say in what the originality of Christianity consists? Are there, in fact, peculiarly Christian ideas? This is an important question for our time. Indeed, it is a paradox peculiar to the human mind that it can grasp the elements and be incapable of embracing the synthesis: epistemological paradox of a science certain in its facts, but inadequate nonetheless: adequate in its theories, but nonetheless uncertain, or the psychological paradox of a self that can be grasped in its parts but is inaccessible in its profound unity. History does not free us from our disquiet in this regard, and to restore the profound originality of the Gospel seems to be an impossible task. We see clearly under what influences, from what syncretism, Christian thought was born. But we also see clearly that, were Christianity to be entirely dismantled into unfamiliar parts, we would even then recognize it to be original, because of a certain resonance, muted more than any that has ever been heard.

If we reflect upon the main themes of Christianity, Incarnation, philosophy of history, the wretchedness and pain of the human condition, we realize that what counts in this context is the substitution of a "Christian" man for a "Greek" one. This difference, which we ill succeed in discerning in the teachings, we experience by comparing Saint Jerome in the desert at odds with temptation, and the young people who used to listen to Socrates.[301] For if indeed Nietzsche is to be believed, if it is accepted that the Greece of darkness which we highlighted at the beginning of this work, the Greece of pessimism, insensible and tragic, was the feature of a strong civilization, we must conclude that Christianity is, in this respect, a renaissance compared to Socratism and its serenity. "Since men cannot provide a cure for death," says Pascal, "they have taken it upon themselves not to think of it at all." The whole task of Christianity is to combat this idleness of heart. Christian man is thus defined and, at the same time, a civilization. Ch. Guignebert's *Early Christianity* speaks of Christian thought as if it were a religion "of fanatics, the hopeless and tramps." What he says is true, but not as its author intends it.

Be that as it may, when Saint Augustine died, Christianity had become a philosophy. It is now sufficiently armed to resist the torment where everything founders. For many years now it has remained the only hope and the only real shield against the misfortune of the Western world. In this way Christianity won its catholicity.

NOTES TO DISSERTATION

1. *Meditations* IV, 23: "Everything is fitting for me, my Universe, which fits your purpose. Nothing in your good time is too early or too late for me; everything is fruit for me which your seasons, Nature, bear; from you, in you, to you are all things."

2. Epictetus, *Discourse* 1,7: "If you cannot correct those who do wrong, do not reproach them, for all evil can be corrected; rather, reproach yourself for the fact that you do not have enough eloquence and persistence to set them right." [Camus is, in fact, paraphrasing sentiments expressed by Epictetus in Discourse II, XXVI, 7.]

3. Cf. Aristotle, *Probl.* XVIII, 3 [XVII, 2]: "If human life is a circle, and a circle has neither beginning nor end, we cannot be 'prior' to those who lived in the time of Troy, nor they 'prior' to us by being nearer to the beginning." Quoted by Rougier, *Celse,* chap. II, p. 76 [chap. II, p. 35]; cf. also Plotinus II, IX, 7.

4. Cf. F. Cumont, *les Religions orientales dans le paganisme romain.*

5. During his campaigns in the East Alexander founded more than forty Greek towns.

6. "Euhemerized": neologism, derived from Euhemerus, the Greek mythographer, for whom the gods were human beings who had been divinized by the fear of their fellow creatures. (R.Q.)

7. Cf. "The new man" in the purification rites of Eleusis; "the goddess Brimo has given birth to Brimos." *Refutations:* V, 8. Cf. Plutarch, *On Isis,* 27 in Loisy: *les mystères païens et le mystère chrétien,* chap. IV, p. 139.

   After checking and stifling the wrath of Typhon [Isis] did not want the conflicts she had undergone to fall into oblivion and silence. She therefore instituted initiation rites of a very simple kind, so as to represent, by means of images, allegories and symbolic scenes, the sufferings she had sustained during her struggle.

   [The first sentence of this quotation is to be found, as Archambault points out (*Camus' Hellenic Sources,* p. 73), on p. 72 of *les mystères païens et le mystère chrétien;* Camus' second sentence misquotes what Loisy writes on page 141 of this same work: "Elle institua donc des initiations très *saintes* ou seraient représentées par des images, des allégories et par des scènes figurées les souffrances de *jadis"* (Emphasis added).]

8. Cf. Loisy, *op. cit.,* chap. 1.

9. Cf. Cumont, *op. cit.,* appendix, *les Mystères de Bacchus.* [It is by no means clear what Camus is referring to at this point, for the work which he cites does not contain an appendix. He may, however, have had in mind either Cumont's *les mystères païens et le mystère chrétien,* chapter II, the first part of which deals with the mysteries of Dionysus, or his *Lux Perpetua.*

Chapter V of this latter work is concerned with "Greek cults" and has a section (pp. 250-59) devoted specifically to Bacchus.]

10. Cumont, chap. III.

11. Loisy, chap. II.

12. *Bulletin de la Société française de Philosophie* (March 1931). *Revue de métaphysique et de morale* (Bréhier) (April 1931); *id.* July 1932 (Souriau).

13. That is, toward the middle of the first century.

14. Émile Bréhier, The History of Philosophy, *The Hellenistic and Roman Age,* p. 214.

15. P. de Labriolle, la Réaction païenne (Paris 1934).

16. P. de Labriolle, *Histoire de la littérature latine chrétienne.*

17. On the imminence of this parousia cf. *Mark,* VIII, 39; XVIII, 30; *Matt.,* X, 23; XII, 27-28; XXIV, 34. *Luke,* IX, 26-27, XXI, 32. Cf. also the *Vigilate; Matt.,* XXIV, 42-44; XXV, 13; *Luke,* XII, 37-40. [*Matt.* XII, 27-28 should read *Matt.* XVI, 27-28.]

18. P. de Labriolle, *op. cit.,* p. 49 [p. 104]:
    "Imbued with the feeling that the world was going to end in a short time (this belief is known to have been held by the first generation of Christians in its entirety, but they would appear to have held it with a degree of intensity that was altogether peculiar to themselves) they wanted . . ."

19. *Job* VII, 5-6.

20. *Job* II, 9; III, 3; X, 8; X, 21-22; XII, 23; XVII, 10-16; XXI, 23-26; XXX, 23.

21. *Passim,* but especially II, 17; III, 19-21; XII, 1-8.

22. Cf. Renan, *The Life of Jesus,* chap. XXV, p. 438:
    The suffering of crucifixion was particularly excruciating because it was possible to live for three or four days in that awful condition. The bleeding of the hands came to an end and was not fatal. The true cause of death was the unnatural position of the body, which brought with it a horrible disturbance of the circulation, dreadful pains in the head and heart, and finally rigidity of the limbs.

23. Porphyry, *Philosophy from Oracles,* in Saint Augustine, *City of God* XIX, 23.

24. Porphyry, quoted by P. de Labriolle, *la Réaction païenne,* p. 211 [271].

25. *Matt.,* VIII, 22. *Matt.,* X, 21-22. *Matt.,* X, 35-37. *Matt.,* XII, 46-50. *Luke,* III, 34; XIV, 26-33. [*Luke* III, 34 should read *Mark* III, 34.]

26. *Luke,* XIV, 26-28 [*Luke* XIV, 26].

27. *Mark,* X, 18.

28. *Romans,* III, 23.

29. *John,* 1, 8; *Corinth.,* X, 13; *Matthew,* XII, 21-23; *id.* XIX, 25-26.

30. VII, 15-24 [VII, 15-23].

31. *Pensées,* no. 199.

32. *Sol.* 1, 2, 7.

33. *Wisdom*, X, 10: "When a righteous man fled from his brother's wrath, she guided him on straight paths; she showed him the Kingdom of God, and gave him knowledge of holy things." [The Latin "sanctorum" is rendered here by the French "choses saintes"; it is often taken, in this context, to refer to angels.]

34. *Luke* XII, 14. *Matt.*, CVIII, 11. *Matt.*, XX, 28.

35. *Colossians* II, 18.

36. *Matt.*, XVIII, 3, 4; XIX, 16. *Mc.*, X, 14, 15. [*Matt.*, XIX, 16 should read *Matt.*, XIX, 15.]

37. VI, 4 [V, 4]

38. *Matt.*: XIV, 33; XII, 58; XV, 28. [*Matt.*, XII, 58 should read *Matt.*, XIII, 58.]

39. *Matt.*: X, 16-18; XX, 1-16; XXV, 14-23. [Two of these references are puzzling, for the passages to which they refer do not relate in any obvious way to the point Camus makes. *Matt.* X, 16-18 is concerned with the mission of the apostles, while *Matt.* XXV, 14-23 recounts the parable of the talents.]

40. *Matt.*, XX, 46; XXV, 34-36. *Mc.*, X, 17, *Luc.*, X, 24.

41. *Col.*, I, 15. *Corinth.*, XV, 45. *Rom.*, I, 4.

42. *Rom.*, I, 20; VIII, 28. *Eph.*, I, 45; III, 11. *Timo* I, 9. [*Eph.*, I, 45, should read *Eph.*, I, 4 and 5; and *Timo* I, 9 should read *Timo* II, 1, 9.]

43. *Rom.*, V, 12; 14 & 15-17; VI, 23.

44. *Rom.*, III, 20. *Rom.*, V, 13. *Rom.*, VII, 7-8.

45. *Rom.*, I, 3; IV, 4. [*Rom.*, IV, 4 should read *Gal* IV, 4.]

46. *Rom.*, III, 25, VI, 6. *Cor.*, VI, 20. *Gal.*, III, 13.

47. Celse, *Discours vrai*. Trans. Rougier: IV, 41. [Rougier: IV, 41 should read II, IV, 41.]

48. Porphyre, *Contre les Chrétiens*. Fragment 77 *in* P. de Labriolle, *la Réaction païenne*, p. 274.

49. *Fragment 84—id.*

50. Tixeront, *History of Dogmas*, chap. III, "the testimony of the Apostolic Fathers."

51. *Id.*, chap. III, p. 115 [1, III, p. 104]: "The title 'apostolic Fathers' is given to the ecclesiastical writers who lived at the end of the first century, or during the first half of the second century. They are supposed to have received from the apostles or their immediate disciples directly the teaching that they pass on."

52. Or "Didache."

53. XXXI, 6, *apud.* Tixeront, III, 2 [1, III, 2].

54. XLIV, *id.*

55. XXXII, 3, 4, *id.*

56. XXXIII, 1, *id.*

57. For all that follows cf. Tixeront, III, 5 [1, III, 5].

58. *To the inhabitants of Smyrna*, I, 1.

59. *Eph.*, XX, 2.
60. *Eph.*, VII, 2.
61. *Smyrna*, I, 1, 2.
62. *Smyrna*, II.
63. *Smyrna*, III.
64. *Smyrna*, VI, 1.
65. *Eph.*, VIII, 2.
66. *Rom.*, VII, 2.
67. Tixeront, *op. cit.*, III, 8 [1, III, 8].
68. V, 1; VII, 3, 5.
69. XI, xi, 1-8.
70. I, 1. *ap.* Tixeront, III, 7 [1, III, 7].
71. Tixeront, III, 3 and 4 [1, III, 3 and 4].
72. *Manduc*, [*Mandata*] IV, 3.
73. *Similit.*, IV, 4.
74. Tixeront, *op. cit.*, III, 6 [1, III, 6].
75. Between 180 and 203.
76. De Faye, *Clément d'Alexandrie*, livre II, chap. II.
77. *Miscellanies*, VII, 80.
78. *Miscellanies*, I, 43.
79. VI, 93.
80. *On Prescription Against Heretics*, VII.
81. *Miscellanies*, I, 18 [I, 1]
82. *To the Colossians*, II, 8.
83. *De Reditu suo*, I, 389, in Rougier, *Celse*, p. 112 [p. 53]
84. *Discours vrai*, III, 37 [III, 87].
85. *John*, III, 16, 36; IV, 14.
86. V, 19, 26.
87. Puech, *les Apologistes grecs du IIe siècle*, id. Tixeront *op. cit.*, V, 1 [I, 5, 1].
88. *Apol.*, II, 13.
89. *Apol.*, I, 44, 59, Tatian, *Oration against the Greeks*, 40, Minucius Felix, *op. cit.*, 34. Tertullian, *Apologet.*, 47. Clement of Alexandria, *Miscellanies*, 1, 28; VI, 44; VI, 153; VI, 159.
90. *Apologet.*, II, 13, 8, 10.
91. Justin, *Dialogue with Trypho*: 16, 17, 108, 122, etc. *Apology*: I, 31-36.
92. *Dialog.*, 63ff.
93. *Oration against the Greeks* (165).
94. *Derision of Gentile Philosophers* (3rd century).
95. *la Réaction païenne*: second part, chap. II.

96. Cf. Boissier, *la Religion romaine*, preface, vol. I, IX: "paganism tries to refashion itself, taking as its model the religion that threatens it and that it combats."

97. Compare especially the episode of the daughter of Jairus (*Luke*, VII, 40) [*Luke*, VIII, 40] and the *Vie d'Apollonius*, IV, 45 (p. 184 of Chassaing's translation).

98. *The Trinity*, I, 1, 3.

99. *Acts*, XVII, 16 [XVII, 23].

100. II, 9.

101. From the beginning of the second century to the end of the third century.

102. First half of the second century.

103. Cf. in Buddhism, a related form of Amidism.

104. De Faye, *Gnostiques et Gnosticisme*, I, chap. II. Amelineau, *Essai sur le Gnosticisme égyptien*.

105. Cf. *Homer's Hymn to Demeter*, 480-83: "Happy is the man who has seen these things while living on earth. But he who has not been initiated into the holy ceremonies and he who has participated in them will never have the same destiny after death in the vast darkness."

106. *Comm. in Rom.*, V; *Hom. in. Luc.*, I; *Comm. in Matt.*, XXXVIII.

107. *Against Heresies*, XXIV, 6, 72c.

108. De Faye, *op. cit.*, page 31.

109. Quoted by De Faye, chap. I. [chap. I, p. 24].

110. Cf. De Faye, *op. cit.*, chap. I [chap. I, pp. 26-27].

111. Book VII.

112. VII, p. 125 [VII, XIII] in Amelineau, *op. cit.*, II, 2.

113. Quoted by Amelineau, p. 135. Compare with the ancient Egyptian beliefs: "The rebels become immovable objects for millions of years," quoted in Amelineau, p. 152.

114. De Faye, *op. cit.*, conclusion pp. 460-63 [pp. 463-66].

115. In Tertullian (*Against Marcion*), Clement of Alexandria (*Miscellanies* III); Origen (*On First Principles*, book II, chap. IV and V) and Philaster (*Epiphanius pseudo Tertullian*); Irenaeus.

116. De Faye, *op. cit.*, I, 4.

117. In *Against Marcion*, chap. VIII [I, 3]. Cf. also *Against Marcion* I, 16: " . . . the sole resource left to them is to divide things into the two classes of visible and invisible, with two gods for their authors, and so to claim the invisible things for their own (the supreme) God," and I, 17; I, 6.

118. *Luke*, V, 36.

119. *Luke*, VI, 43.

120. De Faye, p. 130.

121. Tertullian, *Against Marcion* IV, 6.

122. V, 12-14; V, 27-32; VII, 9, 10; XI and XVI [XVI, 12]; XVIII, 19.

123. *Refutations* I, 7, p. 20.

124. P. 340, lines 12-15 [VII, X].

125. VII, 22 [VII, IX].

126. *Refutations* and *Miscellanies*, XIII [*Miscellanies* IV, 13].

127. De Faye, *op. cit.*, I, 2. Amelineau, *op. cit.*, III, 1, 2, 3, 4, 5.

128. The twelve dedicated to the acting Spirit; the ten, the perfect number according to the Pythagoreans, dedicated to the perfect God.

129. De Faye, chap. II [part II, chap. II]

130. I. 2.

131. Cf. De Faye, *op. cit.*, p. 238.

132. Cf. Amelineau, *op. cit.*, p. 219. De Faye, *op. cit.*, p. 45.

133. XIII, 85, in De Faye, *op. cit.*, p. 42 [IV, XIII, 89].

134. Quoted by the author of the *Dialogue against the Marcionites*. Amelineau, *op. cit.*, p. 230.

135. This at least is the name given to them by De Faye.

136. V, 8 [V, 3].

137. V, 16 [V, 12].

138. V, 15 [V, 14].

139. Quoted by De Faye, *op. cit.*, p. 191.

140. Quoted by De Faye, *op. cit.*, p. 217.

141. Quoted by De Faye, p. 269.

142. In Toussaint, *Saint Paul et l'Hellénisme*. chap. I.

143. De Cherubim, pp. 115-16; Matter, *Histoire du Gnosticisme*, I, chap. V [I, 1, p. 60].

144. M. Matter, *id* [I,1, p. 61].

145. Cf. Bréhier, *les idées philosophiques et religieuses de Philo d'Alexandrie*, part 2, "Dieu, les Intermédiaires et le Monde."

146. *Id.* Part 3, "Le culte spirituel et le progrès moral."

147. J. Guitton, *le Temps et l'Eternité chez Plotin et Saint Augustin*, chap. II, 1, p. 27 [II, 1, p. 71].

148. Compare *Enn.* I [I, 6, 7], " . . . they alone shall attain it . . . who strip themselves of their clothing," and the description of the soul's journey in the mysteries of Mithra; M. Cumont, *The Mysteries of Mithra*, pp. 114 ff. [pp. 144 ff.].

149. Cf. Arnou, *le Désir de Dieu dans la philosophie de Plotin* [p. 52].

150. III, 7, 13; V, 1, 9.

151. Cf. I, 1, 12: "The soul cannot sin. Why then is it punished?"

152. I, 2, 2: "For a thing becomes better because it is limited and because, subject to measure, it leaves the domain of beings which do not have measure and limit."

153. I, 3, 1.

154. V, 8, 7.

155. Cf. also the misuse of a "Metaphysics of Light" in Plotinus. Light is the boundary of the corporeal and incorporeal.
156. VI, 7, 12.
157. II, 9, 16.
158. VI, 9, 1.
159. Cf. especially this passage: for the religious role of the hypostases: V, 1 on the three hypostases. Cf. on their explicative value: V, 3, on the knowing hypostases.
160. VI, 6 [V, 1, 6]: "Everything that is begotten longs for and loves the being which has begotten it."
161. V, 1, 6.
162. V, 2, 6.
163. V, 1, 6; V, 2; V, 3, 4.
164. VI, 7. 35.
165. III, 8, 10.
166. I, 6, 6: "We must therefore employ similar methods in order to inquire into the Good and the Beautiful, the Ugly and the Bad. We must first say that the Beautiful is also the Good."
167. VI, 8, 9.
168. VI, 2.
169. Cf. also VI, 7 [VI, 7, 17]: "From the time when life directs its glances toward it, it is unlimited; once life has seen it, it is limited." . . . "When it looks at the One it immediately receives limit, determination, form . . . ; this life which has received a limit is Intellect."
170. VI, 7, 15.
171. V, 2, conclusion.
172. V, 1, 6.
173. V, 4, 1.
174. III, 8, 10.
175. II, 1, 4 [V, 8, 4]. We also quote, in a footnote because of its length, a text whose imagery and clarity throw light on this aspect of Plotinus' thought. VI, 8, 9:

> Suppose that in our visible world, each part remained what it is without commingling, but that all parts came together, so that if one part appeared, for example the fixed spheres, the sun and other stars would immediately follow; in it, as on a transparent sphere, the earth, the sea and all the animals are seen; in effect, then, all things are seen. Imagine then the presence of such a sphere in the soul. Keep that image and picture another like sphere set aside from the mass. Exclude also the differences of position and of the material image; do not be content with picturing a second sphere smaller than the first . . . All are each

and each is all; all together are different in their powers; but they
all form a unique being with multiple power.

176. VI, 7, 14.
177. Principal texts: (a) in general: IV, 3, 4, 5. (b) definition: I, 8, 14; III, 4,
3; IV, 6, 31; IV, 8, 7; IV, 8, 3; VI, 7, 35. (c) analysis: III, 8, 5; IV, 3, 4, 9;
IV, 9. (d) relationship between the World-Soul and individual souls: III,
1, 14; IV, 3, 5 and 6; IV, 3, 12; IV, 3, 17; IV, 8, 6; IV, 9, 8; VI, 1, 2; V,
2, 7; VI, 4, 16; VI, 5, 7; VI, 1, 7. [Many of these references are confusing.
Camus refers to *Enneads* IV, 6, 31; III, 1, 4; IV, 9, 8 and V, 2, 7, none of
which exists. He claims, moreover, that VI, 1, 2 and VI, 1, 7, for example,
are obviously relevant to the question of the relationships between the
World-Soul and individual souls, and this is by no means the case. IV,
6, 31 should perhaps read IV, 3, 4; III, 4 may well be III, 2, 14; IV, 9, 8
is perhaps VI, 9, 8 and V, 3, 7 should almost certainly read V, 2, 2.]
178. IV, 8, 7.
179. V, 4, 2.
180. III, 2 and 3.
181. IV, 3, 4, 5, "Difficulties about the soul."
182. IV, 9, 5.
183. Note on IV, 3, p. 17.
184. IV, 3, 4.
185. IV, 3, 8.
186. IV, 4, 3.
187. IV, 3, 8.
188. IV, 3, 12; IV, 3, 17; IV, 8, 5.
189. IV, 3, 13; VI, 7, 7; V, 2, 7.
190. III, 12, 4, 5 [IV, 1, 2; IV, 4, 5].
191. IV, 3, 14.
192. VI, 5, 10.
193. IV, 3, 8.
194. II, 5, 5.
195. VI, 5, 10.
196. II, 3, 9.
197. V, 5, 12.
198. I, 2, 7; VI, 3, 16; VI, 9, 7.
199. VI, 7, 22.
200. VI, 7, 22. Translation Arnou, *le Désir de Dieu dans la philosophie de Plotin*, p. 82
[pp. 86-87].
201. VI, 7. 16.
202. III, 5, 9.
203. Edw. Caird: " . . . the philosophy of Plotinus is the condemnation of
Greek dualism, just because it is he who carries it to its utmost point."

The Evolution of Theology in the Greek Philosophers, vol. II, pp. 210 and 393 [vol. II, p. 315].

204. V, 1, 1.
205. V, 5, 9.
206. Again VI, 5, 12: "It does not have to come in order to be present. You are the one who have gone away; to depart is not to leave it in order to go elsewhere; for it is there. But, although remaining altogether close to it, you have turned away from it."
207. Compare with Christian mysticism. Suso ex. no. 54 [*l'exemplaire*, 54e]: "It is to be at the same time in all things and outside of all things. That is why a teacher has said that God is like a circle whose centre is everywhere and whose circumference is nowhere."
208. Arnou, *op. cit.*, p. 191 [p. 91].
209. V, 5, 8.
210. I, 6, 8.
211. Porphyre, *Life of Plotinus*, 23.
212. Principal texts: IV, 8, 1; VI, 9, 9; VI, 7, 39; VI, 8, 19.
213. IV, 8, 1.
214. Perhaps a sect of Disciples of the Mother: II, 9, 10; II, 9, 12.
215. II, 9, 5.
216. II, 9, 9.
217. II, 9, 18.
218. II, 9, 15.
219. II, 9, 5 especially II, 9, 17: " . . . it is not really possible for anything to be beautiful outwardly, but ugly inwardly."
220. II, 9, 16.
221. II, 9, 9.
222. II, 9, 18.
223. II, 9, 15, conclusion.
224. II, 9, 4; II, 9, 11.
225. Saint Jérôme, Chronique d'Eusèbe, *Manuscrit de Macarius*.
226. Fragment 4 quoted by de Labriolle, *la Réaction païenne*, p. 256.
227. Frag. 73 in Labriolle, *op. cit.*, p. 212 [p. 272].
228. Frag. 52 in Labriolle, *op. cit.*, p. 272.
229. *Corinthians*, VII, 31.
230. Frag. 34 in Labriolle, *op. cit.*, p. 260.
231. Frag. 94 in Labriolle, *op. cit.*, p. 287 [p. 277].
232. Fragments 23, 35, 49, 54, 55 in Labriolle, *op. cit.*, p. 287.
233. It is here that the question of the orientalism of Plotinus is said to arise.
234. For the history of Arianism, cf. Tixeront, *History of Dogmas*, vol. II, chap. II.
235. VIII, 22 [*Provbs.* VIII, 22].

236. J. XIV, 28.
237. J. XVII, 3.
238. J. V, 19; also J. XXI, 33, 38; *Luke*, II, 52; *Matt.*, XXVI, 39; *Phil.* 19; *Hebs.*, I, 9.
239. J. X, 30.
240. J. X, 38.
241. J. XII, 45.
242. In Hefele, *History of the Councils*, I, pp. 443, 444 [Book II, chap. II, p. 294].
243. No. 25.
244. Plotinus died in 270.
245. Saint Basil: *Homilies on the precept "Observance*," par. 7, and Eusebius of Caesarea, *Evangelical Preparation* XII, 17: "It is the radiance of a light which escapes from it without disturbing its tranquility."
246. I, 6, On beauty; III, 6, On providence [III, 3]; III, 4, On our allotted guardian spirit; IV, 3, On difficulties about the soul; 6, On the three primary hypostases [V, 1]; V, 6, The principle beyond being does not think.
247. Alfaric, *l'Évolution intellectuelle de Saint Augustin.*
248. *Conf.* VIII, chap. 9 [VII, 9].
249. 354, 430.
250. *Conf.* VIII, chap. 1 [VIII, 2]: "I was still firmly held in thraldom by a woman."
251. Cf. Salvian, *Government of God*, Latin Patrology, VII, 16-17: "... overflowing with vices, seething with iniquity, men benumbed with depravity and swollen with food stank of foul pleasure." [Camus paraphrases at this point what Salvian writes in his *Government of God*, P.L. 53, VII, 16-17:
    I see a city burning with every kind of iniquity; filled with riches, but more with vice; men surpassing each other in the villainy of their depravity; some struggling to outdo in their rapacity; others to outdo in impurity; some drowsy with wine; others distended with too much food; some (bedecked) with flowers; others besmeared with oil; all wasted by varied kinds of indolence and luxury and almost all prostrate in the death of their sins.]
252. "He persuaded me that I ought to trust more in men that taught than in those that ordained obedience." *Conf.* VII, 67, 24. Tes. col. 739. [The passage to which Camus refers at this point is not to be found in the *Confessions*. In *The Happy Life* I, 1, 4, however, Saint Augustine writes:
    From the age of nineteen, having read in the school of rhetoric that book of Cicero's called *Hortensius*, I was inflamed by such a great love of philosophy that I considered devoting myself to it at once. Yet I was not free of these mists which could confuse my course, and I confess that for some quite a while I was led astray, with my eyes fixed on those stars that sink into the ocean. A childish superstition determined me from thorough investigation, and, as soon as I was more courageous, *I threw off the darkness*

> *and learned to trust more in men that taught than in those that ordained obedience.* (Emphasis added.)]

253. *The Happy Life* 4 [*Confessions* VII, 7].

254. *Conf.* VII, col. 152 P.L., vol. 33 col. 737 [*Conf.* VII, 5 P.L. 32, col. 737]. Cf. also on the fear of death: *Conf.* VI, 16; VII, 19-26; *Sol.* I, 16; II, 1 [*Sol.* I, 9, 16; II, 1, 1]. [In *Confessions* VII, 5, Saint Augustine writes: "Such thoughts I turned over within my wretched breast which was overburdened with the most biting concern about the fear of death and (my) failure to discover truth."]

255. J. Martin, *Philon* (1907), p. 67: "The Fathers naturally continue, after Saint Paul, to employ the language which Greek and Alexandrian speculation had created; and their use of this language expressed truths which neither Philo nor any Alexandrian had grasped" and Puech, *les Apologistes grecs* . . . (1912), p. 297 [pp. 296-97]: "the essential fact is that the teaching of the Apologists is initially religious and not philosophic; they believe first in Jesus, Son of God. And then they explain his divinity by saying that the Word existed before Jesus." And finally le Breton, *les Origines du Dogme de la Trinité* (1910), p. 521: "If the theology of the Logos appears so profoundly transformed [in Saint John], it is because its application to the person of Jesus made it necessary for it to undergo these transformations."

256. *On the Nature of the Good:* IV P.L., vol. 42, col. 553.

257. *Against Julian:* III, 206 P.L., vol. 45; col. 334. [*Incomplete Work Against the Second Reply of Julian,* III, 206, P.L., vol. 45, col. 1334.]

258. *The Free Choice of the Will:* L3, chap. 18, no. 51; P.L., 32-1268.

259. *On John.* V, 1; P.L., 18; vol. 35: col. 414 [col. 1414], and also *Sermon* 156, II, 12; P.L., vol. 38: col. 856: "When I say to you: without the help of God you do nothing, I am saying that you do nothing good, for without the help of God the freedom you have is the freedom to do what is evil."

260. The *City of God* V, 18, 3; P.L., vol. 41; vol. 165, *id.* V. 19, P.L., vol. 41, col. 165-166; *Letters* 138, III, 17; P.L., vol. 33, col. 33; *On Patience*, XXVII, 25; P.L., vol. 40; col. 624. *On the Grace of Christ*, XXIV, 25; P.L., vol. 44, *id.* 376.

261. The *City of God* XXI, 16 P.L., vol. 41, col. 770 and XIX, 25 chap., entitled: "There could not be true virtues where there is no true religion" (vol. 41, col. 656). Cf. also *On Various Questions* 83, 66 P.L., vol. 40, col. 63.

262. Especially *On Various Questions*, book I, 2. vol. 40, col. III.

263. On the metaphysical plane. In the domain of psychology Saint Augustine admits free will.

264. *On Various Questions* I, 2, 16: P.L., vol. 40; col. 160, 161.

265. For the works of Pelagius (*Commentary on the Epistles of Saint Paul; Letter to Demetrias; Handbook on Faith to Pope Innocent*) and those of Julian and Celestius, P.L., vol. XXX. [The writings of Julian and Celestius, and the *Handbook on Faith* of Pelagius are, in fact, to be found in volume XLV of Migne's Latin Patrology.]

266. Julian, in Aug., *Against Julian;* 1, 78; P.L., vol. 45, col. 1101 [*Incomplete Work Against the Second Reply of Julian* 1, 78-1, 79; P.L., vol. 45, col. 1102].
267. Pelagius, in Aug., *On Nature and Grace,* Cf. also *On the Grace of Christ* I, 5. *On the Deeds of Pelagius.*
268. In Aug., *On the Deeds of Pelagius* 23 [XI, 23].
269. *To Demetrias,* 8, 17.
270. *Ap.* August., *On the Grace of Christ,* I, 27, 30.
271. *Ap.* Tixeront, *History of Dogmas,* chap. XI [III, XI].
272. *Rom.* VII, 25.
273. *On Genesis Against the Manichees* II, VIII, 32 [II, XXI, 32].
274. *Admonition and Grace* [XII, 33].
275. *Psalm* L, Book of Job. XIX, 4; *Ephesians,* II, 3, especially on *Romans* V, 12; *John,* III, 5.
276. *Against Julian* I, 50, 54, vol. 45, col. 1072 [Incomplete Work Against the Second Reply of Julian]. *Id.* The *City of God,* XXII, 22; I, 3. [The passage to which the last of these references refers is irrelevant to the point Camus makes. He would have done better to have referred to the *City of God* XIX, 5 ff., or even to III, 3 of this same work.]
277. "Universa massa perditionis" ("Wholescale mass of perdition"). *To Simplicius on various questions* 1, *question* II, 16. [This should read: "una quaedam massa peccati" ("One single mass of sin.")]
278. *Against Julian* III, 199 P.L., vol. 45, col. 1333 [*Incomplete Work Against the Second Reply of Julian* III, 199].
279. *On the Predestination of the Saints* 5, 7, 22 [II, 5; III, 7; XI, 22].
280. *Letters* CCXVII.
281. *Letters* CLXXXVI, 7 [III, 7].
282. *Enchiridion* XCVIII and XCIX. *Letters* CLXXXVI, 15. *On the Gift of Persistence,* 17 [VIII, 17].
283. *On Grace and Free Will* 4. [II, 4].
284. *Enn.* IV, III, 24.
285. *On Various Questions* LXXXIII, qu. 46, No. 2, P.L., vol. 40, col. 30.
286. *On Various Questions* LXXXIII, qu. 46, No. 2, P.L., vol. 40, col. 30.
287. "I think, therefore he is." If this has been compared to the *cogito,* it is also because Augustine's God is an inner God.
288. Compare *Enn.* V, 7, 3; VI, 8, 3.
289. *The Trinity,* IV, ch. I, No. 3, P.L, vol. 42, col. 888.
290. *Against the Preachings of the Arians* 3 [I, 3].
291. *Against Maximinus* II, 10 [II, 10, 2].
292. *The Trinity,* II, 8, 9, P.L, vol. 42, col. 85. [These quotations are taken not, as Camus claims, from *The Trinity,* but from Tixeront's *History of Dogmas,* II, p. 362. *The Trinity,* II, 8 and 9, moreover, are to be found not in Migne's *Latin Patrology,* vol. 42, col. 85, but in columns 849 and 850.]
293. *The Trinity,* VI, 9, vol. 42, col. 93 [VI, 1, P.L., vol. 42, col. 929].

294. *Sermon* CXC, 2.
295. *Sermon* CLXXXVI, 1.
296. *Conf.* X, chap. XL.
297. E. Gilson, *The Christian Philosophy of Saint Augustine*, conclusion.
298. *Tractate on John* 29, 6 P.L., vol. 35, col. 1630. ["Si non potes intelligere, crede ut intelligas, praecedit fides, sequitur intellectus. Ergo noli quaerere intelligere ut *credas*, sed crede ut intelligas." (Emphasis added) Moreover, while the second sentence of this quotation is to be found, as Paul Archambault correctly points out (*op.cit.*, p. 149), in Augustine's tractate on John 29, 6, its first sentence belongs to *Sermon* 118, 1.]
299. *The Lord's Sermon on the Mount* 1, chap. III, no. 10, P.L., vol. 1233, col. 1233.
300. The first systematic treatise on Christian morality, that of Ambrose, written in the second half of the fourth century, is based not on the Gospels but on Cicero's *Duties.*
301. And *Letter* XXII, 7:

> "I, yes I, who from fear of hell had condemned myself to such a prison, inhabited only by scorpions and wild beasts, often imagined that I had been transported into the midst of girls as they danced. My face was pale from fasting and my mind was hot with desire." In P. De Labriolle, *Histoire de la littérature latine chrétienne*, p. 451 [503].

Chapter IX

Bibliography Of Dissertation

The Supporters of Christianity

Loisy.	*Les Mystères païens et le mystère chrétien.* Paris, 1919.
Cumont.	*Les Religions orientales dans le paganisme romain*, 1907.
Cumont.	*Les Mystères de Mithra.*
Foucart.	*Recherches sur l'origine et la nature des mystères d'Eleusis*, 1895.
Foucart.	*Les Associations religieuses chez les grecs.*
Gernet et Boulanger.	*Le Génie grec dans la Religion*, Paris, 1932.

Alexandrian Metaphysics

a. Texts:

Plotin.	*Ennéades I to VI,* 5 inclusive, trans. Bréhier; VI, 6 to VI, 9, trans. Bouillet.
Porphyre.	*Vie de Plotin,* vol. I of the Bréhier trans.
Proclus.	*Commentaires du Parménide,* trans. Chaignet, 3 vol.
Damasius.	*Des principes,* trans. Chaignet, 1898.

b. Studies:

Vacherot.	*Histoire de la philosophie d'Alexandrie.* 3 vol., 1846-1851.
Simon.	*Id.* 2 vol., 1843-1845.
Ravaisson.	*Essai sur la métaphysique d'Aristote.*
Bois.	*Essai sur les origines de la philosophie judéo-alexandrine,* Toulouse, 1890.
Bret.	*Essai historique et critique sur l'école juive d'Alexandrie.*

Bréhier.	*Les Idées philosophiques et religieuses de Philon d'Alexandrie*, Paris, 1908.
Kurppe.	*Philon et la Patristique* in "Essais d'histoire": Philosophie, Paris, 1902.
Bréhier.	*La Philosophie de Plotin*, Paris, 1903.
Arnou.	*Le Désir de Dieu dans la philosophie de Plotin*, Paris, 1921.
Guyot.	*L'Infinité divine depuis Philon le Juif jusqu'à Plotin*, Paris, 1908.
Picavet.	*"Hypostases plotiniennes et Trinité chrétienne,"* Annuaire de l'Ecole des Hautes-Etudes, 1917.
Guitton.	*Le Temps et l'Eternité chez Plotin et Saint Augustin*, Paris, 1933.
Picavet.	*Plotin et les Mystères d'Eleusis*, Paris, 1903.
Cochez.	*Les Religions de l'Empire dans la philosophie de Plotin*, 1913.
Cochez.	*"Plotin et les Mystères d'Isis," Revue néoscolastique*, 1911.
C. Elsee.	*Neoplatonism in relation to Christianity*, Cambridge, 1908.
Inge.	*The Philosophy of Plotinus*, London, 1918.
Lindsay.	*The Philosophy of Plotinus*, 1902.
Fuller.	*The Problem of Evil in Plotinus*, Cambridge, 1912.
Caird.	*The Evolution of Theology in the Greek Philosophers*. 2 vol., Glasgow, 1904. *Plotin*: II, pp. 210-346.

Gnosticism

a. Studies:

De Faye.	*Introduction à l'étude du Gnosticisme*, Paris, 1903.
	Gnostiques et Gnosticisme, Paris, 1913.
	Clément d'Alexandrie, 2nd ed. Paris, 1898.
Matter.	*Histoire critique du Gnosticisme*, 2 vol., 2nd ed., Paris, 1844.
Mansel.	*The Gnostic Heresies*.
King.	*The Gnostics*.
Salmon.	*Gnosticisme*.
Amelineau.	*Essai sur le Gnosticisme égyptien*, Guimet, XIV.
De Beausobre.	*Histoire du Manichéisme*, 2 vol., 1739-1744.
Cumont.	*Recherches sur le Manichéisme*. I: 'la Cosmogonie manichéenne d'après Theodore Bar. Khoni', Brussels, 1908.
Alfaric.	*Les Ecritures manichéennes*.

b. Texts. Cf. especially:

Tertullian.   *The Prescription against Heresies* in Migne's *Latin Patrology*, vol. II, col. 10 to 72.
Against Marcion—id., col. 239 to 468.
Against Valentinus, col. 523-524.

Evolution Of Christianity

General Works:

Tixeront.   *Histoire des Dogmes dans l'antiquité chrétienne*, 3 vol., Paris, 1915, 1919, 1921.
P. De Labriolle.   *Histoire de la littérature latine chrétienne*, Paris, 1920. 2nd ed., 1923.
Puech.   *Histoire de la littérature grecque chrétienne, jusqu'à la fin du IVe siècle*, 3 vol., 1928-1930.
Puech.   *Les Apologistes grecs du IIe siècle de notre ère*, Paris, 1912.
Le Breton.   *Les Origines du dogme de la Trinité*, 1920, 1923 ed.

Hellenism And Christianity

a. Studies:

Havet.   *Le Christianisme et ses origines*, 4 vol., Paris, 1800-1884.
Aubié.   *Les Chrétiens de l'Empire romain de la fin des Antonins au début du IIIe siècle*, Paris, 1881.
Boissier.   *La Fin du paganisme*, 4th ed. 1903.
Corbière.   *Le Christianisme et la fin de la philosophie antique*, Paris, 1921.
Toussaint.   *L'Hellénisme et l'Apôtre Paul.*
Lenain De Tillemont. *Mémoires pour servir à l'Histoire ecclésiastique des six premiers siècles*, 1702.
Dourif.   *Du Stoïcisme et Du Christianisme . . .* , Paris, 1863.
Bréhier.   "Hellénisme et Christianisme aux premiers siècles de notre ère," *Revue philosophique*, 27-5-35.
T. R. Glover.   *The Influence of Christ in the Ancient World.*

b. Polemics:

P. De Labriolle.   *La Réaction païenne*, Paris, 1934.
Aubié.   *La Polémique païenne à la fin du IIe siècle*, Paris, 1878.

Rougier.   *Celse ou le conflit de la civilisation antique et du christianisme primitif*, Paris, 1925 (avec traduction du *Discours vrai* de Celse).

Paul Allard.   *Julien l'Apostat*, 3 vol., Paris, 1900-1903.

                       Julien l'Apostat, oeuvres, Bridez edition, Paris, 1932.

c. On Saint Augustine:

In the methodical and almost complete bibliography in Gilson: *Introduction à l'étude de Saint Augustin*, Paris, 1931.

I. Works—Migne: *Latin Patrology*, vols. XXII to XL inclusive. Chief works mentioned in this work.

  (a) *Confessions*, vol. XXXII, col. 659 to 905.

   City of God, vol. XXXVIII, col. 13 to 806.

   Soliloquies, vol. XXXVII, col. 863 to 902.

   Meditations, vol. XXXVII, col. 901 to 944.

   The Happy Life, vol. XXXII, col. 959 to 977.

  (b) Against the Heresies:

   On Two Souls Against the Manichaeans, vol. XXXIX, col. 93 to 112.

   Against Fortunatus the Manichaean, vol. XXXIX, col. 111 to 130.

   Against Adimantus the Disciple of Mani, vol. XXXIX, col. 129 to 174.

   On the Nature of the Good Against the Manichaeans, vol. XXXIX, col. 551 to 578.

   Against Julian, vol. XXXIX, col. 1094 to 1612.

   On Nature and Grace, vol. XLI, col. 199 to 248.

   On the Deeds of Pelagius, vol. XLI, col. 319 to 360.

   On the Grace of Christ and Original Sin, vol. XLI, col. 359 to 416.

   On Grace and Free Will, vol. XLI, col. 881 - 914.

  (c) *Letters*, vol. XXXIII.

  (d) *Sermons*, vol. XXXVI.

II. General Studies.

E. Gilson.	*Introduction à l'étude de saint Augustin*, Paris, 1931.
Portalié.	Article "Saint Augustin" in *Dictionnaire de Théologie catholique*. Vol. I, col. 2268-2472, 1902.
Nourrisson.	*La Philosophie de saint Augustin*, 2 vol., 2nd ed., 1809.
Alfaric.	*L'Évolution intellectuelle de saint Augustin*, vol. I: *Du Manichéisme au Néoplatonisme*, 1918.
Boyer.	*L'Idée de vérité dans la philosophie de saint Augustin*, Paris, 1920.
	Christianisme et Néoplatonisme dans la formation de saint Augustin, Paris, 1920.
J. Martin.	*Saint Augustin*, 1901.
Grandgeorge.	*Saint Augustin et le Néoplatonisme*, 1896.
Cayré.	*La Contemplation augustinienne*, Paris, 1927.

NOTION OF CHRISTIAN PHILOSOPHY

E. Gilson.	"La Notion de philosophie chrétienne" in *Bulletin de la Société française de philosophie*, March 1931.
E. Bréhier.	"Le Problème de la philosophie chrétienne," *Revue de métaphysique et de morale*, April 1931.
Souriau.	"Y a-t-il une philosophie chrétienne?" *Revue de métaphysique et de morale*, July 1932.
E. Gilson.	*L'Esprit de la philosophie médiévale*. 2 vol., Paris, 1932. Chap. I: "Le Problème de la philosophie chrétienne."

CONCLUSION

Camus, as we have seen, was greatly concerned, even as a young man, with "la condition humaine" of Malraux, and with the closely-related theme of human salvation.[1] The depth of this concern is clearly evidenced in *Métaphysique chrétienne et Néoplatonisme*, which examines Christian, Gnostic and Plotinian views on the nature and destiny of man.[2] "Exile" and the "kingdom" are also major themes of *Le Mythe de Sisyphe* and *L'Etranger* in which Camus couples his absurdist view of life with an unquestionably "Hellenic" view of human destiny.

Camus' early philosophy is an absurdist one. Human life, in the opinion of this author, is meaningless. The meaning of life which Camus denies is not, however, of some diffuse or indefinable kind: it is, on the contrary, a particular kind of meaning, namely, that which is attributed to life by all those who, like Camus himself, believe that man possesses deep within his nature the desire for communion with God but who, unlike Camus, believe that God exists and that He answers to man's need of Him. In Camus' opinion there is no God, nor is there any evidence pointing to His existence; to accept religious faith is to endorse the view that man's ultimate destiny lies outside of this world, a view that Camus finds unacceptable.

> "I desire to know God and the soul," says Saint Augustine, "nothing more—nothing whatever." This is true also, and in large measure, of the Gospels, where all that matters is the Kingdom of God, which can be attained only by renouncing so much that belongs to this world. The idea of the Kingdom of God does not first appear in the New Testament. The Jews were already familiar with the word and what it represented. In the Gospels, however, this kingdom has nothing terrestrial about it. It is spiritual. It is the contemplation of God himself.[3]

Man's existence, Camus maintains, *is* absurd, and fidelity to the human condition demands that he accept the finality of death and give to his limited existence its sole proper meaning, by aspiring only toward mastery of his own kingdom.

> As it is formulated toward the first centuries of our time, Hellenism implies that man is self-sufficient and that he himself has the ability to explain the universe and his destiny. His temples are built to his stature. In a certain sense the Greeks believed that existence could be justified by reference to sport and to beauty. The shape of their hills, or a young man running on a beach, revealed to them the whole secret of the universe. Their gospel said: our kingdom is of this world. It is the "Everything is fitting for me, my Universe which fits your purpose" of Marcus Aurelius.[4]

To promote authentic existence is "to live and to create in the very midst of the desert." This is what Camus calls, in the language of *Le Mythe de Sisyphe,* "revolt."

The philosophy of *Le Mythe de Sisyphe* and *L'Etranger* is, however, a highly inadequate one, for that "revolt," which is advocated in the name of authenticity, entails *"la passion"* and *"la liberté"*; and while "freedom" is the equivalent of licence, "intensity" or passion is no more than the hedonistic enjoyment of life that almost invariably accompanies the moral indifferentism of the rebel. This is a philosophy which reposes upon the ethical thought of Nietzsche, as its authority; it emphasizes human freedom at the entire expense of moral responsibility. In *Le Mythe de Sisyphe,* therefore, Camus tells us that there are, in the eyes of *"l'homme absurde,"* responsible people but no guilty ones; in *L'Etranger,* Meursault insists that the murder of the Arab is neither a sin nor a crime.

Camus' thinking on the absurd, from which this ethic emanates, is also seriously flawed, for he bases his absurdism on two assumptions, to each of which he is fully and equally committed: that man is made for the Absolute and that God does not exist. Yet his atheism, which is essentially that of Nietzsche, remains unproven, since religion need not be Apollonian and is not necessarily inimical to man's desire for moral autonomy. Christian thought, which preoccupied Camus throughout his life, does not, of course, deny man his final end of beatitude after death. For many religious thinkers, however, "admission to bliss is at once the ultimate end of human striving, the reward merited by fidelity to moral duty, and the fulfillment of all the human capacities for joy."[5]

Moreover, the human nostalgia for the Absolute is a factor that Camus leaves entirely unexplained, whether in religious or in secular terms. His position in this regard contrasts very strongly with that of Paul Ricoeur, for example, who compares the phenomenological interpretation of religious consciousness with the psychoanalytic one of Freud and argues, very convincingly, that the understanding of man's openness to the Transcendant requires both an "archaeology" and a "teleology" of the human subject.[6] Mackey is therefore correct when he claims that the "naïve agnosticism" of *Le Mythe de Sisyphe* is the product, in large measure, of Camus' refusal seriously to consider the evidence that religious men have always offered for their convictions.[7] He is also correct when he goes on to add:

> The atheistic existentialists who say that the theistic existentialists jump in far too facile a fashion from their description of man's need for God to the affirmation that God exists and that man's destiny is bound up with God make an almost

equally facile use of this same need, if in the opposite direction. They have never quite squarely faced up to the implications of the fact that the need for the absolute *is* the deepest need, the most insidious desire in man.[8]

Camus' early philosophy, for all its faults, is a profoundly valuable one, for it underlines, in both literary and philosophical genres, and therefore in a manner particularly appropriate to our time, the point that was so strongly emphasized by Saint Augustine: that the desire for totality is the essential human dimension. Modern man, no less than his ancient and medieval counterparts, carries with him, as Plotinus put it, the memory of a lost homeland. He is therefore a being who, as Jean Guitton intimates, lives in time but longs for eternity, one who, in a very profound sense, is an exile even within his own terrestrial kingdom.

The soul must plunge into its own origins, the remembrance of which it bears within itself . . . We must not batten on what is not the soul, though it is in the soul; rather, we must return to that homeland, *the remembrance of which tinges our souls' disquiet.*[9]

This is the feature of the human condition which Camus continued to stress, not only in his novel *La Peste* and in his philosophical treatise *L'Homme révolté,* but in that series of literary essays, published as late as 1957, which comprise *L'Exil et le royaume.* It is impossible, therefore, to avoid the conclusion that while much of Camus' intellectual output is of a literary kind, a great deal of this literary work is unquestionably philosophical.

NOTES AND REFERENCES

CHAPTER I

1. Camus' notebook entry, dated February 21, 1941 reads: "Finished *Sisyphus*. The three absurds are now complete." The "three absurds" are *Le Mythe de Sisyphe*, *L'Etranger* and *Caligula*. Page references for Camus' writings are given to the Pléiade edition of his works and to the relevant English translations listed in the bibliography. Where I have found the English translations to be inaccurate, or where such do not exist, I have provided my own translations and included the relevant French quotations in the notes.

   The Pléiade edition of Camus' works is in two volumes. The first of these volumes is entitled *Essais;* the second bears the title *Théâtre, récits, nouvelles*. This edition does not include the *Carnets* nor *La Mort heureuse*.

2. In the preface to the first English edition of *Le Mythe de Sisyphe* (1946), Camus writes:

   > For me, *The Myth of Sisyphus* marks the beginning of an idea which I was to pursue in *The Rebel*. It attempts to resolve the problem of suicide, as *the Rebel* attempts to resolve that of murder, in both cases without the aid of eternal values . . . the fundamental subject of *The Myth of Sisyphus* is this: it is legitimate and necessary to wonder whether life has a meaning; therefore it is legitimate to meet the problem of suicide face to face.

3. *Le Mythe de Sisyphe*, in *Essais*, p. 100 (trans. p. 12).

4. *Ibid.*, p. 119 (trans. p. 32).

5. See Jean Paul Sartre, "An Explication of *the Stranger*," in Germaine Brée's *Camus: A Collection of Critical Essays*, pp. 108-121.

6. *Le Mythe de Sisyphe*, in *Essais*, p. 105 (trans. p. 17).

7. John Cruickshank, for example, in his *Albert Camus and The Literature of Revolt*, p. 49, tells us that "intellectual experience of the absurd is the experience of a person who has expected—no doubt on the basis of his own experience—a chaos impervious to reason. The absurd is the conclusion arrived at by those who have assumed the possibility of a total explanation of existence by the mind but who discover instead an unbridgeable gulf between rationality and experience." R. D. Gorchov, in *Albert Camus' Concept of Absurdity*, pp. 94-95, writes:

   > Having stated examples of strangeness, Camus proceeds to offer the reader his definition of the word: it means *déraisonnable*, without reason.

It may also be defined as irrational. This word is the adjective employed to describe the world as it presents itself to rational scrutiny. Absurdity may therefore be characterized as the complete otherness of reason and the world.

8.   *Le Mythe de Sisyphe*, in *Essais*, p. 113 (trans. p. 26).

9.   *Ibid.*, p. 110 (trans. pp. 22-23).

10. *Ibid.*, p. 113 (trans. p. 26).

11. *Ibid.*, p. 111 (trans. p. 24).

12. Sartre writes ("Explication," p. 117):

> But what are the particular occasions that create this uneasiness in us? The *Myth of Sisyphus* gives us an example:
>
> > A man is talking on the telephone. We cannot hear him behind the glass partition, but we can see his senseless mimicry. We wonder why he is alive! This answers the question almost too well, for the example reveals a certain bias in the author. The questioning of a man who is telephoning and whom we cannot hear is really only *relatively* absurd, because it is part of an incomplete circuit. Listen in on an extension, however, and the circuit is completed; human activity recovers its meaning. Therefore, one would have, in all honesty, to admit that there are only relative absurdities and only in relation to absolute rationalities.

13. *Le Mythe de Sisyphe*, in *Essais*, p. 110 (trans. p. 23). Emphasis added.

14. *Summa Theologiae* I^a II^{ae}, qu. 3, art. 1.

15. J. P. Mackey, "Christianity and Albert Camus," p. 394.

16. Gorchov, "Albert Camus' Concept of Absurdity," p. 94.

17. Cruickshank, *Albert Camus*, p. 49.

18. Sartre, *Explication*, p. 109.

19. Mackey, "Christianity and Albert Camus," p. 393. (Emphasis added) The point which Mackey makes at some length is expressed briefly by Roger Quilliot in his introduction to Camus' *Métaphysique chrétienne et Néoplatonisme*, when he says that "pour le jeune Camus la religion était, ou bien une affaire de vieille femme, un divertissement devant la mort, ou bien l'expression vague des élans de jeunesse vers quelque chose de plus grand qui soi, *l'obscur désir de se survivre et de donner un sens à l'existence: bref, le sens du tragique et du sacré*." (Emphasis added)

20. P. McCarthy, *Camus: A Critical Analysis of His Life and Work*, p. 147.

21. *Le Mythe de Sisyphe*, in *Essais*, pp. 140-141 (trans. pp. 56-57).

22. *Le Mythe de Sisyphe*, in *Essais*, pp. 183-184 (trans. pp. 97-98).

23. Cf. *Essais*, pp. 125-126 (trans. pp. 39-40). When dealing with "absurd creation," moreover, Camus commends Dostoevsky for posing the "absurd problem" in, for example, *The Brothers Karamazov*, but criticizes him severely for his "existential leap."

24. *Métaphysique chrétienne et Néoplatonisme*, in *Essais*, pp. 1304-1305.

25. I say "philosophic influence" because there were other influences at work as well. Roger Quilliot, for example, points out that: "D'une certaine façon, Camus était à la fois étranger à l'esprit religieux et profondément marqué par l'inquiétude métaphysique."

26. See *The Range of Reason*, p. 104.

27. This is a view that Camus frequently expresses, not only for his diploma thesis but in the *Carnets* as well, for his notebooks often refer, in terms that are highly reminiscent of Nietzsche, to the importance of life in *this* world. An entry of June 1937, for example, reads: " . . . Pointlessness of the problem of immortality. We are interested in our destiny, admittedly. But *before*, not after."

28. Herbert Lottman tells us that in 1943 Jean Paulhan met with François Mauriac to discuss the award of the *Grand Prix de Littérature* of the French Academy. (Mauriac had been a member of the Academy since 1933.) Paulhan argued strongly that this award should be given to Camus for *L'Etranger*, which, he said, had as its subject the question, "How can I love my mother (or my wife) if I don't love God?"

    Lottman also tells us that while "in the first major review of *L'Etranger*, Sartre would recognize its existential quality . . . a Finnish economic geographer would tell the author of this book that he saw in the beach scene, when sunstruck Meursault pulled the trigger, a textbook example of the effect of climate on population" (*Albert Camus: A Biography*, p. 244).

    The extraordinarily naive view that Meursault shot the Arab "quite literally . . . because of the sun" is one that is endorsed by Hazel Barnes in *The Literature of Possibility*, p. 183.

29. Cf. the introduction to the first English edition of *L'Etranger* (London: H. Hamilton, 1946).

30. Christiane Galindo was the sister of Pierre Galindo, to whom Camus dedicated "Le Minotaur ou La Halte d'Oran."

31. Cf. *Albert Camus: A Biography*, pp. 193-94. On page 250 of this same work Lottman tells us that in 1941

    > Gaston Gallimard was ready to publish *L'Etranger* immediately, and he so informed Camus through Malraux in November—Gaston personally had found it remarkable. Paulhan confessed that he too liked the book very much, but he would be less enthusiastic about *Le Mythe de Sisyphe*.

    > Still, Camus had not submitted *L'Etranger* as a single work, but as part of a "series," something [Pascal] Pia had made clear to Paulhan. But in Paris they were less sure that such a publishing program was advisable. Indeed, because of the paper shortage, it was practically impossible.... Meanwhile Malraux promised to try to see that *Mythe* was published simultaneously with *L'Etranger* . . . without the chapter on Jewish Franz Kafka. (That would be published separately in a free-zone magazine.) Of *Caligula* nothing would be said immediately; later Gallimard would offer to publish it after *Mythe*, but by then (September 1942) its author felt that more work needed to be done on it and he preferred to wait. *Caligula* finally appeared in book form in 1944.

32. Cf. *Caligula*, in *Théâtre, récits, nouvelles*, p. 16 (trans. p. 34).

33. Cf. *L'Etranger* in *Théâtre, récits, nouvelles*, pp. 1205-6 (trans. p. 112).
34. A notebook entry for 1942 reads: "Three persons entered into the making of *The Outsider*: two men (of whom one was myself) and one woman."
35. *Explication*, p. 108.
36. *Carnets*, 1942.
37. *L'Etranger* in *Théâtre, récits, nouvelles*, p. 1156 (trans. p. 48).
38. *Ibid.*, pp. 1115-16 (trans. pp. 47-48).
39. See, for example, Conor Cruise O'Brien's treatment of Meursault's honesty in his *Camus*, pp. 20-23, and John Cruickshank's reflections, entitled "Art and the Novel," in his *Albert Camus*, pp. 142-63.
40. *Explication*, p. 114. It is interesting to note that Sartre continues: "The order in which the two works appeared seems to confirm this hypothesis. *The Stranger*, the first to appear, plunges us without comment into the "climate" of the absurd; the essay then comes and illumines the landscape."

     This is also inaccurate, however, for Camus, as we have seen, had never intended these two works to be published separately, but to appear together as a series on the absurd. The reason they were not published simultaneously was a purely pragmatic one: the difficulties faced by Gallimard as a result of the paper shortage in France during the war.
41. An entry in Camus' notebooks, dated 1942, refers to Meursault's meeting with the chaplain as "a privileged place in which the very disjointed character finally took on some form of unity."
42. *L'Etranger* in *Théâtre, récits, nouvelles*, pp. 1210-11. (trans. pp. 118-19).
43. *Ibid.*, pp. 1208-9 (trans. pp. 115-16).
44. *Ibid.*, pp. 1175-76 (trans. pp. 73-74). Emphasis added on "idea."
45. *Ibid.*, p. 1209 (trans. p. 117).
46. *Ibid.*, pp. 1207-8 (trans. pp. 114-15).
47. See Mackey, "Christianity and Albert Camus," p. 394.
48. *L'Etranger* in *Théâtre, récits, nouvelles*, pp. 1175 (trans. pp. 72-73).
49. *Ibid.*
50. *Ibid.*
51. *Explication*, p. 110.
52. See "Heidegger and Modern Existentialism," published in *Men of Ideas*, pp. 74-95.

CHAPTER II

1. See *Symposium* 28 (Syracuse University Press, Syracuse, New York, 1974). The only complete English translation of Nietzsche is the 18-volume *Complete Works of Friedrich Nietzsche* (ed. Oscar Levy), to which all references are given. New translations of individual works are listed in J. P. Stern, *Nietzsche*, pp. 158-59. References to the Schlechta edition are given in notes and in the bibliography.

2. This remark is to be found in Nietzsche's unpublished notes for 1886. It is quoted by Elizabeth Förster-Nietzsche in her introduction to *The Birth of Tragedy.*

3. W. Kaufmann, in opposition to most commentators on Nietzsche, claims that this should read "pre-platonic Greece." See *Nietzsche: Philosopher, Psychologist, Antichrist,* pp. 342-60.

4. *The Twilight of the Idols,* p. 16 (*Werke II,* pp. 323-96).

5. *Ibid.,* p. 12.

6. *Ibid.,* p. 11.

7. *Ibid.,* p. 14.

8. *Ibid.,* p. 12.

9. *The Will to Power,* II, p. 36 (*Der Wille zur Macht,* ed. Gast, Stuttgart: Kröner Verlag, 1964).

10. *The Twilight of the Idols,* p. 17.

11. *The Will to Power,* II, p. 36.

12. *The Twilight of the Idols,* p. 9.

13. *Ibid.,* II, p. 114.

14. *Ibid.,* VIII, p. 43.

15. *The Will to Power,* I, p. 327.

16. *Ibid.,* II, p. 408.

17. *Ibid.,* I, p. 328.

18. *The Genealogy of Morals,* p. 114 (*Werke II,* pp. 175-288).

19. *Ibid.,* p. 147.

20. *Ibid.,* pp. 154-55.

21. *Beyond Good and Evil,* p. 83 (*Werke II,* pp. 9-173).

22. *Thus Spake Zarathustra,* p. 387 (*Werke I,* pp. 545-778).

23. See *Letters and Papers from Prison,* pp. 156-157.

24. See *The New Reformation,* pp. 106-22.

25. See A. MacIntyre and P. Ricoeur, *The Religious Significance of Atheism.*

26. *Ecce Homo,* p. 139 (*Werke II,* pp. 399-481).

27. *Zarathustra,* p. 259.

28. *The Twilight of the Idols,* 35, p. 87.

29. *The Antichrist,* p. 131 (*Werke II,* pp. 483-545).

30. *The Will to Power,* I, p. 207.

31. *The Birth of Tragedy,* p. 9 (*Werke I,* pp. 7-110).

32. *Thus Spake Zarathustra,* p. 219.

33. To E. Nietzsche, Bonn, 11 June, 1865.

34. *Beyond Good and Evil,* p. 96.

35. *The Will to Power,* I, p. 208.

36. *The Genealogy of Morals,* p. 168.

37. *Ecce Homo,* p. 91.

38. Vol. I, p. 122.

39. *Beyond Good and Evil,* p. 123.
40. *Ibid.*
41. *Ibid.,* pp. 124-25.
42. *Ibid.,* p. 125.
43. *Ibid.,* p. 127.
44. *Beyond Good and Evil,* p. 227.
45. *Ibid.,* p. 230.
46. "The judgment 'good' did not originate among those to whom goodness was shown. Much rather has it been the good themselves, that is, the aristocratic, the powerful, the high-stationed, the high-minded, who have felt that they themselves were good, that is to say of the first order" (pp. 19-20).
47. *Ibid.,* p. 20.
48. *Ibid.,* p. 21.
49. *Ibid.,* pp. 22-23.
50. "I believe that I can explain the Latin *bonus* as the 'warrior': my hypothesis is that I am right in deriving *bonus* from an older *duonus* (compare *bellus=duellum=duenlum,* in which the word *duonus* appears to me to be contained). *Bonus* accordingly is the man of discord, of variance, '*Entzweiung*' (*duo*) as the warrior: one sees what in ancient Rome 'the good' meant for a man. Must not our actual German word *gut* mean 'the *godlike,* the man of godlike race' and be identical with the national name (originally the nobles' name) of the Goths?" (p. 26).
51. To Peter Gast, Turin, 31 May 1888.
52. *The Genealogy of Morals,* p. 34.
53. *Ibid.,* p. 55.
54. *Ibid.,* p. 30.
55. *Ibid.,* p. 39.
56. *Ibid.,* p. 38.
57. In *The Will to Power,* I, p. 109, he writes: "Moral valuations [*sic*] regarded as a history of lies and the art of calumny in the service of the will to power (of the will of the herd, which rises against stronger men)."
58. *The Genealogy of Morals,* p. 10.
59. *The Will to Power,* I, p. 278.

CHAPTER III

1. *La Peste,* in Pléiade, *Théâtre récits, nouvelles,* p. 1294 (trans. p. 78).
2. Cf. Pléiade, *Essais,* pp. 444-45.
3. Camus writes: The only great Christian thinker who has looked *directly* at the problem of evil is Saint Augustine. And he drew from it the terrible "Nemo bonus." Since then, Christianity has endeavoured to find provisional solutions to the problem. The result is before our eyes. For it is the result. Men have taken

some time over it, but today they are suffering from a poison they drank 2,000 years ago. They are either worn out by evil or resigned to it, which amounts to the same thing. At least, they cannot stand any more lies on this subject.

4. This interview is published in *Pléiade, Essais*, p. 380. Camus says: "I would be slow to say, however, as you do, that Christian faith is a surrender. Does this word describe someone like Saint Augustine or Pascal? Honesty consists in judging a doctrine by its summits and not by its side effects."

5. The essence of this famous Augustinian defence is expressed very simply by Paneloux *La Peste* (*Pléiade, Théâtre, récits nouvelles*, p. 1296): "Calamity has come on you, my brethren, and, my brethren, you deserved it" (trans. p. 80).

6. This talk is published in *Pléiade, Essais*, pp. 371-75.

7. *Camus' Hellenic Sources*, p. 152.

8. Camus writes:

> Ce n'est pas moi qui ai inventé la misère de la créature, ni les terribles formules de la malédiction divine. Ce n'est pas moi qui ai crié ce *Nemo Bonus*, ni la damnation des enfants sans baptême. Ce n'est pas moi qui ai dit que l'homme était incapable de se sauver tout seul et que du fond de son abaissement il n'avait d'espérance que dans la grâce de Dieu.

9. Camus contributed to *Diario* of 6 August 1949 a short article entitled *The Contribution of Existentialism*. He writes:

> It is a serious mistake to treat with such levity philosophical research as serious as existentialism. It has its origins in Saint Augustine, and its chief contribution knowledge consists, undoubtedly, in the impressive richness of its method. Existentialism is, above all, a method.

The method to which Camus refers at this point is, as we shall see, that of "interiority." It is our contention, however, that Camus' existentialism owes to Saint Augustine not merely the latter's "method" but what the Augustinian *reditus* revealed to Augustine, namely that man is made for the Transcendent.

10. This is the only work of Camus that treats of Augustinian thought. There is no evidence to suggest that he read any of Augustine's writings after 1936. A *carnet* entry dated January 1951, however, suggests that he continued to attach great importance to this work, for it indicates a desire on the part of Camus to revise and publish it: "Reprendre le passage de l'hellénisme au christianisme, véritable et seul tournant de l'histoire." The bibliography that is appended to Camus' study suggests, moreover, that he had consulted a great many original sources in preparation for his thesis. It lists, for example, the *Confessions* and the *City of God* as well as *The Happy Life*, the *Soliloquies* and some of Augustine's letters and sermons.

The extent to which Camus did in fact consult the primary sources has been seriously questioned, however, by Archambault, who argues that "nearly all of Camus' references to 'original texts' were found in secondary sources and uncritically copied." During his student days, Archambault insists, Camus had "gathered, at best, a certain veneer of Augustinian culture" (*Camus' Hellenic Sources*, p. 165). At the same time, however, Archambault concedes—and this is a crucial point—that Camus "had probably read parts or all of the *Confessions*," that he had gained "a general knowledge of several important Augustinian works" and that, while this knowledge was "usually derived from secondary sources," these latter "sources" were the relevant works of such eminent

Augustinian scholars as Tixeront, Grandgeorge and Gilson. Archambault also allows that "it would be excessive to pretend that the entire chapter on Augustine is plagiarized," that "some of the work is unequivocally Camus' own," and that it was Camus' personal reflections on Augustine's thought which led him to criticize the "unwarranted conclusions" of Alfaric on the extent of Augustine's Platonism (*Camus' Hellenic Sources*, p. 149). As we shall see the importance of the latter point could not be overestimated.

11. Cf. *Métaphysique chrétienne* . . . , in *Essais*, p. 1294.

12. *Ibid.*, p. 1296.

13. *Ibid.*

14. *Ibid.*

15. *Ibid.*, p. 1297.

16. *Ibid.*

17. *Ibid.*, pp. 1297-98.

18. *Ibid.*, p. 1302.

19. *The Trinity* IV, 1, 3.

20. Cf. *Métaphysique chrétienne* . . . , in *Essais*, p. 1304.

21. *Ibid.*, p. 1303.

22. *Camus' Hellenic Sources*, p. 141.

23. *Métaphysique chrétienne*, in *Essais*, p. 1303.

24. *Ibid.*, p. 1305.

25. *Ibid.*, p. 1306.

26. *Ibid.*, pp. 1309-10.

27. On the question of the ineffability of God, for example, Camus compares Augustine's *Sermon* 117,5 and the *City of God* IX, 16 with *Ennead* VI, 9, 5 of Plotinus. Camus also draws attention to the theme of God's eternity in Plotinus and Augustine and compares *Confessions* XI.13 with *Ennead* III, 6, 7.

28. Cf. *Métaphysique chrétienne* . . . , in *Essais*, p. 1293.

29. The most celebrated exposition of the view that Augustine was converted in 386 not to Christianity but to Platonism is to be found in Prosper Alfaric's *L'Evolution intellectuelle de saint Augustin.*

30. Camus is wrong in one very important respect, for Augustine never had the feeling of having left Christianity and he reverenced Christ as "Sapientia" in every point in his development. All recent students of Augustine's conversion are in agreement on this vital point.

31. Cf. *Métaphysique chrétienne* . . . , in *Essais*, p. 1282-83.

32. *Ibid.*, pp. 1295-96.

> Ce que Saint Augustin exigeait à côté de la Foi, c'était la vérité, à côté des dogmes, une métaphysique. Et avec lui le Christianisme tout entier. Mais s'il adopte un moment le Néoplatonisme ce fut bientôt pour le transfigurer. Et avec lui le Christianisme tout entier.
>
> C'est donc cette place donnée au Christ et à l'Incarnation dans l'originalité du Christianisme qu'il faut retenir chez lui. Ce sont des

formules et des thèmes qu'il a demandés au Néoplatonisme. La figure
de Jésus et le problème de la Rédemption vont tout transfigurer.

33. This was a point that Camus constantly stressed. In a *carnet* entry dated 1942,
for example, he insists that even the denial of God's existence does not rid a
man of his longing for totality, or of the need to respond authentically to the
absurdity of his existence:
Development of the absurd:

1. If the fundamental concern is the need for unity;
2. If the world (or God) cannot satisfy this;

Man must make a unity for himself, either by turning away from the
world or within the world. This restores both an ethic and an austere
rule of life, which still have to be defined.

34. In this thesis Camus identifies Christianity with the thought of Augustine
(Christianity, he says, reached its highest point in Augustinian thought), and
criticizes with extraordinary virulence, as he does in most of his other writings,
what he takes to be major Christian doctrines. The second part of "Christian
Metaphysics," for example, contains a scathing attack upon the notion of
Original Sin, which, Camus claims, is destructive of human autonomy and
implies universal damnation. And in the third chapter of this same thesis Camus
criticizes Augustine's teaching on the importance of faith.

Camus does not criticize, however, in this study or in any of his other
works, Augustine's persistent claim that man is made for God. This is an
extraordinarily significant fact, which suggests that Camus accepted the accu-
racy of the anthropological speculations that he found in Augustine's writings.
Archambault is therefore mistaken when he says (*Camus' Hellenic Sources*, p. 167)
that Camus disagreed "on every major point" with the man whom he once
described as "that other African," and when he adds: "It could be that nothing
in Camus would have been different had he never heard of Augustine."

35. Tarsicius J. van Bavel points out in "The Anthropology of Augustine," p. 35,
that

a complete presentation of Saint Augustine's anthropology would
include his teaching on creation; freedom and sin; relationship between body and soul; emotional life; desire and fear; interiority; epistemology; willing and loving; moral and social life; the image of God
in man; and death.

It scarcely needs to be emphasized, therefore, that the considerations to
be found in this chapter are incomplete. They will, however, throw some light
on Augustine's philosophy of man as expressed for the most part in the
philosophical dialogues, written at Cassiciacum in the period 386-387, and
therefore on his concept of natural desire for God, which, as we have seen,
played such an important role in Camus' case for the absurdity of human
existence.

In the lack of a complete critical edition of the Augustine's works, I have
consulted the best available edition of each of the writings on which the
following pages are based: the revised Skutella edition of *Confessions*; the *Corpus*

Christianorum edition of the *City of God;* the *Corpus Scriptorum Ecclesiasticorum Latinorum* (CSEL) for the remainder.

Where I have quoted Augustine in English, I have made use, for the most part, of the translations to be found in the Fathers of the Church series. (See general bibliography for detailed references.)

36. N.J.J. Balthasar, "La vie intérieure de saint Augustin à Cassiciacum," pp. 407-30.

37. Van Bavel, "The Anthropology of Augustine," p. 2. The central importance of the method of interiority can be grasped only in its internal and intimate relationship to the Augustinian dialectic: *intelligentia, amor* and *desiderium* seek to become ordered (*amor ordinatus*) through adhesion to the ordering force of reality, in its movement of return from multiplicity and dispersion to unity. In this dialectical self-expression, the *mens* ascends from the *exterior* (or *inferior*) to itself (*interior*), and passes through inwardly to its beyond, the *superior*: God, as *veritas, pulchrum* and *summum bonum.*

38. This point is well made by Stanislaus Grabowski in *The All Present God*, p. 272:

> Summarily, Saint Augustine's position may be stated thus: there is one fundamental law of life, and that is the urge for happiness; the diverse functions of the soul, even those which appear to be purely theoretical, cannot be unrelated to this fundamental desire in man. Thus conduct and intellect, morality and theoretical knowledge must participate and cooperate in the actions and life of one striving to be happy. And who is there without this relentless urge for happiness?

> This work covers much more extensively the area treated by Grabowski, "Saint Augustine and the Presence of God," pp. 336-58.

39. *The Happy Life* II, 10.

40. It is significant in this regard that when discussing the philosophical concerns of the ancient philosophers in the *City of God* XIX, Augustine points out that the question which divided the many schools of thought to which Varro referred in *Libri Antiquitatum* was not: Do all men seek happiness? Rather, it was the question: In what does happiness consist? An obvious conclusion is also to be drawn from his assertion, in chapter 12 of the same work, that even those who choose to engage in battle do so in order to attain the happiness that comes with peace. And this, of course, echoes the question posed in the *Confessions* X, 20, 29: "Surely, the happy life is this: what all men desire and [such that] there is absolutely no one who does not desire it?" The centrality of happiness in the *memoria*, or consciousness, is discussed in *Confessions* X, 20-23.

41. *The Free Choice of the Will* I, 14, 30.

42. *The Christian Philosophy of Saint Augustine*, p. 101.

43. *Answer to Sceptics* I, 2, 6 (*Contra Academicos*).

44. *Ibid.*, I, 3, 1.

45. *Ibid.*, I, 2, 6. The same views are expressed by Augustine in *Answer to Sceptics* III, 1. It seems to me, therefore, that Charles Boyer is right to stress the importance of truth in Augustine's philosophy. He writes, on the very first page of *L'Idée de vérité dans la philosophie de saint Augustin*:

> A chaque page de saint Augustin, on lit le mot de vérité . . .

A cette insistance on devine une inspiration fondamentale qui, dans un esprit comme celui d'Augustin, ne peut venir que du centre même de sa philosophie.

46. *Answer to Sceptics* I, 3 is entirely devoted to the question: "Is the mere search for truth sufficient for happiness?"

47. *Ibid.*, I, 2, 6.

48. *Ibid.*, I, 3, 9.

49. *Ibid.*, I, 3, 7.

50. *The Happy Life* II, 14. The *Confessions* show clearly that Augustine could find no happiness without the knowledge of truth. At I, 19, 30 for example, he speaks of the love of truth that he experienced even as an infant, and at VI, 4, 5 he makes it clear that what led him to accept the teachings of the Manichaeans was the fact they appeared to provide him with a rational presentation of truth. Gilson therefore expresses the thought of Augustine very accurately when he says that "there is nothing men prefer to knowledge of the truth, so much so that the idea of a happiness in which we should enjoy well-being and yet be in error seems to us a contradiction in terms" (*The Christian Philosophy of Saint Augustine*, p. 101).

51. *Soliloquies* I, 3, 8.

52. Knowledge of God and knowledge of oneself are, of course, interrelated in the *Soliloquies*. This point is made with exceptional clarity by G. Verbeke in his "Connaissance de soi et connaissance de Dieu chez saint Augustin," pp. 495-515, where he points out that Augustine's *"noverim me, noverim te"* should be understood in a reciprocal sense: Verbeke claims that there is

> un rapport réciproque entre la connaissance de soi et la connaissance de Dieu, en ce sens que la connaissance de soi serait indispensable pour arriver à la connaissance de Dieu et que d'autre part, cette dernière connaissance serait nécessaire afin de se connaître tel qu'on est réellement.

53. *Soliloquies* I, 5, 11. This point is also made by Augustine in the *City of God* IV, 25 and is reinforced in book XIX, 4 of the same work, where he takes issue with the view that the *summum bonum* is to be found in man himself.

54. *The Happy Life,* II, 12.

55. *Ibid.*, IV, 35.

56. Augustine's formal treatment of the relationship between knowledge (*scientia*) and wisdom (*sapientia*) is to be found in *The Trinity* XII-XIV. An excellent account of this relationship is given by Vernon J. Bourke in *Augustine's Quest of Wisdom*, p. 215, and in his brief but excellent article, "Wisdom in the Gnoseology of Saint Augustine," in *Augustinus* 3 (1958), pp. 331-36. In the latter article Bourke rightly emphasizes that in the Augustinian hierarchy of being the soul, which is immutable in place but mutable in time, occupies a place midway between God, who is absolutely immutable, and material things, which are mutable in both time and place.

    Much of what Bourke says is, however, put very succinctly by Augustine himself in *The Trinity* XII, 15:

> . . . this is the correct distinction between wisdom and science, that to wisdom belongs the intellectual cognition of eternal things, but to

> science the reasonable cognition of temporal things. (. . . haec est
> sapientiae et scientiae recta distinctio, ut ad sapientiam pertineat
> aeternarum rerum cognitio intellectualis, ad scientiam vero temporal-
> ium rerum cognitio rationalis).

57. *The Happy Life*, IV, 27.

58. *The Free Choice of the Will*, II, 13, 35. *Confessions* IV, 4, 8 tells us that Augustine's reading of Cicero's *Hortensius* in the year 373 inflamed the young man with a love of "philosophy." This is literally correct, for what the *Hortensius* (which is mentioned explicitly in three of the Cassiciacum dialogues) instilled in him was a desire not for the truth, but for wisdom.

59. These questions are discussed by Augustine in *Answer to Sceptics*, *The Free Choice of the Will* and *Divine Providence and the Problem of Evil*. It is therefore with the relevant parts of these works that the remainder of this chapter will, to a considerable extent at any rate, be concerned.

60. The crucial epistemological problem for the mature Augustine is: "How can we attain to certainty?" It is one that entails a consideration of his treatment of divine illumination and that therefore goes well beyond the scope of this chapter.

61. *Confessions* V, 10, 19.

62. In *Retractions* I, 1, 1 Augustine writes:

> . . . before my baptism I wrote, first of all, against the Academics or
> about the Academics, so that, with the most forceful reasons possible,
> I might remove from my mind—because they were disturbing me—
> their arguments which in many men instill a despair of finding truth
> and prevent a wise man from giving assent to anything or approving
> anything at all as clear and certain, since to them everything seems
> obscure and uncertain. With the help and mercy of the Lord, this has
> been accomplished.

63. It would be difficult to overestimate the importance of *Answer to Sceptics* in Augustine's thought. *The Trinity* XV, 12, 21 makes it clear that he regarded its arguments as definitive, and in the *Enchiridion* XX, 7 he tells us that these arguments paved the way for his pursuit of philosophy.

64. *Answer to Sceptics* III, 10, 23.

65. *Ibid.*, III, 11, 26.

66. *The Free Choice of the Will* II, 12, 34.

67. In *The True Religion*, XXXIX, 73 (written about the same time as *The Free Choice of the Will*), Augustine employs a similar argument. It, however, is designed to establish not that doubt presupposes the existence of a person who is in doubt, but that the sceptic, who doubts whether there is such a thing as truth, knows at least one truth, namely, that he doubts whether truth exists.

68. There are, of course, marked resemblances between the "*Cogito, ergo sum*" of Descartes and Augustine's "*Si fallor, sum.*" These resemblances are stressed by Gilson on pages 41-43 of his monumental work on Augustine. It is important to point out at the same time that their "intuitions" are, in some important respects, very dissimilar. The most important of these dissimilarities is, perhaps, that while there is for Descartes only one basic certainty, there are for Augustine no less than three. This point is made by B. S. Bubacz: "Saint

Augustine's *'si fallor, sum,'* " *Augustinian Studies* 9 (1978), pp. 35-44, as well as by John A. Mourant: "The Cogitos: *Augustinian and Cartesian,*" *Augustinian Studies* 10 (1979), pp. 27-42. Gilson devotes a lengthy discussion to the positions of Augustine and Descartes in "The Future of Augustinian Metaphysics," published in *A Monument to St. Augustine* (London: Sheed and Ward, 1945), pp. 287-315.

69. *The Free Choice of the Will,* II, 3, 7. It is significant that in the very same passage in which he affirms the apodicticity of his *"Si fallor, sum,"* Augustine insists that it is clear to a man not only that he is, but that he lives and understands, since he could not know with certainty that he existed unless he were alive, and it would not be clear to him that he was alive if he did not understand.

70. Attention has already been drawn to the fact that Augustine regarded the refutation of the sceptics which he delivered in *Answer to Sceptics* as definitive. It seems to me that he considered that of *The Free Choice of the Will* to be equally conclusive, for the argument of that work, II, 3, 7, reaffirms the intuition of life which is first expressed in *The Happy Life,* II, 7, together with the intuition of thought, which makes its first appearance in the *Soliloquies,* II, 1, 1 but reappears virtually unaltered, both in the *City of God* XI, 26, and in *The Trinity* X, 10, 14. It is significant too that it is reinforced in *The Trinity* XV, 12, 21, by Augustine's dismissal of the sceptics' claim that a man might be asleep and might therefore be merely dreaming that he exists, lives and understands.

71. The *City of God* XI, 26.

72. It can, of course, be misleading to speak in this context of a natural knowledge of God. It need not be misleading to do so, however, for Augustine's views on the relationship between faith and reason, as expressed, for example, in *Divine Providence* II, 5, make it clear that in his opinion faith does not dispense with the requirement for rational explanation. An excellent account of Augustine's views on the relationship between reason and revelation, as expressed in *Divine Providence,* is to be found in Ragnar Holte, *Béatitude et Sagesse,* pp. 321-27.

73. This passage is quoted by L. De Mondadon from the *Dictionnaire de Théologie catholique,* I, pp. 2-5, in his own article "De la connaissance de soi-même à la connaissance de Dieu," *Recherches de Science Religieuse* 4 (1913), p. 148.

74. *L'Idée de vérité dans la philosophie de Saint Augustin,* p. 50.

75. The tendency to compress Augustine's argument into a few lines is not one that is to be found merely among French scholars, it is also present in many English-speaking philosophers. Vernon Bourke, for example, in his "Invalid Proofs for God's Existence," p. 40, puts it as follows:

> Saint Augustine argued that men make eternally true judgments, such as that seven plus three equals ten. He then asserted that the eternal truth of these judgments cannot come from bodies or finite spirits, because they are mutable and temporal. So, he concluded that such eternally true judgments depend on God, and therefore God must exist.

76. *The Free Choice of the Will,* II, 3, 7.

77. *Ibid.,* II, 6, 13.

78. *Ibid.,* II, 6, 14.

79. In Augustine's view there is an intelligible sphere of absolute truths; this implies the existence of a Ground of truth, " . . . the Truth, in whom and by whom and

through whom all those things are true which are true" (*Soliloquies*, I, 1, 3). The opening sentence of *The Free Choice of the Will*, II, 12, 33 therefore reads: "You would in no way deny, then, that there exists unchangeable truth *that embraces all things that are immutably true*." (Emphasis added) (Quapropter nullo modo negaveris esse incommutabilem veritatem, haec omnia quae incommutabiliter vera sunt continentem. . . .)

80.   *The Free Choice of the Will*, II, 12, 33-34.

81.   *Ibid.*, II, 15, 39.

82.   Augustine's most mature reflections on this crucial question are to be found in *The Trinity* IX, 10, 14, where he articulates his most profound and systematic thinking on man as *imago Dei*. All of creation, he insists, reflects the God who made it, but only man is made in His image. To be *imago Dei* is to be a creature endowed with mind (*mens*) and intelligence (*ratio*). More precisely, it is to be a creature whose soul has within it not only *memoria Dei, intelligentia Dei* and *amor Dei*, but also the ability to perfect itself by growing in the knowledge and love of God. Augustine writes in *The Trinity* XIV, 17, 23: "Whoever, then, is being renewed in the Knowledge of God, and in justice and holiness of truth, by making progress from day to day, transfers his love from temporal to eternal things, from visible to intelligible things, from carnal to spiritual things."

83.   *The Happy Life*, II, 7.

84.   *Ibid.*, II, 8.

85.   *Ibid.*, IV, 35.

86.   Augustine writes, at the very beginning of this work, the Latin title of which is *De Ordine*:

> . . . there is nothing that the most gifted minds search out more eagerly,
> . . . there is nothing that these are more desirous of hearing and learning
> than how it is that God has a care for human affairs, and nevertheless
> perversity is so serious and widespread that it must seem unattributable
> not only to God's governance, but even to a hireling's management, if
> indeed such management could be attributed to a hireling.

87.   *Divine Providence*, II, 19, 49.

88.   *Ibid.*, I, 5, 14 and I, 6, 15.

89.   *Ibid.*, I, 7, 17.

90.   "Dieu présent au coeur," in *Année Théologique Augustinienne* 2 (1951), pp. 117-30, p. 19.

91.   *Divine Providence*, I, 10, 28.

92.   *Ibid.*, I, 9, 27.

93.   One is immediately reminded at this point of the *City of God* XIX, 13, 1, where Augustine, after defining order as "an arrangement of like and unlike things, whereby each of them is disposed in its proper place," immediately goes on to link *"ordo"* with *"lex," "pax"* and, indeed, *"societas."* One is reminded also of the many occasions in the *Confessions* and *Commentaries on the Psalms* in which Augustine identifies happiness with the peace that follows the attainment of Truth.

94.   In Augustine's thought there is, of course, no separation of man's faculties from one another. To grow in knowledge of God is therefore to grow in the love of Him as well. This point is well made by F. J. Thonnard, "La Vie affective de

l'âme selon saint Augustin," p. 41, when he says that for the human soul *"la sagesse"* is *"le bien."*

95. *Divine Providence*, I, 2, 5.

96. *Ibid.*, II, 19, 51. Augustine's reflections on the nature and destiny of man, as expressed in *Divine Providence*, are obviously Platonic. There can be little doubt that the immediate source of this Platonism was the *Enneads* of Plotinus, particularly *Ennead* I, 6, the treatise "On the beautiful," and V, 1 which deals with the three principal hypostases.

   The debt that Augustine owed to Plotinus for his view on the place of the soul in creation and its ascent to God is well illustrated by S. Connolly, "The Platonism of Augustine's Ascent to God," *Irish Ecclesiastical Record* 78 (1952), pp. 43-44, and "The Ascent in the Philosophy of Plotinus," *Irish Ecclesiastical Record* 81, (1954), pp. 120-33. In the first of these articles, Connolly argues very convincingly that the *"libri Platonicorum"* of *Confessions* VII, 9, 13 are for the most part the *Enneads* of Plotinus; in the second he establishes conclusively that both "the constituent elements" of the ascent and "its structure as a whole" are accounted for by the influence of the *Enneads*.

   There can be little doubt that the *libri* included some writings of Porphyry, with whom Augustine shared an interest in comparative religion.

97. *The Christian Philosophy of Saint Augustine*, p. 249.

98. *Soliloquies*, I, 5, 2.

99. This point is strongly emphasized by R. Ackworth, "St. Augustine and the Teleological Argument for the Immortality of the Soul," *The Downside Review* 75 (1957), pp. 215-21.

100. *The Happy Life*, II, 35.

101. *Retractions*, I, 4, 3.

102. Much has been made by scholars of the importance of Augustine's *Commentary on Psalm 41* for an understanding of this and other aspects of the saint's anthropology. Cuthbert Butler, for example, makes a great deal of it in his *History of Western Mysticism*, pp. 20-26, as does J. Maréchal, in "La vision de Dieu au sommet de la contemplation d'après saint Augustin," *Nouvelle Revue Théologique* 2 (1930), pp. 89-109, 192-213. It is significant, however, that Augustine also emphasizes this point when commenting on numerous other Psalms. His *Commentary on Psalm 32*, for example, is in this regard extraordinarily instructive in its application of *imago Dei* to human nature.

103. In *Sermon 241*, for example, Augustine describes the passage by which the soul rises from the knowledge of material things to, as it were, the natural knowledge of God. But it is clear, even in this passage, that the soul's search for a philosophic knowledge of God is viewed in the context of its natural desire for the Beatific Vision.

104. *Confessions* VII, 17, 23, for example, tells us that even the mystical vision of God, which in Augustine's view is obviously superior to the natural knowledge of Him, is fleeting. It is therefore a mere adumbration of the Beatitude that awaits man.

105. The *City of God* XIX, 20.(Quam ob rem summum bonum civitatis Dei cum sit aeterna pax atque perfecta, non per quam mortales transeant nascendo atque moriendo, sed in qua immortales maneant nihil adversi omnino patiendo; quis

est qui illam vitam vel beatissimam neget, vel in ejus comparatione istam, quae
hic agitur, quantislibet animi et corporis externarumque rerum bonis plena sit,
non miserrimam judicet?)

106.   Camus stresses the absurdity of life not only in *Le Mythe de Sisyphe* and *L'Etranger*,
but also in *Caligula* and *Le Malentendu*. In *Cross Purpose*, Martha, for example, longs
to escape from the "dark country" and the "dreary tavern" in which she lives, to
"the sea and the sunlight." Her desire for happiness is frustrated, however, by
the "natural order of things" in which death, of course, has the central role. And
in *Théâtre, récits, nouvelles*, pages 107-8, Caligula says quite explicitly:

> If I'd had the moon, if love were enough, all might have been different.
> But where could I quench this thirst? What human heart, what God,
> would have for me the depth of a great lake? There's nothing in this
> world, or in the other, made to my stature. And yet I know, and you
> too know, that all I need is for the impossible to be! I've reached for it
> at the confines of the world, in the secret places of my heart. I've
> stretched out my hands, but it's always you I find, you only, confronting
> me, and I've come to hate you. (trans. p. 97)

CHAPTER IV

1. In *Le Mythe de Sisyphe, Essais*, p. 137.

2. In *Le Mythe de Sisyphe, Essais*, p. 144.

3. *Ibid.*, p. 117 (trans. p.31).

4. *Ibid.*, p. 128 (trans. p. 43).

5. *Essais*, pp. 125-26.

6. *Ibid.*, p. 131.

7. That this is indeed "a casual reading" of *Le Mythe de Sisyphe* will be made clear in
the concluding section of this chapter.

8. *Le Mythe de Sisyphe* in *Essais*, pp. 134-35 (trans. p. 50).

9. *Ibid.*, p. 135 (trans. p. 50).

10. In *Camus* (p. 146), Patrick McCarthy claims that "superficially, *Sisyphe* is a book
about suicide, but in reality Camus has already banished the temptation of
suicide by deciding not to publish *La Mort heureuse*, which was an apology for
suicide." This, however, was unlikely to have been Camus' reason for not
publishing *La Mort heureuse*; Herbert Lottman is almost certainly correct when
he says that Camus was unhappy with this work for literary reasons: "It seemed
badly-assimilated Montherlant" (*Albert Camus: A Biography*, p. 172).

11. *Le Mythe de Sisyphe*, in *Essais*, p. 138 (trans. p. 53).

12. *Ibid.*, (trans. p. 54).

13. Conor Cruise O'Brien is typical in this respect. In *Camus* (p. 32), he writes: "The
real significance, and the source of the appeal, of the work of this period is not
one of revolt, but of affirmation." This however is a misleading statement, for
"revolt" is, as we shall see, a largely positive stance.

14. *Le Mythe de Sisyphe*, in *Essais*, p. 138 (trans. p. 53).

15. *Ibid.*, (trans. p. 54).

16. *Ibid.*, (trans. p. 53).

17. *Ibid.*, p. 139 (trans. p. 54).

18. *Ibid.*, p. 113 (trans. p. 26).

19. *Ibid.*, p. 120 (trans. p. 34).

20. *Ibid.*

21. *Ibid.*, p. 121 (trans. p. 34).

22. *Ibid.*

23. In *Le Mythe de Sisyphe, Essais*, p. 145 (trans. p. 62) Camus writes: "Thus I draw from the absurd three consequences, which are my revolt, my freedom and my passion."

24. *Ibid.*, p. 139 (trans. p. 54).

25. Camus' notebook entry, dated December 1938, reads: "Men have the illusion that they are free. But when they are sentenced to death they lose this illusion. The whole problem lies in whether or not it is real in the first place." And an entry dated August 1939 reads: "The only liberty possible is a liberty as regards death."

26. *Le Mythe de Sisyphe*, in *Essais*, p. 142 (trans. pp. 58-59).

27. J. P. Mackey, "Christianity and Albert Camus," p. 395.

28. *Le Mythe de Sisyphe*, in *Essais*, p. 142 (trans. p. 59).

29. *Ibid.*, pp. 149-50 (trans. pp. 64-65). This is a point which Camus makes often. For example, a notebook entry dated August 1938 reads:

    . . . The really free man is the one who, accepting death as it is, at the same time accepts its consequences—that is to say, the abolition of all life's traditional values. Ivan Karamazov's "Everything is permitted" is the only expression there is of a coherent liberty. *And we must follow out all the consequences of his remark.* (Emphasis added.)

30. *Le Mythe*, in *Essais*, pp. 149-50 (trans. p. 65).

    In *Camus* Patrick McCarthy writes (p. 63):

    In *Le Mythe de Sisyphe* Camus asserts the need for limits. The most interesting part of Camus' thought seems to be the flat rejection of violence. In *Sisyphe* lucidity tells us that there can be no pantheistic universe and no conquest of the moon. *So it is useless to gun down Zagreus or to murder idle patricians.* "We cannot condone violence unless it is clear-sighted," says Camus, who feels that violence is rarely clear-sighted. The sophisticate in Camus is speaking; this is the un-Algerian Camus who invokes limits to correct the violence of his fellow Algerians. (Emphasis added.)

    What McCarthy says here is simply inaccurate, for it is not *Le Mythe de Sisyphe* but rather *Caligula* that asserts the need for limits. "I have chosen a wrong path, a path that leads to nothing," says the emperor. "My freedom is not the right one." Nor does Camus conclude from our inability to find absolutes that limits should be imposed. He simply insists that there is no contradiction involved in holding, at the same time, that limits can be imposed on the conduct of the absurd man and that the absurdist ethic implies that all is permitted.

This is a point which Cruickshank also appears to have missed, for while he is correct in saying that for Camus "innocence and complete freedom of action go together," he implies that *Le Mythe de Sisyphe* is consistent on this point. For he goes on to say (p. 67) that "in writings published a few years later, *however*, particularly in his *Lettres à un ami allemand*, Camus rejects his first interpretation of innocence and accepts the fact of limitation and responsibility even in the context of the absurd." (Emphasis added.)

31. *Le Mythe de Sisyphe*, in *Essais*, pp. 145-46 (trans. p. 62).

32. The influence of Nietzsche on Camus' early work is alluded to by, for example, Roger Quilliot and Philip Thody. The former claims, in fact, that Nietzsche was, for the young Camus, "the law and the prophets"; the latter says that "many of Camus's criticisms of Nietzsche's nihilism (in *L'Homme révolté*) seem equally applicable to his own earlier attitudes." (*Carnets 1935-42*, p. 143).

Thody, in fact, refers in this connection to a notebook entry of May 1938 that says that Nietzsche "condemns the Reformation which saves Christianity from the principles of life and love that Cesare Borgia was infusing into it. The Pope Borgia was finally justifying Christianity." And he continues:

> The reference here seems to be to section 61 of *The Antichrist, A Criticism of Christianity*, which reads as follows: "I see a spectacle so rich in meaning and so wonderfully paradoxical to boot, that it would be enough to make all the gods of Olympus rock with immortal laughter,—Cesar Borgia as Pope . . . Do you understand me? . . . . Very well then, this would have been the triumph which *I* alone am longing for today:—this would have *swept* Christianity *away* . . . . But . . . . Luther saw the corruption of the Papacy when the very reverse stared him in the face: the old corruption, *peccatum originale*, Christianity *no* longer sat upon the Papal chair! But Life! the triumph of Life! The great yea to all lofty, beautiful and daring things. . . . ."

Thody also draws attention to the fact that Camus quotes Nietzsche's statement, from *Twilight of the Idols*, that "the tragic artist says 'yes' to everything terrible and problematical."

33. *Explication*, p. 109.

34. In *Le Mythe de Sisyphe* Camus describes "revolt" as "the certainty of a crushing fate, *without the resignation that ought to accompany it*" (emphasis added), and at the end of *L'Etranger* Meursault makes it clear that he is happy and would continue to live, if that were possible.

35. *L'Etranger*, p. 1210 (trans. p. 118).

36. *Ibid.*, p. 1210 (trans. p. 117).

37. *Ibid.*, p. 1207 (trans. p. 114).

38. *Ibid.*, p. 1210 (trans. p. 118). This freedom is, of course, of a very limited kind, but in Meursault's view it is the only freedom that is available to him.

39. This is described in *Le Mythe de Sisyphe* as "la passion." The kind of life it entails is depicted by Jean Baptiste Clamence in the second chapter of Camus' *La Chute*.

40. L'Etranger, in *Théâtre, récits, nouvelles*, p. 1210 (trans. p. 118).

41. *Ibid.*, pp. 1208-9, 1175-76 (trans. pp. 115-16, 73-74).

42. See, for example, John Cruickshank, *Albert Camus and the Literature of Revolt*, pp. 142-43, and Conor Cruise O'Brien, *Camus*, pp. 20-22.
43. *Camus*, p. 21.
44. Ibid., pp. 22-46.
45. *Ibid.*, pp. 20-21.
46. Ibid., p. 21. The essay from which O'Brien quotes at this point is "The World of the Man Condemned to Death." It is to be found in *Camus: A Collection of Critical Essays*, ed. Germaine Brée, pp. 92-107.
47. O'Brien, *Camus*, pp. 21-22.
48. This is what Camus refers to in his notebooks as "the truth." For example, an entry dated 1938 reads: "Here, the absurd is perfectly clear. It is the opposite of irrationality. It is the plain and simple truth."
49. *L'Etranger*, in *Théâtre, récits, nouvelles*, p. 1148 (trans. p. 40). Emphasis added.
50. *Ibid.*, pp. 1210-11 (trans. pp. 118-19).
51. *Camus*, p. 24.
52. This was the "really important thing" he would have told the court, had he been given the opportunity.
53. *Camus.*, p. 25.
54. *L'Etranger*, in *Théâtre, récits, nouvelles*, p. 1168 (trans. p. 64). Emphasis added. There are other passages which express Meursault's absurdist philosophy. It finds a cogent, though less obvious, expression in the assertion to which we have already referred, that the murder of the Arab was a "criminal offence" but not a crime.
55. *Ibid.*, p. 1131 (trans. p. 18).

CHAPTER V

1. Walter Kaufmann in *Nietzsche* (p. 101) refers to this problem as Nietzsche's "greatest and most persistent" one.
2. *The Young Nietzsche*, p. 278.
3. *The Birth of Tragedy, An Attempt at Self-Criticism*, p. 11.
4. *Ibid.*, p. 61.
5. *Ibid.*, p. 62.
6. *The Drama of Atheist Humanism*, p. 38.
7. A.H.J. Knight, *Some Aspects of the Life and Work of Nietzsche*, p. 54.
8. *Ecce Homo*, p. 70.
9. *Ibid.*, p. 69.
10. *The Birth of Tragedy*, p. 83.
11. *The Will to Power*, II, p. 239.
12. *Ibid.*, II, p. 289.
13. In his essay "Nietzsche: Art and Intellectual Inquiry," published in *Nietzsche: Imagery and Thought* (pp. 1-32), Peter Pütz, after suggesting, as other commen-

tators have done, that there are three stages in the development of Nietzsche's philosophy, writes:

> The beginning of the third phase is announced at the end of *The Joyful Science* (1882). If *Human, All Too Human* commenced with an expression of faith in chemistry, in this work the joyful scientist scorns number and calculation, seeing and grasping, as "coarseness" and "idiocy" (II, 249) . . . then from Zarathustra on not only are all demands for a scientific or historical interpretation of the world superseded, but even the heroism of truth at any price is drowned out by the laughter of buffoons, by the mocking wisdom of those who have seen through the little tricks of science, by the rhythmic stamping of the dancer. Now, instead of "unpretentious truths" the great philosophical and visionary themes hold the field: "the will to power," "eternal recurrence," the "great man," "breeding," and so forth. After the "yes" of Zarathustra the transvaluation of values begins, Nietzsche's great essay in metaphysics. Art is rehabilitated and given a positive function as the opponent of devitalizing knowledge: "Art and nothing but art." Art is the great enabler of life, the great temptress to life, the great stimulant of life (III, 692).

14. See G. W. Cunningham, "Nietzsche on the Philosopher," *The Philosophical Review* 54 (1945), pp. 155-72.
15. *The Will to Power*, I, p. 383.
16. *Ibid.*, I, p. 384.
17. *Beyond Good and Evil*, p. 8.
18. *Ibid.*, p. 152.
19. *Zarathustra*, pp. 239-40.
20. *Beyond Good and Evil*, p. 228.
21. *Nietzsche*, pp. 152-179.
22. *Beyond Good and Evil*, pp. 10-12.
23. *The Will to Power*, II, p. 110.
24. *Beyond Good and Evil*, pp. 25-28.
25. *The Will to Power*, II, pp. 205-6.
26. *Beyond Good and Evil*, pp. 51-52. It is interesting to note, in this regard, the claim made by Nietzsche in *The Will to Power* (II, p. 152) that all organic processes can be "shown to be but forms of the fundamental will, the will to power, and buds thereof."
27. G. A. Morgan, *What Nietzsche Means*, p. 60.
28. *The Will to Power*, II, p. 159.
29. *Ibid.*, p. 125.
30. *Ibid.*, p. 124.
31. *Ibid.*, p. 128.
32. *Ibid.*, p. 157.
33. *Ibid.*, p. 125.
34. *Ibid.*, p. 159.
35. *Ibid.*, pp. 124-25.

36. *Zarathustra*, p. 119.

37. *Ibid.*, p. 136.

38. In *The Lonely Nietzsche* (p. 279), his sister, Frau Förster-Nietzsche, writes:

    Nietzsche finally came to regard the interplay of all natural forces as conditioned by a "will to power"—the master morality, as it were: he saw in Nature not the "will to life" (Schopenhauer), but a will to the exaltation of life: not a "struggle for existence" (Darwin), but a struggle for a nobler, stronger, existence: not "the instinct of self-preservation" (Spinoza), but the instinct of self-augmentation; not "love and strife" (Empedocles), but the contest for victory and supremacy.

    And on p. 319 of the same work she makes two further points that are important in the present context: first, that for Nietzsche the will to power was "the principle [through which] the tangled skein of life might best be unravelled"; secondly, that in his plan for *The Will to Power*, Nietzsche referred to this principle as "an interpretation of all that happens."

39. Morgan, *What Nietzsche Means*, p. 66.

40. *Ibid.*, pp. 66-67.

41. *Ibid.*, p. 67.

42. *Ibid.*, p. 221.

43. *Ibid.*, p. 235.

44. *Ibid.*, p. 207.

45. The terminology is that of T. H. Huxley. In *Evolution and Ethics*, p. 31, he refers to "propounders of what are called the 'ethics of evolution,' when the 'evolution of ethics' would usually better express the object of their speculations."

46. *Ibid.*, p. 7. This point is made even more strongly on pp. 33-34 of the same work; Huxley writes:

    The practice of that which is ethically best—what we call goodness or virtue—involves a course of conduct which in all respects is opposed to that which leads to success in the cosmic struggle for existence. In place of ruthless self-assertion it demands self-restraint. . . . It repudiates the gladiatorial theory of existence. Laws and moral precepts are directed to the end of curbing the cosmic process and reminding the individual of his duty to the community, to the protection and influence of which he owes, if not existence itself, at least the life of something better than a brutal savage.

47. These words are quoted by Frau Förster-Nietzsche in *The Lonely Nietzsche* (p. 330), from a private note of Dr. Richard Oehler.

48. Scholars such as Kaufmann, Taylor and Stack have attempted in recent years "to salvage this 'will to power' for traditional moral philosophy by claiming that Nietzsche conceived of it as 'the will to overcome oneself.' " This, as J. P. Stern points out (*Nietzsche*, p. 84), "would place him [Nietzsche] squarely in the same tradition as St. Paul, Spinoza and Schopenhauer." The interpretation of Nietzsche's ethical thought adopted, for example, by Stack seems to me to be a strangely benign one that, while supported by some of Nietzsche's assertions, simply does not represent the central thrust of his attack upon conventional morality. Stack's reflections on this aspect of Nietzsche's philosophy do not, in any case, concur with the Promethean view of Nietzsche adopted by Camus.

49. Camus' endorsement of Nietzsche's immoralism ended, of course, with the humanism of *Lettres à un ami allemand* (1945) and *La Peste* (1947). *L'Homme révolté* (1951), moreover, contains a long section in which Camus criticizes Nietzsche for advocating a limitless freedom which, he insists, is incompatible with the demands of authentic rebellion. "Without law there is no freedom. If fate is not guided by superior values, if chance is king then there is nothing but the step in the dark and the appalling freedom of the blind" (trans. p. 62).

CHAPTER VI

1. Cruickshank, *Albert Camus and the Literature of Revolt*, p. 47.

2. *Ibid.*, p. 48.

3. *Le Mythe de Sisyphe*, in *Essais*, p. 139 (trans. p. 54). Camus writes: "That revolt gives life its value. Spread out over the whole length of a life, it restores its majesty to that life."

4. Cruickshank, *Camus*, pp. 62-63.

5. *Ibid.*, pp. 63-65.

6. In *Le Mythe de Sisyphe* (*Essais*, p. 137; trans. p. 52) Camus writes: "Is one going to die, escape by the leap, rebuild a mansion of ideas and forms to one's own scale? Is one on the contrary going to take up the heartrending and marvellous wager of the absurd?"

7. In *Le Mythe de Sisyphe*, in *Essais*, p. 139 (trans. p. 54).

8. *Ibid.*, p. 134 (trans. pp. 49-50).

9. *Métaphysique chrétienne . . .* , in *Essais*, p. 1228.

10. *Ibid.*, p. 1236.

11. *Ibid.*, p. 1222.

12. Cruickshank, *Albert Camus*, p. 67.

13. *Ibid.*, p. 71.

14. *Ibid.*

15. This is a point which Camus argues at some length in *Le Mythe de Sisyphe* (*Essais*, pp. 139-42; trans. pp. 56-57). It is one which he often makes, moreover, in his notebooks.

    An entry dated August 1938, for example, reads: "The only liberty possible is a liberty as regards death. This really free man is the one who, accepting death as it is, at the same time accepts its consequences."

    And in December of the same year he writes: "Men have the illusion that they are free. But when they are sentenced to death they lose the allusion. The whole problem lies in whether or not it is real in the first place."

16. Cruickshank, *Camus.*, p. 84. Cruickshank's criticisms are to be found in detail on pp. 84-86.

17. J. P. Mackey, "Christianity and Albert Camus," pp. 395-96. A similar point is beautifully made by Jean Sarocchi in the notes that he appends to the English translation of *La Mort heureuse* (1973, p. 129):

Purity of heart is one of the major problems in Camus. He attempts to distinguish it from virtue. . . . Kierkegaard annoyed Camus by linking it with virtue or goodness: "For Kierkegaard purity of heart is oneness, unity. But it is unity and goodness." (*Carnets*, II, p. 36). Camus' entire moral development is located within this problematic conjunction.

18. Cruickshank, *Camus.*, p. 43.

19. *Ibid.*, p. 42.

20. It is one which, as far as I can tell, is expressed by no one other than Cruickshank. The evidence which he adduces for it is to be found in a brief preliminary note to *Le Mythe de Sisyphe* and in *L'Enigme*.

21. Camus writes:

> Written fifteen years ago, in 1940, amidst the French and European disaster, this book [*The Myth of Sisyphus*] declares that even within the limits of nihilism it is possible to find the means to proceed beyond nihilism. In all the books I have written since, I have attempted to pursue this direction. Although *The Myth of Sisyphus* poses mortal problems, it sums itself up for me as a lucid invitation to live and to create, in the very midst of the desert.

22. It is important to remember that *Le Mythe de Sisyphe* ends with a discussion of that myth. And Sisyphus is, of course, commended by Camus not merely for acknowledging his absurd condition but for having accepted his meaningless task, thereby conferring upon it the only kind of meaning it could have. The essay closes with the words: "One must imagine Sisyphus happy."

23. A footnote in *Le Mythe de Sisyphe*, in *Essais*, p. 130 (trans. p. 45) reads: "Even the most rigorous epistemologies imply metaphysics. And to such a degree that the metaphysic of many contemporary thinkers consists in having nothing but an epistemology."

24. Lottman, *Albert Camus: A Biography*, pp. 244-45.

CHAPTER VII

1. Camus' *Discours de la Suède*, the published version of his Nobel Prize speech and lecture, is dedicated to his former teacher. It is addressed to "*Monsieur* Louis Germain."

2. Camus is said to have been particularly good at French literature and mathematics, the two most important subjects of the examination he was to take at the end of his studies at the *Ecole Communale*.

3. Entry to the *lycée* marked the end of Camus' formal religious education. Neither of his parents was a practising Catholic; he himself had been baptized and had received his first Holy Communion at the age of eleven, in accordance with the wishes of his grandmother. It is important to realize, however, that Camus continued all his life to be, in a very real sense, a profoundly religious man. Those who, like Louis Bénisti and Max-Pol Fouchet, had known him at an early age tell us that during his time at the *lycée* Camus read the Bible, reflected upon the mystics and, like Nietzsche, was fascinated with the person of Jesus.

4. Students of sufficient ability often spent seven years of study at a *lycée*. The first six of these years culminated in the *baccalauréat*, the diploma that was required for admission to the French institutions of higher education. The final year was that of the *hypokhâgne*. Had Camus' progress through the *lycée* been a conventional one, he would, of course, have entered the University of Algiers as a full-time student in October 1931. His entry to university was delayed, however, by the first attack of tuberculosis which occurred in December 1930 or January 1931, and made it necessary for him to repeat the final year of his studies for the *baccalauréat*.

   The tuberculosis from which Camus suffered for most of his life had, moreover, more serious consequences, and this even at the academic level. The most obvious, and indeed the most important, of these consequences was that it made it impossible for him to take the *agrégation* (due to the health requirement under French university regulations), and so deprived him of a career as a university teacher. His formal studies in philosophy ended with the *diplôme d'études supérieures* of 1936.

5. In mainland France two years of preparation were necessary for the élite French institutions such as the *Ecole Normale Supérieure*. These were called respectively *hypokhâgne* and *khâgne*. Only the first of these years was open to Algerian students.

6. Camus had begun to attend the university on a part-time basis in his final year at the *lycée*.

7. All *lycée* students of this period, whether of France or Algiers, employed Armand Cuvillier's *Manuel de philosophie*, which afforded them some knowledge of the major philosophers. It was here that Camus was introduced, though at a very elementary level, to, for example, the work of Schopenhauer and Nietzsche.

8. Examinations were not an important feature of life at the *lycée*. Those which marked the end of the hypokhâgne were, in fact, superfluous. (Lottman, to whom I am indebted for some of the details provided in this chapter, recounts that two of Camus' fellow students of 1932-33 returned to Oran without even sitting for their examinations.) Students were, however, required during their final year to submit frequent dissertations, and these largely of a philosophic nature.

9. The works in question are *La Mort dans l'âme*, *L'Envers et l'endroit* and *L'Homme révolté*. Camus also wrote a preface to the second edition of Grenier's *Les Iles*. He was never to see this preface in print, however, for the relevant edition of Grenier's most famous work had not been published at the time of Camus' death.

10. The writings of Malraux did not, of course, form part of the syllabus for the *baccalauréat* of this period, nor did they appear on the *hypokhâgne* program, vague as this program was. Camus' general interest in French literature, however, which he owed for the most part to his teachers at the *lycée*, led him to read many authors whose works did not appear on the conventional syllabus. And among the writers with whom Camus became acquainted were Gide and Malraux. He is known to have discovered the former's *Nourritures terrestres* at the age of 16 and to have read Gide's *Les Faux-monnayeurs* during his studies at the *lycée*. Camus was familiar too with Malraux's *La Tentation de l'Occident* (1926), *Les Conquérants* (1928) and *La Voie royale* (1930). It was, however, Malraux's *La Condition humaine* (1933) that most influenced Camus.

11. Even before arriving in Algiers Grenier had gained something of a reputation, not only as a teacher but also as a writer, for he had published in *Ecrits*, to which the young Malraux had contributed his *D'une Jeunesse européenne*, an essay entitled *"Interiora Rerum."* It was during his stay in Algiers that Grenier made his name, however, as a regular contributor to *La Nouvelle Revue Française* and as the author of *Les Iles* and *Inspirations méditerranéennes.*

12. In 1932 Grenier persuaded the editors of the school magazine *Sud* to publish a series of articles written by students of his *lycée* philosophy class. It is interesting that Camus himself contributed four essays to *Sud* at this time and that some of them treat of Nietzschean and Bergsonian themes.

13. The second edition of *Les Iles* was published shortly after Camus' death in January 1960. Its preface, written by Camus the previous year, contains an explicit acknowledgment on the part of its author of what he owed to his former teacher. This work, says Camus, taught him what even Gide's *Nourritures terrestres* had not done, namely that the joys of this life, while very real, are nonetheless fleeting ones and that man's nostalgia for a more permanent happiness affords him a glimpse of "the sacred" and "the divine."

14. Camus became a student of philosophy of the University of Algiers in October 1933. Its programme of studies required that he take, first, the *Licence de philosophie*, which was awarded after two years to those students who had taken the four certificates required for this degree, and then, at the end of his third year, the *Diplôme d'études supérieures*, for which he was required to submit a dissertation. Camus took his *certificat de morale et sociologie* immediately upon entering the university (he had, it seems, done the required study during his *hypokhâgne* year) and his *certificat de psychologie* in June 1934. In the following year he obtained his *certificat d'études littéraires* and his *certificat de logique et philosophie générale.*

15. Réné Poirier was born in 1900 and had, like Grenier, obtained his *agrégation* in 1922. He taught for some years at a *lycée* in Chartres, before being appointed, first, to the University of Montpellier, and then, at the age of 33, to the newly established chair of philosophy at the University of Algiers. As professor of philosophy there he did virtually all the teaching for the *licence* and was responsible for the supervision of all postgraduate studies. It was Poirier who suggested in 1935 that Camus consult Jean Guitton's *Le Temps et l'Eternité chez Plotin et Saint Augustin* before choosing a suitable topic for his diploma.

    Poirier is reported to have been an excellent teacher who showed considerably less interest in modern philosophy than in traditional thought. It is hardly surprising therefore that he exerted relatively little influence on Camus, who was attracted much more to Grenier's reflections on Spinoza than to Poirier's lectures on logic and psychology.

16. The influence which Grenier exerted on Camus did not end with the latter's departure from the *lycée*. He was, in fact, Poirier's assistant at the University of Algiers during the years 1933 to 1935 and introduced Camus, during that period, to the thought of, for example, Plato and Chestov, as well as to peripheral subjects such as Hindu philosophy and Taoism. Such was Grenier's influence on Camus, indeed, that the latter first decided, on the advice of his mentor, to devote his diploma dissertation to Indian philosophy. It was later,

at the insistence of Poirier, that Camus opted apparently but not in fact for a very different topic.

17. Camus, as we have seen, agrees with Saint Augustine that man is made for God. He insists, however, as Nietzsche did, that man's sole kingdom is to be located in *this* world.

  Camus' quest for an "island within an island" is reflected not only in "Métaphysique chrétienne et Néoplatonisme," but in, for example, *L'Été à Alger* where he poses the question: "is there anything odd in finding again, on earth, that union for which Plotinus longed?" (*Pléiade*, Essais, p. 75).

18. The term Hellenism is, Camus himself acknowledges, a notoriously vague one. The difficulty of defining the "Greek spirit" for the purpose of his study, however, is not, in Camus' view, an insuperable one, for in Pléiade, *Essais*, p. 1225, he writes:

  On the other hand, there can be no doubt that a certain number of chosen themes are discernible in any civilization, and that it is possible, with the help of Socratic thought, to trace within Greek philosophy a certain number of privileged patterns whose composition implies precisely what is called Hellenism. Something in Greek thought prefigures Christianity, while at the same time something else rejects it in advance. (Mais, d'un autre côté, il est bien certain qu'on peut dégager d'une civilisation un certain nombre de thèmes favoris, et, le socratisme aidant, de calquer à l'intérieur de la pensée grecque un certain nombre de dessins privilégiés dont la composition inspire précisément ce que l'on appelle l'hellénisme. Quelque chose dans la pensée grecque préfigure le Christianisme dans le même temps qu'autre chose le rejette à l'avance).

19. See P. Archambault, *Camus' Hellenic Sources*, p. 66.

20. *Métaphysique chrétienne* . . . , in *Essais*, p. 1231.

21. *Ibid.*, p. 1232.

22. *Ibid.*, p. 1234.

23. *Ibid.*, pp. 1237-38.

24. *Ibid.*, p. 1238.

25. *Ibid.*, p. 1243.

26. *Ibid.*, p. 1240.

27. *Ibid.*, p. 1241.

28. *Ibid.*, p. 1246.

29. *Ibid.*

30. *Ibid.*, p. 1248.

31. *Ibid.*, p. 1249.

32. *Ibid.*, p. 1250.

33. *Ibid.*, p. 1251.

34. *Ibid.*, p. 1250.

35. *Ibid.*, pp. 1252-53.

36. *Ibid.*, p. 1256.

37. *Ibid.*, p. 1261.

38. *Ibid.*, p. 1265. "L'influence chrétienne ici réside moins dans un ensemble de doctrines que dans un état d'esprit et une orientation."
39. *Ibid.*, p. 1268.
40. *Ibid.*
41. *Ibid.*
42. *Ibid.*, p. 1269.
43. *Ibid.*, p. 1270.
44. *Ibid.*, p. 1271.
45. *Ibid.*, p. 1272.

Si le monde est beau, c'est que quelque chose y vit. Mais c'est aussi que quelque chose l'ordonne. Cet esprit qui l'anime c'est l'âme du monde. Le principe supérieur qui limite cette vie dans des cadres déterminés c'est l'intelligence. Mais l'unité d'un ordre est toujours supérieure à cet ordre. Il y a donc un troisième principe supérieur à l' intelligence et qui est l'Un.

46. *Ibid.*, p. 1273.
47. *Ibid.*, p. 1274.
48. *Ibid.*, p. 1275.
49. *Ibid.*, p. 1273.
50. *Ibid.*
51. *Ibid.*, p. 1283.
52. *Ibid.*, p. 1273.
53. *Ibid.*, p. 1285.
54. *Ibid.*, p. 1287.
55. *Ibid.*
56. *Ibid.*, p. 1288.
57. *Ibid.*, p. 1289.
58. *Ibid.*, p. 1291.

. . . ce que le Néoplatonisme a fourni au Christianisme pour son évolution postérieure, c'est une méthode et une direction de pensée.

Une direction de pensée parce qu'en lui fournissant des cadres déjà façonnés aux pensées religieuses, il l'orientait forcément vers les façons de voir à l'intérieur desquelles ces cadres avaient été créés. C'est vers la conciliation d'une métaphysique et d'une foi primitive que la pensée alexandrine encourage le Christianisme à marcher. Mais ici, il y avait peu à faire, le mouvement était donné. Mais la méthode arrivait à point. C'est en effet selon le principe de participation que le Christianisme va résoudre ses grands problèmes, Incarnation et Trinité.

59. *Ibid.*, p. 1293.
60. *Ibid.*

CONCLUSION

1. The theme which Camus chose for his diploma dissertation was, Jean Grenier insists, one in which its author had always been interested. Grenier writes (*Camus*, p. 42): "L'histoire des idées ne l'avait pas orienté vers telle doctrine plutôt que vers telle autre, bien qu'une lettre de lui témoigne que la rencontre de l'hellénisme et du christianisme était pour lui un sujet de méditation."

2. When dealing with Neoplatonism in his *Mémoire*, Camus insists, for example, that Plotinus was concerned not only with "the rational explanation of things," but with "the destiny of the soul" as well. And in his treatment of Gnosticism, which he describes as a "Christian heresy," Camus writes:

   They [the Gnostics] are without exception pessimistic about the world. They look to God with very great zeal, while nonetheless making Him inaccessible. . . . Gnosticism sees in knowledge a means of salvation. In this respect it is Greek, for it wants that which enlightens to regenerate at the same time. It elaborates a Greek theory of grace.

   Ils sont tous pessimistes à l'égard du monde. C'est avec une très vive ferveur qu'ils s'adressent au Dieu qu'ils font pourtant inaccessible. . . . Le Gnosticisme voit dans la connaissance un moyen de salut. En cela il est Grec car il veut que ce qui illumine, régénère du même coup. Ce qu'il élabore, c'est une théorie grecque de la grâce.

3. *Métaphysique chrétienne et Néoplatonisme*, in Pléiade, *Essais*, p. 1235.

4. *Ibid.*, p. 1225.

5. E. D'Arcy, *Conscience And Its Right to Freedom*, p. 213.

6. P. Ricoeur, *De l'interprétation: essai sur Freud*.

7. J. P. Mackey, *Christianity and Albert Camus*, p. 399.

8. *Ibid.*, pp. 401-2.

9. *Métaphysique chrétienne et Néoplatonisme*, in Pléiade, *Essais* pp.1285:

   . . . pour s'élever à Dieu, il faille rentrer en soi. Portant en elle le reflet de ses origines l'âme doit s'y plonger. De Dieu à Dieu, tel est son voyage pendant la génération. Il ne faut pas vivre de ce qui dans l'âme mais il faut se purifier c'est-à-dire se laver de ce qui s'est attaché à l'âme n'est pas l'âme mais retourner dans cette patrie *dont le souvenir colore parfois nos inquiétudes d'âme.* (Emphasis added.)

BIBLIOGRAPHY

For the purposes of convenient consultation, this bibliography is divided into four sections: Augustine, Camus, Nietzsche, and General.

AUGUSTINE

(a) *Works*

AUGUSTINE, St.   *Soliloquia*, Migne, *Pat. Lat.*, vol. XXXII, cols. 869-904, 1877.

. . .   *De Beata Vita* (C.S.E.L., vol. LXIII, sect. 1, par. III). 1922.

. . .   *De Ordine* (C.S.E.L., vol. LXIII, sect. 1, par. III), 1922.

. . .   *De Civitate Dei*, C.C., vols. XLVII, XLVIII, 1955

. . .   *Ennarrationes in Psalmos* I-L, C.C., vol. XXXVIII, par. X, 1, 1956.

. . .   *Ennarrationes in Psalmos* LI-C, C.C., vol. XXXIX, par. X, 2. 1956.

. . .   *De Doctrina Christiana; De Vera Religione*, C.C., vol. XXXII, 1962.

. . .   *De Doctrina Christiana* (C.S.E.L., vol. LXXX, sect. VI, par. VI), 1963.

. . .   *De Trinitate I-XII*, C.C., vol. L. par. XVI, I, 1968.

. . .   *De Trinitate XIII-XV*, C.C., vol. LII, par. XVI, 2, 1968.

. . .   *Enchiridion*, C.C., vol. XLVI, par. XIII, 2, 1969.

. . .   *Confessionum Libri XIII*, ed. M. Skutella. Bibliotheca Teubneriana, Leipzig 1934; revised edition, Stuttgart (Teubner), 1969.

. . .   *Contra Academicos; De Libero Arbitrio*, C.C., vol. XXIX, 1970.

. . .   *Retractationes*, C.C., vol. LVII, 1984.

C.C. = Corpus Christianorum, Series Latina (Turnhout: Brepols, 1953-)

C.S.E.L. = Corpus Scriptorum Ecclesiasticorum Latinorum, (Vienna 1866-).

Migne, *Pat. Lat.*= Patrologiae Cursus Completus, Series Latina, ed. J. P. Migne (Paris, 1844-).

English Translations

Ancient Christian Writers: The Works of the Fathers in Translation, ed. J. Quasten and J. C. Plumpe. Westminster, Md.: Newman Press, 1946- .

Fathers of the Church, ed. L. Schopp, D. J. Deferrari, et al. Washington: Catholic University of America Press, 1947- .

Earlier Works. Selected and trans. with an introduction by J.H.S. Burleigh. London: S.C.M. Press, 1953.

Later Works. Selected and trans. by John Burnaby. London: S.C.M. Press, 1955.

A Select Library of the Nicene and Post-Nicene Fathers of the Christian Church, ed. P. Schopp. Grand Rapids, MI: Eerdmans, 1971-1980.

A comprehensive bibliography of Saint Augustine's writings, in Latin and English translation, is to be found in Christopher Kirwan's *Augustine*, p. 228-33.

(b) *Secondary Literature on Augustine*

ACKWORTH, R   "St. Augustine and the Teleological Argument for the Immortality of the Soul," *The Downside Review* 75 (1957), pp. 215-21.

ALFARIC, P.   *L'Évolution intellectuelle de S. Augustin.* Paris: E. Nourry, 1918.

BALTHASAR, N.   "La Vie intérieure de Saint Augustin à Cassiciacum," *Giornale di Metafisica* 9 (1954), pp. 407-30.

BATTENHOUSE,
   R. W. (ed.)   *A Companion to the Study of St. Augustine.* New York: Oxford University Press, 1955.

BECKER, A.   *L'Appel des béatitudes.* Paris: Editions Saint-Paul, 1977.

BEIERWALTES, W.   *Regio beatitudinis: Augustine's Concept of Happiness.* The St. Augustine Lecture 1980, Villanova: Villanova Press.

BONNER, G.   *St. Augustine of Hippo, Life and Controversies.* London: Student Christian Movement Press, 1963.

BOURKE, V. J.   *Augustine's Quest of Wisdom.* Milwaukee, WI: Bruce, 1945.

. . .   "Invalid Proofs for God's Existence," *Proceedings of the American Catholic Philosophical Association* 28 (1954), pp. 36-49.

. . .   "Saint Augustine and the Cosmic Soul," *Giornale di Metafisica* 9 (1954), pp. 431-40.

. . .   "Wisdom in the Gnoseology of Saint Augustine," *Augustinus* 3 (1958), pp. 331-36.

BOYER, C.   "La preuve de Dieu Augustinienne," *Archives de philosophie* 7 (1930), pp. 105-41.

. . .   *L'Idée de vérité dans la philosophie de Saint Augustin.* Paris: Beauchesne, 1921.

BROWN, P.   *Augustine of Hippo: A Biography.* London: Faber, 1967.

BUBACZ, B. S.   "St. Augustine's 'Si Fallor, Sum,' " *Augustinian Studies* 9 (1978), pp. 35-44.

BURNABY, J.   *Amor Dei: A Study of the Religion of Saint Augustine.* London: Hodder and Stoughton, 1938.

BUTLER, C.   *Western Mysticism.* London: Constable, 1967.

CAYRE, F.   "Dieu présent au coeur," *Année Théologique Augustinienne* 11 (1951), pp. 117-30.

. . .   *Les Sources de l'amour divin. La divine présence d'après Saint Augustin.* Paris: Desclée de Brouwer, 1933.

CHADWICK, H.   *Augustine.* Oxford: Oxford University Press, 1986.

CLARKE, Mary T.   "The Psychology of Marius Victorinus," *Augustinian Studies* 5 (1974), pp. 149-66.

CONNOLLY, S.   "The Platonism of Augustine's 'Ascent' to God, I," *Irish Ecclesiastical Record* 78 (1952), pp. 44-53.

. . .   "St. Augustine's 'Ascent' to God, II," *Irish Ecclesiastical Record* 80 (1953), pp. 28-36.

. . .   "St. Augustine's 'Ascent' to God, III. The Ascent in the Philosophy of Plotinus," *Irish Ecclesiastical Record* 81 (1954), pp. 120-33.

. . .   "St. Augustine's 'Ascent' to God, IV. The Structure of the 'Ascent,' " *Irish Ecclesiastical Record* 81 (1954), pp. 260-69.

COURCELLE, P.   *Recherches sur les "Confessions" de S. Augustin.* Paris: E. de Boccard, 1950.

D'ARCY, M., et al.   *A Monument to Saint Augustine.* London: Sheed & Ward, 1945.

DE MONDADON,
L.   "De la connaissance de soi-même à la connaissance de
            Dieu," *Recherches de Science Religieuse* 4(1913), pp. 148-
            56.
ESSER, Gerard.   "The Augustinian Proof for God's Existence and the
            Thomistic Fourth Way," *Proceedings of the American
            Catholic Philosophical Association* 28 (1954), pp. 194-
            207.
FAY, T.A.   "*Imago Dei.* Augustine's Metaphysics of Man," *Antonianum*
            49 (1974), pp. 173-97.
GILSON, E.   *The Christian Philosophy of Saint Augustine.* London:
            Gollancz, 1961.
GRABOWSKI, S.   "St. Augustine and the Presence of God," *Theological
            Studies* 13 (1956), pp. 336-58.
    . . .   *The All-Present God: A Study in St. Augustine.* St. Louis:
            Herder, 1954.
GRANDGEORGE,
L.   *Saint Augustin et le Néo-Platonisme.* Paris: E. Leroux, 1896.
GUARDINI, R.   *The Conversion of St. Augustine.* Chicago: Regnery, 1960.
GUITTON, J.   *Le Temps et l'Eternité chez Plotin et Saint Augustin.* Paris:
            Bovin, 1933.
HAGENDAHL, H.   *Augustine and the Latin Classics.* 2 vols. Göteborg: Elander,
            1977.
HEIJKE, J.   "The Image of God According to St. Augustine," *Folia*
            10 (1956), pp. 3-11.
HOLTE, R.   *Béatitude et sagesse: Saint Augustine et le problème de la fin de
            l'homme dans la philosophie ancienne.* Paris: Études
            Augustiniennes, 1962.
KIRWAN,
Christopher.   *Saint Augustine.* London: Routledge, 1988.
KOWALCZYK, S.   "La Conception de l'homme chez Saint Augustin,"
            Giornale di Metafisica 27 (1972), pp. 199-211.
    . . .   "La Métaphysique du bien selon l'acceptation de St.
            Augustin," *Estudios Augustinianos* (1973), pp. 31-51.
LEHRBERGER,
James.   "Intelligo Ut Credam: St. Augustine's Confessions,"
            Thomist 52 (1988), pp. 23-39.
MAERTENS, G.   "Augustine's Image of Man," *Studia Verbeke XVIII*
            (Louvain) (1976), pp. 175-98.

MANDOUZE, A.   *Saint Augustin: l'aventure de la raison et de la grâce.* Paris: Études Augustiniennes, 1968.

MARECHAL, J.   "La Vision de Dieu au sommet de la contemplation d'après Saint Augustin," *Nouvelle Revue Théologique* 2 (1930), pp. 89-109, 192-213.

MARROU, H. I.   *Saint Augustine.* New York: Harper and Row, 1957.

MOURANT, J. A.   "The Cogitos: Augustinian and Cartesian," *Augustinian Studies* 10 (1979), pp. 27-42.

O'CONNELL, R. J.   "The *Enneads* and Saint Augustine's Image of Happiness," *Vigiliae Christianae* 17 (1963), pp. 129-64.

O'MEARA, J.   *The Young Augustine.* London: Longmans, Green & Co., 1954.

PORTALIE, E.   *A Guide to the Thought of Saint Augustine.* Introduction by Vernon J. Bourke, trans. by Ralph J. Bastian. London: Burns & Oates, 1975.

PRZYWARA, E.   *An Augustine Synthesis.* Introduction by C. C. Martindale. London: Sheed & Ward, 1936, 1977.

RAWSON, E.   *Cicero. A Portrait.* Bristol: Bristol Classical Press, 1975.

RIGBY, Paul.   *Original Sin in Saint Augustine's "Confessions."* Ottawa: University of Ottawa Press, 1987.

RUSSELL, R. P.   "Cicero's *Hortensius* and the Problem of Riches in St. Augustine," *Augustinian Studies* 7 (1976), pp. 56-68.

SALMON, E.   "The Nature of Man in St. Augustine's Thought," *Proceedings of the American Catholic Philosophical Association* 25 (1955), pp. 25-41.

TESKE, Roland J.   "The Aim of Augustine's Proof that God Truly Is," *International Philosophical Quarterly* 26 (1986), pp. 253-68.

TESTARD, M.   *Saint Augustin et Cicéron,* vol. 1, *Cicéron dans la formation et dans l'oeuvre de S. Augustin.* Paris: Études Augustiniennes, 1958.

THONNARD, F. J.   "La Vie affective de l'âme selon Saint Augustin," *Année Théologique Augustinienne* 13 (1953), pp. 33-65.

VAN BAVEL, T. J.   "The Anthropology of Augustine," *Louvain Studies* 5 (1974), pp. 34-47..

VERBEKE, G.   "Connaissance de soi et connaissance de Dieu chez Saint Augustin," *Augustiniana* 4 (1954), pp. 495-515.

CAMUS

(a) *Works*

CAMUS, Albert.   *Théâtre, récits, nouvelles*. Preface by Jean Grenier. Texts arranged and annotated by Roger Quilliot. Paris: Bibliothèque de la Pléiade, Gallimard, 1962.

. . .   *Essais*. Introduction by R. Quilliot. Texts arranged and annotated by R. Quilliot and L. Faucon, Paris: Gallimard, 1965.

. . .   *Métaphysique chrétienne et Néoplatonisme*, in *Camus*. Essays, ed. R. Quilliot. Paris: Pléiade, Gallimard, 1970 (original 1936).

. . .   *L'Envers et l'endroit*. Algiers: Charlot, 1937; Paris: Gallimard, 1958.

. . .   *Noces*. Algiers: Charlot, 1939.

. . .   *L'Etranger*. Paris: Gallimard, 1942.

. . .   *Le Mythe de Sisyphe*. Paris: Gallimard, 1942.

. . .   *Le Malentendu*. Paris: Gallimard, 1944.

. . .   *Caligula*. Paris: Gallimard, 1944.

. . .   *Lettres à un ami allemand*. Paris: Gallimard, 1945.

. . .   *La Peste*. Paris: Gallimard, 1947.

. . .   *Actuelles I* (Chroniques 1944-1948). Paris: Gallimard, 1950.

. . .   *Les Justes*. Paris: Gallimard, 1950.

. . .   *L'Homme révolté*. Paris: Gallimard, 1951.

. . .   *Actuelles II* (Chroniques 1948-1953). Paris: Gallimard, 1953.

. . .   *L'Eté*. Paris: Gallimard, 1954.

. . .   *La Chute*. Paris: Gallimard, 1956.

. . .   *L'Exil et le royaume*. Paris: Gallimard, 1957.

. . .   *Actuelles III* (Chroniques algériennes, 1939-1958). Paris: Gallimard, 1958.

. . .   *Les Possédés*. Paris: Gallimard, 1959.

. . .   *Carnets, mai-février*, 1935-1942. Paris: Gallimard, 1962.

. . .   *Carnets, janvier-mars*, 1942-1951. Paris: Gallimard, 1964.

. . .   *La Mort heureuse*. Introduction and notes by Jean Sarocchi. Paris: Gallimard, 1971.

CAMUS, Albert, and GRENIER, Jean.

Correspondance 1932-1960. Preface and notes by Marguerite Dobrenne. Paris: Gallimard, 1981.

English Translations

CAMUS, Albert.　　*The Fall*. Trans. by Justin O'Brien. Harmondsworth: Penguin Books, 1957.

. . .　　*The Plague*. Trans. from the French by Stuart Gilbert. Harmondsworth: Penguin Books, 1960.

. . .　　*The Outsider*. Trans. by Stuart Gilbert with introduction by Cyril Connolly. Harmondsworth: Penguin Books, 1961.

. . .　　*Exile and the Kingdom*. Trans. by Justin O'Brien. Harmondsworth: Penguin Books, 1962. Reprinted 1964.

. . .　　*Notebooks: 1935-1942*. Trans. from the French with an introduction and notes by Philip Thody. London: Hamish Hamilton, 1963.

. . .　　*Caligula and Cross Purpose*. Trans. by Stuart Gilbert. Introduction by John Cruickshank. Harmondsworth: Penguin Books, 1965.

. . .　　*Notebooks: 1942-1951*. Trans. from the French with an introduction and notes by Philip Thody. London: Hamish Hamilton, 1966.

. . .　　*Selected Essays and Notebooks*. Edited and trans. by Philip Thody. Harmondsworth: Penguin Books, 1970.

. . .　　*The Just* and *The Possessed*. Trans. by Henry James and Justin O'Brien. Harmondsworth: Penguin Books, 1970.

. . .　　*The Rebel. An Essay on Man in Revolt*. Trans. by Anthony Bower with a foreword by Sir Herbert Read. Harmondsworth: Penguin Modern Classics, 1971.

. . .　　*A Happy Death*. Trans. from the French by Richard Howard. Afterword and notes by Jean Sarocchi. Harmondsworth: Penguin Books, 1973.

. . .　　*The Myth of Sisyphus*. Trans. from the French by Justin O'Brien. Harmondsworth: Penguin Books, 1975.

(b) *Secondary Literature on Camus*

ARCHAMBAULT,
P.   "Albert Camus et la métaphysique chrétienne," in R.
                    Gay-Croiser, *Albert Camus* (1980), pp. 210-217.
. . .   "Augustin et Camus," *Recherches Augustiniennes* vol. VI
                    (1969), pp. 195-221.
. . .   *Camus' Hellenic Sources*. Chapel Hill: University of North
                    Carolina Press, 1972.
BARNES, Hazel E.   *The Literature of Possibility*. London: Tavistock Press, 1961.
BRÉE, G.   *Camus*. New Brunswick: Rutgers University Press, 1959.
BRÉE, G., ed.   *A Collection of Critical Essays*. Englewood Cliffs, NJ:
                    Prentice Hall, 1962.
BRIOSI, A.   "Sartre et le caractère 'classique' de *L'Etranger*," in R.
                    Gay-Croisier, *Albert Camus* (1980), pp. 235-242.
CHAMPIGNY, R.   *Sur un héros païen*. Paris: Gallimard, 1959.
CROCHET, M.   *Les Mythes dans l'oeuvre de Camus*. Paris: Editions
                    Universitaire, 1973.
CRUICKSHANK,
John.   *Albert Camus and the Literature of Revolt*, London: Oxford
                    University Press, 1959.
FITCH, B.   "Le Paradigme herméneutique chez Camus," in R.
                    Gay-Crosier, *Albert Camus* (1980), pp. 32-44.
. . .   *The Narcissistic Text. A Reading of Camus's Fiction*. Toronto:
                    University of Toronto Press, 1982.
GAY-CROSIER, R.,
ed.   *Albert Camus 1980*. Second International Conference. 21-
                    30 February, 1980. Gainesville: University of
                    Florida Press, 1980.
GORCHOV, R.D.   "*Albert Camus' Concept of Absurdity*." Yale University Ph.D.
                    diss., 1976. Xerox University Microfilms, Ann
                    Arbor, MI, 1981.
GRENIER, Jean.   *Albert Camus*. Paris: Gallimard, 1968.
HARDY, G. G.   "Happiness Beyond the Absurd: The Existentialist
                    Quest of Camus," *Philosophy Today* 23 (Winter
                    1979), pp. 367-79.
KOVACS, George.   "The Philosophy of Death in Albert Camus," *Proceedings
                    of the American Catholic Philosophical Association* 49
                    (1975), pp. 189-97.

. . .   "The Search for Meaning in Albert Camus," *Proceedings of the American Catholic Philosophical Association* 10 (1987), pp. 121-139.

LAZERE, D.   *The Unique Creation of Albert Camus.* New Haven: Yale University Press, 1973.

LEBESQUE,
Morvan.   *Albert Camus par lui-même.* (Ecrivains de Toujours.) Paris: Éditions du Seuil, 1963.

LOTTMAN,
Herbert R.   *Albert Camus: A Biography.* London: Weidenfeld and Nicolson, 1979.

MACKEY, James P. "Christianity and Albert Camus," *Studies* LV (1966), pp. 392-402.

MAILHOT, L.   *Albert Camus ou l'imagination du désert.* Montreal: University of Montreal Presses, 1973.

MAQUET, G.   *Albert Camus ou l'invincible été.* Paris: Debresse, Nouvelles Éditions,1956.

McCARTHY,
Patrick.   *Camus: A Critical Analysis of His Life and Work.* London: Hamish Hamilton, 1982.

. . .   *Camus: The Stranger.* Cambridge: Cambridge University Press, 1988.

MIJUSKOVIC, Ben. "Camus and the Problem of Evil," *Sophia* 14-15 (1975-1976), pp. 11-19.

NEWELL, J. David. "Camus on the Will to Happiness," *Philosophy Today* 23 (1979), pp. 380-85.

NGUYEN-VAN-HUY,
P.   *La Métaphysique du bonheur chez Albert Camus.* Neuchâtel: A La Baconnière, 1968.

NOYER-WEIDNER, A. "Structure et sens de 'L'Étranger,' " *Albert Camus* (1980), pp. 72-85.

O'BRIEN, C. C.   *Camus.* London: Fontana 1970.

PARKER, E.   *Albert Camus: The Artist in the Arena.* Madison: University of Wisconsin Press, 1966.

PRATT, B.   *L'Evangile selon Albert Camus.* Paris: José Corti, 1980.

QUILLIOT, R.   *La Mer et les prisons.* Essay on Albert Camus. Paris: Gallimard, 1970.

SARTRE, Jean-Paul. "Explication de *L'Etranger*," J.-P. Sartre, *Situations*, I. Essais critiques (1947), pp. 92-112. Paris: Gallimard, 1947.

SHAW, Daniel.   "Absurdity and Suicide: A Reexamination," *Philosophical Research Archives* 11 (1985), pp. 209-23.

SMITH, Edward T.   "Original Innocence in a Passionate Universe: The Moral Anthropology of Camus," *Thomist* 42 (1978), pp. 69-94.

SPRINTZEN, David.   *Camus: A Critical Examination.* Philadelphia: Temple University Press, 1988.

THODY, Philip.   *Albert Camus: A Study of His Work.* New York: Macmillan, 1957.

WEYEMBERGH, M.   "Camus et Nietzsche: Evolution d'une affinité," *Albert Camus* (1980), pp. 221-30.

ZUCKER, Richard.   "The Happiness of Sisyphus," *Kinesis* 16 (1987), pp. 41-65.

NIETZSCHE

(a) *Works*

The works of Friedrich Nietzsche are published in two volumes by Carl Hanswer Verlag, Munich:

Friedrich Nietzsche. Work in Two Volumes. Ed. by Karl Schlechta, second edition, Munich, 1973. *The Will to Power* is not included; this posthumous work, assembled from the *Nachlass*, is published by Kröner Verlag, Stuttgart: *The Will to Power: Attempt at a Transvaluation of All Values.* Selected and arranged by Peter Gast, with the assistance of E. Förster-Nietzsche, Stuttgart, 1964.

English Translations

The Complete Works of Friedrich Nietzsche. The first complete and authorized English translation. Edited by Dr. Oscar Levy. Edinburgh: J. N. Foulis, 1909-13, 18 vols.

Vol. 1:   *The Birth of Tragedy, or Hellenism and Pessimism.* Trans. by Wm. A. Haussmann. (With an introduction by Elizabeth Förster-Nietzsche, trans. by A.M. Ludovici), 1909.

Vol. 2:   *Early Greek Philosophy, and Other Essays.* Trans. by Maximilian A. Mügge, 1911.

Vol. 3:   *On the Future of our Educational Institutions. Homer and Classical Philology.* Trans. with an introd. by J. M. Kennedy, 1909.

Vols. 4, 5:	*Thoughts out of Season* (part 1 trans. by Anthony M. Ludovici; part 2 trans. by Adrian Collins), 1909.
Vols. 6, 7:	*Human, All-too-Human* (part 1 trans. by Helen Zimmern; part 2 trans. by Paul V. Cohn), 1909, 1911.
Vol. 8:	*The Case of Wagner*, 3rd ed. trans. by A. M. Ludovici. *We Philologists*, trans. by J. M. Kennedy, 1911.
Vol. 9:	*The Dawn of Day*, trans. by J. M. Kennedy, 1911.
Vol. 10:	*The Joyful Wisdom*, 2nd ed. trans. by Thomas Common with poetry rendered by Paul V. Cohn and Maude D. Petre, 1910.
Vol. 11:	*Thus Spoke Zarathustra*, trans. by Thomas Common (introd. by Mrs. Förster-Nietzsche. Notes on "Thus Spoke Zarathustra" by A. M. Ludovici), 1909.
Vol. 12:	*Beyond Good and Evil*, 2nd ed., trans. by Helen Zimmern, 1909.
Vol. 13:	*The Genealogy of Morals*, trans. by Horace B. Samuel. "Peoples and Countries," fragment (trans. by J. M. Kennedy), 1910.
Vols. 14, 15:	*The Will to Power*, trans. by A. M. Ludovici. 1909, 1910.
Vol. 16:	*The Twilight of the Idols . . . the Antichrist.* Notes on Zarathustra and Eternal Recurrence. Trans. by A. M. Ludovici, 1911.
Vol. 17:	*Ecce Homo*, trans. by A. M. Ludovici. Poetry rendered by Paul V. Cohn (and others) . . . *Hymn to Life*, composed by Nietzsche, 1911.
Vol. 18:	*Index to Nietzsche.* Compiled by Robert Guppy. Vocabulary of foreign quotations. Trans. by Paul V. Cohn with an introductory essay: "The Nietzsche Movement in England" by O. Levy, 1913.

Recent translations

Because the Levy translation has been subjected to scholarly criticism, notably by W. Kaufmann, we make reference to the following newer translations:

Nietzsche. Unpublished Letters, trans. and ed. by Karl F. Leidecker. London: Peter Owen, 1960.

The Birth of Tragedy and *The Case of Wagner* (The Wagner Case), trans. by W. Kaufmann. New York: Vintage Books, 1967.

The Will to Power, trans by W. Kaufmann and R. J. Hollingdale. New York: Viking Books, 1968.

Thus Spoke Zarathustra, trans. by W. Kaufmann. New York: Viking Books, 1966. Trans. by R. J. Hollingdale. Harmondsworth: Penguin Books, 1969.

Beyond Good and Evil: Prelude to a Philosophy of the Future, trans. by W. Kaufmann. New York: Vintage Books, 1973. Trans by R. J. Hollingdale. Harmondsworth: Penguin Books, 1973.

The Portable Nietzsche, trans. by W. Kaufman. New York: Viking Books, 1973. Contains translations of *Thus Spoke Zarathustra*, *Twilight of the Idols*, *The Antichrist* and *Nietzsche Contra Wagner*.

A Genealogy of Morals and *Ecce Homo*, trans. by W. Kaufmann and R. J. Hollingdale. New York: Vintage Books, 1973.

The Gay Science (The Joyous Science), trans. by W. Kaufmann. New York: Vintage Books, 1974.

A Nietzsche Reader, trans. by R. J. Hollingdale. Harmondsworth: Penguin Books, 1977.

Daybreak: Thoughts on the Prejudices of Morality, trans. by R. J. Hollingdale, introd. by Michael Tanner. Cambridge: Cambridge University Press, 1982.

Untimely Meditations, trans. by R. J. Hollingdale, introd. by J. P. Stern. Cambridge: Cambridge University Press, 1983.

(b) *Secondary Literature on Nietzsche*

ANDLER, Charles.   *Nietzsche: sa vie et sa pensée.* 3 vols. Paris: Editions Bossard, 1922-1931.

BRANDES, George.   *Friedrich Nietzsche.* London: Heinemann, 1914.

BRINTON, Crane.   *Nietzsche.* Cambridge, MA: Harvard University Press, 1941.

CLAIR, André.   "Formation de la conscience et constitution de la moralité selon *La généalogie de la morale* de Nietzsche," *Revue des Sciences philosophiques et théologiques* 62 (1978), pp. 395-418.

CLARKE, Maudemarie. *Nietzsche's Attack on Morality.* Ann Arbor, MI: University Microfilms International, 1981.

COPLESTON, F. C.   *Friedrich Nietzsche, Philosopher of Culture.* London: Burns & Oates, 1942.

. . .   *St. Thomas and Nietzsche.* Oxford: Blackfriars, 1944
                  (1955).

CUNNINGHAM,

G. W.   "Nietzsche on the Philosopher," *The Philosophical Review*
                  54 (1945), pp. 155-72.

DAVEY, Nicholas J. R. "Heidegger's Interpretation of Nietzsche: The Will to
                  Power as Art," *Journal of The British Society for Phenom-
                  enology* 12 (1981), pp. 267-74.

DELEUZE, Gilles. *Nietzsche and Philosophy.* Trans. by Hugh Tomlinson.
                  London: Athlone Press, 1983.

DURR, V. ed.   *Nietzsche: Literature and Values.* Madison: Univ. of
                  Wisconsin Press, 1988.

FÖRSTER-NIETZSCHE,

Elizabeth.   *The Young Nietzsche.* Trans. by A. M. Ludovici. London:
                  W. Heinemann, 1912.

. . .   *The Lonely Nietzsche.* Trans. by Paul V. Cohn. London:
                  W. Heinemann, 1915.

HIGGINS, Kathleen

M.   *Nietzsche's Zarathustra.* Temple University Press, 1987.

HOLLINGDALE, R. J. *Nietzsche.* London: Routledge and Kegan Paul, 1973.

HUNT, Lester H. *Nietzsche and the Origin of Virtue.* London: Routledge,
                  1991.

KAUFMANN, W.   *Nietzsche: Philosopher, Psychologist, Antichrist.* Princeton NJ:
                  Princeton University Press, 1950.

. . .   "Nietzsche and Existentialism," *Symposium* 28 (1974),
                  pp. 7-16.

KNIGHT, A.H.J.   *Some Aspects of the Life and Work of Nietzsche.* Cambridge:
                  Cambridge University Press, 1983.

LAMPERT, Laurence. *Nietzsche's Teaching.* New Haven, CT: Yale University
                  Press, 1987.

LEIGH, James G. "Deleuze, Nietzsche and the Eternal Return," *Philosophy
                  Today* 22 (1978), pp. 206-23.

LINGIS, Alphonso. "The Last Form of 'The Will to Power,'" *Philosophy
                  Today* 22 (1978), pp. 193-205.

MAGNUS, Bernd.   *Nietzsche's Existential Imperative.* Bloomington: Indiana Uni-
                  versity Press, 1978.

. . .   "Nietzsche's Philosophy in 1988: The Will to Power
                  and the Übermensch," *Journal of the History of Philos-
                  ophy* 24 (1986), pp. 79-98.

MAY, R.   "Nietzsche's Contribution to Psychology," *Symposium*
                  28 (1974), pp. 58-73.

MILLER, J. H.   "The Disarticulation of the Self in Nietzsche," *The Monist* 64 (1981), pp. 247-61.

MORGAN, G. A.   *What Nietzsche Means.* New York: Harper Torchbooks, 1965.

NEHAMAS, A.   "The Eternal Recurrence," *The Philosophical Review* 89 (1980), pp. 331-56.

.   .   .   *Nietzsche: Life as Literature.* Cambridge MA: Harvard University Press, 1985.

ORR, Stephen.   "The Inconsequentiality of Moral Values in Nietzsche's Philosophy," *Kinesis* 17 (1987), pp. 33-47.

PASLEY, M. (ed.)   *Nietzsche: Imagery and Thought: A collection of essays.* London: Methuen, 1978.

SCHACHT, R.   "Nietzsche's Second Thoughts about Art," *The Monist* 64 (1981), pp. 231-46.

SILK, M. S., and
    STERN J. P.   *Nietzsche on Tragedy.* Cambridge: Cambridge University Press, 1981.

SMALL, Robin.   "Nietzsche's God," *Philosophy Today* 26 (1982), pp. 41-53.

SOLOMON,
    Robert C., ed.   *Nietzsche: A Collection of Critical Essays.* Notre Dame: University of Notre Dame Press, 1980.

STACK, George J.   *Nietzsche: Man, Knowledge, and Will to Power.* Brookline, MA: Longwood Press, 1991.

STAMBAUGH, J.   *Nietzsche's Thought of Eternal Return.* Baltimore: Johns Hopkins University Press, 1972.

STEFFNEY, John.   "Existentialism's Legacy of Nothingness," *Philosophy Today* 21 (1977), pp. 216-26.

STERN, J. P.   *Nietzsche.* London: Fontana, 1978.

.   .   .   *A Study of Nietzsche.* Cambridge: Cambridge University Press, 1979.

STEWART, H.L.   *Nietzsche and the Ideals of Modern Germany.* London: Arnold, 1915.

THIBON, G.   *Nietzsche ou le déclin de l'esprit.* Lyon: Lardanchet, 1948.

WILLIAMS, Meredith   "Transcendence and Return: The Overcoming of Philosophy in Nietzsche and Wittgenstein," *International Philosophical Quarterly* 28 (1988), pp. 403-19.

GENERAL WORKS

AMELINEAU, E.   *Essai sur le gnosticisme égyptien, ses développements et son origine égyptienne.* Paris: E. Leroux, 1887.

ARISTOTLE.   *Metaphysics. (The Works of Aristotle,* vol. 8, Oxford translation), 2nd ed. Oxford: Oxford University Press, 1928.

ARMSTRONG, A. H. "Salvation, Plotinian and Christian," *Downside Review* 75 (Spring 1957), pp. 126-39.

ARMSTRONG,
    A. H., ed.   *The Cambridge History of Late Greek and Early Medieval Philosophy.* Cambridge: Cambridge University Press, 1967.

ARNOU, R.   *Le Désir de Dieu dans la philosophie de Plotin.* Paris: F. Alcan, 1921.

BERGSON, H.   *The Two Sources of Morality and Religion.* Trans. by R. Ashley Audra and Cloudesey Brereton. London: Macmillan, 1935.

BOISSIER, M.L.A.G.   *La Religion romaine d'Auguste aux Antonins.* 2 vols. Paris, 1874.

BREHIER, E.   *Les Idées philosophiques et religieuses de Philon d'Alexandre.* Paris: A. Picard, 1908.

. . .   *La Philosophie de Plotin.* Paris: Boivin, 1928.

. . .   "Le Problème de la philosophie chrétienne," *Revue de métaphysique et de morale* 38 (1931), pp. 133-62.

. . .   *The History of Philosophy.* Trans. by Joseph Thomas and Wade Baskin. 7 vols. Chicago: University of Chicago Press, 1963-69.

CAIRD, E.   *The Evolution of Theology in the Greek Philosophers.* 2 vol. Glasgow: J. Maclehose & Sons, 1904.

CELSUS.   *On the True Doctrine: A Discourse Against the Christians.* Trans. with a general introd. by R. Joseph Hoffmann. New York: Oxford University Press, 1987.

CUMONT, F.V.M.   *The Mysteries of Mithra.* Trans. from the 2nd revised French ed. by Thomas J. McCormack. London: Kegan Paul, Trench, Truber & Co., 1903.

. . .   *Les Religions orientales dans le paganisme romain.* Paris: E. Leroux, 1906.

. . .   *Lux Perpetua,* Paris: P. Geuthner, 1949.

D'ARCY, E.   *Conscience and Its Right to Freedom*, London: Sheed and Ward, 1961.

DE FAYE, E.   *Clément d'Alexandrie. Etude sur les rapports du Christianisme et de la philosophie grecque au IIe siècle.* Paris: E. Leroux, 1898.

. . .   *Gnostiques et gnosticisme. Etude critique des documents du gnosticisme chrétien aux IIe et IIIe siècles.* Paris: P. Geuthner, 1925.

DE LABRIOLLE, P.   *History and Literature of Christianity from Tertullian to Boethius.* Trans. by Herbert Walsh et al. London: Kegan Paul & Co., 1924.

. . .   *La Réaction païenne. Etude sur la polémique anti-chrétienne du Ier au VIe siècle.* Paris, 1934.

DOSTOEVSKY, F.   *Crime and Punishment.* Trans. from the Russian by Constance Garnett. London: Heinemann, 1914.

. . .   *The Possessed.* Trans. from the Russian by Constance Garnett. London: Heinemann, 1914.

. . .   *The Brothers Karamazov.* Trans. from the Russian by Constance Garnett. London: Heinemann, 1958.

EPICTETUS.   *The Discourses as Reported by Arrian, the Manual and Fragments.* With an English trans. by W. A. Oldfather. London: Heinemann, 1925-28; 2 vol. (Loeb Classical Library).

FEUERBACH, L.   *The Essence of Christianity.* London: Harper and Row, 1957.

FULLER, B.A.G.   *The Problem of Evil in Plotinus.* Cambridge: Cambridge University Press, 1912.

GIDE, A.P.G.   *The Counterfeiters.* Trans. by Dorothy Bussy. Harmondsworth: Penguin Books, 1970.

. . .   *Fruits of the Earth.* Trans. by Dorothy Bussy. Harmondsworth: Penguin Books, 1970.

GILSON, E.   *The Spirit of Medieval Philosophy.* Trans. by A.H.C. Downes. London: Sheed & Ward, 1936.

. . .   *History of Christian Philosophy in the Middle Ages.* London: Sheed & Ward, 1955.

GRENIER, J.   *Les Iles,* Paris: Gallimard, 1947.

HEFELE, Karl Joseph.   *A History of Christian Councils,* from the original documents. Trans. and edited by W. R. Clark. Edinburgh: T. & T. Clark, 1871-96.

HOMER.   *The Homeric Hymns.* Trans. by Apostolos N.
                       Athanassakis. Baltimore: The Johns Hopkins
                       University Press, 1976.

HUXLEY, T. H.   *Evolution and Ethics: The Romanes Lecture.* London:
                       Macmillan, 1893.

INGE, W. R.   *The Philosophy of Plotinus,* 3rd ed. 2 vol. London:
                       Longmans & Co., 1929.

JUKA, S.   "L'Humain et l'absolu dans 'Les Iles' de Jean Grenier,"
                       Revue de Métaphysique et de Morale 82 (4) (1977),
                       pp. 528-49.

KIERKEGAARD,
    Søren.   *Fear and Trembling and the Sickness unto Death,* 2nd ed.
                       Princeton, NJ: Princeton University Press, 1954.
    . . .   *Stages on Life's Way.* Trans. by Walter Lowrie. New
                       York, Schocken Books, 1967.

LE BRETON, Jules.   *History of the Dogma of the Trinity, from its origins to the Coun-*
                       cil of Nicaea. Trans. by Algar Thorold from the 8th
                       ed. London: Burns Oates & Co., 1939.

LOISY, A.   *Les Mystères païens et le mystère chrétien.* Paris: E. Nourry,
                       1914.

LUBAC, H. de   *The Drama of Atheist Humanism.* Trans. by Edith W. Riley.
                       London: Sheed & Ward, 1967.

MacINTYRE, A., and
    RICOEUR, P.   *The Religious Significance of Atheism.* New York: Columbia
                       University Press, 1969.

MAGEE, B. ed.   *Men of Ideas. Some Creators of Contemporary Philosophy.*
                       London: BBC, 1978.

MALRAUX, A.   *La Condition humaine.* Paris: Gallimard, 1946.
    . . .   *La Tentation de l'Occident.* Paris: Grasset, 1951.
    . . .   *The Conquerors.* Trans. by Winifred Stephens Whale.
                       Boston: Beacon Press, 1956.

MARITAIN, J.   *The Range of Reason.* London: Bles, 1953.

MATTER, Jacques.   *Histoire critique du Gnosticisme et de son influence sur les sectes reli-*
                       gieuses et philosophiques des six premiers siècles de l'Ere
                       Chrétienne. Strasbourg: V. Levraut; Paris: P.
                       Bertrand, 1843-1844.

MINUCIUS, Felix.   *Octavius* in the Ante-Nicene Fathers, vol. IV. Ed. by
                       Alexander Roberts and James Donaldson. Grand
                       Rapids, MI: Eerdmans, 1972.

ORIGEN.   *De Principiis* in the Ante-Nicene Fathers, vol. IV. Ed. by
                   Alexander Roberts and James Donaldson. Grand
                   Rapids, MI: Eerdmans, 1972.

PASCAL, B.   *Pensées.* Trans. with an introd. by A. J. Krailsheimer.
                   Harmondsworth: Penguin Books, 1966.

PLATO.   *The Symposium.* A new trans. by W. Hamilton.
                   Harmondsworth: Penguin Books, 1951.

. . .   *The Republic.* Trans. with an introduction by
                   W. Hamilton. Harmondsworth: Penguin Books,
                   1974.

PLOTINUS.   *The Enneads.* Trans. by S. MacKenna. 3rd ed., rev. by B.
                   S. Page. Foreword by E. R. Dodds. London: Faber,
                   1962.

PLUTARCH.   *De Iside et Osiride.* Edited with an introduction, trans. and
                   commentary by J. Gwyn Griffiths. Cardiff: Uni-
                   versity of Wales Press, 1970.

POJMAN, L. P.   *Religious Belief and the Will.* London: Routledge & Kegan
                   Paul, 1986.

PUECH, A.   *Les Apologistes grecs du IIᵉ siècle de notre ère.* Paris: Hachette,
                   1912.

RENAN, Ernest.   *The Life of Jesus.* With an introduction by John Haynes
                   Holmes. New York: Modern Library, 1955.

RICOEUR, P.   *De l'interprétation: essai sur Freud.* Paris: Éditions du Seuil,
                   1965.

SALVIAN.   *The Government of God.* Trans. by Jeremiah F. O'Sullivan.
                   Washington, D.C.: Catholic University of
                   America Press, 1947.

SPINOZA,
    Benedict.   *Ethics and "De Intellectus emendatione."* Trans. by A. Boyle
                   with an introduction by G. Santayana. London:
                   Dent, 1910.

. . .   *Selections.* Ed. by John Wild. New York: Scribners, 1930.

SOURIAU, Michel.   "Y a-t-il une philosophie chrétienne?," *Revue de
                   Métaphysique et de morale* 39 (1932), pp. 353-385.

THOMAS AQUINAS,
    St.   *Basic Writings of Saint Thomas Aquinas,* vol. I. Edited and
                   annotated with an introd. by Anton C. Pegis.
                   New York: Random House, 1945.

TIXERONT, L. J.   *History of Dogmas.* Trans. from the 5th French ed. by
                   H.L.B. 3 vol. St. Louis, MO: B. Herder, 1910-16.

TOUSSAINT, C.   *L'Hellénisme et l'apôtre Paul.* Paris: E. Nourry, 1921.

SELECT INDEX OF NAMES

DATE DUE

MAY 1 2 2000		
APR 3 0 2001		
	MAY 0 9 1996	
JUL 1 9 2005		

Demco, Inc. 38-293